WITCHES

Wicked, Wild & Wonderful

WITCHES

Wicked, Wild & Wonderful

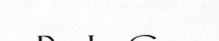

Edited by Paula Guran

○
PRIME BOOKS

FOR MY NEW "FAMILIAR": NALA

"Hasn't this cat got anything better to do? Couldn't you give him
something to read?"—Shepherd "Shep" Henderson (James Stewart)
in *Bell, Book and Candle* (1958)
Screenplay by Daniel Taradash,
Based on the Play by John Van Druten

Contents

⌒

Introduction

In any quest for magic, in any search for sorcery, witchery, legerdemain, first check the human spirit.—Rod Serling, "Dust," *The Twilight Zone*

One of the most common characters to be found in fantasy, there are many fictional variations of the witch icon and similar diversity in the themes and meanings represented. The versatility and richness of the image continues to grow, as does the popularity of modern interpretations.

The idea of witchcraft can be found in nearly every culture and its folklore. This anthology explores only a few permutations of the fictional witch and primarily in the context of Western tradition.

Our concept of the witch is not only extremely broad, it is also contradictory.

There is the stereotypical cackling "old hag" riding a broomstick and stirring her cauldron. She often lives alone with a black cat as her familiar. The incarnation of evil, she can hex you or cast a spell that makes your cow go dry—or worse. Sometimes she doesn't even exhibit magical powers; her sorcery is measured by how she cruelly preys on the innocent.

But we also know the "good witch": wise-woman and healer, the elder who possesses helpful knowledge—sometimes arcane and occult, sometimes merely practical—and provides guidance and protection. The good witch helps heroes, saves the day with her own heroism, or assists rightful rulers to regain thrones and rule well. She is often an important figure in the life of a young person.

The witch has her place in history-based or pseudo-Medieval epics, alternate universes, pastoral settings, urban bustle, suburban neighborhoods, and just about any era or locale imaginable.

Warts and beaked noses under pointy hats personify one archetype, but witches can also be beautiful: seductive and dangerous; an attractive or plain wise-women/healer; exotic, sexy, and literally bewitching; spunky and cute; chic business witch; urban punk; the girl next door or the demon of your nightmares—the witch has infinite variety.

Humble and helpful or powerful and manipulative; peasant, queen, or suburbanite—a witch can be the ultimate loner, need a coven, have a family, be part of an international organization, or anything in between. She can be aged or ageless. Lately teen-aged witches, full of juvenile conflict as well as the challenges of dealing with their powers and/or destiny, have started to inhabit a subgenre of their own.

"She" can even be a "he."

Witches can be normal humans who agree to a pact with the Devil in order to practice black magic and subvert souls. Or they can simply be mortals who learn the craft of magic, no Satanic deal needed. Witches may be thoroughly human practitioners of a particular religion. There are also hereditary witches born with special powers. In some fantasy witches are a separate species.

Whether born with supernatural abilities or having acquired them, witches may keep their powers hidden from the misunderstandings and prejudices of the mundane world. Or they may be "out of the broom closet" and openly practice witchcraft. Some of the latter live in worlds where witchcraft is part of the natural order of things

A great deal of modern fictional witchcraft has been influenced by various neopagan and Wiccan beliefs—including communion with a tri-part goddess. "Domestic" witches—women with magical powers, but who marry or love humans, is another predominately twentieth century invention.

Unlike other fantastic beings who capture our imagination, witches are not fundamentally supernatural creatures. Vampires? They are no longer human and cannot walk among us during daylight hours (at least not without special provision). Werewolves possess an animal nature usually connected with the full moon. Fairies, although they can look like us, have never been human. Ghosts were once human but, having been transformed, no longer belong to the world of the living. Witches, though, are either humans who practice magic or are born with special abilities, but are otherwise indistinguishable from the rest of us. Witches can live among us without ever revealing their extraordinary powers.

As Stefan Dziemianowicz wrote in 1995: "For all their remarkable powers, [witches] are accessible, and sometimes vulnerable. It is this dual nature that makes witches so fascinating—and frightening."

But as accessible and indistinguishable as they may be—witches are still "other." Historically, those persecuted as witches, Dziemianowicz reminds us, "shared one common stigma: the perception they differed in subtle and insidious ways . . . their greatest transgression was their simple nonconformity." Being an outsider is a risky business.

Nowadays, witches can still be wicked, but they often are used to personify very human evil. After all, we don't really fear the Devil or uncanny monsters so much as we fear our fellow humans: our own capacity for evil is all too apparent. Fairy tales have been sanitized and given happy endings, but the core truths remain real. Parents abandon their children (and worse), people kill for no reason, power is often misused in horrendous ways, there are cruel and painful dangers in the deep, dark forests of our lives. In modern society, it never hurts to be the fairest or the most skilled or the cleverest. It also helps to know the right people, be special in some way, or find luck in unlikely places. Most of us kiss a few frogs along the way. We may meet up with helpful witches or encounter witches who can destroy us.

In fantasy these days, more often than not, witches are the "good guys." Freed from centuries of patriarchy, witches—mostly female—have become a wonderful symbol of the empowered woman. The troubled real world we live in seems to need the power of magic to solve its problems—rationality just isn't enough to kick twenty-first century evil's ass.

And perhaps we now recognize the "other" in ourselves—our own wild differences, our personal uniqueness—more readily and are willing to learn from it rather than fear it. As with any fantasy icon, through witches, readers can recognize their connection to the rest of humanity as well as discover truths about themselves.

I hope you find—through the marvelous imaginations of these writers and their amazing stories—some magic of your own.

Paula Guran
October 2011

Delia Sherman's delightfully domestic modern witchcraft tale takes its title from Walpurgis Night, a spring festival celebrated on April 30 or May 1 in many Northern and Central European countries. The holiday's name comes from Saint Walpurga, an eighth century English missionary to the Germanic tribes. Walpurga was canonized on May 1 around 870. The first of May (or thereabouts) had a long pagan tradition as a time for spring fertility festivals marking the end of the winter in the Northern hemisphere. Conveniently, Walpurga became a patron saint of pregnant women, good crops, and a protector of peasants, so attaching her name helped Christianize the heathen spring fling. The eve of May Day came to be known as Walpurga's Night (Walpurgisnacht in German and Dutch). The holiday was (and is) seen in some regions as a night when the barriers between the mundane and the supernatural could be easily breached—like All Hallow's Eve (which comes exactly six months later). Evil spirits are driven away with loud noises, bonfires, singing, drinking, dancing, and general revelry. In Germany it was particularly associated as a night when witches gathered. Walpurgis Night also coincides with Beltane, a Gaelic festival similarly celebrated in Scotland and Ireland.

Walpurgis Afternoon
Delia Sherman

The big thing about the new people moving into the old Pratt place at Number 400 was that they got away with it at all. Our neighborhood is big on historical integrity. The newest house on the block was built in 1910, and you can't even change the paint-scheme on your house without recourse to preservation committee studies and zoning board hearings.

The old Pratt place had generated a tedious number of such hearings over the years—I'd even been to some of the more recent ones. Old Mrs. Pratt had let it go pretty much to seed, and when she passed away, there was trouble about clearing the title so it could be sold, and then it burned down.

Naturally a bunch of developers went after the land—a three-acre property in a professional neighborhood twenty minutes from downtown is something like a Holy Grail to developers. But their lawyers couldn't get the title cleared either, and the end of it was that the old Pratt place never did get built on. By the time Geoff and I moved next door, the place was an empty lot. The neighborhood kids played Bad Guys and Good Guys there after school and the neighborhood cats preyed on its endless supply of mice and voles. I'm not talking eyesore, here; just a big shady plot of land overgrown with bamboo, rhododendrons, wildly rambling roses, and some nice old trees, most notably an immensely ancient copper beech big enough to dwarf any normal-sized house.

It certainly dwarfs ours.

Last spring all that changed overnight, literally. When Geoff and I turned in, we lived next door to an empty lot. When we got up, we didn't. I have to tell you, it came as quite a shock first thing on a Monday morning, and I wasn't even the one who discovered it. Geoff was.

Geoff's the designated keeper of the window because he insists on sleeping with it open and I hate getting up into a draft. Actually, I hate getting up, period. It's a blessing, really, that Geoff can't boil water without burning it, or I'd never be up before ten. As it is, I eke out every second of warm unconsciousness I can while Geoff shuffles across the floor and *thunks* down the sash and takes his shower. On that particular morning, his shuffle ended not with a *thunk*, but with a gasp.

"Holy shit," he said.

I sat up in bed and groped for my robe. When we were in grad school, Geoff had quite a mouth on him, but fatherhood and two decades of college teaching have toned him down a lot. These days, he usually keeps his swearing for Supreme Court decisions and departmental politics.

"Get up, Evie. You gotta see this."

So I got up and went to the window, and there it was, big as life and twice as natural, a real *Victorian Homes* centerfold, set back from the street and just the right size to balance the copper beech. Red tile roof, golden brown clapboards, miles of scarlet-and-gold gingerbread draped over dozens of eaves, balconies, and dormers. A witch's hat tower, a wrap-around porch, and a massive carriage house. With a cupola on it. Nothing succeeds like excess, I always say.

"Holy shit."

"Watch your mouth, Evie," said Geoff automatically.

I like to think of myself as a fairly sensible woman. I don't imagine things, I face facts, I hadn't gotten hysterical when my fourteen-year-old daughter asked me about birth control. Surely there was some perfectly rational explanation for this phenomenon. All I had to do was think of it.

"It's a hallucination," I said. "Victorian houses don't go up overnight. People do have hallucinations. We're having a hallucination. Q.E.D."

"It's not a hallucination," Geoff said.

Geoff teaches intellectual history at the university and tends to disagree, on principle, with everything everyone says. Someone says the sky is blue, he says it isn't. And then he explains why. "This has none of the earmarks of a hallucination," he went on. "We aren't in a heightened emotional state, not expecting a miracle, not drugged, not part of a mob, not starving, not sense deprived. Besides, there's a clothesline in the yard with laundry hanging on it. Nobody hallucinates long underwear."

I looked where he was pointing, and sure enough, a pair of scarlet long johns was kicking and waving from an umbrella-shaped drying-rack, along with a couple pairs of women's panties, two oxford-cloth shirts hung up by their collars, and a gold-and-black print caftan. There was also what was arguably the most beautifully designed perennial bed I'd ever seen basking in the early morning sun. As I was squinting at the delphiniums, a side door opened and a woman came out with a wicker clothesbasket propped on her hip. She was wearing shorts and a T-shirt, had fairish hair pulled back in a bushy tail, and struck me as being a little long in the tooth to be going barefoot and braless.

"Nice legs," said Geoff.

I snapped down the window. "Pull the shades before you get in the shower," I said. "It looks to me like our new neighbors get a nice, clear shot of our bathroom from their third floor."

In our neighborhood, we pride ourselves on minding our own business and not each other's—live and let live, as long as you keep your dog, your kids, and your lawn under control. If you don't, someone calls you or drops you a note, and if that doesn't make you straighten up and fly right, well, you're likely to get a call from the town council about that extension you neglected to get a variance for. Needless to say, the house at Number 400 fell way outside all our usual coping mechanisms. If some contractor had shown up at dawn with bulldozers and two-by-fours, I could have called the police or our councilwoman or someone and got an injunction. How do you get an injunction against a physical impossibility?

The first phone call came at about eight-thirty: Susan Morrison, whose back yard abuts the Pratt place.

"Reality check time," said Susan. "Do we have new neighbors or do we not?"

"Looks like it to me," I said.

Silence. Then she sighed. "Yeah. So. Can Kimmy sit for Jason Friday night?"

Typical. If you can't deal with it, pretend it doesn't exist, like when one couple down the street got the bright idea of turning their front lawn into a wildflower meadow. The trouble is, a Victorian mansion is a lot harder to ignore than even the wildest meadow. The phone rang all morning with hysterical calls from women who hadn't spoken to us since Geoff's brief tenure as president of the neighborhood association.

After several fruitless sessions of what's-the-world-coming-to, I turned on the machine and went out to the garden to put in the beans. Planting them in May was pushing it, but I needed the therapy. For me, gardening's the most soothing activity on Earth. When you plant a bean, you get a bean, not an azalea or a cabbage. When you see that bean covered with icky little orange things, you know they're Mexican bean beetle larvae and go for the pyrethrum. Or you do if you're paying attention. It always astonishes me how oblivious even the garden club ladies can be to a plant's needs and preferences.

Sure, there are nasty surprises, like the winter that the mice ate all the Apricot Beauty tulip bulbs. But mostly you know where you are with a garden. If you put the work in, you'll get satisfaction out, which is more than can be said of marriages or careers.

This time though, digging and raking and planting failed to work their usual magic. Every time I glanced up, there was Number 400, serene and comfortable, the shrubs established and the paint chipping just a little around the windows, exactly as if it had been there forever instead of less than twelve hours.

I'm not big on the inexplicable. Fantasy makes me nervous. In fact, fiction makes me nervous. I like facts and plenty of them. That's why I wanted to be a botanist. I wanted to know everything there was to know about how plants worked, why azaleas like acid soil and peonies like wood ash and how you might be able to get them to grow next to each other. I even went to graduate school and took organic chemistry. Then I met Geoff, fell in love, and traded in my Ph.D. for an M-R-S, with a minor in

Mommy. None of these events (except possibly falling in love with Geoff) fundamentally shook my allegiance to provable, palpable facts. The house next door was palpable, all right, but it shouldn't have been. By the time Kim got home from school that afternoon, I had a headache from trying to figure out how it got to be there.

Kim is my daughter. She reads fantasy, likes animals a lot more than she likes people, and is a big fan of Buffy the Vampire Slayer. Because of Kim, we have two dogs (Spike and Willow), a cockatiel (Frodo), and a lop-eared Belgian rabbit (Big Bad), plus the overflow of semi-wild cats (Balin, Dwalin, Bifur, and Bombur) from the Pratt place, all of which she feeds and looks after with truly astonishing dedication.

Three-thirty on the nose, the screen door slammed and Kim careened into the kitchen with Spike and Willow bouncing ecstatically around her feet.

"Whaddya think of the new house, Mom? Who do you think lives there? Do they have pets?"

I laid out her after-school sliced apple and cheese and answered the question I could answer. "There's at least one woman—she was hanging out laundry this morning. No sign of children or pets, but it's early days yet."

"Isn't it just the coolest thing in the universe, Mom? Real magic, right next door. Just like Buffy!"

"Without the vampires, I hope. Kim, there's no such thing as magic. There's probably a perfectly simple explanation."

"But, Mom!"

"But nothing. You need to call Mrs. Morrison. She wants to know if you can sit for Jason on Friday night. And Big Bad's looking shaggy. He needs to be brushed."

That was Monday.

Tuesday morning, our street looked like the Expressway at rush hour. It's a miracle there wasn't an accident. Everybody in town must have driven by, slowing down as they passed Number 400 and craning out the car window. Things quieted down in the middle of the day when everyone was at work, but come 4:30 or so, the joggers started and the walkers and more cars. About 6:00, the police pulled up in front of the house, at which point everyone stopped pretending to be nonchalant and held their breath. Two cops disappeared into the house, came out again a few minutes later, and left without talking to anybody. They were holding cookies and looking bewildered.

The traffic let up on Wednesday. Kim found a kitten (Hermione) in the wildflower garden and Geoff came home full of the latest in a series of personality conflicts with his department head, which gave everyone something other than Number 400 to talk about over dinner.

Thursday, Lucille Flint baked one of her coffee cakes and went over to do the Welcome Wagon thing.

Lucille's our local Good Neighbor. Someone moves in, has a baby, marries, dies, and there's Lucille, Johnny-on-the-spot with a coffee cake in her hands and the proper Hallmark sentiment on her lips. Lucille has the time for this kind of thing because she doesn't have a regular job. All right, neither do I, but I write a gardener's advice column for the local paper, so I'm not exactly idle. There's the garden, too. Besides, I'm not the kind of person who likes sitting around in other people's kitchens drinking watery instant and hearing the stories of their lives. Lucille is.

Anyway. Thursday morning, I researched the diseases of roses for my column. I'm lucky with roses. Mine never come down with black spot, and the Japanese beetles prefer Susan Morrison's yard to mine. Weeds, however, are not so obliging. When I'd finished googling "powdery mildew," I went out to tackle the rose bed.

Usually, I don't mind weeding. My mind wanders, my hands get dirty. I can almost feel my plants settling deeper into the soil as I root out the competition. But my rose bed is on the property line between us and the Pratt place. What if the house disappeared again, or someone wanted to chat? I'm not big into chatting. On the other hand, there was shepherd's purse in the rose bed, and shepherd's purse can be a wild Indian once you let it get established, so I gritted my teeth, grabbed my Cape Cod weeder, and got down to it.

Just as I was starting to relax, I heard footsteps passing on the walk and pushed the rose canes aside just in time to see Lucille Flint climbing the stone steps to Number 400. I watched her ring the doorbell, but I didn't see who answered because I ducked down behind a bushy Gloire de Dijon. If Lucille doesn't care who knows she's a busybody, that's her business.

After twenty-five minutes, I'd weeded and cultivated those roses to a fare-thee-well, and was backing out when I heard the screen door, followed by Lucille telling someone how lovely their home was, and thanks again for the scrumptious pie.

I caught her up under the copper beech.

"Evie dear, you're all out of breath," she said. "My, that's a nasty tear in your shirt."

"Come in, Lucille," I said. "Have a cup of coffee."

She followed me inside without comment, and accepted a cup of microwaved coffee and a slice of date-and-nut cake.

She took a bite, coughed a little, and grabbed for the coffee.

"It is pretty awful, isn't it?" I said apologetically. "I baked it last week for some PTA thing at Kim's school and forgot to take it."

"Never mind. I'm full of cherry pie from next door." She leaned over the stale cake and lowered her voice. "The cherries were fresh, Evie."

My mouth dropped open. "Fresh cherries? In May? You're kidding."

Lucille nodded, satisfied at my reaction. "Nope. There was a bowl of them on the table, leaves and all. What's more, there was corn on the draining-board. Fresh corn. In the husk. With the silk still on it."

"No!"

"Yes." Lucille sat back and took another sip of coffee. "Mind you, there could be a perfectly ordinary explanation. Ophelia's a horticulturist, after all. Maybe she's got greenhouses out back. Heaven knows there's enough room for several."

I shook my head. "I've never heard of corn growing in a greenhouse."

"And I've never heard of a house appearing in an empty lot overnight," Lucille said tartly. "About that, there's nothing I can tell you. They're not exactly forthcoming, if you know what I mean."

I was impressed. I knew how hard it was to avoid answering Lucille's questions, even about the most personal things. She just kind of picked at you, in the nicest possible way, until you unraveled. It's one of the reasons I didn't hang out with her much.

"So, who are they?"

"Rachel Abrams and Ophelia Canderel. I think they're lesbians. They feel like family together, and you can take it from me, they're not sisters."

Fine. We're a liberal suburb, we can cope with lesbians. "Children?"

Lucille shrugged. "I don't know. There were drawings on the fridge, but no toys."

"Inconclusive evidence," I agreed. "What did you talk about?"

She made a face. "Pie crust. The Perkins's wildflower meadow. They like it. Burney." Burney was Lucille's husband, an unpleasant old fart who disapproved of everything in the world except his equally unpleasant terrier, Homer. "Electricians. They want a fixture put up in the front hall. Then Rachel tried to tell me about her work in artificial intelligence, but I couldn't understand a word she said."

From where I was sitting, I had an excellent view of Number 400's wisteria-covered carriage house with its double doors ajar on an awe-inspiring array of garden tackle. "Artificial intelligence must pay well," I said.

Lucille shrugged. "There has to be family money somewhere. You ought to see the front hall, not to mention the kitchen. It looks like something out of a magazine."

"What are they doing here?"

"That's the forty-thousand-dollar question, isn't it?"

We drained the cold dregs of our coffee, contemplating the mystery of why a horticulturist and an artificial intelligence wonk would choose our quiet, tree-lined suburb to park their house in. It seemed a more solvable mystery than how they'd transported it there in the first place.

Lucille took off to make Burney his noontime franks and beans and I tried to get my column roughed out. But I couldn't settle to my computer, not with that Victorian enigma sitting on the other side of my rose bed. Every once in a while, I'd see a shadow passing behind a window or hear a door bang. I gave up trying to make the disposal of diseased foliage interesting and went out to poke around in the garden. I was elbow-deep in the viburnum, pruning out deadwood, when I heard someone calling.

It was a woman, standing on the other side of my roses. She was big, solidly curved, and dressed in bright flowered overalls. Her hair was braided with shiny gold ribbon into dozens of tiny plaits tied off with little metal beads. Her skin was a deep matte brown, like antique mahogany. Despite the overalls, she was astonishingly beautiful.

I dropped the pruning shears. "Damn," I said. "Sorry," I said. "You surprised me." I felt my cheeks heat. The woman smiled at me serenely and beckoned.

I don't like new people and I don't like being put on the spot, but I've got my pride. I picked up my pruning shears, untangled myself from the viburnum, and marched across the lawn to meet my new neighbor.

She said her name was Ophelia Canderel, and she'd been admiring my garden. Would I like to see hers?

I certainly would.

If I'd met Ophelia at a party, I'd have been totally tongue-tied. She was beautiful, she was big, and frankly, there just aren't enough people of color in our neighborhood for me to have gotten over my Liberal nervousness around them. This particular woman of color, however, spoke fluent Universal Gardener and her garden was a gardener's garden, full of horticultural experiments and puzzles and stuff to talk about. Within about three minutes, she was asking my advice about the gnarly brown larvae infesting her bee balm, and I was filling her in on the peculiarities of our local microclimate. By the time we'd inspected every flower and shrub in the front yard, I was more comfortable with her than I was with the local garden club ladies. We were alike, Ophelia and I.

We were discussing the care and feeding of peonies in an acid soil when Ophelia said, "Would you like to see my shrubbery?"

Usually when I hear the word "shrubbery" I think of a semi-formal arrangement of rhodies and azaleas, lilacs and viburnum, with a potentilla perhaps, or a butterfly bush for late summer color. The bed should be deep enough to give everything room to spread and there should be a statue in it, or maybe a sundial. Neat, but not anal—that's what you should aim for in a shrubbery.

Ophelia sure had the not-anal part down pat. The shrubs didn't merely spread. They rioted. And what with the trees and the orchids and the ferns and the vines, I couldn't begin to judge the border's depth. The hibiscus and the bamboo were okay, although I wouldn't have risked them myself. But to plant bougainvillea and poinsettias, coconut palms and frangipani this far north was simply tempting fate. And the statue! I'd never seen anything remotely like it, not outside of a museum, anyway. No head to speak of, breasts like footballs, a belly like a watermelon, and a phallus like an overgrown zucchini, the whole thing weathered with the rains of a thousand years or more.

I glanced at Ophelia. "Impressive," I said.

She turned a critical eye on it. "You don't think it's too much? Rachel says it is, but she's a minimalist. This is my little bit of home, and I love it."

"It's a lot," I admitted. Accuracy prompted me to add, "It suits you."

I still didn't understand how Ophelia had gotten a tropical rainforest to flourish in a temperate climate.

I was trying to find a nice way to ask her about it when she said, "You're a real find, Evie. Rachel's working, or I'd call her to come down. She really wants to meet you."

"Next time," I said, wondering what on earth I'd find to talk about with a specialist on artificial intelligence. "Um. Does Rachel garden?"

Ophelia laughed. "No way—her talent is not for living things. But I made a garden for her. Would you like to see it?"

I was only dying to, although I couldn't help wondering what kind of exotica I was letting myself in for. A desertscape? Tundra? Curiosity won. "Sure," I said. "Lead on."

We stopped on the way to visit the vegetable garden. It looked fairly ordinary, although the tomatoes were more August than May, and the beans more late June. I didn't see any corn and I didn't see any greenhouses. After a brief sidebar on insecticidal soaps, Ophelia led me behind the carriage house. The unmistakable sound of quacking fell on my ears.

"We aren't zoned for ducks," I said, startled.

"We are," said Ophelia. "Now. How do you like Rachel's garden?"

A prospect of brown reeds with a silvery river meandering through it stretched through where the Morrison's back yard ought to be, all the way to a boundless expanse of ocean. In the marsh it was April, with a crisp salt wind blowing back from the water and ruffling the brown reeds and the white-flowering shad and the pale green unfurling sweetfern. Mallards splashed and dabbled along the meander. A solitary great egret stood among the reeds, the fringes of its white courting shawl blowing around one black and knobbly leg. As I watched, open-mouthed, the egret unfurled its other leg from its breast feathers, trod at the reeds, and lowered its golden bill to feed.

~

I got home late. Kim was in the basement with the animals, and the chicken I was planning to make for dinner was still in the freezer. Thanking heaven for modern technology, I defrosted the chicken in the microwave, chopped veggies, seasoned, mixed, and got the whole mess in the oven just as Geoff walked in the door. He wasn't happy about eating forty-five minutes late, but he was mostly over it by bedtime.

That was Thursday.

Friday, I saw Ophelia and Rachel pulling out of their driveway in one of those old cars that has huge fenders and a running board. They returned after lunch, the back seat full of groceries. They and the groceries disappeared through the kitchen door, and there was no further sign of them until late afternoon, when Rachel opened one of the quarter-round windows in the attic and energetically shook the dust out of a small, patterned carpet.

On Saturday, the invitation came.

It stood out among the flyers, book orders, and requests for money that usually came through our mail-slot, a five-by-eight silvery-blue envelope that smelled faintly of sandalwood. It was was addressed to the Gordon Family in a precise italic hand.

I opened it and read:

Rachel Esther Abrams and Ophelia Desirée Candarel
Request the Honor of Your Presence
at the
Celebration of their Marriage.
Sunday, May 24 at 3 p.m.
There will be refreshments before and after the Ceremony.

I was still staring at it when the doorbell rang. It was Lucille, looking fit to burst, holding an invitation just like mine.

"Come in, Lucille. There's plenty of coffee left."

I don't think I'd ever seen Lucille in such a state. You'd think someone had invited her to parade naked down Main Street at noon.

"Well, write and tell them you can't come," I said. "They're just being neighborly, for Pete's sake. It's not like they can't get married if you're not there."

"I know. It's just . . . It puts me in a funny position, that's all. Burney's a founding member of Normal Marriage for Normal People. He wouldn't like it at all if he knew I'd been invited to a lesbian wedding."

"So don't tell him. If you want to go, just tell him the new neighbors have invited you to an open house on Sunday, and you know for a fact that we're going to be there."

Lucille smiled. Burney hated Geoff almost as much as Geoff hated Burney. "It's a thought," she said. "Are you going?"

"I don't see why not. Who knows? I might learn something."

∼

The Sunday of the wedding, I took forever to dress. Kim thought it was funny, but Geoff threatened to bail if I didn't quit fussing. "It's a lesbian wedding, for pity's sake. It's going to be full of middle-aged dykes with ugly haircuts. Nobody's going to care what you look like."

"I care," said Kim. "And I think that jacket is wicked cool."

I'd bought the jacket at a little Indian store in the Square and not worn it since. When I got it away from the Square's atmosphere of collegiate funk it looked, I don't know, too Sixties, too artsy, too bright for a forty-something suburban matron. It was basically purple, with teal blue and gold and fuchsia flowers all over it and brass buttons shaped like parrots. Shaking my head, I started to unfasten the parrots.

Geoff exploded. "I swear to God, Evie, if you change again, that's it. It's not like I want to go. I've got papers to correct: don't have time for this"—he glanced at Kim—"nonsense. Either we go or we stay. But we do it now."

Kim touched my arm. "It's you, Mom. Come on."

So I came on, my jacket flashing neon in the sunlight. By the time we hit the sidewalk, I felt like a tropical floral display; I was ready to bolt home and hide under the bed.

"Great," said Geoff. "Not a car in sight. If we're the only ones here, I'm leaving."

"I don't think that's going to be a problem," I said.

Beyond the copper beech, I saw a colorful crowd milling around as purposefully as bees, bearing chairs and flowers and ribbons. As we came closer, it became clear that Geoff couldn't have been more wrong about the wedding guests. There wasn't an ugly haircut in sight, although there were some pretty startling dye-jobs. The dress code could best be described as eclectic, with a slight bias toward floating fabrics and rich, bright colors. My jacket felt right at home.

Geoff was muttering about not knowing anybody when Lucille appeared, looking festive in Laura Ashley chintz.

"Isn't this fun?" she said, with every sign of sincerity. "I've never met such interesting people. And friendly! They make me feel right at home. Come over here and join the gang."

She dragged us toward the long side-yard, which sloped down to a lavishly blooming double-flowering cherry underplanted with peonies. Which shouldn't have been in bloom at the same time as the cherry, but I was getting used to the vagaries of Ophelia's garden. A willowy young person in chartreuse lace claimed Lucille's attention, and they went off together. The three of us stood in a slightly awkward knot at the edge of the crowd, which occasionally threw out a few guests who eddied around us briefly before retreating.

"How are those spells of yours, dear? Any better?" inquired a solicitous voice in my ear, and, "Oh!" when I jumped. "You're not Elvira, are you? Sorry."

Geoff's grip was cutting off the circulation above my elbow. "This was not one of your better ideas, Evie. We're surrounded by weirdos. Did you see that guy in the skirt? I think we should take Kimmy home."

A tall black man with a flattop and a diamond in his left ear appeared, pried Geoff's hand from my arm, and shook it warmly. "Dr. Gordon? Ophelia told me to be looking out for you. I've read *The Anarchists*, you see, and I can't tell you how much I admired it."

Geoff actually blushed. Before the subject got too painful to talk about, he used to say that for a history of anarchism, his one book had had a remarkably elite readership: three members of the tenure review committee, two reviewers for scholarly journals, and his wife. "Thanks," he said.

Geoff's fan grinned, clearly delighted. "Maybe we can talk at the reception," he said. "Right now I need to find you a place to sit. They look like they're just about ready to roll."

~

It was a lovely wedding.

I don't know exactly what I was expecting, but I was mildly surprised to see a rabbi and a wedding canopy. Ophelia was an enormous rose in crimson draperies. Rachel was a calla lily in cream linen. Their heads were tastefully wreathed in oak and ivy leaves. There were the usual prayers and promises and tears; when the rabbi pronounced them married, they kissed and horns sounded a triumphant fanfare.

Kim poked me in the side. "Mom? Who's playing those horns?"

"I don't know. Maybe it's a recording."

"I don't think so," Kim said. "I think it's the tree. Isn't this just about the coolest thing ever?"

We were on our feet again. The chairs had disappeared and people were dancing. A cheerful bearded man grabbed Kim's hand to pull her into the line. Geoff grabbed her and pulled her back.

"Dad!" Kim wailed. "I want to dance!"

"I've got a pile of papers to correct before class tomorrow," Geoff said. "And if I know you, there's some homework you've put off until tonight. We have to go home now."

"We can't leave yet," I objected. "We haven't congratulated the brides."

Geoff's jaw tensed. "So go congratulate them," he said. "Kim and I will wait for you here."

Kim looked mutinous. I gave her the eye. This wasn't the time or the place to object. Like Geoff, Kim had no inhibitions about airing the family linen in public, but I had enough for all three of us.

"Dr. Gordon. There you are." *The Anarchists* fan popped up between us. "I've been looking all over for you. Come have a drink and let me tell you how brilliant you are."

Geoff smiled modestly. "You're being way too generous," he said. "Did you read Peterson's piece in *The Review?*"

"Asshole," said the man dismissively. Geoff slapped him on the back, and a minute later, they were halfway to the house, laughing as if they'd known each other for years. Thank heaven for the male ego.

"Dance?" said Kim.

"Go for it," I said. "I'm going to get some champagne and kiss the brides."

The brides were nowhere to be found. The champagne, a young girl informed me, was in the kitchen. So I entered Number 400 for the first time, coming through the mudroom into a large, oak-paneled hall. To my left a staircase with an ornately carved oak banister rose to an art-glass window. Ahead was a semicircular fireplace with a carved bench on one side and a door that probably led to the kitchen on the other. Between me and the door was an assortment of brightly dressed strangers, talking and laughing.

I edged around them, passing two curtained doors and a bronze statue of Alice and the Red Queen. Puzzle fragments of conversation rose out of the general buzz:

"My pearls? Thank you, my dear, but you know they're only stimulated."

"And *then* it just went 'poof'! A perfectly good frog, and it just went 'poof'!"

" . . . and then Tallulah says to the bishop, she says, 'Love your drag, darling, but your purse is on fire.' Don't you love it? 'Your purse is on fire'!"

The kitchen itself was blessedly empty except for a stout gentleman in a tuxedo, and a striking woman in a peach silk pantsuit, who was tending an array of champagne bottles and a cut-glass bowl full of bright blue punch. Curious, I picked up a cup of punch and sniffed at it. The woman smiled up at me through a caterpillary fringe of false lashes.

"Pure witch's brew," she said in one of those Lauren Bacall come-hither voices I've always envied. "But what can you do? It's the *specialité de la maison*."

The tuxedoed man laughed. "Don't mind Silver, Mrs. Gordon. He just likes to tease. Ophelia's punch is wonderful."

"Only if you like Ty-dee Bowl," said Silver, tipping a sapphire stream into another cup. "You know, honey, you shouldn't stand around with your mouth open like that. Think of the flies."

Several guests entered in plenty of time to catch this exchange. Determined to preserve my cool, I took a gulp of the punch. It tasted fruity and made my mouth prickle, and then it hit my stomach like a firecracker. So much for cool. I choked and gasped.

"I tried to warn you," Silver said. "You'd better switch to champagne." Now I knew Silver was a man, I could see that his hands and wrists were big for the rest of her—him. I could feel my face burning with punch and mortification.

"No, thank you," I said faintly. "Maybe some water?"

The stout man handed me a glass. I sipped gratefully. "You're Ophelia and Rachel's neighbor, aren't you?" he said. "Lovely garden. You must be proud of that asparagus bed."

"I was, until I saw Ophelia's."

"Ooh, listen to the green-eyed monster," Silver cooed. "Don't be jealous, honey. Ophelia's the best. Nobody understands plants like Ophelia."

"I'm not jealous," I said with dignity. "I'm wistful. There's a difference."

Then, just when I thought it couldn't possibly get any worse, Geoff appeared, looking stunningly unprofessorial, with one side of his shirt collar turned up and his dark hair flopped over his eyes.

"Hey, Evie. Who knew a couple of dykes would know how to throw a wedding?"

You'd think after sixteen years of living with Geoff, I'd know whether or not he was an alcoholic. But I don't. He doesn't go on binges, he doesn't get drunk at every party we go to, and I'm pretty sure he doesn't drink on the sly. What I do know is that drinking doesn't make him more fun to be around.

I took his arm. "I'm glad you're enjoying yourself," I said brightly. "Too bad we have to leave."

"Leave? Who said anything about leaving? We just got here."

"Your papers," I said. "Remember?"

"Screw my papers," said Geoff and held out his empty cup to Silver. "This punch is dy-no-mite."

"What about your students?"

"I'll tell 'em I didn't feel like reading their stupid essays. That'll fix their little red wagons. Boring as hell anyway. Fill 'er up, beautiful," he told Silver.

Silver considered him gravely. "Geoff, darling," he said. "A little bird tells me that there's an absolutely delicious argument going on in the smoking room. They'll never forgive you if you don't come play."

Geoff favored Silver with a leer that made me wish I were somewhere else. "Only if you play too," he said. "What's it about?"

Silver waved a pink-tipped hand. "Something about theoretical versus practical anarchy. Right, Rodney?"

"I believe so," said the stout gentleman agreeably.

A martial gleam rose in Geoff's eye. "Let me at 'em."

Silver's pale eyes turned to me, solemn and concerned. "You don't mind, do you, honey?"

I shrugged. With luck, the smoking-room crowd would be drunk too, and nobody would remember who said what. I just hoped none of the anarchists had a violent temper.

"We'll return him intact," Silver said. "I promise." And they were gone, Silver trailing fragrantly from Geoff's arm.

While I was wondering whether I'd said that thing about the anarchists or only thought it, I felt a tap on my shoulder—the stout gentleman, Rodney.

"Mrs. Gordon, Rachel and Ophelia would like to see you and young Kimberly in the study. If you'll please step this way?"

His manner had shifted from wedding guest to old-fashioned butler. Properly intimidated, I trailed him to the front hall. It was empty now, except for Lucille and the young person in chartreuse lace, who were huddled together on the bench by the fireplace. The young person was talking earnestly and Lucille was listening and nodding and sipping punch. Neither of them paid any attention to us or to the music coming from behind one of the curtained doors. I saw Kim at the foot of the stairs, examining the newel post.

It was well worth examining: a screaming griffin with every feather and every curl beautifully articulated and its head polished smooth and black as ebony. Rodney gave it a brief, seemingly unconscious caress as he started up the steps. When Kim followed suit, I thought I saw the carved eye blink.

I must have made a noise, because Rodney halted his slow ascent and gazed down at me, standing open-mouthed below. "Lovely piece of work, isn't it? We call it the house guardian. A joke, of course."

"Of course," I echoed. "Cute."

~

It seemed to me that the house had more rooms than it ought to. Through open doors, I glimpsed libraries, salons, parlors, bedrooms. We passed through a stone cloister where discouraged-looking ficuses in tubs shed their leaves on the cracked pavement and into a green-scummed pool. I don't know what shocked me more: the cloister or the state of its plants. Maybe Ophelia's green thumb didn't extend to houseplants.

As far as I could tell, Kim took all this completely in stride. She bounded along like a dog in the woods, peeking in an open door here, pausing to look at a picture there, and pelting Rodney with questions I wouldn't have dreamed of asking, like "Are there kids here?" "What about pets?" "How many people live here, anyway?"

"It depends," was Rodney's unvarying answer. "Step this way, please."

Our trek ended in a wall covered by a huge South American tapestry of three women making pots. Rodney pulled the tapestry aside, revealing an iron-banded oak door that would have done a medieval castle proud. "The study," he said, and opened the door on a flight of ladder-like steps rising steeply into the shadows.

His voice and gesture reminded me irresistibly of one of those horror movies in which a laconic butler leads the hapless heroine to a forbidding door and invites her to step inside. I didn't know which of three impulses was stronger: to laugh, to run, or, like the heroine, to forge on and see what happened next.

It's some indication of the state I was in that Kim got by me and through the door before I could stop her.

I don't like feeling helpless and I don't like feeling pressured. I really don't like being tricked, manipulated, and herded. Left to myself, I'd have turned around and taken my chances on finding my way out of the maze of corridors. But I wasn't going to leave without my daughter, so I hitched up my wedding-appropriate long skirt and started up the steps.

The stairs were every bit as steep as they looked. I floundered up gracelessly, emerging into a huge space sparsely furnished with a beat-up rolltop desk, a wingback chair and a swan-neck rocker on a threadbare Oriental rug at one end, and some cluttered door-on-sawhorse tables on the other. Ophelia and Rachel, still dressed in their bridal finery, were sitting in the chair and the rocker respectively, holding steaming mugs and talking to Kim, who was incandescent with excitement.

"Oh, there you are," said Ophelia as I stumbled up the last step. "Would you like some tea?"

"No, thank you," I said stiffly. "Kim, I think it's time to go home now."

Kim protested, vigorously. Rachel cast Ophelia an unreadable look.

"It'll be fine, love," Ophelia said soothingly. "Mrs. Gordon's upset, and who could blame her? Evie, I don't believe you've actually met Rachel."

Where I come from, social niceties trump everything. Without actually meaning to, I found I was shaking Rachel's hand and congratulating her on her marriage. Close up, she was a handsome woman, with a decided nose, deep lines around her mouth, and the measuring gaze of a gardener examining an unfamiliar insect on her tomato leaves. I didn't ask her to call me Evie.

Ophelia touched my hand. "Never mind," she said soothingly. "Have some tea. You'll feel better."

Next thing I knew, I was sitting on a chair that hadn't been there a moment before, eating a lemon cookie from a plate I didn't see arrive, and drinking Lapsang Souchong from a cup that appeared when Ophelia reached for it. Just for the record, I didn't feel better at all. I felt as if I'd taken a step that wasn't there, or perhaps failed to take one that was: out of balance, out of place, out of control.

Kim, restless as a cat, was snooping around among the long tables.

"What's with the flying fish?" she asked.

"They're for Rachel's new experiment," said Ophelia. "She thinks she can bring the dead to life again."

"You better let me tell it, Ophie," Rachel said. "I don't want Mrs. Gordon thinking I'm some kind of mad scientist."

In fact, I wasn't thinking at all, except that I was in way over my head.

"I'm working on animating extinct species," Rachel said. "I'm particularly interested in dodos and passenger pigeons, but eventually, I'd like to work up to bison and maybe woolly mammoths."

"Won't that create ecological problems?" Kim objected. "I mean, they're way big, and we don't know much about their habits or what they ate or anything."

There was a silence while Rachel and Ophelia traded family-joke smiles.

"That's why we need you," Rachel said.

Kim looked as though she'd been given the pony she'd been agitating for since fourth grade. Her jaw dropped. Her eyes sparkled. And I lost it.

"Will somebody please tell me what the hell you're talking about?" I said. "I've been patient. I followed your pal Rodney through more rooms than Versailles and I didn't run screaming, and believe me when I tell you I wanted to. I've drunk your tea and listened to your so-called explanations, and I still don't know what's going on."

Kim turned to me with a look of blank astonishment. "Come on, Mom. I can't believe you don't know that Ophelia and Rachel are witches. It's perfectly obvious."

"We prefer not to use the W-word," Rachel said. "Like most labels, it's misleading and inaccurate. We're just people with natural scientific ability who have been trained to ask the right questions."

Ophelia nodded. "We learn to ask the things themselves. They always know. Do you see?"

"No," I said. "All I see is a roomful of junk and a garden that doesn't care what season it is."

"Very well," said Rachel, and rose from her chair. "If you'll just come over here, Mrs. Gordon, I'll try to clear everything up."

At the table of the flying fish, Ophelia arranged us in a semi-circle, with Rachel in a teacherly position beside the exhibits. These seemed to be A) the fish and B) one of those Japanese good-luck cats with one paw curled up by its ear and a bright enameled bib.

"As you know," Rachel said, "my field is artificial intelligence. What that means, essentially, is that I can animate the inanimate. Observe." She caressed the porcelain cat between its ears. For two breaths, nothing happened. Then the cat lowered its paw and stretched itself luxuriously. The light glinted off its bulging sides; its curly red mouth and wide painted eyes were expressionless.

"Sweet," Kim breathed.

"It's not really alive," Rachel said, stroking the cat's shiny back. "It's still porcelain. If it jumps off the table, it'll break."

"Can I pet it?" Kim asked.

"No!" Rachel and I said in firm and perfect unison.

"Why not?"

"Because I'd like you to help me with an experiment." Rachel looked me straight in the eye. "I'm not really comfortable with words," she said. "I prefer demonstrations. What I'm going to do is hold Kim's hand and touch the fish. That's all."

"And what happens then?" Kim asked eagerly.

Rachel smiled at her. "Well, we'll see, won't we? Are you okay with this, Mrs. Gordon?"

It sounded harmless enough, and Kim was already reaching for Rachel's hand. "Go ahead," I said.

Their hands met palm to palm. Rachel closed her eyes. She frowned in concentration and the atmosphere tightened around us. I yawned to unblock my ears.

Rachel laid her free hand on one of the fish.

It twitched, head jerking galvanically; its wings fanned open and shut.

Kim gave a little grunt, which snapped my attention away from the fish. She was pale and sweating a little—

I started to go to her, but I couldn't. Someone was holding me back.

"It's okay, Evie," Ophelia said soothingly. "Kim's fine, really. Rachel knows what she's doing."

"Kim's pale," I said, calm as the eye of a storm. "She looks like she's going to throw up. She's not fine. Let me go to my daughter, Ophelia, or I swear you'll regret it."

"Believe me, it's not safe for you to touch them right now. You have to trust us."

My Great-Aunt Fanny I'll trust you, I thought, and willed myself to relax in her grip. "Okay," I said shakily. "I believe you. It's just, I wish you'd warned me."

"We wanted to tell you," Ophelia said. "But we were afraid you wouldn't believe us. We were afraid you would think we were a couple of nuts. You see, Kim has the potential to be an important zoologist—if she has the proper training. Rachel's a wonderful teacher, and you can see for yourself how complementary their disciplines are. Working together, they . . . "

I don't know what she thought Kim and Rachel could accomplish, because the second she was more interested in what she was saying than in holding onto me, I was out of her hands and pulling Kim away from the witch who, as far as I could tell, was draining her dry.

That was the plan, anyway.

As soon as I touched Kim, the room came alive.

It started with the flying fish leaping off the table and buzzing past us on Saran Wrap wings. The porcelain cat thumped down from the table and, far from breaking, twined itself around Kim's ankles, purring hollowly. An iron plied itself over a pile of papers, smoothing out the creases. The teddy bear growled at it and ran to hide behind a toaster.

If that wasn't enough, my jacket burst into bloom.

It's kind of hard to describe what it's like to wear a tropical forest. Damp, for one thing. Bright. Loud. Uncomfortable. Very, very uncomfortable. Overstimulating. There were flowers and parrots screeching (yes, the flowers, too—or maybe that was me). It seemed to go on for a long time, kind of like giving birth. At first, I was overwhelmed by the chaos of growth and sound, unsure whether I was the forest or the forest was me. Slowly I realized that it didn't have to be chaos, and that if I just pulled myself together, I could make sense of it. That flower went there, for instance, and the teal one went there. That parrot belonged on that vine and everything needed to be smaller and stiller and less extravagantly colored. Like that.

Gradually, the forest receded. I was still holding Kim, who promptly bent over and threw up on the floor.

"There," I said hoarsely, "I told you she was going to be sick."

Ophelia picked up Rachel and carried her back to her wingchair. "You be quiet, you," she said over her shoulder. "Heaven knows what you've done to Rachel. I told you not to touch them."

Ignoring my own nausea, I supported Kim over to the rocker and deposited her in it. "You might have told me why," I snapped. "I don't know why people can't just explain things instead of making me guess. It's not like I can read minds, you know. Now, are you going to conjure us up a glass of water, or do I have to go find the kitchen?"

Rachel had recovered herself enough to give a shaky laugh. "Hell, you could conjure it yourself, with a little practice. Ophie, darling, calm down. I'm fine."

Ophelia stopped fussing over her wife long enough to snatch a glass of cool mint tea from the air and hand it to me. She wouldn't meet my eyes, and she was scowling. "I told you she was going to be difficult. Of all the damn-fool, pigheaded . . . "

"Hush, love," Rachel said. "There's no harm done, and now we know just where we stand. I'd rather have a nice cup of tea than listen to you cursing out Mrs. Gordon for just trying to be a good mother." She turned her head to look at me. "Very impressive, by the way. We knew you had to be like Ophie, because of the garden, but we didn't know the half of it. You've got a kick like a mule, Mrs. Gordon."

I must have been staring at her like one of the flying fish. Here I thought I'd half-killed her, and she was giving me a smile that looked perfectly genuine.

I smiled cautiously in return. "Thank you," I said.

Kim pulled at the sleeve of my jacket. "Hey, Mom, that was awesome. I guess you're a witch, huh?"

I wanted to deny it, but I couldn't. The fact was that the pattern of flowers on my jacket was different and the colors were muted, the flowers more English garden than tropical paradise. There were only three buttons, and they were larks, not parrots. And I felt different. Clearer? More whole? I don't know—different. Even though I didn't know how the magic worked or how to control it, I couldn't ignore the fact—the palpable, provable fact—it was there.

"Yeah," I said. "I guess I am."

"Me, too," my daughter said. "What's Dad going to say?"

I thought for a minute. "Nothing, honey. Because we're not going to tell him."

~

We didn't, either. And we're not going to. There's no useful purpose served by telling people truths they aren't equipped to accept. Geoff's pretty oblivious, anyway. It's true that in the hung-over aftermath of Ophelia's blue punch, he announced that he thought the new neighbors might be a bad influence, but he couldn't actually forbid Kim and me to hang out with them because it would look homophobic.

Kim's over at Number 400 most Saturday afternoons, learning how to be a zoologist. She's making good progress. There was an episode with zombie mice I don't like to think about, and a crisis when the porcelain cat broke falling out of a tree. But she's learning patience, control, and discipline, which are all excellent things for a girl of fourteen to learn. She and Rachel have reanimated a pair of passenger pigeons, but they haven't had any luck in breeding them yet.

Lucille's the biggest surprise. It turns out that all her nosy-parkerism was a case of ingrown witchiness. Now she's studying with Silver, of all people, to be a psychologist. But that's not the surprise. The surprise is that she left Burney and moved into Number 400, where she has a room draped with chintz and a gray cat named Jezebel and is as happy as a clam at high tide.

I'm over there a lot, too, learning to be a horticulturist. Ophelia says I'm a quick study, but I have to learn to trust my instincts. Who knew I had instincts? I thought I was just good at looking things up.

I'm working on my own garden now. I'm the only one who can find it without being invited in. It's an English kind of garden, like the gardens in books I loved as a child. It has a stone wall with a low door in it, a little central lawn, and a perennial border full of foxgloves and Sweet William and Michelmas daisies. Veronica blooms in the cracks of the wall, and periwinkle carpets the beds where old-fashioned fragrant roses nod heavily to every passing breeze. There's a small wilderness of rowan trees, and a neat shrubbery embracing a pond stocked with fish as bright as copper pennies. Among the dusty-smelling boxwood, I've put a statue of a woman holding a basket planted with stonecrop. She's dressed in a jacket incised with flowers and vines and closed with three buttons shaped like parrots. The fourth button sits on her shoulder, clacking its beak companionably and preening its brazen feathers. I'm thinking of adding a duck pond next, or maybe a wilderness for Kim's menagerie.

Witches don't have to worry about zoning laws.

～

A woman with magical powers—skilled at martial arts and occult detection—who has a vampire as a lover with whom she fights the forces of evil in an urban setting where, unknown to most humans, there are many who are not human . . .

*As familiar as that plotline may sound in 2012, this story was published in 1989 and introduced Diana Tregarde, an American witch whose witchcraft has a great deal in common with modern neopagan Wiccan beliefs. She is also a "Guardian"—charged with protecting the Earth and all its creatures—a designation that gives her access to more magical power than most witches. Protecting others isn't a paying job, however, so Diana writes romance novels for a living. "Nightside" only hints at the characters and world Mercedes Lackey created for three novels—*Burning Water *(1989),* Children of the Night *(1990),* Jinx High *(1991)—a novella, and another short story. The novels were published by Tor as "horror" and, according to Lackey, did not sell well. She declined to write more.*

Diana Tregarde can be viewed as yet another in a long line of fictional protectors of humanity with occult powers, but she was also one of the first modern "kick-ass" heroines who are now so popular.

Nightside
Mercedes Lackey

It was early spring, but the wind held no hint of verdancy, not even the promise of it—it was chill and odorless, and there were ghosts of dead leaves skittering before it. A few of them jittered into the pool of weak yellow light cast by the aging streetlamp—a converted gaslight that was a relic of the previous century. It was old and tired, its pea-green paint flaking away; as weary as this neighborhood, which was older still. Across the street loomed an ancient church, its congregation dwindled over the years to a handful of little old women and men who appeared like scrawny blackbirds every Sunday, and then scattered back to the shabby houses that stood to either side of it until Sunday should come again. On the side of the street that the lamp tried (and failed) to illuminate, was the cemetery.

Like the neighborhood, it was very old—in this case, fifty years shy of being classified as "Colonial." There were few empty gravesites now, and most of those belonged to the same little old ladies and men that had lived and would die here. It was protected from vandals by a thorny hedge as well as a ten-foot wrought-iron fence. Within its confines, as seen through the leafless branches of the hedge, granite cenotaphs and enormous Victorian monuments hulked shapelessly against the bare sliver of a waning moon.

The church across the street was dark and silent; the houses up and down the block showed few lights, if any. There was no reason for anyone of this neighborhood to be out in the night.

So the young woman waiting beneath the lamppost seemed that much more out-of-place.

Nor could she be considered a typical resident of this neighborhood by any stretch of the imagination—for one thing, she was young; perhaps in her mid-twenties, but no more. Her clothing was neat but casual, too casual for someone visiting an elderly relative. She wore dark, knee-high boots, old, soft jeans tucked into their tops, and a thin windbreaker open at the front to show a leotard beneath. Her attire was far too light to be any real protection against the bite of the wind, yet she seemed unaware of the cold. Her hair was long, down to her waist, and straight—in the uncertain light of the lamp it was an indeterminate shadow, and it fell down her back like a waterfall. Her eyes were large and oddly slanted, but not Oriental; catlike, rather. Even the way she held herself was feline; poised, expectant—a graceful tension like a dancer's or a hunting predator's. She was not watching for something—no, her eyes were unfocused with concentration. She was *listening*.

A soft whistle, barely audible, carried down the street on the chill wind. The tune was of a piece with the neighborhood—old and time-worn.

Many of the residents would have smiled in recollection to hear "Lili Marlene" again.

The tension left the girl as she swung around the lamppost by one hand to face the direction of the whistle. She waved, and a welcoming smile warmed her eyes.

The whistler stepped into the edge of the circle of light. He, too, was dusky of eye and hair—and heartbreakingly handsome. He wore only dark jeans and a black turtleneck, no coat at all—but like the young woman, he didn't seem to notice the cold. There was an impish glint in his eyes as he finished the tune with a flourish.

"A flair for the dramatic, Diana, *mon cherie*?" he said mockingly. "Would that you were here for the same purpose as the lovely Lili! Alas, I fear my luck cannot be so good . . . "

She laughed. His eyes warmed at the throaty chuckle. "Andre," she chided, "don't you ever think of anything else?"

"Am I not a son of the City of Light? I must uphold her reputation, *mais non*?" The young woman raised an ironic brow. He shrugged. "Ah well—since it is you who seek me, I fear I must be all business. A pity. Well, what lures you to my side this unseasonable night? What horror has *Mademoiselle* Tregarde unearthed this time?"

Diana Tregarde sobered instantly, the laughter fleeing her eyes. "I'm afraid you picked the right word this time, Andre. It is a horror. The trouble is, I don't know what kind."

"Say on. I wait in breathless anticipation." His expression was mocking as he leaned against the lamppost, and he feigned a yawn.

Diana scowled at him and her eyes darkened with anger. He raised an eyebrow of his own. "If this weren't so serious," she threatened, "I'd be tempted to pop you one—Andre, people are dying out there. There's a 'Ripper' loose in New York."

He shrugged, and shifted restlessly from one foot to the other. "So? This is new? Tell me when there is not! That sort of criminal is as common to the city as a rat. Let your police earn their salaries and capture him."

Her expression hardened. She folded her arms tightly across the thin nylon of her windbreaker; her lips tightened a little. "Use your head, Andre! If this was an ordinary slasher-killer, would I be involved?"

He examined his fingernails with care. "And what is it that makes it *extraordinaire*, eh?"

"The victims had no souls."

"I was not aware," he replied wryly, "that the dead possessed such things anymore."

She growled under her breath, and tossed her head impatiently. The wind caught her hair and whipped it around her throat. "You are *deliberately* being difficult! I have half a mind—"

It finally seemed to penetrate the young man's mind that she was truly angry—and truly frightened, though she was doing her best to conceal the fact; his expression became contrite. "Forgive me, *cherie*. I *am* being recalcitrant."

"You're being a pain in the ass," she replied acidly. "Would I have come to you if I wasn't already out of my depth?"

"Well—" he admitted. "No. But—this business of souls, *cherie*, how can you determine such a thing? I find it most difficult to believe."

She shivered, and her eyes went brooding. "So did I. Trust me, my friend, I know what I'm talking about. There isn't a shred of doubt in my mind. There are at least six victims who no longer exist in any fashion anymore."

The young man finally evidenced alarm. "But—how?" he said, bewildered. "How is such a thing possible?"

She shook her head violently, clenching her hands on the sleeves of her jacket as if by doing so she could protect herself from an unseen—but not unfelt—danger. "I don't know, I don't know! It seems incredible even now—I keep thinking it's a nightmare, but—Andre, it's real, it's not my imagination—" Her voice rose a little with each word, and Andre's sharp eyes rested for a moment on her trembling hands.

"*Eh bien,*" he sighed, "I believe you. So there is something about that devours souls—and mutilates bodies as well, since you mentioned a 'Ripper' persona?"

She nodded.

"Was the devouring before or after the mutilation?"

"Before, I think—it's not easy to judge." She shivered in a way that had nothing to do with the cold.

"And you came into this how?"

"Whatever it is, it took the friend of a friend; I—happened to be there to see the body afterwards, and I knew immediately there was something wrong. When I unshielded and used the Sight—"

"Bad." He made it a statement.

"Worse. I—I can't describe what it felt like. There were still residual emotions, things left behind when—" Her jaw clenched. "Then when I started checking further I found out about the other five victims—that what I had discovered was no fluke. Andre, whatever it is, it has to be stopped." She laughed again, but this time there was no humor in it. "After all, you could say stopping it is in my job description."

He nodded soberly. "And so you become involved. Well enough, if you must hunt this thing, so must I." He became all business. "Tell me of the history. When, and where, and who does it take?"

She bit her lip. "'Where'—there's no pattern. 'Who' seems to be mostly a matter of opportunity; the only clue is that the victims were always out on the street and entirely alone, there were no witnesses whatsoever, so the thing needs total privacy and apparently can't strike wherever at will. And 'when'—is moon-dark."

"Bad." He shook his head. "I have no clue at the moment. The *loup-garou* I know, and others, but I know nothing that hunts beneath the dark moon."

She grimaced. "You think I do? That's why I need your help; you're sensitive enough to feel something out of the ordinary, and you can watch and hunt undetected. I can't. And I'm not sure I want to go trolling for this thing alone—without knowing what it is, I could end up as a late-night snack for it. But if that's what I have to do, I will."

Anger blazed up in his face like a cold fire. "You go hunting alone for this creature over my dead body!"

"That's a little redundant, isn't it?" Her smile was weak, but genuine again.

"Pah!" he dismissed her attempt at humor with a wave of his hand. "Tomorrow is the first night of moon-dark; I shall go a-hunting. *You* remain at home, else I shall be most wroth with you. I know where to find you, should I learn anything of note."

"You ought to—" Diana began, but she spoke to the empty air.

The next night was warmer, and Diana had gone to bed with her windows open to drive out some of the stale odors the long winter had left in her apartment. Not that the air of New York City was exactly fresh, but it was better than what the heating system kept recycling through the building. She didn't particularly like leaving her defenses open while she slept, but the lingering memory of Katy Rourk's fish wafting through the halls as she came in from shopping had decided her. Better exhaust fumes than burned haddock.

She hadn't had an easy time falling asleep, and when she finally managed to do so, tossed restlessly, her dreams uneasy and readily broken—

—as by the sound of someone in the room.

Before the intruder crossed even half the distance between the window and her bed, she was wide awake, and moving. She threw herself out of bed, somersaulted across her bedroom, and wound up crouched beside the door, one hand on the light switch, the other holding a polished dagger she'd taken from beneath her pillow. As the lights came on, she saw Andre standing in the center of the bedroom, blinking in surprise, wearing a sheepish grin.

Relief made her knees go weak. "Andre, you idiot!" She tried to control her tone, but her voice was shrill and cracked a little. "You could have been killed!"

He spread his hands wide in a placating gesture. "Now, Diana—"

"'Now Diana' my eye!" she growled. "Even you would have a hard time getting around a severed spine!" She stood up slowly, shaking from head to toe with released tension.

"I didn't wish to wake you," he said, crestfallen.

She closed her eyes and took several long, deep, calming breaths; focusing on a mantra, moving herself back into stillness until she knew she would be able to reply without screaming at him.

"Don't," she said carefully, "Ever. Do. That. Again." She punctuated the last word by driving the dagger she held into the doorframe.

"*Certainement, ma petite,*" he replied, his eyes widening a little as he began to calculate how fast she'd moved. "The next time I come in your window when you sleep, I shall blow a trumpet first."

"You'd be a *lot* safer. I'd be a lot happier," she said crossly, pulling the dagger loose with a snap of her wrist. She palmed the light switch and dimmed the lamps down to where they would be comfortable to his light-sensitive eyes, then crossed the room, the plush brown carpet warm and soft under her bare feet. She bent slightly, and put the silver-plated dagger back under her pillow. Then with a sigh she folded her long legs beneath her to sit on her rumpled bed. This was the first time Andre had ever caught her asleep, and she was irritated far beyond what her disturbed dreams warranted. She was somewhat obsessed with her privacy and with keeping her night-boundaries unbreached—she and Andre were off-and-on lovers, but she'd never let him stay any length of time.

He approached the antique wooden bed slowly. "*Cherie*, this was no idle visit—"

"I should bloody well hope not!" she interrupted, trying to soothe her jangled nerves by combing the tangles out of her hair with her fingers.

"—I have seen your killer."

She froze.

"It is nothing I have ever seen or heard of before."

She clenched her hands on the strand of hair they held, ignoring the pull. "Go on—"

"It—no, *he*—I could not detect until he made his first kill tonight. I found him then, found him just before he took his hunting-shape, or I never would have discovered him at all; for when he is in that shape there is nothing about him that I could sense that marked him as different. So ordinary—a man, an Asian; Japanese, I think, and like many others—not young, not old; not fat, not thin. So unremarkable as to be invisible. I followed him—he was so normal I found it difficult to believe what my own eyes had seen a moment before; then, not ten minutes later, he found yet another victim and—fed again."

He closed his eyes, his face thoughtful. "As I said, I have never seen or heard of his like, yet—yet there was something familiar about him. I cannot even tell you what it was, and yet it was familiar."

"You said you saw him attack—*how*, Andre?" She leaned forward, her face tight with urgency as the bed creaked a little beneath her.

"The second quarry was—the—is it 'bag lady' you say?" At her nod he continued. "He smiled at her—just smiled, that was all. She froze like the frightened rabbit. Then he—changed—into dark, dark smoke; only smoke, nothing more. The smoke enveloped the old woman until I could see her no longer. Then—he fed. I—I can understand your feelings now, *cherie*. It was—nothing to the eye, but—what I felt *within*—"

"Now you see," she said gravely.

"*Mais oui*, and you have no more argument from me. This thing is abomination, and must be ended."

"The question is—" She grimaced.

"How? I have given some thought to this. One cannot fight smoke. But in his hunting form—I think perhaps he is vulnerable to physical measures. As you say, even I would have difficulty in dealing with a severed spine or crushed brain. I think maybe it would be the same for him. Have you the courage to play the wounded bird, *ma petite*?" He sat beside her on the edge of the bed and regarded her with solemn and worried eyes.

She considered that for a moment. "Play bait while you wait for him to move in? It sounds like the best plan to me—it wouldn't be the first time I've done that, and I'm not exactly helpless, you know," she replied, twisting a strand of hair around her fingers.

"I think you have finally proved that to me tonight!" There was a hint of laughter in his eyes again, as well as chagrin. "I shall never again make the mistake of thinking you to he a fragile flower. *Bien*. Is tomorrow night too soon for you?"

"Tonight wouldn't be too soon," she stated flatly.

"Except that he has already gone to lair, having fed twice." He took one of her hands, freeing it from the lock of hair she had twisted about it. "No, we rest—I know where he is to be found, and tomorrow night we face him at full strength." Abruptly he grinned. "*Cherie*, I have read one of your books—"

She winced, and closed her eyes in a grimace. "Oh Lord—I was afraid you'd ferret out one of my pseudonyms. You're as bad as the Elephant's Child when it comes to 'satiable curiosity.'"

"It was hardly difficult to guess the author when she used one of my favorite expressions for the title—and then described me so very intimately not three pages from the beginning."

Her expression was woeful. "Oh no! Not that one!"

He shook an admonishing finger at her. "I do not think it kind to make me the villain, and all because I told you I spent a good deal of the Regency in London."

"But—but—Andre, these things follow formulas, I didn't really have a choice—anybody French in a Regency romance has to be either an expatriate aristocrat or a villain—" She bit her lip and looked pleadingly at him. "—I needed a villain and I didn't have a clue—I was in the middle of that phony medium thing and I had a deadline—and—" Her words thinned down to a whisper, "—to tell you the truth, I didn't think you'd ever find out. You—you aren't angry, are you?"

He lifted the hair away from her shoulder, cupped his hand beneath her chin and moved close beside her. "I *think* I may possibly be induced to forgive you—"

The near-chuckle in his voice told her she hadn't offended him. Reassured by that, she looked up at him, slyly. "Oh?"

"You could—" He slid her gown off her shoulder a little, and ran an inquisitive finger from the tip of her shoulder blade to just behind her ear "—write another, and let me play the hero—"

"Have you any—suggestions?" she replied, finding it difficult to reply when his mouth followed where his finger had been.

"In that 'Burning Passions' series, perhaps?"

She pushed him away, laughing. "The soft-core porn for housewives? Andre, you can't be serious!"

"Never more," he pulled her back. "Think of how enjoyable the research would be—"

She grabbed his hand again before it could resume its explorations. "Aren't we supposed to be resting?"

He stopped for a moment, and his face and eyes were deadly serious.

"*Cherie*, we must face this thing at strength. You need sleep—and to relax. Can you think of any better way to relax body and spirit than—"

"No," she admitted. "I always sleep like a rock when you get done with me."

"Well then. And I—I have needs; I have not tended to those needs for too long, if I am to have full strength, and I should not care to meet this creature at less than that."

"Excuses, excuses—" She briefly contemplated getting up long enough to take care of the lights—then decided a little waste of energy was worth it, and extinguished them with a thought. "C'mere, you—let's do some research."

He laughed deep in his throat as they reached for one another with the same eager hunger.

~

She woke late the next morning—so late that in a half hour it would have been "afternoon"—and lay quietly for a long, contented moment before wriggling out of the tumble of bedclothes and Andre. No fear of waking him—he wouldn't rouse until the sun went down. She arranged him a bit more comfortably and tucked him in, thinking that he looked absurdly young with his hair all rumpled and those long, dark lashes of his lying against his cheeks—he looked much better this morning, now that she was in a position to pay attention. Last night he'd been pretty pale and hungry-thin. She shook her head over him. Someday his gallantry was going to get him into trouble. "Idiot—" she whispered, touching his forehead, "—all you ever have to do is *ask*—"

But there were other things to take care of—and to think of. A fight to get ready for; and she had a premonition it wasn't going to be an easy one.

So she showered and changed into a leotard, and took herself into her barren studio at the back of the apartment to run through her *katas* three times—once slow, twice at full speed—and then into some Tai Chi exercises to rebalance everything. She followed that with a half hour of meditation, then cast a circle and charged herself with all of the Power she thought she could safely carry.

Without knowing what it was she was to face, that was all she could do, really—that, and have a really good dinner—

She showered and changed again into a bright red sweatsuit and was just finishing dinner when the sun set and Andre strolled into the white-painted kitchen, shirtless, and blinking sleepily.

She gulped the last bite of her liver and waggled her fingers at him. "If you want a shower, you'd better get a fast one—I want to get in place before he comes out for the night."

He sighed happily over the prospect of a hot shower. "The perfect way to start one's day. *Petite*, you may have difficulty in dislodging me now that you have let me stay overnight—"

She showed her teeth. "Don't count your chickens, kiddo. I can be very nasty!"

"*Ma petite—I—*" He suddenly sobered, and looked at her with haunted eyes.

She saw his expression and abruptly stopped teasing. "Andre—please don't say it—I can't give you any better answer now than I could when you first asked—if I—cared for you as more than a friend."

He sighed again, less happily. "Then I will say no more, because you wish it—but—what of this notion—would you permit me to stay with you? No more than that. I could be of some use to you, I think, and I would take nothing from you that you did not offer first. I do not like it that you are so much alone. It did not matter when we first met, but you are collecting powerful enemies, *cherie*."

"I—" She wouldn't look at him, but only at her hands, clenched white-knuckled on the table.

"Unless there are others—" he prompted, hesitantly.

"No—no, there isn't anyone but you." She sat in silence for a moment, then glanced back up at him with one eyebrow lifted sardonically. "You *do* rather spoil a girl for anyone else's attentions."

He was genuinely startled. "*Mille pardons, cherie*," he stuttered, "I—I did not know—"

She managed a feeble chuckle. "Oh Andre, you idiot—I *like* being spoiled! I don't get many things that are just for me—" she sighed, then gave in to his pleading eyes. "All right then, move in if you want."

"It is what *you* want that concerns me."

"I want," she said, very softly. "Just—the commitment—don't ask for it. I've got responsibilities as well as Power, you know that; I—can't see how to balance them with what you offered before—"

"Enough," he silenced her with a wave of his hand. "The words are unsaid, we will speak of this no more unless you wish it. I seek the embrace of warm water—"

She turned her mind to the dangers ahead, resolutely pushing the dangers he represented into the back of her mind. "And I will go bail the car out of the garage."

~

He waited until he was belted in on the passenger's side of the car to comment on her outfit. "I did not know you planned to race him, Diana," he said with a quirk of one corner of his mouth.

"Urban camouflage," she replied, dodging two taxis and a kamikaze panel truck. "Joggers are everywhere, and they run at night a lot in deserted neighborhoods. Cops won't wonder about me or try to stop me, and our boy won't be surprised to see me alone. One of his other victims was out running. His boyfriend thought he'd had a heart attack. Poor thing. He wasn't one of us, so I didn't enlighten him. There are some things it's better the survivors don't know."

"*Oui*. Left here, *cherie*."

The traffic thinned down to a trickle, then to nothing. There are odd little islands in New York at night; places as deserted as the loneliest country road. The area where Andre directed her was one such; by day it was small warehouses, one-floor factories, an odd store or two. None of them had enough business to warrant running second or third shifts, and the neighborhood had not been gentrified yet, so no one actually lived here. There were a handful of night watchmen, perhaps, but most of these places depended on locks, burglar alarms, and dogs that were released at night to keep out intruders.

"There—" Andre pointed at a building that appeared to be home to several small manufactories. "He took the smoke-form and went to roost in the elevator control house at the top. That is why I did not advise going against him by day."

"Is he there now?" Diana peered up through the glare of sodium-vapor lights, but couldn't make out the top of the building.

Andre closed his eyes, a frown of concentration creasing his forehead. "No," he said after a moment. "I think he has gone hunting."

She repressed a shiver. "Then it's time to play bait."

Diana found a parking space marked dimly with the legend "President"— she thought it unlikely it would be wanted within the next few hours. It was deep in the shadow of the building Andre had pointed out, and her car was dead-black; with any luck, cops coming by wouldn't even notice it was there and start to wonder.

She hopped out, locking her door behind her, now looking exactly like the lone jogger she was pretending to be, and set off at an easy pace. She did not look back.

If absolutely necessary, she knew she'd be able to keep this up for hours. She decided to take all the north-south streets first, then weave back along the east-west. Before the first hour was up she was wishing she'd dared bring a "walk-thing"—every street was like every other street; blank brick walls broken by dusty, barred windows and metal doors, alleys with only the occasional dumpster visible, refuse blowing along the gutters. She was bored; her nervousness had worn off, and she was lonely. She ran from light to darkness, from darkness to light, and saw and heard nothing but the occasional rat.

Then he struck, just when she was beginning to get a little careless. Careless enough not to see him arrive.

One moment there was nothing, the next, he was before her, waiting halfway down the block. She knew it was him—he was exactly as Andre had described him, a nondescript Asian man in a dark windbreaker and slacks. He was tall for an Asian—taller than she by several inches. His appearance nearly startled her into stopping—then she remembered that she was supposed to be an innocent jogger, and resumed her steady trot.

She knew he meant her to see him, he was standing directly beneath the streetlight and right in the middle of the sidewalk. She would have to swerve out of her path to avoid him.

She started to do just that, ignoring him as any real jogger would have—when he raised his head and smiled at her.

She was stopped dead in her tracks by the purest terror she had ever felt in her life. She froze, as all of his other victims must have—unable to think, unable to cry out, unable to run. Her legs had gone numb, and nothing existed for her but that terrible smile and those hard, black eyes that had no bottom—

Then the smile vanished, and the eyes flinched away. Diana could move again, and staggered back against the brick wall of the building behind her, her breath coming in harsh pants, the brick rough and comforting in its reality beneath her hands.

"Diana?" It was Andre's voice behind her.

"I'm—all right—" she said, not at all sure that she really was.

Andre strode silently past her, face grim and purposeful. The man seemed to sense his purpose, and smiled again—

But Andre never faltered for even the barest moment.

The smile wavered and faded; the man fell back a step or two, surprised that his weapon had failed him—

Then he scowled, and pulled something out of the sleeve of his windbreaker; and to Diana's surprise, charged straight for Andre, his sneakered feet scuffing on the cement—

And something suddenly blurring about his right hand. As it connected with Andre's upraised left arm, Diana realized what it was—almost too late.

"Andre—he has nunchuks—they're *wood*," she cried out urgently as Andre grunted in unexpected pain. "He can kill you with them! Get the hell out of here!"

Andre needed no second warning. In the blink of an eye, he was gone.

Leaving Diana to face the creature alone.

She dropped into guard-stance as he regarded her thoughtfully, still making no sound, not even of heavy breathing. In a moment he seemed to make up his mind, and came for her.

At least he didn't smile again in that terrible way—perhaps the weapon was only effective once.

She hoped fervently he wouldn't try again—as an empath, she was doubly-vulnerable to a weapon forged of fear.

They circled each other warily, like two cats preparing to fight—then Diana thought she saw an opening—and took it.

And quickly came to the conclusion that she was overmatched, as he sent her tumbling with a badly bruised shin. The next few moments reinforced that conclusion as he continued unscathed while she picked up injury after painful injury.

She was a brown-belt in karate, but he was a black-belt in kung fu, and the contest was a pathetically uneven match. She knew before very long that he was toying with her—and while he still swung the wooden nunchuks, Andre did not dare move in close enough to help.

She realized (as fear dried her mouth, she grew more and more winded, and she searched frantically for a means of escape) that she was as good as dead.

If only she could get those damn 'chuks away from him!

And as she ducked and stumbled against the curb, narrowly avoiding the strike he made, an idea came to her. He knew from her moves—as she knew from his—that she was no amateur. He would never expect an amateur's move from her—something truly stupid and suicidal—

So the next time he swung at her, she stood her ground. As the 'chuk came at her she took one step forward, smashing his nose with the heel of her right hand and lifting her left to intercept the flying baton.

As it connected with her left hand with a sickening crunch, she whirled and folded her entire body around hand and weapon, and went limp, carrying it away from him.

She collapsed in a heap at his feet, hand afire with pain, eyes blurring with it, and waited for either death or salvation.

And salvation in the form of Andre rose behind her attacker. With one *savate* kick he broke the man's back; Diana could hear it cracking like green wood—and before her assailant could collapse, a second double-handed blow sent him crashing into the brick wall, head crushed like an eggshell.

Diana struggled to her feet, and waited for some arcane transformation. Nothing.

She staggered to the corpse, face flat and expressionless—a sign she was suppressing pain and shock with utterly implacable iron will. Andre began to move forward as if to stop her, then backed off again at the look in her eyes.

She bent slightly, just enough to touch the shoulder of the body with her good hand—and released the Power.

Andre pulled her back to safety as the corpse exploded into flame, burning as if it had been soaked in oil. She watched the flames for one moment, wooden-faced; then abruptly collapsed.

Andre caught her easily before she could hurt herself further, lifting her in his arms as if she weighed no more than a kitten. "*Ma pauvre petite*," he murmured, heading back towards the car at a swift but silent run, "It is the hospital for you, I think—"

"Saint-Francis—" she gasped, every step jarring her hand and bringing tears of pain to her eyes, "One of us—is on the night staff—Dr. Crane—"

"*Bien*," he replied. "Now be silent."

"But—how are you—"

"In your car, foolish one. I have the keys you left in it."

"But—"

"I can drive."

"But—"

"*And* I have a license. Will you be silent?"

"How?" she said, disobeying him.

"Night school," he replied succinctly, reaching the car, putting her briefly on her feet to unlock the passenger-side door, then lifting her into it. "You are not the only one who knows of urban camouflage."

This time she did not reply—mostly because she had fainted from pain.

～

The emergency room was empty—for which Andre was very grateful. His invocation of Dr. Crane brought a thin, bearded young man around to the tiny examining cubicle in record time.

"Good god almighty! What did you tangle with, a bus?" he exclaimed, when stripping the sweatsuit jacket and pants revealed that there was little of Diana that was not battered and black-and-blue.

Andre wrinkled his nose at the acrid antiseptic odors around them, and replied shortly. "No. Your 'Ripper.'"

The startled gaze the doctor fastened on him revealed that Andre had scored. "Who—won?" he asked at last.

"We did. I do not think he will prey upon anyone again."

The doctor's eyes closed briefly; Andre read prayerful thankfulness on his face as he sighed with relief. Then he returned to business. "You must be Andre, right? Anything I can supply?"

Andre laughed at the hesitation in his voice. "Fear not, your blood supply is quite safe, and I am unharmed. It is Diana who needs you."

The relief on the doctor's face made Andre laugh again.

Dr. Crane ignored him. "Right," he said, turning to the work he knew best.

~

She was lightheaded and groggy with the Demerol Dr. Crane had given her as Andre deftly stripped her and tucked her into her bed; she'd dozed all the way home in the car.

"I just wish I knew what that thing was—" she said inconsequentially, as he arranged her arm in its light Fiberglas cast a little more comfortably. "—I won't be happy until I *know*—"

"Then you are about to be happy, *cherie*, for I have had the brainstorm." Andre ducked into the living room and emerged with a dusty leatherbound book. "Remember I said there was something familiar about it? Now I think I know what it was." He consulted the index, and turned pages rapidly—found the place he sought, and read for a few moments. "As I thought—listen. 'The *gaki*—also known as the Japanese vampire—takes its nourishment only from the living. There are many kinds of *gaki*, extracting their sustenance from a wide variety of sources. The most harmless are the "perfume" and "music" *gaki*; they are by far the most common. Far deadlier are those that require blood, flesh, or souls.'"

"Souls?"

"Just so. 'To feed, or when at rest, they take their normal form of a dense cloud of dark smoke. At other times, like the *kitsune*, they take on the form of a human being. Unlike the *kitsune*, however, there is no way to distinguish them in this form from any other human. In the smoke form, they are invulnerable—in the human form, however, they can be killed; but to permanently destroy them, the body must be burned—preferably in conjunction with or solely by Power.' I said there was something familiar about it—it seems to have been a kind of distant cousin." Andre's mouth smiled, but his eyes reflected only a long-abiding bitterness.

"There is no way you have any relationship with that—thing!" she said forcefully. "It had no more honor, heart, or soul than a rabid beast!"

"I—I thank you, *cherie*," he said, slowly, the warmth returning to his eyes. "There are not many who would think as you do."

"Their own closed-minded stupidity."

"To change the subject—what was it made you burn it as you did? I would have abandoned it. It seemed dead enough."

"I don't know—it just seemed the thing to do," she yawned. "Sometimes my instincts just work . . . right . . . "

Suddenly her eyes seemed too leaden to keep open.

"Like they did with you . . . " She fought against exhaustion and the drug, trying to keep both at bay.

But without success. Sleep claimed her for its own.

He watched her for the rest of the night, until the leaden lethargy of his own limbs told him dawn was near. He had already decided not to share her bed, lest any movement on his part cause her pain. Instead, he made up a pallet on the floor beside her.

He stood over her broodingly while he in his turn fought slumber, and touched her face gently. "Well—" he whispered, holding off torpor far deeper and heavier than hers could ever be—while she was mortal. "You are not aware to hear, so I may say what I will and you cannot forbid. Dream; sleep and dream—I shall see you safe—my only love."

And he took his place beside her, to lie motionless until night should come again.

~

There's a deep association with Scandinavian mythology in this story, but Elizabeth Bear also offers an aspect of the witch that is probably more common today than ever: the benign healer and protector, the wise "good witch." The tradition lies in the English "cunning folk" (men or women) who practiced folk magic. Similar figures are found in other western European countries: French devins-guérisseurs *and* leveurs de sorts, *Danish* kloge folk, *Dutch* toverdokters *or* duivelbanners, *German* Hexenmeister *or* Kräuterhexen, *Spanish* curanderos, *Portuguese* saludadores; *in Swedish they were called* klok gumma *and* klok gubbe, *which translate as "wise woman" and "wise man." In some areas these people functioned as folk healers into the twentieth century. For most of history, cunning folk were rarely persecuted as witches, for the simple reason that most common people felt what they did was helpful and useful, whereas other witches were thought to do harm.*

The Cold Blacksmith
Elizabeth Bear

"Old man, old man, do you tinker?"

Weyland Smith raised up his head from his anvil, the heat rolling beads of sweat across his face and his sparsely forested scalp, but he never stopped swinging his hammer. The ropy muscles of his chest knotted and released with every blow, and the clamor of steel on steel echoed from the trees. The hammer looked to weigh as much as the smith, but he handled it like a bit of cork on a twig. He worked in a glade, out of doors, by a deep cold well, just right for quenching and full of magic fish. Whoever had spoken was still under the shade of the trees, only a shadow to one who squinted through the glare of the sun.

"Happen I'm a blacksmith, miss," he said.

As if he could be anything else, in his leather apron, sweating over forge and anvil in the noonday sun, limping on a lamed leg.

"Do you take mending, old man?" she asked, stepping forth into the light.

He thought the girl might be pretty enough in a country manner, her features a plump-cheeked outline under the black silk veil pinned to the corners of her hat. Not a patch on his own long-lost swan-maiden Olrun, though Olrun had left him after seven years to go with her two sisters, and his two brothers had gone with them as well, leaving Weyland alone.

But Weyland kept her ring and with it her promise. And for seven times seven years to the seventh times, he'd kept it, seduced it back when it was stolen away, held it to his heart in fair weather and foul. Olrun's promise-ring. Olrun's promise to return.

Olrun who had been fair as ice, with shoulders like a blacksmith, shoulders like a giantess.

This girl could not be less like her. Her hair was black and it wasn't pinned, all those gleaming curls a-tumble across the shoulders of a dress that matched her hair and veil and hat. A little linen sack in her left hand was just the natural color, and something in it chimed when she shifted. Something not too big. He heard it despite the tolling of the hammer that never stopped.

"I'll do what I'm paid to." He let his hammer rest, and shifted his grip on the tongs. His wife's ring slid on its chain around his neck, catching on chest hair. He couldn't wear it on his hand when he hammered. "And if'n 'tis mending I'm paid for, I'll mend what's flawed."

She came across the knotty turf in little quick steps like a hobbled horse—as if it was her lamed, and not him—and while he turned to thrust the bent metal that would soon be a steel horse-collar into the coals again she passed her hand over his bench beside the anvil.

He couldn't release the bellows until the coals glowed red as currant jelly, but there was a clink and when her hand withdrew it left behind two golden coins. Two coins for two hands, for two pockets, for two eyes.

Wiping his hands on his matted beard, he turned from the forge, then lifted a coin to his mouth. It dented under his teeth, and he weighed its heaviness in his hand. "A lot for a bit of tinkering."

"Worth it if you get it done," she said, and upended her sack upon his bench.

A dozen or so curved transparent shards tumbled red as forge-coals into the hot noon light, jingling and tinkling. Gingerly, he reached out and prodded one with a forefinger, surprised by the warmth.

"My heart," the woman said. "'Tis broken. Fix it for me."

He drew his hand back. "I don't know nowt about women's hearts, broken or t'otherwise."

"You're the Weyland Smith, aren't you?"

"Aye, miss." The collar would need more heating. He turned away, to pump the bellows again.

"You took my gold." She planted her fists on her hips. "You can't refuse a task, Weyland Smith. Once you've taken money for it. It's your geas."

"Keep tha coin," he said, and pushed them at her with a fingertip. "I'm a smith. Not never a matchmaker, nor a glassblower."

"They say you made jewels from dead men's eyes, once. And it was a blacksmith broke my heart. It's only right one should mend it, too."

He leaned on the bellows, pumping hard.

She turned away, in a whisper of black satin as her skirts swung heavy by her shoes. "You took my coin," she said, before she walked back into the shadows. "So fix my heart."

～

Firstly, he began with a crucible, and heating the shards in his forge. The heart melted, all right, though hotter than he would have guessed. He scooped the glass on a bit of rod stock and rolled it on his anvil, then scraped the gather off with a flat-edged blade and shaped it into a smooth ruby-bright oval the size of his fist.

The heart crazed as it cooled. It fell to pieces when he touched it with his glove, and he was left with only a mound of shivered glass.

That was unfortunate. There had been the chance that the geas would grant some mysterious assistance, that he would guess correctly and whatever he tried first would work. An off chance, but stranger things happened with magic and his magic was making.

Not this time. Whether it was because he was a blacksmith and not a matchmaker or because he was a blacksmith and not a glassblower, he was not sure. But hearts, glass hearts, were outside his idiom and outside his magic.

He would have to see the witch.

～

The witch must have known he was coming, as she always seemed to know. She awaited him in the doorway of her pleasant cottage by the wildflower meadow, more wildflowers—daisies and buttercups—waving among the long grasses of the turfed roof. A nanny goat grazed beside the chimney, her long coat as white as the milk that stretched her udder pink and shiny. He saw no kid.

The witch was as dark as the goat was white, her black, black hair shot with silver and braided back in a wrist-thick queue. Her skirts were kilted up over her green kirtle, and she handed Weyland a pottery cup before he ever entered her door. It smelled of hops and honey and spices, and steam curled from the top: spiced heated ale.

"I have to see to the milking," she said. "Would you fetch my stool while I coax Heidrún off the roof?"

"She's shrunk," Weyland said, but he balanced his cup in one hand and limped inside the door to haul the stool out, for the witch's convenience.

The witch clucked. "Haven't we all?"

By the time Weyland emerged, the goat was down in the dooryard, munching a reward of bruised apples, and the witch had found her bucket and was waiting for the stool. Weyland set the cup on the ledge of the open window and seated the witch with a little bit of ceremony, helping her with her skirts. She smiled and patted his arm, and bent to the milking while he went to retrieve his ale.

Once upon a time, what rang on the bottom of the empty pail would have been mead, sweet honeyed liquor fit for gods. But times had changed, were always changing, and the streams that stung from between the witch's strong fingers were rich and creamy white.

"So what have you come for, Weyland Smith?" she asked, when the pail was a quarter full and the milk hissed in the pail rather than sang.

"I'm wanting a spell as'll mend a broken heart," he said.

Her braid slid over her shoulder, hanging down. She flipped it back without lifting her head. "I hadn't thought you had it in you to fall in love again," she said, her voice lilting with the tease.

"'Tisn't my heart as is broken."

That did raise her chin, and her fingers stilled on Heidrún's udder. Her gaze met his; her eyebrows lifted across the fine-lined arch of her forehead. "Tricky," she said. "A heart's a wheel," she said. "Bent is bent. It can't be mended. And even worse—" She smiled, and tossed the fugitive braid back again. "—if it's not your heart you're after fixing."

"Din't I know it?" he said, and sipped the ale, his wife's ring—worn now—clicking on the cup as his fingers tightened.

Heidrún had finished her apples. She tossed her head, long ivory horns brushing the pale silken floss of her back, and the witch laughed and remembered to milk again. "What will you give me if I help?"

The milk didn't ring in the pail any more, but the gold rang fine on the dooryard stones.

The witch barely glanced at it. "I don't want your gold, blacksmith."

"I din't want for hers, neither," Weyland said. "'Tis the half of what she gave." He didn't stoop to retrieve the coin, though the witch snaked a soft-shoed foot from under her kirtle and skipped it back to him, bouncing it over the cobbles.

"What can I pay?" he asked, when the witch met his protests with a shrug.

"I didn't say I could help you." The latest pull dripped milk into the pail rather than spurting. The witch tugged the bucket clear and patted Heidrún on the flank, leaning forward with her elbows on her knees and the pail between her ankles while the nanny clattered over cobbles to bound back up onto the roof. In a moment, the goat was beside the chimney again, munching buttercups as if she hadn't just had a meal of apples. A large, fluffy black-and-white cat emerged from the house and began twining the legs of the stool, miaowing.

"Question 'tisn't what tha can or can't do," he said sourly. "'Tis what tha will or won't."

The witch lifted the pail and splashed milk on the stones for the cat to lap. And then she stood, bearing the pail in her hands, and shrugged. "You could pay me a Name. I collect those."

"If'n I had one."

"There's your own," she countered, and balanced the pail on her hip as she sauntered toward the house. He followed. "But people are always more disinclined to part with what belongs to them than what doesn't, don't you find?"

He grunted. She held the door for him, with her heel, and kicked it shut when he had passed. The cottage was dim and cool inside, with only a few embers banked on the hearth. He sat when she gestured him onto the bench, and not before. "No names," he said.

"Will you barter your body, then?"

She said it over her shoulder, like a commonplace. He twisted a boot on the rushes covering a rammed-earth floor and laughed. "And what'd a bonny lass like thaself want with a gammy-legged, fusty, coal-black smith?"

"To say I've had one?" She plunged her hands into the washbasin and scrubbed them to the elbow, then turned and leaned against the stand. When she caught sight of his expression, she laughed as well. "You're sure it's not your heart that's broken, Smith?"

"Not this sennight." He scowled around the rim of his cup, and was still scowling as she set bread and cheese before him. Others might find her intimidating, but Weyland Smith wore the promise-ring of Olrun the Valkyrie. No witch could mortify him. Not even one who kept Heidrún—who had dined on the leaves of the World Ash—as a milch-goat.

The witch broke his gaze on the excuse of tucking an escaped strand of his long gray ponytail behind her ear, and relented. "Make me a cauldron," she said. "An iron cauldron. And I'll tell you the secret, Weyland Smith."

"Done," he said, and drew his dagger to slice the bread.

She sat down across the trestle. "Don't you want your answer?"

He stopped with his blade in the loaf, looking up. "I've not paid."

"You'll take my answer," she said. She took his cup, and dipped more ale from the pot warming over those few banked coals. "I know your contract is good."

He shook his head at the smile that curved her lips, and snorted. "Someone'll find out tha geas one day, enchantress. And may tha never rest easy again. So tell me then. How might I mend a lass's broken heart?"

"You can't," the witch said, easily. "You can replace it with another, or you can forge it anew. But it cannot be mended. Not like *that*."

"Gerrawa with tha," Weyland said. "I tried reforging it. 'Tis glass."

"And glass will cut you," the witch said, and snapped her fingers. "Like that."

⁓

He made the cauldron while he was thinking, since it needed the blast furnace and a casting pour but not finesse. *If glass will cut and shatter, perhaps a heart should be made of tougher stuff*, he decided as he broke the mold.

⁓

Secondly, he began by heating the bar stock. While it rested in the coals, between pumping at the bellows, he slid the shards into a leathern bag, slicing his palms—though not deep enough to bleed through heavy callus. He wiggled Olrun's ring off his right hand and strung it on its chain, then broke the heart to powder with his smallest hammer. It didn't take much work. The heart was fragile enough that Weyland wondered if there wasn't something wrong with the glass.

When it had done, he shook the powder from the pouch and ground it finer in the pestle he used to macerate carbon, until it was reduced to a pale-pink silica dust. He thought he'd better use all of it, to be sure, so he mixed it in with the carbon and hammered it into the heated bar stock for seven nights and seven days, folding and folding again as he would for a sword-blade, or an axe, something that needed to take a resilient temper to back a striking edge.

It wasn't a blade he made of his iron, though, now that he'd forged it into steel. What he did was pound the bar into a rod, never allowing it to cool, never pausing hammer—and then he drew the rod through a die to square and smooth it, and twisted the thick wire that resulted into a gorgeous fist-big filigree.

The steel had a reddish color, not like rust but as if the traces of gold that had imparted brilliance to the ruby glass heart had somehow transferred that tint into the steel. It was a beautiful thing, a cage for a bird no bigger than Weyland's thumb, with cunning hinges so one could open it like a box, and such was his magic that despite all the glass and iron that had gone into making it, it spanned no more and weighed no more than would have a heart of meat.

He heated it cherry-red again, and when it glowed he quenched it in the well to give it resilience and set its form.

~

He wore his ring on his wedding finger when he put it on the next morning, and he let the forge lie cold—or as cold as it could lie, with seven days' heat baked into metal and stone. It was the eighth day of the forging, and a fortnight since he'd taken the girl's coin.

She didn't disappoint. She was along before midday.

She came right out into the sunlight this time, rather than lingering under the hazel trees, and though she still wore black it was topped by a different hat, this one with feathers. "Old man," she said, "have you done as I asked?"

Reverently, he reached under the block that held his smaller anvil, and brought up a doeskin swaddle. The suede draped over his hands, clinging and soft as a maiden's breast, and he held his breath as he laid the package on the anvil and limped back, his left leg dragging a little. He picked up his hammer and pretended to look to the forge, unwilling to be seen watching the lady.

She made a little cry as she came forward, neither glad nor sorrowful, but rather tight, as if she couldn't keep all her hope and anticipation pent in her breast any longer. She reached out with hands clad in cheveril and brushed open the doeskin—

Only to freeze when her touch revealed metal. "This heart doesn't beat," she said, as she let the wrappings fall.

Weyland turned to her, his hands twisted before his apron, wringing the haft of his hammer so his ring bit into his flesh. "It'll not shatter, lass, I swear."

"It doesn't beat," she repeated. She stepped away, her hands curled at her sides in their black kid gloves. "This heart is no use to me, blacksmith."

∼

He borrowed the witch's magic goat, which like him—and the witch—had been more than half a God once and wasn't much more than a fairy story now, and he harnessed her to a sturdy little cart he made to haul the witch's cauldron. He delivered it in the sunny morning, when the dew was still damp on the grass, and he brought the heart to show.

"It's a very good heart," the witch said, turning it in her hands. "The latch in particular is cunning. Nothing would get in or out of a heart like that if you didn't show it the way." She bounced it on her palms. "Light for its size, too. A girl could be proud of a heart like this."

"She'll have none," Weyland said. "Says as it doesn't beat."

"Beat? Of course it doesn't beat," the witch scoffed. "There isn't any love in it. And you can't put that there for her."

"But I mun do," Weyland said, and took the thing back from her hands.

∼

For thirdly, he broke Olrun's ring. The gold was soft and fine; it flattened with one blow of the hammer, and by the third or fourth strike, it spread across his leather-padded anvil like a puddle of blood, rose-red in the light of the forge. By the time the sun brushed the treetops in its descent, he'd pounded the ring into a sheet of gold so fine it floated on his breath.

He painted the heart with gesso, and when that was dried he made bole, a rabbit-skin glue mixed with clay that formed the surface for the gilt to cling to.

With a brush, he lifted the gold leaf, bit by bit, and sealed it painstakingly to the heart. And when he had finished and set the brushes and the burnishers aside—when his love was sealed up within like the steel under the gold—the iron cage began to beat.

∼

"It was a blacksmith broke my heart," the black girl said. "You'd think a blacksmith could do a better job on mending it."

"It beats," he said, and set it rocking with a burn-scarred, callused fingertip. " 'Tis bonny. And it shan't break."

"It's cold," she complained, her breath pushing her veil out a little over her lips. "Make it warm."

"I'd not wonder tha blacksmith left tha. The heart tha started with were colder," he said.

~

For fourthly, he opened up his breast and took his own heart out, and locked it in the cage. The latch was cunning, and he worked it with thumbs slippery with the red, red blood. Afterwards, he stitched his chest up with cat-gut and an iron needle and pulled a clean shirt on, and let the forge sit cold.

~

He expected a visitor, and she arrived on time. He laid the heart before her, red as red, red blood in its red-gilt iron cage, and she lifted it on the tips of her fingers and held it to her ear to listen to it beat.

And she smiled.

~

When she was gone, he couldn't face his forge, or the anvil with the vacant chain draped over the horn, or the chill in his fingertips. So he went to see the witch.

She was sweeping the dooryard when he came up on her, and she laid the broom aside at once when she saw his face. "So it's done," she said, and brought him inside the door.

The cup she brought him was warmer than his hands. He drank, and licked hot droplets from his moustache after.

"It weren't easy," he said.

She sat down opposite, elbows on the table, and nodded in sympathy. "It never is," she said. "How do you feel?"

"Frozen cold. Colder'n Hell. I should've gone with her."

"Or she should have stayed with you."

He hid his face in the cup. "She weren't coming back."

"No," the witch said. "She wasn't." She sliced bread, and buttered him a piece. It sat on the planks before him, and he didn't touch it. "It'll grow back, you know. Now that it's cut out cleanly. It'll heal in time."

He grunted, and finished the last of the ale. "And then?" he asked, as the cup clicked on the boards.

"And then you'll sooner or later most likely wish it hadn't," the witch said, and when he laughed and reached for the bread she got up to fetch him another ale.

~

Ruby's "conjure hand"—also known as a mojo, a gris-gris bag, or several other names—is a magic charm with traditions in West African culture brought to the New World by enslaved Africans. A sort of "prayer in a bag," the contents vary depending on what the conjurer wants to achieve; inclusion of personal items make the charm stronger. As in Ellen Klages' story, the color of the bag often has meaning, too. Red or pink flannel might be used for a love hand, white for fertility, orange for change or warning. "Feeding" the hand—alcohol, cologne, bodily fluids, various oils—is needed because the mojo, once created, is a live spirit requiring sustenance. The power of its magic is derived from spiritual inheritance: one's ancestors can help or protect one through the mojo. The stronger the belief, the more powerful the trust in the magic, the better it works.

Basement Magic
Ellen Klages

Mary Louise Whittaker believes in magic. She knows that somewhere, somewhere else, there must be dragons and princes, wands and wishes. Especially wishes. And happily ever after. Ever after is not now.

Her mother died in a car accident when Mary Louise was still a toddler. She misses her mother fiercely but abstractly. Her memories are less a coherent portrait than a mosaic of disconnected details: soft skin that smelled of lavender; a bright voice singing "Sweet and Low" in the night darkness; bubbles at bath time; dark curls; zwieback.

Her childhood has been kneaded, but not shaped, by the series of well-meaning middle-aged women her father has hired to tend her. He is busy climbing the corporate ladder, and is absent even when he is at home. She does not miss him. He remarried when she was five, and they moved into a two-story Tudor in one of the better suburbs of Detroit. Kitty, the new Mrs. Ted Whittaker, is a former Miss Bloomfield Hills, a vain divorcee with a towering mass of blond curls in a shade not her own. In the wild, her kind is inclined to eat their young.

Kitty might have tolerated her new stepdaughter had she been sweet and cuddly, a slick-magazine cherub. But at six, Mary Louise is an odd, solitary child. She has unruly red hair the color of Fiestaware, the dishes that might have been radioactive, and small round pink glasses that make her blue eyes seem large and slightly distant. She did not walk until she was almost two, and propels herself with a quick shuffle-duckling gait that is both urgent and awkward.

One spring morning, Mary Louise is camped in one of her favorite spots, the window seat in the guest bedroom. It is a stage set of a room, one that no one else ever visits. She leans against the wall, a thick book with lush illustrations propped up on her bare knees. Bright sunlight, filtered through the leaves of the oak outside, is broken into geometric patterns by the mullioned windows, dappling the floral cushion in front of her.

The book is almost bigger than her lap, and she holds it open with one elbow, the other anchoring her Bankie, a square of pale blue flannel with pale blue satin edging that once swaddled her infant self, carried home from the hospital. It is raveled and graying, both tattered and beloved. The thumb of her blanket arm rests in her mouth in a comforting manner. Mary Louise is studying a picture of a witch with purple robes and hair as black as midnight when she hears voices in the hall. The door to the guest room is open a crack, so she can hear clearly, but cannot see or be seen. One of the voices is Kitty's. She is explaining something about the linen closet, so it is probably a new cleaning lady. They have had six since they moved in.

Mary Louise sits very still and doesn't turn the page, because it is stiff paper and might make a noise. But the door opens anyway, and she hears Kitty say, "This is the guest room. Now unless we've got company—and I'll let you know—it just needs to be dusted and the linens aired once a week. It has an—oh, there you are," she says, coming in the doorway, as if she has been looking all over for Mary Louise, which she has not.

Kitty turns and says to the air behind her, "This is my husband's daughter, Mary Louise. She's not in school yet. She's small for her age, and her birthday is in December, so we decided to hold her back a year. She never does much, just sits and reads. I'm sure she won't be a bother. Will you?" She turns and looks at Mary Louise but does not wait for an answer. "And this is Ruby. She's going to take care of the house for us."

The woman who stands behind Kitty nods, but makes no move to enter the room. She is tall, taller than Kitty, with skin the color of gingerbread.

Ruby wears a white uniform and a pair of white Keds. She is older, there are lines around her eyes and her mouth, but her hair is sleek and black, black as midnight.

Kitty looks at her small gold watch. "Oh, dear. I've got to get going or I'll be late for my hair appointment." She looks back at Mary Louise. "Your father and I are going out tonight, but Ruby will make you some dinner, and Mrs. Banks will be here about six." Mrs. Banks is one of the babysitters, an older woman in a dark dress who smells like dusty licorice and coos too much. "So be a good girl. And for god's sake get that thumb out of your mouth. Do you want your teeth to grow in crooked, too?"

Mary Louise says nothing, but withdraws her damp puckered thumb and folds both hands in her lap. She looks up at Kitty, her eyes expressionless, until her stepmother looks away. "Well, an-y-wa-y," Kitty says, drawing the word out to four syllables, "I've really got to be going." She turns and leaves the room, brushing by Ruby, who stands silently just outside the doorway.

Ruby watches Kitty go, and when the high heels have clattered onto the tiles at the bottom of the stairs, she turns and looks at Mary Louise. "You a quiet little mouse, ain't you?" she asks in a soft, low voice.

Mary Louise shrugs. She sits very still in the window seat and waits for Ruby to leave. She does not look down at her book, because it is rude to look away when a grownup might still be talking to you. But none of the cleaning ladies talk to her, except to ask her to move out of the way, as if she were furniture.

"Yes siree, a quiet little mouse," Ruby says again. "Well, Miss Mouse, I'm fixin to go downstairs and make me a grilled cheese sandwich for lunch. If you like, I can cook you up one too. I make a mighty fine grilled cheese sandwich." Mary Louise is startled by the offer. Grilled cheese is one of her very favorite foods. She thinks for a minute, then closes her book and tucks Bankie securely under one arm. She slowly follows Ruby down the wide front stairs, her small green-socked feet making no sound at all on the thick beige carpet.

It is the best grilled cheese sandwich Mary Louise has ever eaten. The outside is golden brown and so crisp it crackles under her teeth. The cheese is melted so that it soaks into the bread on the inside, just a little. There are no burnt spots at all. Mary Louise thanks Ruby and returns to her book.

The house is large, and Mary Louise knows all the best hiding places. She does not like being where Kitty can find her, where their paths might cross. Before Ruby came, Mary Louise didn't go down to the basement very much. Not by herself. It is an old house, and the basement is damp and musty, with heavy stone walls and banished, battered furniture. It is not a comfortable place, nor a safe one. There is the furnace, roaring fire, and the cans of paint and bleach and other frightful potions. Poisons. Years of soap flakes, lint, and furnace soot coat the walls like household lichen.

The basement is a place between the worlds, within Kitty's domain, but beneath her notice. Now, in the daytime, it is Ruby's, and Mary Louise is happy there. Ruby is not like other grownups. Ruby talks to her in a regular voice, not a scold, nor the singsong Mrs. Banks uses, as if Mary Louise is a tiny baby. Ruby lets her sit and watch while she irons, or sorts the laundry, or runs the sheets through the mangle. She doesn't sigh when Mary Louise asks her questions.

On the rare occasions when Kitty and Ted are home in the evening, they have dinner in the dining room. Ruby cooks. She comes in late on those days, and then is very busy, and Mary Louise does not get to see her until dinnertime. But the two of them eat in the kitchen, in the breakfast nook. Ruby tells stories, but has to get up every few minutes when Kitty buzzes for her, to bring more water or another fork, or to clear away the salad plates. Ruby smiles when she is talking to Mary Louise, but when the buzzer sounds, her face changes. Not to a frown, but to a kind of blank Ruby mask.

One Tuesday night in early May, Kitty decrees that Mary Louise will eat dinner with them in the dining room, too. They sit at the wide mahogany table on stiff brocade chairs that pick at the backs of her legs. There are too many forks and even though she is very careful, it is hard to cut her meat, and once the heavy silverware skitters across the china with a sound that sets her teeth on edge. Kitty frowns at her.

The grownups talk to each other and Mary Louise just sits. The worst part is that when Ruby comes in and sets a plate down in front of her, there is no smile, just the Ruby mask.

"I don't know how you do it, Ruby," says her father when Ruby comes in to give him a second glass of water. "These pork chops are the best I've ever eaten. You've certainly got the magic touch."

"She does, doesn't she?" says Kitty. "You must tell me your secret."

"Just shake 'em up in flour, salt and pepper, then fry 'em in Crisco," Ruby says.

"That's all?"

"Yes, ma'am."

"Well, isn't that marvelous. I must try that. Thank you, Ruby. You may go now."

"Yes, ma'am." Ruby turns and lets the swinging door between the kitchen and the dining room close behind her. A minute later Mary Louise hears the sound of running water, and the soft clunk of plates being slotted into the racks of the dishwasher.

"Mary Louise, don't put your peas into your mashed potatoes that way. It's not polite to play with your food," Kitty says. Mary Louise sighs. There are too many rules in the dining room.

"Mary Louise, answer me when I speak to you."

"Muhff-mum," Mary Louise says through a mouthful of mashed potatoes.

"Oh, for god's sake. Don't talk with your mouth full. Don't you have any manners at all?"

Caught between two conflicting rules, Mary Louise merely shrugs.

"Is there any more gravy?" her father asks. Kitty leans forward a little and Mary Louise hears the slightly muffled sound of the buzzer in the kitchen. There is a little bump, about the size of an Oreo, under the carpet just beneath Kitty's chair that Kitty presses with her foot. Ruby appears a few seconds later and stands inside the doorway, holding a striped dishcloth in one hand.

"Mr. Whittaker would like some more gravy," says Kitty.

Ruby shakes her head. "Sorry, Miz Whittaker. I put all of it in the gravy boat. There's no more left."

"Oh." Kitty sounds disapproving. "We had plenty of gravy last time."

"Yes, ma'am. But that was a beef roast. Pork chops just don't make as much gravy," Ruby says.

"Oh. Of course. Well, thank you, Ruby."

"Yes ma'am." Ruby pulls the door shut behind her.

"I guess that's all the gravy, Ted," Kitty says, even though he is sitting at the other end of the table, and has heard Ruby himself.

"Tell her to make more next time," he says frowning. "So what did you do today?" He turns his attention to Mary Louise for the first time since they sat down.

"Mostly I read my book," she says. "The fairy tales you gave me for Christmas."

"Well, that's fine," he says. "I need you to call the Taylors and cancel." Mary Louise realizes he is no longer talking to her, and eats the last of her mashed potatoes.

"Why?" Kitty raises an eyebrow. "I thought we were meeting them out at the club on Friday for cocktails."

"Can't. Got to fly down to Florida tomorrow. The space thing. We designed the guidance system for Shepard's capsule, and George wants me to go down with the engineers, talk to the press if the launch is a success."

"Are they really going to shoot a man into space?" Mary Louise asks.

"That's the plan, honey."

"Well, you don't give me much notice," Kitty says, smiling. "But I suppose I can pack a few summer dresses, and get anything else I need down there."

"Sorry, Kit. This trip is just business. No wives."

"No, only to Grand Rapids. Never to Florida," Kitty says, frowning. She takes a long sip of her drink. "So how long will you be gone?"

"Five days, maybe a week. If things go well, Jim and I are going to drive down to Palm Beach and get some golf in."

"I see. Just business." Kitty drums her lacquered fingernails on the tablecloth. "I guess that means I have to call Barb and Mitchell, too. Or had you forgotten my sister's birthday dinner next Tuesday?" Kitty scowls down the table at her husband, who shrugs and takes a bite of his chop.

Kitty drains her drink. The table is silent for a minute, and then she says, "Mary Louise! Don't put your dirty fork on the tablecloth. Put it on the edge of your plate if you're done. Would you like to be excused?"

"Yes, ma'am," says Mary Louise.

~

As soon as she is excused, Mary Louise goes down to the basement to wait. When Ruby is working it smells like a cave full of soap and warm laundry. A little after seven, Ruby comes down the stairs carrying a brown paper lunch sack. She puts it down on the ironing board. "Well, Miss Mouse. I thought I'd see you down here when I got done with the dishes."

"I don't like eating in the dining room," Mary Louise says. "I want to eat in the kitchen with you."

"I like that, too. But your stepmomma says she got to teach you some table manners, so when you grow up you can eat with nice folks."

Mary Louise makes a face, and Ruby laughs.

"They ain't such a bad thing, manners. Come in real handy someday, when you're eatin with folks you want to have like you."

"I guess so," says Mary Louise. "Will you tell me a story?"

"Not tonight, Miss Mouse. It's late, and I gotta get home and give my husband his supper. He got off work half an hour ago, and I told him I'd bring him a pork chop or two if there was any left over." She gestures to the paper bag. "He likes my pork chops even more than your daddy does."

"Not even a little story?" Mary Louise feels like she might cry. Her stomach hurts from having dinner with all the forks.

"Not tonight, sugar. Tomorrow, though, I'll tell you a long one, just to make up." Ruby takes off her white Keds and lines them up next to each other under the big galvanized sink. Then she takes off her apron, looks at a brown gravy stain on the front of it, and crumples it up and tosses it into the pink plastic basket of dirty laundry. She pulls a hanger from the line that stretches across the ceiling over the washer and begins to undo the white buttons on the front of her uniform.

"What's that?" Mary Louise asks. Ruby has rucked the top of her uniform down to her waist and is pulling it over her hips. There is a green string pinned to one bra strap. The end of it disappears into her left armpit.

"What's what? You seen my underwear before."

"Not that. That string." Ruby looks down at her chest.

"Oh. That. I had my auntie make me up a conjure hand."

"Can I see it?" Mary Louise climbs down out of the chair and walks over to where Ruby is standing.

Ruby looks hard at Mary Louise for a minute. "For it to work, it gotta stay a secret. But you good with secrets, so I guess you can take a look. Don't you touch it, though. Anybody but me touch it, all the conjure magic leak right out and it won't work no more." She reaches under her armpit and draws out a small green flannel bag, about the size of a walnut, and holds it in one hand.

Mary Louise stands with her hands clasped tight behind her back so she won't touch it even by accident and stares intently at the bag. It doesn't look like anything magic. Magic is gold rings and gowns spun of moonlight and silver, not a white cotton uniform and a little stained cloth bag. "Is it really magic? Really? What does it do?"

"Well, there's diff'rent kinds of magic. Some conjure bags bring luck. Some protects you. This one, this one gonna bring me money. That's why it's green. Green's the money color. Inside there's a silver dime, so the money knows it belong here, a magnet—that attracts the money right to me—and some roots, wrapped up in a two-dollar bill. Every mornin I gives it a little drink, and after nine days, it gonna bring me my fortune." Ruby looks down at the little bag fondly, then tucks it back under her armpit.

Mary Louise looks up at Ruby and sees something she has never seen on a grownup's face before: Ruby believes. She believes in magic, even if it is armpit magic.

"Wow. How does—"

"Miss Mouse, I got to get home, give my husband his supper." Ruby steps out of her uniform, hangs it on a hanger, then puts on her blue skirt and a cotton blouse.

Mary Louise looks down at the floor. "Okay," she says.

"It's not the end of the world, sugar." Ruby pats Mary Louise on the back of the head, then sits down and puts on her flat black shoes. "I'll be back tomorrow. I got a big pile of laundry to do. You think you might come down here, keep me company? I think I can tell a story and sort the laundry at the same time." She puts on her outdoor coat, a nubby, burnt-orange wool with chipped gold buttons and big square pockets, and ties a scarf around her chin.

"Will you tell me a story about the magic bag?" Mary Louise asks. This time she looks at Ruby and smiles.

"I think I can do that. Gives us both somethin to look forward to. Now scoot on out of here. I gotta turn off the light." She picks up her brown paper sack and pulls the string that hangs down over the ironing board. The light bulb goes out, and the basement is dark except for the twilight filtering in through the high single window. Ruby opens the outside door to the concrete stairs that lead up to the driveway. The air is warmer than the basement.

"Nitey, nite, Miss Mouse," she says, and goes outside.

"G'night Ruby," says Mary Louise, and goes upstairs.

~

When Ruby goes to vacuum the rug in the guest bedroom on Thursday morning, she finds Mary Louise sitting in the window seat, staring out the window.

"Mornin, Miss Mouse. You didn't come down and say hello."

Mary Louise does not answer. She does not even turn around. Ruby pushes the lever on the vacuum and stands it upright, dropping the gray fabric cord she has wrapped around her hand. She walks over to the silent child. "Miss Mouse? Somethin wrong?"

Mary Louise looks up. Her eyes are cold. "Last night I was in bed, reading. Kitty came home. She was in a really bad mood. She told me I read too much and I'll just ruin my eyes—more—reading in bed. She took my book and told me she was going to throw it in the 'cinerator and burn it up." She delivers the words in staccato anger, through clenched teeth.

"She just bein mean to you, sugar." Ruby shakes her head. "She tryin to scare you, but she won't really do that."

"But she *did*!" Mary Louise reaches behind her and holds up her fairy tale book. The picture on the cover is soot-stained, the shiny coating blistered. The gilded edges of the pages are charred and the corners are gone.

"Lord, child, where'd you find that?"

"In the 'cinerator, out back. Where she said. I can still read most of the stories, but it makes my hands all dirty." She holds up her hands, showing her sooty palms.

Ruby shakes her head again. She says, more to herself than to Mary Louise, "I burnt the trash after lunch yesterday. Must of just been coals, come last night."

Mary Louise looks at the ruined book in her lap, then up at Ruby. "It was my favorite book. Why'd she do that?" A tear runs down her cheek.

Ruby sits down on the window seat. "I don't know, Miss Mouse," she says. "I truly don't. Maybe she mad that your daddy gone down to Florida, leave her behind. Some folks, when they're mad, they just gotta whup on somebody, even if it's a little bitty six-year-old child. They whup on somebody else, they forget their own hurts for a while."

"You're bigger than her," says Mary Louise, snuffling. "You could— whup—*her* back. You could tell her that it was bad and wrong what she did."

Ruby shakes her head. "I'm real sorry, Miss Mouse," she says quietly, "But I can't do that."

"Why not?"

" 'Cause she the boss in this house, and if I say anythin crosswise to Miz Kitty, her own queen self, she gonna fire me same as she fire all them other colored ladies used to work for her. And I needs this job. My husband's just workin part-time down to the Sunoco. He tryin to get work in the Ford plant, but they ain't hirin right now. So my paycheck here, that's what's puttin groceries on our table."

"But, but—" Mary Louise begins to cry without a sound. Ruby is the only grownup person she trusts, and Ruby cannot help her.

Ruby looks down at her lap for a long time, then sighs. "I can't say nothin to Miz Kitty. But her bein so mean to you, that ain't right, neither." She puts her arm around the shaking child.

"What about your little bag?" Mary Louise wipes her nose with the back of her hand, leaving a small streak of soot on her cheek.

"What 'bout it?"

"You said some magic is for protecting, didn't you?"

"Some is," Ruby says slowly. "Some is. Now, my momma used to say, 'an egg can't fight with a stone.' And that's the truth. Miz Kitty got the power in this house. More'n you, more'n me. Ain't nothin to do 'bout that. But conjurin—" She thinks for a minute, then lets out a deep breath.

"I think we might could put some protection 'round you, so Miz Kitty can't do you no more misery," Ruby says, frowning a little. "But I ain't sure quite how. See, if it was your house, I'd put a goopher right under the front door. But it ain't. It's your daddy's house, and she married to him legal, so ain't no way to keep her from comin in her own house, even if she is nasty."

"What about my room?" asks Mary Louise.

"Your room? Hmm. Now, that's a different story. I think we can goopher it so she can't do you no harm in there."

Mary Louise wrinkles her nose. "What's a *goopher*?"

Ruby smiles. "Down South Carolina, where my family's from, that's just what they calls a spell, or a hex, a little bit of rootwork."

"Root—?"

Ruby shakes her head. "It don't make no never mind what you calls it, long as you does it right. Now if you done cryin, we got work to do. Can you go out to the garage, to your daddy's toolbox, and get me nine nails? Big ones, all the same size, and bright and shiny as you can find. Can you count that many?"

Mary Louise snorts. "I can count up to *fifty*," she says.

"Good. Then you go get nine shiny nails, fast as you can, and meet me down the hall, by your room."

When Mary Louise gets back upstairs, nine shiny nails clutched tightly in one hand, Ruby is kneeling in front of the door of her bedroom, with a paper of pins from the sewing box, and a can of Drano. Mary Louise hands her the nails.

"These is just perfect," Ruby says. She pours a puddle of Drano into its upturned cap, and dips the tip of one of the nails into it, then pokes the nail under the edge of the hall carpet at the left side of Mary Louise's bedroom door, pushing it deep until not even its head shows.

"Why did you dip the nail in Drano?" Mary Louise asks. She didn't know any of the poison things under the kitchen sink could be magic.

"Don't you touch that, hear? It'll burn you bad, cause it's got lye in it. But lye the best thing for cleanin away any evil that's already been here. Ain't got no Red Devil like back home, but you got to use what you got. The nails and the pins, they made of iron, and iron keep any new evil away from your door." Ruby dips a pin in the Drano as she talks and repeats the poking, alternating nails and pins until she pushes the last pin in at the other edge of the door. "That oughta do it," she says. She pours the few remaining drops of Drano back into the can and screws the lid on tight, then stands up. "Now all we needs to do is set the protectin charm. You know your prayers?" she asks Mary Louise.

"I know 'Now I lay me down to sleep.'"

"Good enough. You get into your room and you kneel down, facin the hall, and say that prayer to the doorway. Say it loud and as best you can. I'm goin to go down and get the sheets out of the dryer. Meet me in Miz Kitty's room when you done."

Mary Louise says her prayers in a loud, clear voice. She doesn't know how this kind of magic spell works, and she isn't sure if she is supposed to say the God Blesses, but she does. She leaves Kitty out and adds Ruby. "And help me to be a good girl, amen," she finishes, and hurries down to her father's room to see what other kinds of magic Ruby knows.

The king-size mattress is bare. Mary Louise lies down on it and rolls over and over three times before falling off the edge onto the carpet. She is just getting up, dusting off the knees of her blue cotton pants, when Ruby appears with an armful of clean sheets, which she dumps onto the bed. Mary Louise lays her face in the middle of the pile. It is still warm and smells like baked cotton. She takes a deep breath.

"You gonna lay there in the laundry all day or help me make this bed?" Ruby asks, laughing.

Mary Louise takes one side of the big flowered sheet and helps Ruby stretch it across the bed and pull the elastic parts over all four corners so it is smooth everywhere.

"Are we going to do a lot more magic?" Mary Louise asks. "I'm getting kind of hungry."

"One more bit, then we can have us some lunch. You want tomato soup?"

"Yes!" says Mary Louise.

"I thought so. Now fetch me a hair from Miz Kitty's hairbrush. See if you can find a nice long one with some dark at the end of it."

Mary Louise goes over to Kitty's dresser and peers at the heavy silver brush. She finds a darker line in the tangle of blond and carefully pulls it out. It is almost a foot long, and the last inch is definitely brown. She carries it over to Ruby, letting it trail through her fingers like the tail of a tiny invisible kite.

"That's good," Ruby says. She reaches into the pocket of her uniform and pulls out a scrap of red felt with three needles stuck into it lengthwise. She pulls the needles out one by one, makes a bundle of them, and wraps it round and round, first with the long strand of Kitty's hair, then with a piece of black thread.

"Hold out your hand," she says.

Mary Louise holds out her hand flat, and Ruby puts the little black-wrapped bundle into it. "Now, you hold this until you get a picture in your head of Miz Kitty burnin up your pretty picture book. And when it nice and strong, you spit. Okay?"

Mary Louise nods. She scrunches up her eyes, remembering, then spits on the needles.

"You got the knack for this," Ruby says, smiling. "It's a gift."

Mary Louise beams. She does not get many compliments, and stores this one away in the most private part of her thoughts. She will visit it regularly over the next few days until its edges are indistinct and there is nothing left but a warm glow labeled RUBY.

"Now put it under this mattress, far as you can reach." Ruby lifts up the edge of the mattress and Mary Louise drops the bundle on the box spring.

"Do you want me to say my prayers again?"

"Not this time, Miss Mouse. Prayers is for protectin. This here is a sufferin hand, bring some of Miz Kitty's meanness back on her own self, and it need another kind of charm. I'll set this one myself." Ruby lowers her voice and begins to chant:

Before the night is over,
Before the day is through.
What you have done to someone else
Will come right back on you.

"There. That ought to do her just fine. Now we gotta make up this bed. Top sheet, blanket, bedspread all smooth and nice, pillows plumped up just so."

"Does that help the magic?" Mary Louise asks. She wants to do it right, and there are almost as many rules as eating in the dining room. But different.

"Not 'zactly. But it makes it look like it 'bout the most beautiful place to sleep Miz Kitty ever seen, make her want to crawl under them sheets and get her beauty rest. Now help me with that top sheet, okay?"

Mary Louise does, and when they have smoothed the last wrinkle out of the bedspread, Ruby looks at the clock. "Shoot. How'd it get to be after one o'clock? Only fifteen minutes before my story comes on. Let's go down and have ourselves some lunch."

In the kitchen, Ruby heats up a can of Campbell's tomato soup, with milk, not water, the way Mary Louise likes it best, then ladles it out into two yellow bowls. She puts them on a metal tray, adds some saltine crackers and a bottle of ginger ale for her, and a lunchbox bag of Fritos and a glass of milk for Mary Louise, and carries the whole tray into the den. Ruby turns on the TV and they sip and crunch their way through half an hour of *As the World Turns*.

During the commercials, Ruby tells Mary Louise who all the people are, and what they've done, which is mostly bad. When they are done with their soup, another story comes on, but they aren't people Ruby knows, so she turns off the TV and carries the dishes back to the kitchen.

"I gotta do the dustin and finish vacuumin, and ain't no way to talk over that kind of noise," Ruby says, handing Mary Louise a handful of Oreos. "So you go off and play by yourself now, and I'll get my chores done before Miz Kitty comes home."

Mary Louise goes up to her room. At 4:30 she hears Kitty come home, but she only changes into out-to-dinner clothes and leaves and doesn't get into bed. Ruby says good-bye when Mrs. Banks comes at 6:00, and Mary Louise eats dinner in the kitchen and goes upstairs at 8:00, when Mrs. Banks starts to watch *Dr. Kildare*.

On her dresser there is a picture of her mother. She is beautiful, with long curls and a silvery white dress. She looks like a queen, so Mary Louise thinks she might be a princess. She lives in a castle, imprisoned by her evil stepmother, the false queen. But now that there is magic, there will be a happy ending. She crawls under the covers and watches her doorway, wondering what will happen when Kitty tries to come into her room, if there will be flames.

~

Kitty begins to scream just before nine Friday morning. Clumps of her hair lie on her pillow like spilled wheat. What is left sprouts from her scalp in irregular clumps, like a crabgrass-infested lawn. Clusters of angry red blisters dot her exposed skin.

By the time Mary Louise runs up from the kitchen, where she is eating a bowl of Kix, Kitty is on the phone. She is talking to her beauty salon. She is shouting, "This is an emergency! An emergency!"

Kitty does not speak to Mary Louise. She leaves the house with a scarf wrapped around her head like a turban, in such a hurry that she does not even bother with lipstick. Mary Louise hears the tires of her T-bird squeal out of the driveway. A shower of gravel hits the side of the house, and then everything is quiet.

Ruby comes upstairs at ten, buttoning the last button on her uniform. Mary Louise is in the breakfast nook, eating a second bowl of Kix. The first one got soggy. She jumps up excitedly when she sees Ruby.

"Miz Kitty already gone?" Ruby asks, her hand on the coffeepot.

"It worked! It worked! Something *bad* happened to her hair. A lot of it fell out, and there are chicken pox where it was. She's at the beauty shop. I think she's going to be there a long time."

Ruby pours herself a cup of coffee. "That so?"

"Uh-huh." Mary Louise grins. "She looks like a *goopher*."

"Well, well, well. That come back on her fast, didn't it? Maybe now she think twice 'bout messin with somebody smaller'n her. But you, Miss Mouse," Ruby wiggles a semi-stern finger at Mary Louise, "don't you go jumpin up and down shoutin 'bout goophers, hear? Magic ain't nothin to be foolin around with. It can bring sickness, bad luck, a whole heap of misery if it ain't done proper. You hear me?"

Mary Louise nods and runs her thumb and finger across her lips, as if she is locking them. But she is still grinning from ear to ear.

~

Kitty comes home from the beauty shop late that afternoon. She is in a very, very bad mood, and still has a scarf around her head. Mary Louise is behind the couch in the den, playing seven dwarfs. She is Snow White and is lying very still, waiting for the prince.

Kitty comes into the den and goes to the bar. She puts two ice cubes in a heavy squat crystal glass, then reaches up on her tiptoes and feels around on the bookshelf until she finds a small brass key. She unlocks the liquor cabinet and fills her glass with brown liquid. She goes to the phone and makes three phone calls, canceling cocktails, dinner, tennis on Saturday. "Sorry," Kitty says. "Under the weather. Raincheck?" When she is finished she refills her glass, replaces the key, and goes upstairs. Mary Louise does not see her again until Sunday.

Mary Louise stays in her room most of the weekend. It seems like a good idea, now that it is safe there. Saturday afternoon she tiptoes down to the kitchen and makes three peanut butter and honey sandwiches. She is not allowed to use the stove. She takes her sandwiches and some Fritos upstairs and touches one of the nails under the carpet, to make sure it is still there. She knows the magic is working, because Kitty doesn't even try to come in, not once.

At seven-thirty on Sunday night, she ventures downstairs again. Kitty's door is shut. The house is quiet. It is time for Disney. *Walt Disney's Wonderful World of Color*. It is her favorite program, the only one that is not black and white, except for *Bonanza*, which comes on after her bedtime.

Mary Louise turns on the big TV that is almost as tall as she is, and sits in the middle of the maroon leather couch in the den. Her feet stick out in front of her, and do not quite reach the edge. There is a commercial for Mr. Clean. He has no hair, like Kitty, and Mary Louise giggles, just a little. Then there are red and blue fireworks over the castle where Sleeping Beauty lives. Mary Louise's thumb wanders up to her mouth, and she rests her cheek on the soft nap of her Bankie.

The show is *Cinderella*, and when the wicked stepmother comes on, Mary Louise thinks of Kitty, but does not giggle. The story unfolds and Mary Louise is bewitched by the colors, by the magic of television. She does not hear the creaking of the stairs. She does not hear the door of the den open, or hear the rattle of ice cubes in an empty crystal glass. She does not see the shadow loom over her until it is too late.

～

It is a sunny Monday morning. Ruby comes in the basement door and changes into her uniform. She switches on the old brown table radio, waits for its tubes to warm up and begin to glow, then turns the yellowed plastic dial until she finds a station that is more music than static. The Marcels are singing "Blue Moon" as she sorts the laundry, and she dances a little on the concrete floor, swinging and swaying as she tosses white cotton panties into one basket and black nylon socks into another.

She fills the washer with a load of whites, adds a measuring cup of Dreft, and turns the dial to Delicate. The song on the radio changes to "Runaway" as she goes over to the wooden cage built into the wall, where the laundry that has been dumped down the upstairs chute gathers.

"As I walk along . . . " Ruby sings as she opens the hinged door with its criss-cross of green painted slats. The plywood box inside is a cube about three feet on a side, filled with a mound of flowered sheets and white terry cloth towels. She pulls a handful of towels off the top of the mound and lets them tumble into the pink plastic basket waiting on the floor below. "An' I wonder. I wa-wa-wa-wa-wuh-un-der," she sings, and then stops when the pile moves on its own, and whimpers.

Ruby parts the sea of sheets to reveal a small head of carrot-red hair.

"Miss Mouse? What on God's green earth you doin in there? I like to bury you in all them sheets!"

A bit more of Mary Louise appears, her hair in tangles, her eyes red-rimmed from crying.

"Is Kitty gone?" she asks.

Ruby nods. "She at the beauty parlor again. What you doin in there? You hidin from Miz Kitty?"

"Uh-huh." Mary Louise sits up and a cascade of hand towels and washcloths tumbles out onto the floor.

"What she done this time?"

"She—she—" Mary Louise bursts into ragged sobs.

Ruby reaches in and puts her hands under Mary Louise's arms, lifting the weeping child out of the pile of laundry. She carries her over to the basement stairs and sits down, cradling her. The tiny child shakes and holds on tight to Ruby's neck, her tears soaking into the white cotton collar. When her tears subside into trembling, Ruby reaches into a pocket and proffers a pale yellow hankie.

"Blow hard," she says gently. Mary Louise does. "Now scooch around front a little so you can sit in my lap." Mary Louise scooches without a word. Ruby strokes her curls for a minute. "Sugar? What she do this time?"

Mary Louise tries to speak, but her voice is still a rusty squeak.

After a few seconds she just holds her tightly clenched fist out in front of her and slowly opens it. In her palm is a wrinkled scrap of pale blue flannel, about the size of a playing card, its edges jagged and irregular.

"Miz Kitty do that?"

"Uh-huh," Mary Louise finds her voice. "I was watching Disney and *she* came in to get another drink. She said Bankie was just a dirty old rag with germs and sucking thumbs was for babies—" Mary Louise pauses to take a breath. "She had scissors and she cut up all of Bankie on the floor. She said next time she'd get bigger scissors and cut off my thumbs! She threw my

Bankie pieces in the toilet and flushed, three times. This one fell under the couch," Mary Louise says, looking at the small scrap, her voice breaking.

Ruby puts an arm around her shaking shoulders and kisses her forehead. "Hush now. Don't you fret. You just sit down here with me. Everything gonna be okay. You gotta—" A buzzing noise from the washer interrupts her. She looks into the laundry area, then down at Mary Louise and sighs. "You take a couple deep breaths. I gotta move the clothes in the washer so they're not all on one side. When I come back, I'm gonna tell you a story. Make you feel better, okay?"

"Okay," says Mary Louise in a small voice. She looks at her lap, not at Ruby, because nothing is really very okay at all.

Ruby comes back a few minutes later and sits down on the step next to Mary Louise. She pulls two small yellow rectangles out of her pocket and hands one to Mary Louise. "I like to set back and hear a story with a stick of Juicy Fruit in my mouth. Helps my ears open up or somethin. How about you?"

"I like Juicy Fruit," Mary Louise admits.

"I thought so. Save the foil. Fold it up and put it in your pocket."

"So I have someplace to put the gum when the flavor's all used up?"

"Maybe. Or maybe we got somethin else to do and that foil might could come in handy. You save it up neat and we'll see."

Mary Louise puts the gum in her mouth and puts the foil in the pocket of her corduroy pants, then folds her hands in her lap and waits.

"Well, now," says Ruby. "Seems that once, a long, long time ago, down South Carolina, there was a little mouse of a girl with red, red hair and big blue eyes."

"Like me?" asks Mary Louise.

"You know, I think she was just about 'zactly like you. Her momma died when she was just a little bit of a girl, and her daddy married hisself a new wife, who was very pretty, but she was mean and lazy. Now, this stepmomma, she didn't much like stayin home to take care of no child weren't really her own and she was awful cruel to that poor little girl. She never gave her enough to eat, and even when it was snowin outside, she just dress her up in thin cotton rags. That child was awful hungry and cold, come winter.

"But her real momma had made her a blanket, a soft blue blanket, and that was the girl's favorite thing in the whole wide world. If she wrapped it around herself and sat real quiet in a corner, she was warm enough, then.

"Now, her stepmomma, she didn't like seein that little girl happy. That little girl had power inside her, and it scared her stepmomma. Scared her so bad that one day she took that child's most favorite special blanket and cut it up into tiny pieces, so it wouldn't be no good for warmin her up at all."

"That was really mean of her," Mary Louise says quietly.

"Yes it was. Awful mean. But you know what that little girl did next? She went into the kitchen, and sat down right next to the cookstove, where it was a little bit warm. She sat there, holdin one of the little scraps from her blanket, and she cried, cause she missed havin her real momma. And when her tears hit the stove, they turned into steam, and she stayed warm as toast the rest of that day. Ain't nothin warmer than steam heat, no siree.

"But when her stepmomma saw her all smilin and warm again, what did that woman do but lock up the woodpile, out of pure spite. See, she ate out in fancy rest'rants all the time, and she never did cook, so it didn't matter to her if there was fire in the stove or not.

"So finally that child dragged her cold self down to the basement. It was mighty chilly down there, but she knew it was someplace her stepmomma wouldn't look for her, cause the basement's where work gets done, and her stepmomma never did do one lick of work.

"That child hid herself back of the old wringer washer, in a dark, dark corner. She was cold, and that little piece of blanket was only big enough to wrap a mouse in. She wished she was warm. She wished and wished and between her own power and that magic blanket, she found her mouse self. Turned right into a little gray mouse, she did. Then she wrapped that piece of soft blue blanket around her and hid herself away just as warm as if she was in a feather bed.

"But soon she heard somebody comin down the wood stairs into the basement, clomp, clomp, clomp. And she thought it was her mean old stepmomma comin to make her life a misery again, so she scampered quick like mice do, back into a little crack in the wall. 'Cept it weren't her stepmomma. It was the cleanin lady, comin down the stairs with a big basket of mendin."

"Is that you?" Mary Louise asks.

"I reckon it was someone pretty much like me," Ruby says, smiling. "And she saw that little mouse over in the corner with that scrap of blue blanket tight around her, and she said, "Scuse me Miss Mouse, but I needs to patch me up this old raggy sweater, and that little piece of blanket is just the right size. Can I have it?'"

"Why would she talk to a mouse?" Mary Louise asks, puzzled.

"Well, now, the lady knew that it wasn't no regular mouse, 'cause she weren't no ordinary cleanin lady, she was a conjure woman too. She could see that magic girl spirit inside the mouse shape clear as day."

"Oh. Okay." Ruby smiles.

"Now, the little mouse-child had to think for a minute, because that piece of blue blanket was 'bout the only thing she loved left in the world. But the lady asked so nice, she gave over her last little scrap of blanket for the mendin and turned back into a little girl.

"Well sir, the spirit inside that blue blanket was powerful strong, even though the pieces got all cut up. So when the lady sewed that blue scrap onto that raggy old sweater, what do you know? It turned into a big warm magic coat, just the size of that little girl. And when she put on that magic coat, it kept her warm and safe, and her stepmomma never could hurt her no more."

"I wish there really was magic," says Mary Louise sadly. "Because she *did* hurt me again."

Ruby sighs. "Magic's there, sugar. It truly is. It just don't always work the way you think it will. That sufferin hand we put in Miz Kitty's bed, it work just fine. It scared her plenty. Trouble is, when she scared, she get mad, and then she get mean, and there ain't no end to it. No tellin what she might take it into her head to cut up next."

"My thumbs," says Mary Louise solemnly. She looks at them as if she is saying good-bye.

"That's what I'm afraid of. Somethin terrible bad. I been thinkin on this over the weekend, and yesterday night I call my Aunt Nancy down in Beaufort, where I'm from. She's the most powerful conjure woman I know, taught me when I was little. I ask her what she'd do, and she says, 'sounds like you all need a Peaceful Home hand, stop all the angry, make things right.'"

"Do we have to make the bed again?" asks Mary Louise.

"No, sugar. This is a wearin hand, like my money hand. 'Cept it's for you to wear. Got lots of special things in it."

"Like what?"

"Well, first we got to weave together a hair charm. A piece of yours, a piece of Miz Kitty's. Hers before the goopher, I think. And we need some dust from the house. And some rosemary from the kitchen. I can get all them when I clean today. The rest is stuff I bet you already got."

"I have magic things?"

"I b'lieve so. That piece of tinfoil from your Juicy Fruit? We need that. And somethin lucky. You got somethin real lucky?"

"I have a penny what got run over by a train," Mary Louise offers.

"Just so. Now the last thing. You know how my little bag's green flannel, 'cause it's a money hand?"

Mary Louise nods.

"Well, for a Peaceful Home hand, we need a square of light blue flannel. You know where I can find one of those?"

Mary Louise's eyes grow wide behind her glasses. "But it's the only piece I've got left."

"I know," Ruby says softly.

"It's like in the story, isn't it?"

"Just like."

"And like in the story, if I give it to you, Kitty can't hurt me ever again?"

"Just like."

Mary Louise opens her fist again and looks at the scrap of blue flannel for a long time. "Okay," she says finally, and gives it to Ruby.

"It'll be all right, Miss Mouse. I b'lieve everything will turn out just fine. Now I gotta finish this laundry and do me some housework. I'll meet you in the kitchen round one-thirty. We'll eat and I'll fix up your hand right after my story."

At two o'clock the last credits of *As the World Turns* disappear from the TV. Ruby and Mary Louise go down to the basement. They lay out all the ingredients on the padded gray surface of the ironing board. Ruby assembles the hand, muttering under her breath from time to time. Mary Louise can't hear the words. Ruby wraps everything in the blue flannel and snares the neck of the walnut-sized bundle with three twists of white string.

"Now all we gotta do is give it a little drink, then you can put it on," she tells Mary Louise.

"Drink of what?"

Ruby frowns. "I been thinkin on that. My Aunt Nancy said best thing is to get me some Peaceful Oil. But I don't know no root doctors up here. Ain't been round Detroit long enough."

"We could look in the phone book."

"Ain't the kind of doctor you finds in the Yellow Pages. Got to know someone who knows someone. And I don't. I told Aunt Nancy that, and she says in that case, reg'lar whiskey'll do just fine. That's what I been givin my money hand. Little bit of my husband's whiskey every mornin for six days now. I don't drink, myself, 'cept maybe a cold beer on a hot summer night. But whiskey's strong magic, comes to conjurin. Problem is, I can't take your hand home with me to give it a drink, 'long with mine."

"Why not?"

"'Cause once it goes round your neck, nobody else can touch it, not even me, else the conjure magic leak right out." Ruby looks at Mary Louise thoughtfully. "What's the most powerful drink you ever had, Miss Mouse?"

Mary Louise hesitates for a second, then says, "Vernor's ginger ale. The bubbles are very strong. They go up my nose and make me sneeze."

Ruby laughs. "I think that just might do. Ain't as powerful as whiskey, but it fits, you bein just a child and all. And there's one last bottle up in the Frigidaire. You go on up now and fetch it."

Mary Louise brings down the yellow and green bottle. Ruby holds her thumb over the opening and sprinkles a little bit on the flannel bag, mumbling some more words that end with "father son and holy ghost amen." Then she ties the white yarn around Mary Louise's neck so that the bag lies under her left armpit, and the string doesn't show.

"This bag's gotta be a secret," she says. "Don't talk about it, and don't let nobody else see it. Can you do that?"

Mary Louise nods. "I dress myself in the morning, and I change into my jammies in the bathroom."

"That's good. Now the next three mornings, before you get dressed, you give your bag a little drink of this Vernor's, and say, 'Lord, bring an end to the evil in this house, amen.' Can you remember that?"

Mary Louise says she can. She hides the bottle of Vernor's behind the leg of her bed. Tuesday morning she sprinkles the bag with Vernor's before putting on her T-shirt. The bag is a little sticky.

But Mary Louise thinks the magic might be working. Kitty has bought a blond wig, a golden honey color. Mary Louise thinks it looks like a helmet, but doesn't say so. Kitty smiles in the mirror at herself and is in a better mood. She leaves Mary Louise alone.

Wednesday morning the bag is even stickier. It pulls at Mary Louise's armpit when she reaches for the box of Kix in the cupboard. Ruby says this is okay.

By Thursday, the Vernor's has been open for too long. It has gone flat and there are no bubbles at all. Mary Louise sprinkles her bag, but worries that it will lose its power. She is afraid the charm will not work, and that Kitty will come and get her. Her thumbs ache in anticipation.

When she goes downstairs Kitty is in her new wig and a green dress. She is going out to a luncheon. She tells Mary Louise that Ruby will not be there until noon, but she will stay to cook dinner. Mary Louise will eat in the dining room tonight, and until then she should be good and not to make a mess. After she is gone, Mary Louise eats some Kix and worries about her thumbs.

When her bowl is empty, she goes into the den, and stands on the desk chair so she can reach the tall books on the bookshelf. They are still over her head, and she cannot see, but her fingers reach. The dust on the tops makes her sneeze; she finds the key on a large black book called *Who's Who in Manufacturing 1960.* The key is brass and old-looking.

Mary Louise unlocks the liquor cabinet and looks at the bottles. Some are brown, some are green. One of the green ones has Toto dogs on it, a black one and a white one, and says SCOTCH WHISKEY. The bottle is half-full and heavy. She spills some on the floor, and her little bag is soaked more than sprinkled, but she thinks this will probably make up for the flat ginger ale.

She puts the green bottle back and carefully turns it so the Toto dogs face out, the way she found it. She climbs back up on the chair and puts the key back up on top of *Manufacturing*, then climbs down.

The little ball is cold and damp under her arm, and smells like medicine. She changes her shirt and feels safer. But she does not want to eat dinner alone with Kitty. That is not safe at all. She thinks for a minute, then smiles. Ruby has shown her how to make a room safe.

There are only five nails left in the jar in the garage. But she doesn't want to keep Kitty *out* of the dining room, just make it safe to eat dinner there. Five is probably fine. She takes the nails into the kitchen and opens the cupboard under the sink. She looks at the Drano. She is not allowed to touch it, not by Kitty's rules, not by babysitter rules, not by Ruby's rules. She looks at the pirate flag man on the side of the can. The poison man. He is bad, bad, bad, and she is scared. But she is more scared of Kitty.

She carries the can over to the doorway between the kitchen and the dining room and kneels down. When she looks close she sees dirt and salt and seeds and bits of things in the thin space between the linoleum and the carpet.

The can is very heavy, and she doesn't think she can pour any Drano into the cap. Not without spilling it. So she tips the can upside down three times, then opens it. There is milky Drano on the inside of the cap. She carefully dips in each nail and pushes them, one by one, under the edge of the dining room carpet. It is hard to push them all the way in, and the two in the middle go crooked and cross over each other a little.

"This is a protectin hand," she says out loud to the nails. Now she needs a prayer, but not a bedtime prayer. A dining room prayer. She thinks hard for a minute, then says, "For what we are about to receive may we be truly thankful amen." Then she puts the Drano back under the sink and washes her hands three times with soap, just to make sure.

Ruby gets there at noon. She gives Mary Louise a quick hug and a smile, and then tells her to scoot until dinnertime, because she has to vacuum and do the kitchen floor and polish the silver. Mary Louise wants to ask Ruby about magic things, but she scoots.

Ruby is mashing potatoes in the kitchen when Kitty comes home. Mary Louise sits in the comer of the breakfast nook, looking at the comics in the paper, still waiting for Ruby to be less busy and come and talk to her. Kitty puts her purse down and goes into the den. Mary Louise hears the rattle of ice cubes. A minute later, Kitty comes into the kitchen. Her glass has an inch of brown liquid in it. Her eyes have an angry look.

"Mary Louise, go to your room. I need to speak to Ruby in private."

Mary Louise gets up without a word and goes into the hall. But she does not go upstairs. She opens the basement door silently and pulls it almost shut behind her. She stands on the top step and listens.

"Ruby, I'm afraid I'm going to have to let you go," says Kitty.

Mary Louise feels her armpits grow icy cold and her eyes begin to sting.

"Ma'am?"

"You've been drinking."

"No, ma'am. I ain't—"

"Don't try to deny it. I know you coloreds have a weakness for it. That's why Mr. Whittaker and I keep the cabinet in the den locked. For your own good. But when I went in there, just now, I found the cabinet door open. I cannot have servants in my house that I do not trust. Is that clear?"

"Yes, ma'am."

Mary Louise waits for Ruby to say something else, but there is silence. "I will pay you through the end of the week, but I think it's best if you leave after dinner tonight." There is a rustling and the snap of Kitty's handbag opening. "There," she says. "I think I've been more than generous, but of course I cannot give you references."

"No, ma'am," says Ruby.

"Very well. Dinner at six. Set two places. Mary Louise will eat with me." Mary Louise hears the sound of Kitty's heels marching off, then the creak of the stairs going up. There is a moment of silence, and the basement door opens.

Ruby looks at Mary Louise and takes her hand. At the bottom of the stairs she sits, and gently pulls Mary Louise down beside her. "Miss Mouse? You got somethin you want to tell me?"

Mary Louise hangs her head.

"You been in your daddy's liquor?"

A tiny nod. "I didn't *drink* any. I just gave my bag a little. The Vernor's was flat and I was afraid the magic wouldn't work. I put the key back. I guess I forgot to lock the door."

"I guess you did."

"I'll tell Kitty it was me," Mary Louise says, her voice on the edge of panic. "You don't have to be fired. I'll tell her."

"Tell her what, Miss Mouse? Tell her you was puttin your daddy's whiskey on a conjure hand?" Ruby shakes her head. "Sugar, you listen to me. Miz Kitty thinks I been drinkin, she just fire me. But she find out I been teachin you black juju magic, she gonna call the po-lice. Better you keep quiet, hear?"

"But it's not fair!"

"Maybe it is, maybe it ain't." Ruby strokes Mary Louise's hair and smiles a sad smile, her eyes as gentle as her hands. "But, see, after she talk to me that way, ain't no way I'm gonna keep workin for Miz Kitty nohow. It be okay, though. My money hand gonna come through. I can feel it. Already startin to, maybe. The Ford plant's hirin again, and my husband's down there today, signin up. Maybe when I gets home, he's gonna tell me good news. May just be."

"You can't *leave* me!" Mary Louise cries.

"I got to. I got my own life."

"Take me with you."

"I can't, sugar." Ruby puts her arms around Mary Louise. "Poor Miss Mouse. You livin in this big old house with nice things all 'round you, 'cept nobody nice to you. But angels watchin out for you. I b'lieve that. Keep you safe till you big enough to make your own way, find your real kin."

"What's kin?"

"Fam'ly. Folks you belong to."

"Are you my kin?"

"Not by blood, sugar. Not hardly. But we're heart kin, maybe. 'Cause I love you in my heart, and I ain't never gonna forget you. That's a promise." Ruby kisses Mary Louise on the forehead and pulls her into a long hug. "Now since Miz Kitty already give me my pay, I 'spect I oughta go up, give her her dinner. I reckon you don't want to eat with her?"

"No."

"I didn't think so. I'll tell her you ain't feelin well, went on up to bed. But I'll come downstairs, say good-bye, 'fore I leave." Ruby stands up and looks fondly down at Mary Louise. "It'll be okay, Miss Mouse. There's miracles every day. Why, last Friday, they put a fella up in space. Imagine that? A man up in space? So ain't nothin impossible, not if you wish just hard as you can. Not if you believe." She rests her hand on Mary Louise's head for a moment, then walks slowly up the stairs and back into the kitchen.

~

Mary Louise sits on the steps and feels like the world is crumbling around her. This is not how the story is supposed to end. This is not happily ever after. She cups her tiny hand around the damp, sticky bag under her arm and closes her eyes and thinks about everything that Ruby has told her. She wishes for the magic to be real.

And it is. There are no sparkles, no gold. This is basement magic, deep and cool. Power that has seeped and puddled, gathered slowly, beneath the notice of queens, like the dreams of small awkward girls. Mary Louise believes with all her heart, and finds the way to her mouse self.

Mouse sits on the bottom step for a minute, a tiny creature with a round pink tail and fur the color of new rust. She blinks her blue eyes, then scampers off the step and across the basement floor. She is quick and clever, scurrying along the baseboards, seeking familiar smells, a small ball of blue flannel trailing behind her.

When she comes to the burnt-orange coat hanging inches from the floor, she leaps. Her tiny claws find purchase in the nubby fabric, and she climbs up to the pocket, wriggles over and in. Mouse burrows into a pale cotton hankie that smells of girl tears and wraps herself tight around the flannel ball that holds her future. She puts her pink nose down on her small pink paws and waits for her true love to come.

~

Kitty sits alone at the wide mahogany table. The ice in her drink has melted. The kitchen is only a few feet away, but she does not get up. She presses the buzzer beneath her feet, to summon Ruby. The buzzer sounds in the kitchen. Kitty waits. Nothing happens. Impatient, she presses on the buzzer with all her weight. It shifts, just a fraction of an inch, and its wire presses against the two lye-tipped nails that have crossed it. The buzzer shorts out with a hiss. The current, diverted from its path to the kitchen, returns to Kitty. She begins to twitch, as if she were covered in stinging ants, and her eyes roll back in her head. In a gesture that is both urgent and awkward, she clutches at the tablecloth, pulling it and the dishes down around her. Kitty Whittaker, a former Miss Bloomfield Hills, falls to her knees and begins to howl wordlessly at the Moon.

∼

Downstairs, Ruby hears the buzzer, then a crash of dishes. She starts to go upstairs, then shrugs. She takes off her white uniform for the last time. She puts on her green skirt and her cotton blouse, leaves the white Keds under the sink, puts on her flat black shoes. She looks in the clothes chute, behind the furnace, calls Mary Louise's name, but there is no answer. She calls again, then, with a sigh, puts on her nubby orange outdoor coat and pulls the light string. The basement is dark behind her as she opens the door and walks out into the soft spring evening.

∼

In Tanith Lee's story, Taisia-Tua is a mysterious witch who comes to the exotic and opulent city of Qon Oshen. The enchantress wears a variety of masks. Masks, although they have a particular meaning in this tale, have more general magical uses as well. Wearing a mask "transforms" the wearer in some way. Rituals and performances by magic-makers wearing masks tapped the power or spirits of animals, ancestors, gods, and "other selves." In many African cultures masks were used to protect against witchcraft and sorcery. Fictional superheroes (or non-super heroes like Zorro and the Scarlet Pimpernel) don masks—supposedly to disguise themselves, but putting on a mask is also part of their transformation from mundane to extraordinary.

Mirage and Magia
Tanith Lee

During the Ninth Dynasty of the Jat Calendar, Taisia-Tua lived at the town of Qon Oshen, in a mansion of masks and mirrors.

At that time, being far inland, and unlinked by road or bridge to any of the great seaports of the Western Peninsula, Qon Oshen was an obscure and fulminating area. Its riches, born of itself and turned back like radiations upon itself, had made it both exotic and psychologically impenetrable to most of those foreigners who very occasionally entered it. Generally, it was come on by air, almost by accident, by riders of galvanic silver and crimson balloon-ships. Held in a clasp of pointed, platinum-colored hills, in which one break only poured to the shore of an iridium lake, Qon Oshen presented latticed towers, phantasmal soaring bridgeways, a game board of square plazas and circular trafficuli. Sometimes, gauzelike clouds, attracted to the chemical and auric emanations of the town, would hang low over it, foaming the tower tops. In a similar manner, the reputation of Taisia-Tua hung over the streets, insubstantial, dreamlike, menacing.

She had come from the north, riding in a high white grasshopper carriage, which strode on fragile legs seven feet in the air. The date of her coming varied depending on who recounted it. Seventeen years ago, ten, the year when Saturo, the demon-god, sent fire, and the cinnamon harvest was lost. Her purpose for arrival was equally elusive. She chose for her dwelling a mansion of rose-red tilework, spiraled about with thin stone balustrades on which squatted antimony toads and jade cats, and enclosed by gates of wrought iron, five yards high. Dark green deciduous, and pale-gray fan-shaped pines spread around the mansion, as if to shield it. After sunset, its windows of stained glass turned slotted eyes of purple, magenta, blue, emerald, and gold upon the town. Within the masking trees and behind the masking windows, the Magia—for everyone had known at once she was an enchantress—paced out the dance moves of her strange and insular life.

One thing was always remembered. On the morning or noon or evening or midnight of her arrival, someone had snatched a glimpse inside the grasshopper carriage. This someone, (a fool, for who but a fool would risk such a glimpse?) had told how there were no windows but that, opposite the seat of lush plum silk, the wall above the driver's keys was all one polished mirror. The only view Taisia-Tua had apparently had, all the way from the north to Qon Oshen, was that of her own self.

"Is she beautiful, then?"

"Most beautiful."

"Not at all beautiful."

"*Ugly.*"

"*Gorgeous.*"

"One cannot be sure. Whenever she passes through the town she is always partly masked or veiled. Nor has anyone ever seen her in the same gown twice, or the same wig (she is always wigged). Even her slippers and her jewelry are ephemeral."

It was usually agreed this diversity might be due to such powers of illusion as an enchantress would possess. Or simply to enormous wealth and extravagance—each of which qualities the town was prepared to admire. Certainly, in whatever clothing or guise, Taisia-Tua Magia was never mistaken for another.

At Midsummer of her first year, whenever that was, at Qon Oshen, she perpetrated her first magic. There were scores of witnesses.

A round moon, yellow as wine, hung over the town, and all the towers and bridgeways seemed to reach and stretch to catch its light. The scent of a thousand peach trees, apricot gardens, lily pools, and jasmine pergolas filled the darkness. Gently feverish with the drunkenness of summer, men and women stole from the inns and the temples—on such nights, even the demon-god might be worshipped—and wandered abroad everywhere. And into Seventh Plaza Taisia-Tua walked with slow measured steps, a moment or so behind the midnight bell. Her gown was black and sewn with peacocks' eyes. Her hair was deepest blue. Her face was white, rouged the softest, most transparent of vermilions at cheekbones and lips, and like violet smolder along the eyelids. This face itself was like a mask, but an extra mask of stiff silver hid her forehead, brows, and the hollows under the painted eyes. Her nails were silver, too, and each of them four inches in length, which presumably indicated these also were unreal. Her feet were gloved in silk mounted on golden soles which went *chink-chink-chink* as she moved. She was unaccompanied, save by her supposed reputation. The crowd in the plaza fell back, muttered, and carefully observed. Instinctively, it seemed, they had always guessed this creature boded them no particular good. But her exoticism was so suitable to the mode, they had as yet no wish to censure.

For some while, the Magia walked about, very slowly, gazing this way and that. She took her time, glancing where she would, paying no apparent heed to any who gazed or glanced at her. She was, naturally, protected by her masks, and perhaps by the tiny looking-glass that hung on a chain from her belt, and which, now and then, she raised, gazing also at herself.

At length, she crossed the plaza to the spot where the three-tiered fountain played, turning now indigo, now orchid. Here a young man was standing, with his friends. He was of the Linla family, one of the highest, richest houses in the town, and his name was Iye. Not merely an aristocrat and rich, either, but exceedingly handsome and popular. To this person the enchantress proceeded, and he, caught in mid-sentence and mid-thought, paused, watching her wide-eyed. When she was some few feet from him, Taisia-Tua halted. She spoke, in a still, curious, lifeless little voice.

"*Follow* me."

Iye Linla turned to his friends, laughing, looking for their support, but they did not laugh at all.

"Magia," said Iye, after a moment, staring her out and faltering, for it was hard to stare out a mask and two masked unblinking eyes. "Magia, I do not follow anyone without good reason. Excuse me, but I have business here."

Taisia-Tua made a very slight gesture, which spread her wide sleeves like the wings of some macabre night butterfly. That was all. Then she turned, and her golden soles went *chink-chink-chink* as she walked away.

One of Iye's friends caught his shoulder. "On no account go after her."

"I? Go after that hag—more likely I would go with demoniac Saturo—"

But already he had taken a step in her direction. Shocked, Iye attempted to secure himself to the ground. Presently, finding he could not, he gripped the wrists and clothing of his companions. But an uncanny bodily motivation possessed him. Like one who is drowning, he slipped inexorably from their grasp. There was no longer any conversation. With expressions of dismay and horror, the friends of Iye Linla beheld him walk after the enchantress, at first reluctantly, soon with a steady, unrelenting stride. Like her dog, it seemed, he would pursue her all the way home. They broke abruptly from their stupor, and ran to summon Iye's father, the Linla kindred and guards. But by the time such forces had been marshaled and brought to the mansion of rose-red tile, the gates were shut, nor did any answer the shouts and knocking, the threats and imprecations, while on their pedestals, the ghostly toads and greenish cats grinned at the sinking moon.

Only one old uncle of the Linla house was heard to remark that a night in bed with a mage-lady might do young Iye no harm at all. He was shortly to repent these words, and half a year later the old man ritually stabbed himself before the family altar because of his ill-omened utterance. For the night passed, and the dawn began to surface like a great shoal of luminous fishes in the east. And a second or so after the sunrise bell, a slim carved door opened in the mansion, and then closed again behind the form of Iye Linla. A second more, and a pair of ironwork gates parted in their turn, but Iye Linla advanced no further than the courtyard. Soon, some of his kindred hastened into the court, others standing by the gates to keep them wide, and hurried the young man from the witch's yard.

On the street, they slapped his cheeks and hands, forced wine between his lips, implored him, cursed him. To no avail. His open eyes were opaque, seldom blinking, indicating blindness. They led him home, where the most eminent physicians and psychologists were called, but none of these made an iota of progress with him. Eventually, Iye's official courtesan stole in to visit him, prepared to try such remedies as her sensual arts had taught her. She had been in the chamber scarcely two minutes when her single piercing shriek brought half the household into the apartment, demanding what new thing was amiss.

Iye's courtesan stood in a rain of her own burnished hair, and of her own weeping, and she said, "His eyes—his eyes—Oh, I looked into his eyes—Saturo has eaten his soul."

"The woman is mad," was the common consensus, but one of the physicians, ignoring this, went to Iye, and himself peered between the young man's lids. This physician then spoke in a hushed and awful manner that brought quiet and terror on the whole room.

"The courtesan is clever. Some strange spell has been worked here, and any may see it that will look. It is usual, when glancing into the eyes of another, to see pictured there, since these lenses are reflective, a minute image of oneself. But in the eyes of Iye Linla I perceive only this: The minute image of Iye Linla himself, and, what is more, I perceive him from the back."

Fear was, in this event, mightier than speculation.

By noon, most of Qon Oshen knew of Iye's peculiar fate, and brooded on it. A re-emergence of the enchantress was expected with misgiving. However, Taisia-Tua did not walk in the town again for several weeks. In her stead, there began to be seen about, in the high skies of twilight or early morning, a mysterious silvery kite, across whose elongated tail were inscribed these words:

IS THERE A GREATER MAGICIAN THAN I?

In Qon Oshen, not one man asked another to whom this kite belonged.

~

It may be supposed, though such deeds were performed in secret, that the Linla family sent to the enchantress's house various embassies, pleas, and warnings, not to mention coffers full of bribes. But the spell, such as it was, was not removed from Iye. He, the hope of his house, remained thereafter like an idiot, who must be tended and fed and laid down to sleep and roused up again, exercised like a beast, and nursed like a baby. Sallow death banners were hung from the Linla gates about the time the kite manifested in the sky. By the autumn's end, another two houses of Qon Oshen were mourning in similar fashion.

At the Chrysanthemum Festival, Taisia-Tua, in a gown like fire, hair like burning coals, wings of cinnabar concealing cheeks and chin, scratched with a turquoise nail-tip the sleeve of a young priest, an acolyte of the Ninth Temple. He was devout and handsome, an intellectual, moreover a son of the aristocratic house of Kli-Sra. Yet he went after the Magia just as Iye Linla had done. And came forth from her mansion after the sunrise bell also just as Iye Linla did, so that in his eyes men beheld the young priest's own image, reversed, and to be seen only from the back.

A month later, (only a month), when the toasted leaves were falling and sailing on the oval ponds and inconsequently rushing along the narrow marble lanes of Qon Oshen, an artist of great fame and genius turned from his scroll, the gilded pen in his hand, and found the Magia behind him, her lower face hidden by a veil of ivory plaques, her clothes embroidered by praying mantises.

"Spare me," the artist said to her, "from whatever fate it is you put on those others you summoned. For the sake of the creative force which is in me, if not from pity because I am a human man."

But—"*Follow* me," she said, and moved away from him. This time the soles on her gloved feet were of wood, and they made a noise like fans snapping shut. The artist crushed the gilded pen in his hand. The nib pierced his palm and his blood fell on the scroll. The pattern it made, such was his talent, was as fair as the considered lines any other might have devised. Yet he had no choice but to obey the witch, and when the morning rose from the lake, he was like the others who had done so.

Sometimes the Magia's kite blew in the skies, sometimes not. Sometimes some swore they had seen it, while others denied it had been visible, but all knew the frightful challenge of its writing:

Is THERE A GREATER MAGICIAN THAN I?

Sometimes a man would vanish from his home, and they would say: "*She* has taken him." This was not always the case. Yet she *did* take. In the pure blue days of winter, when all the town was a miracle of ice, each pinnacle like glass, and to step on the streets seemed likely to break every vista in a myriad pieces, then she would come and go, and men would follow her, and men would return—no longer sensible or living, though alive. And in the spring when the blossoms bubbled over and splashed and cascaded from every wall and walk, then, too, she would work her magic. And in the green, fermenting bottle of summer, in its simmering days and restless nights, and in autumn when the world of the town fell upward through a downfalling of purple and amber leaves—then. Randomly, persistently, seemingly without excuse. Unavoidably, despite war being made against her by the nobility of the place, despite intrigues and jurisdiction, despite the employment of other magicians, whose spells to hers were, as it turned out, like blades of grass standing before the curtain of the cyclone. Despite sorties and attacks of a physical nature. Despite the lunacy of firing a missile from a nearby hill in a reaction of fury and madness of the family Mhey, which had lost to her three of its sons. The rocket exploded by night against the roof of the rose tile mansion with a clap like forty thunders, a rose itself of flame and smoke, to wake most of the town with screams and cries. But running to the spot there were discovered only huge hills of clinker and cooling cinders in the street. The mansion was unscathed, its metals and stones untwisted, its jewelry windows unsmashed, its beasts of antimony and jade leering now downward at those who had come to see.

"Her powers are alarming. Why does she work evil against us?"

"What are her reasons?"

"What is the method of the dreadful spell?"

Qon Oshen prayed for her destruction. They prayed for one to come who would destroy her.

But she preyed upon them like a leopard, and they did not know how, or why.

~

There was a thief in Qon Oshen who was named Locust. Locust was hideous, and very cunning, and partly insane with the insanity of the wise. He slipped in among a gathering of respected rich men, flung off his official-seeming cloak, and laughed at their surprise. Although he was a thief, and had stolen from each of them, and each surmised it, Locust fitted within the oblique ethics of the town, for he was a lord of his trade and admired for the artistry of his evil-doing. If he were ever caught at his work, he knew well they had vowed to condemn him to the Eight Agonizing Deaths. But while he eluded justice, sourly they reveled in his theatrical deeds against their neighbors and bore perforce with those nearer home.

"I, Locust, knowing how well you love me, for a certain sum, will perform a useful task for you."

The rich men turned to glance at each other. Their quick minds had already telepathically received the impression of his next words.

"Excellently deduced, your excellencies. I will pierce into the Magia's mansion, and presently come tell you what goes on there."

Some hours after, when the bow of the moon was raising its eyebrow at him, Locust, lord of thieves, penetrated, by means of burglars' skills and certain sorceries he himself was adept in, the mansion of rose-red tiling. Penetrated and watched, played hide and seek with shades and with more than shades, and escaped to report his news. Though from that hour of revelation, he reckoned himself—in indefinable, subtle, sinister ways—altered. And when, years later, he faltered in his profession, was snatched by the law, and—humiliatingly—pardoned, he claimed he had contracted emanations of the witch's house like a virus, and the ailment had gradually eroded his confidence in himself.

"It was a trick of leaping to get over the gate—my secret. Entering then by a window too small to admit even a cat—for I can occasionally condense and twist my bones in a fashion unnormal, possibly uncivilized, I dealt with such uncanny safeguards as seemed extant by invoking my demon patron, Saturo; we are great friends. I then dropped down into a lobby."

It was afterward remarked how curious it was that a thief might breach the defenses of the mansion which a fire missile could not destroy.

But Locust, then full of his cleverness, did not remark it. He went on to speak of the bewildering aspect the mansion had come, internally, to display. A bewilderment due mainly to the labyrinthine and accumulative and mirage-making and virtually hallucinatory effects that resulted from a multitude of mirrors, set everywhere and overlapping like scales. Mirrors, too, of all shapes, sizes, constructions and substances, from those of sheerest and most reflective glass, to those of polished copper and bronze, to those formed by sheets of water held bizarrely in stasis over underlying sheets of black onyx. A fearful confusion, even madness, might have overcome another, finding himself unguided in the midst of such phenomena. For of course the mirrors did not merely reflect, they reflected into each other. Image rebounded upon image like a hail of crystal bullets fired into infinity. Many times, Locust lost himself, fell to his knees, grew cold, grew heated, grew nauseous, passed near to fainting or screaming, but his own pragmatism saved him. From room to unconscionable room he wended, and with him went thousands of replicas of himself (but, accustomed to his own unbeauty, he did not pay these companions much heed). Here and there an article of science or aesthetics might arrest him, but mostly he was bemused, until hesitating to examine a long-stemmed rose of a singular purple-crimson, he was startled into a yell. Without warning, the flower commenced to spin, and as it spun to peel off glowing droplets, as if it wept fire. A moment more and the door of the mansion, far away through the forest of mirrors, opened with a mysterious sigh. Locust hastily withdrew behind a mirror resembling an enormous eye.

In twenty seconds the Magia came gliding in, lavender-haired and clad in a gown like a wave drawn down from the moon. And behind her stumbled the handsome fourth son of the house of Uqet.

And so Locust the thief came to be the only intimate witness to the spell the Magia wove about her victims.

Firstly she seated herself on a pillow of silk. Then she folded her hands upon her lap, and raised her face, which on that day was masked across eyes and forehead in the plumage of a bird of prey. It seemed she sat and gazed at her visitor as if to attract his attention, gazed with her plumaged eyes, her very porcelain skin, her strawberry mouth, even her long, long nails seemed to gaze at him. She was, Locust explained, an object to rivet the awareness, had it not been for the quantities of mirrors, which plainly distracted the young man, so he did not look at Taisia-Tua the enchantress, but around and around, now into this image of himself, now into that. And soon he began to fumble about the room, peering into his own face in crystal, in platinum, in water, jade, and brass. For perhaps two hours this went on, or maybe it was longer, or less long. But the son of Uqet wavered from looking glass to looking glass, at each snagging upon his own reflection, adhering to it, and his countenance grew stranger and stranger and more wild and—oddly—more fixed, until at last all expression faded from it. And all the while, saying nothing, doing nothing, Taisia-Tua Magia sat at the room's center on the pillow of silk.

Finally the son of Uqet came to stare down into the mirror paving under his feet, and there he ceased to move. Until, after several minutes, he fell abruptly to his knees, and so to his face. And there he lay, breathing mist against his own reflected mouth, and the witch came to her feet and stepped straight out of the chamber. But as she went by him, Locust heard her say aloud: "You are all the same. All the same as he who was before you. Is there no answer?"

This puzzled Locust so much, he left it out of his report.

At the witch's exit, it did occur to the thief to attempt reviving the young man from his trance, but when a few pinches and shakings had failed to cause awakening, Locust abandoned Uqet and used his wits instead to gain departure before the enchantress should locate him.

This story thereafter recited (or most of it), earned much low-voiced meditation from his listeners.

"But did she summon no demon?"

"Did she utter no malody?"

"Did she not employ wand or ring, or other device?"

Uqet was found in the morning, lying in Taisia-Tua's yard: Locust's proof. Uqet's eyes were now a familiar sightless sight.

Immediately a whole tribe of fresh magicians was sent for. Their powers to hers were like wisps of foam blowing before the tidal wave. Not the strongest nor the shrewdest could destroy the horror of her enchantment, nor break a single mirror in her mansion. Houses of antique lineage removed themselves from the vicinity. Some remained, but refused to allow their heirs ever to walk abroad.

They prayed for her destruction. For one to come who would destroy her.

The kite inquired of heaven and earth:

IS THERE A GREATER MAGICIAN THAN I?

In a confusion of datelessness, the years shriveled and fell like the leaves . . .

But though the date of her arrival was uncertain, the date of his arrival was exactly remembered.

It was in the year of the Scorpion, on the day of the blooming of the ancient acacia tree in Thirty-Third Plaza, that only put forth flowers once in every twenty-sixth decade. As the sun began to shine over the towers and bridges, he appeared under the glistening branches of this acacia, seated cross-legged on the ground. The fretwork of light and shadow, and the mothlike blooms of the tree, made it hard to be sure of what he was, or even if he was substantially there. He was indeed discernible first by an unearthly metallic music that sewed a way out through the foliage and ran down the plaza like streams of water, till a crowd began to gather to discover the source.

The music came from a pipe of bone which was linked, as if by an umbilical cord of silver tubing, to a small tablet of lacquer keys. Having observed the reason for the pipe's curious tone, the crowd moved its attention to the piper. Nor was his tone at all usual. The colors of his garments were of blood and sky, the shades, conceivably, of pain and hope. Around his bowed face and over his pale hands as he played hung a cloud of hair dark red as mahogany, but to which the sun rendered its own edging of blood and sky-blue rainbows.

When the music ceased, the crowd would have thrown him cash, but at that moment he raised his head, and revealed he was masked, that a face of alabaster covered his own, a formless blank of face that conveyed only the most innocent wickedness. Although through the long slits of the eyes, something was just detectable, some flicker of life, like two blue ghosts dwelling behind a wall. Then, before the crowd had scarcely formed a thought, he set the instruments of music aside and came to his feet, (which were bare), rose straight and tall and pliant as smoke rising from a fire. He held up one hand and a scarlet bird soared out of his palm. He opened the other hand and an azure bird soared out of that. The two birds dashed together, merged, fell apart in a shattering of gems, rubies, garnets, sapphires, aquamarines, that dewed the pavement for yards around. With involuntary cries of delight and avarice, men bent to pick them up and found peonies and hyacinths instead had rooted in the tiles.

"Then stars spun through the air, and he juggled them—ten stars or twenty."

"Stars by day—day-stars? They were fires he juggled from hand to hand."

"He seemed clothed in fire. All but the white face, like a bowl of white thoughts."

"Then he walked on his hands and made the children laugh."

"A vast throng of people had congregated when he removed several golden fish from the acacia tree. These spread their fins and flew away."

"He turned three somersaults backwards, one after another with no pause."

"The light changed where he was standing."

"Where did he come from?"

"That is speculation. But to our chagrin, many of us saw where he proceeded."

Into the crowd, like the probing of a narrow spear, the presence of the enchantress had pressed its way. They became aware of her as they would become aware of a sudden lowering of the temperature, and, not even looking to see what they had no need or wish to see, they slid from her like water from a blade. She wore violet sewn with beads the color of green ice. All her face, save only the eyes, was caged in an openwork visor of five thin curving horizontal bars of gold. Her hair today was the tint of tarnished orichale.

She stood within the vortex the crowd had made for her, she stood and watched the magician-musician. She watched him produce silver rings from the air, fling them together to represent atoms or universes, and cast them into space in order to balance upside down on his head, catching the rings with his toes. Certainly, she had had some inkling of the array of mages who had been called to Qon Oshen against her. If it struck her that this was like some parody of their arts, some game played with the concept of witchcraft, she did not demonstrate. But that she considered him, contemplated him, was very evident. The crowd duly grew grim and silent, hanging on the edges of her almost tangible concentration as if from spikes. Then, with a hundred muffled exclamations, it beheld the Magia turn without a word and go away again, having approached no one, having failed to issue that foreboding commandment: *Follow* me.

But it seemed this once she had had no necessity to say the ritual aloud. For, taking up the pipe and the tablet of keys, leaving seven or eight phantasms to dissolve on the air, five or six realities—gilded apples, paper animals—to flutter into the hands of waiting children, the masked, red-headed man walked from under the acacia tree, and followed her without being requested.

A few cried out to him, warning or plea. Most hugged their silence, and as he passed them, the nerves tingled in their spines. While long after he had disappeared from view, they heard the dim, clear notes of the pipe start up along the delicate arteries of the town, like new blood running there in the body of Qon Oshen. It seemed he woke music for her as he pursued her and what must be his destruction.

Men lingered in Thirty-Third Plaza. At last, one of the Mhey household spoke out in a tone of fearful satisfaction:

"Whatever else, I think on this occasion she has summoned up a devil to go with her."

"It is Saturo," responded a priest in the crowd, "the demon-god of darkness and fire. Her evil genius come to devour her."

In alarm and excitement, the people gazed about them, wondering if the town would perish in such a confrontation.

~

She never once looked back, and never once, as those persons attested which saw him go by, did he falter, or the long sheaves and rills of notes falter, that issued from the pipe and the tablet of lacquer keys.

Taisia-Tua reached her mansion gates, and they swung shut behind her. Next, a carved door parted and she drew herself inside the house as a hand is drawn into a glove, and the door, too, shut itself firmly. In the space of half a minute the demon, if such he was, Saturo, if so he was called, had reached the iron gates. Whole families and their guards had been unable to breach these gates, just as the rocket had been unable to disunify the architecture. Locust the thief had wriggled in by tricks and incantations, but the law of Balance in magic may have decreed just such a ludicrous loophole should be woven in the fabric of the Magia's safeguards. Or she may have had some need for one at least to spy the sole enchantment she dealt inside her rose-red walls.

He who was supposed to be, and might have been, Saturo, the demon-god of flame and shade, poised then at one of the gates. Even through the blank white mask, any who were near could have heard his soft, unmistakable voice say to the gate:

"Why shut me out, when you wish me to come in?"

And at these words the gate opened itself and he went through it.

And at the carved door he said: "Unless you unlock yourself, how am I to enter?"

The door swung the slender slice of itself inward, and the demon entered the mansion of the witch.

The mirrors hung and burned, and fleered and sheered all about him then, scaled over each other, winking, shifting, promising worlds that were not. Saturo paid no attention to any of them. He walked straight as a panther through the house, and the myriad straight and savage images of him, sky and snow, and the drowning redness of his hair, walked with him—but he never glanced at them.

So he arrived quickly in the room where the rose spun and threw off its fiery tears. And here the enchantress had already seated herself on the pillow of silk. Her face, in its golden cage, was raised to his. Her eyelids were rouged a soft, dull purple, the paint on her skin—a second skin—dazzled. Each of her terrible clawlike nails crossed over another. Her eyes, whose hue and character were obscured, stared. She looked merciless. Or simply devoid of anything, which must, therefore, include mercy.

Saturo the demon advanced to within two feet of her, and seated himself on the patterned floor in front of her. So they stared at each other, like two masked dolls, and neither moved for a very long while.

At length, after this very long while had dripped and melted from the chamber like wax, Taisia-Tua spoke to the demon.

"Can it be you alone are immune to my wonderful magery?"

There was no reply, only the stare of the mask continuing unalleviated, the suspicion of two eyes behind the mask, unblinking. Another season of time went by, and Taisia-Tua said:

"Will you not look about you? See, you are everywhere. Twenty to one hundred replicas of yourself are to be found on every wall, the floor, the ceiling. Why gaze at me, when you might gaze at yourself? Or can it be you are as hideous as that other who broke in here, and like him do not wish to be shown to your own eyes? Remove your mask, let me see to which family of the demons you belong."

"Are you not afraid," said Saturo, "of what kind of face a demon keeps behind a mask?"

"A face of black shadow and formlessness, or of blazing fire. The prayers of the town to be delivered from me have obviously drawn you here. But I am not afraid."

"Then, Taisia-Tua Magia, you yourself may pluck away the mask."

Having said this, he leaned toward her, so close his dark red hair brushed her suddenly uplifted hands, which she had raised as if to ward him off. And as if she could not help herself then, the edges of her monstrous nails met the white mask's edges, and it fell, like half an eggshell, to the floor. It was no face of dark or flame which appeared. But pale and still, and barely human in its beauty, the face looked back at her and the somber pallor of the eyes, that were indeed like two blue ghosts haunting it. It was a cruel face, and kind, compassionate and pitiless, and the antithesis of all masks. And the moment she saw it, never having seen it before, she recognized it, as she had recognized him under the acacia tree. But she said hastily and coldly, as if it were sensible and a protection to say such things to such a creature: "You are more handsome than all the rest. Look into the mirrors. Look into the mirrors and see yourself."

"I would rather," said Saturo, who maybe was not Saturo, "look at you."

"Fool," said the enchantress, in a voice smaller than the smallest bead on her gown. "If you will not surrender to your vanity, how is my magic to work on you?"

"Your magic has worked. Not the magic of your spells. Your own magic."

"Liar," said the witch. "But I see you are bemused, as no other was, by fashion." At this, she pulled the gold cage from her face, and the orichaic wig from her hair—which flew up fine and electric about her head. "See, I am less than you thought," said Taisia-Tua. "Surely you would rather look at yourself?" And she smeared the paint from her face and wiped it clean and pale as paper. "Surely you would rather look at yourself?" And she threw off her jewels, and the nails, and the outer robe of violet, and sat there in the plain undergown. "Surely you would rather look at yourself?" And uncolored and unmasked she sat there and lowered her eyes, which was now the only way she could hide herself. "Surely, surely," she muttered, "you would rather look at yourself."

"Who," said he, quieter than quietness, and much deeper than depth, "hurt you so in the north that you came to this place to revenge yourself forever? Who wounded you so you must plunge knives into others, which certainly remained the same knife, plunged again and again into your own heart? Why did the heart break that now enables these mirrors not to break? Who loved himself so much more than you that you believed you also must learn to love only your own image, since no other could love you, or choose to gaze on you rather than on himself? True of most, which you have proven. Not true of all. What silly game have you been playing, with pain turned into sorcery and vanity turned into a spell? And have you never once laughed, young woman, not even at yourself?"

Her head still bowed, the enchantress whispered, "How do you know these things?"

"Any would know it, that knew you. Perhaps I came in answer to praying, not theirs, but yours. Your prayers of glass and live-dead men."

Then taking her hand he stood up and made her stand with him.

"Look," he said, and now he leaned close enough she could gaze into the two mirrors of his eyes. And there she saw, not another man staring in forever at himself, but, for the first time, her own face gazing back at her—for this is what he saw. And finding this, Taisia-Tua, not the rose, wept, and as everyone of her tears fell from her eyes, there was the sound of mirror-glass breaking somewhere in the house.

While, here and there about Qon Oshen, as the mirrors splintered, inverted images crumbled inside the eyes of young men, and were gone.

Iye Linla yawned and cursed, and called for food. The sons of Mhey came back to themselves and rolled in a riotous heap like inebriated puppies. A priest bellowed, an aristocrat frowned, at discovering themselves propped up like invalids, their relatives bobbing, sobbing, about the bed. Each returned and made vocal his return. In Twenty-First Plaza, an artist rushed from his house, shouting for the parchment with the bloodstain of his genius upon it.

By dusk, when the stars cast their own bright broken glass across the sky, the general opinion was that the witch was dead. And decidedly, none saw that wigged and masked nightmare lady again.

For her own hair was light and fine, and her skin paler yet, and her eyes were gray as the iridium lake. She was much less beautiful, and much more beautiful than all her masks. And in this disguise, her own self, she went away unknown from Qon Oshen, leaving all behind her, missing none of it, for he had said to her: "*Follow* me."

~

A month of plots and uneasiness later, men burst in the doors of the vacant mansion, hurling themselves beneath the grinning toads and the frigid cats of greenish jade, as if afraid to be spat on. But inside they found only the webs of spiders and the shards of exploded mirrors. Not a gem remained, or had ever existed, to appease them. No treasure and no hoard of magery. Her power, by which she had pinned them so dreadfully, was plainly merely their own power, those energies of self-love and curiosity and fear turned back, (ever mirror-fashion), on themselves. Like the reflection of a moon, she had waned, and the mirage sunk away, but not until a year was gone did they sigh with nostalgia for her empire of uncertainty and terror forever lost to them. "When the Magia ruled us, and we trembled," they would boastfully say. They even boasted of the mocking kite, until one evening a sightseer, roaming the witch's mansion—now a feature of great interest in Qon Oshen—came on a scrap of silk, and on the silk a line of writing.

Then Qon Oshen was briefly ashamed of Taisia-Tua Magia. For the writing read: LOVE, LOVE, LOVE THE MAGICIAN IS GREATER, FAR GREATER, THAN I.

~

Theodora's Goss's mysterious Miss Emily Gray and her young pupils employ mirrors in magical ways. We've been raised knowing about the evil witch/queen's magic mirror in "Snow White" and Alice traveling through a looking glass. Most of us think—at least fleetingly—of bad luck when we break a mirror. Covering mirrors after a death is (or was) a common custom in many cultures and religions. There is lore connecting the soul to one's reflection as well as the ability to glimpse the dead. Witches and others are said to be able to see the past and present, or divine the future through mirrors and other reflective surfaces. Mirrors—in jewelry, sewn onto clothing or set in windows— have also been used to repel evil, but they can also captivate. Mirrors reveal the truth, but can also deceive.

Lessons with Miss Gray
Theodora Goss

That summer, we were reporters: intrepid, like Molly McBride of the *Charlotte Observer*, who had ridden an elephant in the Barnum and Bailey Circus, and gone up in a balloon at the Chicago World's Fair, and whose stagecoach had been robbed by Black Bart himself. Although she had told him it would make for a better story, Black Bart had refused to take her purse: he would not rob a lady.

We were sitting in the cottage at the bottom of the Beauforts' garden, on the broken furniture that was kept there. Rose, on the green sofa with the torn upholstery, was chewing on her pencil and trying to decide whether her yak, on the journey she was undertaking through the Himalayas, was a noble animal of almost human intelligence, or a surly and unkempt beast that she could barely control. Emma, in an armchair with a sagging seat, was eating gingerbread and writing the society column, in which Ashton had acquired a number of Dukes and Duchesses. Justina, in another armchair, which did not match—but what was Justina doing there at all? She was two years older than we were, and a *Balfour*, of the Balfours who reminded you, as though you had forgotten, that Lord Balfour had been granted all of Balfour County by James I. And Justina was beautiful. We had been startled when she had approached us, in the gymnasium of the Ashton Ladies' Academy, where all of us except Melody went to school, and said, "Are you writing a newspaper? I'd like to help." There she was, sitting in the armchair, which was missing a leg and had to be propped on an apple crate. It leaned sideways like a sinking ship. She was writing in a script that was more elegant than any of ours—Rose's page was covered with crossings out, and Emma's with gingerbread crumbs—about Serenity Sage, who was, at that moment, trapped in the Caliph's garden, surrounded by the scent of roses and aware that at any moment, the Caliph's eunuchs might find her. She would always, afterward, associate the scent of roses with danger. How, Justina wondered, would Serenity escape? How would she get back to Rome, where the Cardinal, who had hired her, was waiting? Beside him, as he sat in a secret chamber beneath the cathedral, were a trunk filled with gold coins and his hostage: her lover, the revolutionary they called The Mask. We did not, of course, insist that everything in our newspaper be true. How boring that would have been. And Melody was sitting on the other end of the sofa, reading the *Charlotte Observer*, trying to imitate the advertising.

"Soap as white as, as—" she said. "As soap."

"As the snows of the Himalayas," said Rose, who had decided that her yak was surly, and the sunlight on the slopes blinding. But surely her guide, who was intrepid, would lead her to the fabled Forbidden Cities.

"As milk," said Emma. "I wish I had milk. Callie's gingerbread is always dry."

"For goodness sake," said Rose. "Can't you think of anything other than food?"

"As the moon, shining over the sullied streets of London," said Melody, in the voice she used to recite poetry in school.

"What do you know about London?" said Emma. "Make it the streets of Ashton."

"I don't think they're particularly sullied," said Rose.

"Not in front of your house, Miss Rose," said Melody, in another voice altogether. Rose kicked her.

"As the paper on which a lover has written his letter," said Justina. Serenity Sage was sailing down the Tiber.

"If he's written the letter, it's not going to be white," said Emma. "Obviously."

And then we were silent, because no one said "obviously" to a Balfour, although Justina had not noticed. The Mask was about to take off his mask.

"I don't understand," said Melody, in yet another voice, which made even Justina look up. "Lessons in witchcraft," she read, "with Miss Emily Gray. Reasonable rates. And it's right here in Ashton."

"Do you think it's serious?" asked Emma. "Do you think she's teaching real witchcraft? Not just the fake stuff, like Magical Seymour at the market in Brickleford, who pulls Indian-head pennies out of your ears?"

"You're getting crumbs everywhere," said Rose, who was suddenly and inexplicably feeling critical. "Why shouldn't it be real? You can't put false advertising in a newspaper. My father told me that."

And suddenly we all knew, except Justina, who was realizing the Cardinal's treachery, that we were no longer reporters. We were witches.

~

"Where did you say she lived?" asked Melody. We were walking down Elm Street, in a part of town that Melody did not know as well as the rest of us.

"There," said Emma. We didn't understand how Emma managed to know everything, at least about Ashton. Although her mother was a whirlpool of gossip: everything there was to know in Ashton made its way inevitably to her. She had more servants than the rest of us: Mrs. Spraight, the housekeeper, as well as the negro servants, Callie, who cooked, and Henry, who was both gardener and groom. Rose's mother made do with a negro housekeeper, Hannah, and Justine, who lived with her grandmother, old Mrs. Balfour, had only Zelia, a French mulatto who didn't sleep in but came during the day to help out. And Melody—well, Melody was Hannah's niece, and she had no servants at all. She lived with her aunt and her cousin Coralie, who taught at the negro school, across the train tracks. We didn't know how she felt about this—we often didn't know what Melody felt, and when we asked, she didn't always answer.

"Don't you think it's unfair that you have to go to that negro school, with only a dusty yard to play in? Don't you think you should be able to go to the Ashton Lady's Academy, with us? Don't you think—" And her face would shut, like a curtain. So we didn't often ask.

"The brick house, with the roses growing on it," said Emma. "It used to be the Randolph house. She was a witch too, Mrs. Randolph, at least that's what I heard. She died, or her daughter died, or somebody, and afterward all the roses turned as red as blood."

"They're pink," said Melody.

"Well, maybe they've faded. I mean, this was a long time ago, right?" Rose looked at the house. The white trim had been freshly painted, and at each window there were lace curtains. "Are we going in, or not?"

"It looks perfectly respectable," said Emma. "Not at all like a witch's house."

"How do you know what a witch's house looks like?" asked Melody.

"Everyone knows what a witch's house looks like," said Rose. "I think you're all scared. That's why you're not going in."

At that, we all walked up the path and to the front door, although Justina had forgotten where we were and had to be pulled. Justina often forgot where we were, or that the rest of us were there at all. Rose raised her hand to the knocker, which was shaped like a frog—the first sign we had seen that a witch might, indeed, be within—waited for a moment, then knocked.

"Good afternoon," said a woman in a gray dress, with white hair. She looked like your grandmother, the one who baked you gingerbread and knitted socks. Or like a schoolteacher, as proper as a handkerchief. Behind her stood a ghost.

~

That summer, we each had a secret that we were keeping from the others.

Rose's secret was that she wanted to fly. She had books hidden under her bed, books on birds and balloons and gliders, on everything that flew. She read every story that she could find about flight—Icarus, and the Island of Laputa, and the stories of Mr. Verne. There was no reason to keep this a secret—the rest of us would not have particularly cared, although Melody might have said that if God intended us to fly, he would have given us wings. Her aunt had said that to a passing preacher, who had told the negro people to rise up, rise up, as equal children of God. And Justina might have looked even more absent than usual, with the words "away, away" singing through her head. But Rose would have been miserable if she had told: it was the only secret she had, and it gave her days, and especially nights, when she was exploring the surface of the moon, meaning. And what if her mother found out? Elizabeth Caldwell's lips would thin into an elegant line, and Rose would see in her eyes the distance between their house with its peeling paint, beneath a locust tree that scattered its seedpods over the lawn each spring, and the house where her mother had grown up, in Boston. She would see the distance between herself and the girl who had grown up in that house, in lace dresses, playing the piano or embroidering on silk, a girl who had never been rude or disobedient. Who had never, so far as Rose knew, wanted to climb the Himalayas, or to fly.

Justina's secret was that her grandmother, the respectable Mrs. Balfour who, when she appeared in the Balfour pew at the Episcopal Church, resembled an ageing Queen Victoria, was going mad. Two nights ago, she had emptied the contents of her chamberpot over the mahogany suite in the parlor, spreading them over the antimacassars, over the Aubusson carpet. Justina had washed everything herself, so Zelia would not find out. And Zelia had apparently not found out, although the smell— She still had a bruise where her grandmother had gripped her arm and whispered, "Do you see the Devil, with his hooves like a goat's and his tongue like a lizard's? *I can.*" "Away, away" the words sang through her head, and she imagined herself as Serenity Sage, at the mercy of the Cardinal, but with a curved dagger she had stolen from the Caliph hidden in her garter. Then she would be away, away indeed, sailing across the Mediterranean, with the wind blowing her hair like a golden flag.

Emma's secret was that her mother had locked the pantry. Adeline Beaufort had been a Balfour—Emma was Justina's second or third cousin— and no daughter of hers was going to be *fat*. For two weeks now she had been bribing Callie, with rings, hair ribbons, even the garnet necklace that her father had given her as a birthday present. That morning, she had traded a pair of earrings for gingerbread. Callie was terrified of Mrs. Beaufort. "Lordy, Emma, don't tempt me again! She'll have me whipped, like in the old slave days," she had whispered. But she could not resist fine things, even if she had to keep them under a floorboard, as Emma could not resist her hunger. They were trapped, like a couple of magpies, fearful and desiring.

Melody's secret was that she wanted to go to college. There was a negro college in Atlanta that admitted women, the preacher had told her. So they could be teachers, for the betterment of the negro race. Because white teachers went to college, and why should only negro children be taught by high school graduates—if that? And Melody wanted to better the negro race. Sometimes she wondered if she should be with us at all, instead of with the other girls in her school—perhaps, as her aunt often said, she should stick with her own. But her own filled her with a sense of both loyalty and despair. Why couldn't those girls look beyond Ashton, beyond the boys they would one day marry, and the families they would work for? And there was a streak of pragmatism in this, as in many of her actions, because the rest of us checked books out of the library for her, more books than even we read. She had never been told that colored folk could not enter the library, but colored folk never did, and what if she was told to leave? Then she would know she was not welcome, which was worse than suspecting she would not be. So every morning, after her chores were done and before school, when other girls were still ironing their dresses and curling their hair, she went to the houses of the wealthy negro families, of the Jeffersons, who traded tobacco and were, if the truth be told, the wealthiest family in Ashton, and the Beauforts, whose daughters were, as everyone knew, Emma's fourth or fifth cousins, and cleaned. She put the money she earned, wrapped in an old set of her aunt's drawers, in a hole at the back of her closet. For college.

~

The ghost was, of course, a girl, and we all knew her, except Justina. She lived near the railroad tracks, by the abandoned tobacco factory that not even the Jeffersons used anymore, with her father. He was a drunkard. We did not know her name, but we could identify her without it. She was the ghost, the white girl, the albino: white hair, white face, and thin white hands sticking out from the sleeves of a dress that was too short, that she must have outgrown several years ago. Only her eyes, beneath her white eyebrows, had color, and those were a startling blue. Her feet were bare, and dirty.

We knew that we weren't supposed to play with her, because she was poor, and probably an idiot. What else could that lack of coloring mean, but idiocy? There was an asylum in Charlotte—her father should be persuaded to put her there, for her own good. But he was a drunkard, and could even Reverend Hewes persuade a drunkard? He rarely let her out. Look at the girl—did he remember to feed her? She looked like she lived on air. Adeline Beaufort and Elizabeth Caldwell agreed: it would be for her own good. Really a mercy, for such a creature.

"Come inside, girls," said Miss Gray. "But mind you wipe your feet. I won't have dirt in the front hall."

It was certainly respectable. The parlor looked like the Beauforts', but even more filled with what Emma later told us were bibelots or *objets d'art*: china shepherdesses guarding their china sheep; cranberry-colored vases filled with pink roses and sprays of honeysuckle; and painted boxes, on one of which Justina, who had studied French history that year, recognized Marie Antoinette. And there were cats. We did not notice them, initially—

they had a way of being inconspicuous, which Miss Gray later told us was their own magic, a cat magic. But we would blink, and there would be a cat, on the sofa where we were about to sit, or on the mantel where we had just looked. "How they keep from knocking down all those—music boxes and whatnots, I don't know," Emma said afterward. But we didn't say anything then. We didn't know what to say.

"Please sit down, girls." We did so cautiously, trying to keep our knees away from the rickety tables, with their lace doilies and china dogs. Trying to remember that we were in a witch's house. "I've made some lemonade, and Emma will be pleased to hear that I've baked walnut bars, and those cream horns she likes." There was also an angel cake, like a white sponge, and a Devil's Food cake covered with chocolate frosting, and a jellyroll with strawberry jelly, and meringues. We ate although Melody whispered that one should never, ever eat in a witch's house. The ghost ate too, cutting her slice of angel cake into small pieces with the side of her fork and eating them slowly, one by one.

"Another slice, Melody, Justina, Rose?" We did not wonder how she knew our names. She was a witch. It would have been stranger, wouldn't it, if she hadn't known? We shook our heads, except for Emma, who ate the last of the jellyroll.

"Then it's time to discuss your lessons. Please follow me into the laboratory."

It must have been a kitchen, once, but now the kitchen table was covered with a collection of objects in neat rows and piles: scissors; a mouse in a cage; balls of string, the sort used in gardens to tie up tomatoes; a kitchen scale; feathers, blue and green and yellow; spectacles, most of them cracked; a crystal ball; seashells; the bones of a small alligator, held together with wire; candles of various lengths; butterfly wings; a plait of hair that Rose thought must have come from a horse—she liked horses, because on their backs she felt as though she were flying; some fountain pens; a nest with three speckled eggs; and silver spoons. At least, that's what we remembered afterward, when we tried to make a list. We sat around the table on what must have once been kitchen chairs, with uncomfortable wooden backs, while Miss Gray stood and lectured to us, exactly like Miss Harris in Rhetoric and Elocution.

"Once," said Miss Gray, "witchcraft was seen as a—well, a craft, to be taught by apprenticeship and practiced by intuition. Nowadays, we know that witchcraft is a science. Specific actions will yield specific results. Rose, please don't slouch in your chair. Being a witch should not prevent you from behaving like a lady. Justina, your elbow has disarranged Mortimer, a South American alligator, or the remains thereof. A witch is always respectful, even to inanimate objects. Please pay attention. As I was saying, nowadays witchcraft is regarded as a science, as reliable, for an experienced practitioner, as predicting the weather. It is this science—not the hocus-pocus of those terrible women in *Macbeth*, who are more to be pitied than feared in their delusion—that I propose to teach you. We shall begin tomorrow. Please be prompt—I dislike tardiness."

As we walked down the garden path, away from the Randolph house, Emma said to the ghost, "How did you know about the lessons?"

"My Papa was sleeping under the *Observer*," she said. Her voice was a rusty whisper, as though she had almost forgotten how to use it.

"Here, I don't want this," said Emma, handing her the last cream horn, somewhat crumbled, which she had been keeping in her pocket.

None of us realized until afterward that Miss Gray had never told us what time to come.

~

"The first lesson," said Miss Gray, "is to see yourselves."

We were looking into mirrors, old mirrors speckled at the edges, in tarnished gold frames—Justina's had a crack across her forehead, and Emma stared into a shaving-glass. Justina thought, "I look like her. My mother looked like her. They say my mother died of influenza, but perhaps she died at the asylum in Charlotte, chained to her bed, clawing at her hair and crying because of the lizards. Perhaps all the Balfours go mad, from marrying each other. Is that why Father left?" Because to the best of her knowledge, her father was in Italy, perhaps in Rome, where Serenity glared out through the bars of her prison, so far beneath the cathedral that no daylight crept between the stones, at the Inquisitor and his men, monks all, but with pistols at their sides. Justina looked into her eyes, large and dark, for signs of madness.

Rose scowled, which did not improve her appearance. What would she have looked like, if she had taken after the Winslows rather than her father? She imagined her mother and her aunt Catherine, who had never married. How daunting it must have been, taking for a moment her father's perspective, to marry that austere delicacy, which could only have come from the City of Winter. In Boston, her mother had told her, it snowed all winter long. Rose imagined it as a city of perpetual silence, where the snow muffled all sounds except for the tinkling of bells, sleigh bells and the bells of churches built from blocks of ice. Within the houses, also built of ice, sat ladies and gentlemen, calm, serene, with noses like icicles, conversing politely—probably about the weather. And none of them were as polite or precise as her mother or her aunt Catherine, the daughters of the Snow Queen. When they drove in their sleigh, drawn by a yak, they wore capes of egret feathers. If she were more like them, more like a Snow Princess, instead of—sunburnt and ungainly—would she, Rose wondered, love me then?

Emma imagined herself getting fatter and fatter, her face stretching until she could no longer see herself in the shaving glass. If she suddenly burst, what would happen? She would ooze over Ashton like molasses, covering the streets. Her father would call the men who were harvesting tobacco, call them from the fields to gather her in buckets and then tubs. They would give her to the women, who would spread her over buttered bread, and the children would eat her for breakfast. She shook her head, trying to clear away the horrifying image.

Melody thought, "Lord, let me never wish for whiter skin, or a skinnier nose, or eyes like Emma's, as blue as the summer sky, no matter what."

We did not know what the ghost thought, but as she stared into her mirror, she shook her head, and we understood. Who can look into a mirror without shaking her head? Except Miss Gray.

"No, no, girls," said Miss Gray. "All of the sciences require exact observation, particularly witchcraft. You must learn to see, not what you expect to see, but what is actually *there*. Now look again."

It was Melody who saw first. Of course she had been practicing: Melody always practiced. It was hot even for July—the flowers in all the gardens of Ashton were drooping, except for the flowers in Miss Gray's garden. But in the laboratory it was cool. We were drinking lemonade. We were heartily sick of looking into mirrors.

"Come, girls," said Miss Gray. "I would like you to see what Melody has accomplished." We looked into Melody's mirror: butterflies. Butterflies everywhere, all the colors of sunrise, Swallowtails and Sulfurs, Harvesters and Leafwings, Fritillaries, Emperors, and Blues, like pieces of silk that were suddenly wings—silk from evening gowns that Emma's mother might have worn, or Rose's. "O latest born and loveliest visions far of all Olympus' faded hierarchy! Butterflies are symbols of the soul," said Miss Gray. "And also of poetry. You, Melody, are a poet."

"That's stupid," said Melody.

"But nevertheless true," said Miss Gray.

"It's like—a garden, or a park," said Emma, when she too saw. And we could also see it, a lawn beneath maple trees whose leaves were beginning to turn red and gold. They were spaced at regular intervals along a gravel path, and both lawn and path were covered with leaves that had already fallen. The lawn sloped down to a pond whose surface reflected the branches above. Beside the path stood a bench, whose seat was also covered with leaves. On either side of the bench were stone urns, with lichen growing over them, and further along the path we could see the statue of a woman, partially nude. She was dressed in a stone scarf and bits of moss.

"How boring," said Emma, although the rest of us would have liked to go there, at least for the afternoon, it was so peaceful.

And then, for days, we saw nothing. But finally, in the ghost's mirror, appeared the ghost of a mouse, small and gray, staring at us with black eyes.

"He's hungry," said the ghost. Emma handed her a piece of gingerbread, and she nibbled it gratefully, although we knew that wasn't what she meant. And from then on, we called her Mouse.

"If you'd only apply yourself, Rose, I'm sure you could do it," said Miss Gray, as Miss Osborn, the mathematics teacher, had said at the end of the school year while giving out marks. Rose scowled again, certain that she could not. And it was Justina whom we saw next.

"It's only a book," she said. It was a large book, bound in crimson leather with gilding on its spine, and a gilt title on the cover: *Justina*.

"Open it," said Miss Gray.

"How?" But she was already reaching into the mirror, opening the book at random—to a page that began, "And so, Justina opened the book." The rest of the page was blank. "Who writes in it?" asked Justina, as the words " 'Who writes in it,' asked Justina" wrote themselves across the page.

"That's enough for now," said Miss Gray as she reached into the mirror and closed the book. "Let's not get ahead of ourselves."

On the day that Rose finally saw herself, the rest of us were grinding bones into powder and putting the powder into jars labeled lizard, bat, frog. Mouse was sewing wings on a taxidermed mouse.

"That's it?" asked Rose, outraged. "I've been practicing all this time for a stupid rosebush? It doesn't even have roses. It's all thorns."

"Wait," said Miss Gray. "It's early yet for roses," although the pink roses—La Reine, she had told us—were blooming over the sides of the Randolph house, and their perfume filled the laboratory.

Sitting in the cottage afterward, we agreed: the first lesson had been disappointing. But we rather liked grinding bones.

~

Rose's heart swung in her chest like a pendulum when Miss Gray said, "It's time you learned how to fly." She told us to meet in the woods, at the edge of Slater's Pond. Mouse was late, she was almost always late. As we stood waiting for her, Emma whispered, "Do you think we're going to use broomsticks? Witches use broomsticks, right?"

Miss Gray, who had been looking away from us and into the woods, presumably for Mouse, turned and said, "Although Emma seems to have forgotten, I trust the rest of you remember that a lady never whispers. The use of a broomstick, although traditional, arose from historical rather than magical necessity. All that a witch needs to fly is a tree branch—the correct tree branch, carefully trained. It must have fallen, preferably in a storm—we are fortunate, this summer, to have had so many storms—and the tree from which it fell must be compatible with the witch. The principle is a scientific one: a branch, which has evolved to exist high above the earth, waving in the wind, desires to return to that height. Therefore, with the proper encouragement, it has the ability to carry the witch up into the air, which we experience as flying. Historically, witches have disguised their branches as brooms, to hide them from—those authorities who did not understand that witchcraft is a science. It is part of the lamentable history of prejudice against rational thinking. I myself, when I worked with Galileo— Sophia, I'm afraid you're late again."

"I'm sorry," mumbled Mouse, and we walked off into the woods, each separately searching for our branches, with Miss Gray's voice calling instructions and encouragement through the trees.

Justina's branch was a loblolly pine, which only she could ride: it kicked and bucked like an untrained colt. Melody rode a tulip poplar that looked too large for her. It moved like a cart horse, but she said that it was so steady, she always felt safe. Rose found an Osage-orange that looked particularly attractive, with its glossy leaves and three dried oranges, now brown, still attached, but they did not agree—she liked to soar over the treetops, and it preferred to navigate through the trees, within a reasonable distance of the ground. When she flew too high, it would prick her with its thorns. So she gave it to Emma, who rode it until the end of summer and afterward asked Henry to carve a walking stick out of it, so she would not forget her flying lessons. Rose finally settled on a winged elm, which she said helped her loop-de-loop, a maneuver only she would try. Mouse took longer than all of us to find her branch: she was scared of flying, we could see that. Finally, Miss Gray gave her a shadbush, which never flew too high and seemed as skittish as she was. Miss Gray herself flew on a sassafras, which never misbehaved. She rode side-saddle, with her back straight and her skirt sweeping out behind her, in a steady canter.

"Straighten your back," she would say, as we flew, carefully at first and then with increasing confidence, over the pasture beneath Slocumb's Bluff, the highest point in Ashton. "Rose, you look like a hunchback. Melody, you must ride your branch with spirit. Think of yourself as Hippolyta riding her favorite horse to war."

"Who's Hippolyta?" asked Emma, gripping her branch as tightly as she could. She had just avoided an encounter with the rocky side of the bluff. Mouse was the most frightened, but Emma was the most cautious of us.

"Queen of the Amazons," said Melody, attempting to dodge two Monarchs. Since the day she had seen herself in the mirror, butterflies had come to her, wherever she was. They sat on her shoulders, and early one morning, when she was cleaning the mirror in Elspeth Jefferson's bedroom, she saw that they had settled on her hair, like a crown.

That day, none of us were being Amazon queens. Rose was flying close to the side of the bluff and over the Himalayas, in a cloak of egret feathers. She could see the yak she had once ridden, sulking beneath her. She was, for the first time she could remember, perfectly happy. Somewhere among those peaks were the Forbidden Cities. She could see the first of them, the City of Winter, where the Snow Queen ruled in isolated splendor and the Princesses Elizabeth and Caroline rode thought the city streets in a sleigh drawn by leopards as white as snow. She flew upward, over the towers of the city, which were shining in the sunlight. And there were the people, serene and splendid, looking up at her, startled to see her flying above them with her cloak of egret feathers streaming out behind her, although they were too polite to shout. But then one and another raised their hands to wave to her, and the bells on their wrists jingled, like sleigh bells.

She raised her hand to wave back, and plunged down the side of the bluff.

"What were you thinking!" said Emma, when Rose was sitting on a boulder at the bottom of the bluff, with her ankle bound up in Miss Gray's scarf.

"I pulled out of it, didn't I?" said Rose.

"But you almost didn't," said Melody. "You really should be more careful."

Rose snorted, and we knew what Miss Gray would say to that. A lady never snorts. But Miss Gray had other problems to take care of.

"Justina!" she called, but Justina wasn't listening. Serenity Sage was floating over the Alps in a balloon. In a castle in Switzerland, The Mask was waiting for her. He had not been captured by the Inquisition after all, and knowing that he was free had given her the resolve to starve herself until she was slender enough to slip through the prison bars, and then up through the darkness of the stone passages under the cathedral. There, through a rosewood fretwork, she had seen the secret rites of the Inquisition, and they had marked her soul forever. But today she was free and flying in the sunlight over the mountains. For three days now, her grandmother had been sick. Zelia had been sitting with her, Zelia had taken care of everything, and the cut on Justina's shoulder was healing, although the paperweight with a view of the Brighton Pavilion would never be the same. Three days, three days of freedom, thought Serenity, watching the mountains below, which looked like a bouquet of white roses.

"Justina!" called Miss Emily. "Are you simply going to float up into the sky? Stop at once."

The loblolly stopped, although Justina almost didn't. She lurched forward and looked around, startled, at Miss Gray.

"I don't want to be an Amazon queen," said Emma, watching from below, "and I don't want to learn to fly."

"How can you not want to fly?" asked Rose.

"Because I'm not you. How can you never remember to comb your hair?"

Rose ran her fingers through her hair, which did look like it had been in a whirlwind.

"Stop arguing," said Melody. "I'm worried about Mouse."

"She's doing all right," said Rose. What Mouse lacked in courage, she made up for in determination: she was sputtering over the meadow, her thin legs stuck out on either sides of the branch, her body bent forward to make it go faster, her hair falling into her face.

"That's not what I'm worried about," said Melody. "Have you noticed how thin she's getting?"

"You'd be so much better if you practiced," said Rose. "Melody practices. That's why she's the best flyer, after me and Justina."

"I don't think you're so much better than Justina," said Emma.

"You're not listening," said Melody. "I said—" but just then a flock of Painted Ladies rose about her, so thick that she had to brush them away with her hands.

We all learned to fly, although it took longer than we expected, and by the time we could all soar over the bluff—except Emma, who preferred to stay close to the ground—the summer storms had passed. We could feel, in the colder updrafts, the coming of autumn.

Despite what Emma had said, Rose was the best of us, the most accomplished flyer. She had explored the Himalayas, had found each of the Forbidden Cities hidden among their peaks, including the city that was simply a stone maze, the City of Birds, where she had practiced speaking bird language, and the temporary and evanescent City of Clouds.

~

Autumn was coming, and these were the things we knew: how to, in a mirror or still pond, see Historical Scenes (although we were heartily sick of the Battle of Waterloo and the Death of Cleopatra, which Miss Gray seemed to particularly enjoy); summon various animals, including possums, squirrels, sparrows, and stray dogs; turn small pebbles into gold and turn gold into small pebbles (to which we had lost another pair of Emma's earrings); and speak with birds. We could now speak to the crows that lived in the trees beside the Beaufort's cottage, although they never said anything interesting. It was always about whose daughter was marrying whom, and how that changed the rules of precedence, which were particularly arcane among crows.

We thought of them first, when we decided to do something about Mouse.

"Can't we ask the birds? Maybe they know where she is." Melody sat curled in a corner of the green sofa, like one of Miss Gray's cats. "We haven't seen her for days." But the crows, who told us everything they knew about mice, knew nothing about Mouse.

"Try the mirror," said Justina. "If we can watch the Battle of Waterloo over and over, surely we can see where Mouse has gone." We were startled: since we had learned how to fly, Justina had seemed more distant than ever, and although she still spent mornings with us at the cottage, she always seemed to be somewhere else.

The only mirror in the cottage had once been in the Beauforts' front hall; it was tall and in a gilt frame, the sort of hall mirror that had been fashionable when old Mrs. Balfour and Mrs. Beaufort, Emma's grandmother, had ruled the social world of Ashton, whose front halls had to be widened to accommodate their crinolines. When Adeline Beaufort entered the house after Grandma Beaufort's funeral, she said, "That mirror has to go."

Justina wiped the dust from it with her handkerchief, which turned as gray and furry as a mouse.

"Please," she said, as politely as Miss Gray had taught us, because one should always be polite, even to dead alligators, "show us Mouse."

"Not Cleopatra again!" said Emma. We were sitting around Justina, who sat on the floor in front of the mirror. "You know, I don't think she's beautiful at all. I don't know what Mark Anthony saw in her."

"Please show us America," said Justina. "And nowadays, not in historical times." We were no longer looking at the obelisks of Egypt, but at a group of teepees, with Indians sitting around doing what Indians did, we supposed, when they weren't scalping settlers. We had all learned in school that Indians collected scalps like Rose's mother collected Minton figurines.

"Thank you," said Justina. "But here in Ashton." We saw a city, with buildings three or four stories high and crowds in the streets, milling around the trolleys and their teams of horses. "That's New York," said Melody, and we remembered that she had lived there, once—when her mother was still alive. Then ships in a harbor, their sails raised against the sky, and then Emma's mother, staring into a mirror, so that we started back, almost expecting to see ourselves reflected behind her. She spread Dr. Bronner's Youth Cream over her cheeks and what they call the décolletage, and then slapped herself to raise the circulation. She leaned toward the mirror and touched the skin under her eyes, anxiously.

Emma turned red. "Parents are so stupid."

"Yes, thank you," said Justina patiently, "but we really want to see Mouse. No, that's—what's Miss Gray doing with Zelia?" They were walking in the Balfour's garden, their heads bent together, talking as though they were planning—what?

And there, finally, was Mouse.

We saw at once why Mouse had been missing our lessons with Miss Gray: she was tied up. There was a rope tied around one of her ankles, with a knot as large as the ankle itself.

"It looks like—the dungeons of the Inquisition," said Justine.

"It looks like the old slave house at the Caldwell plantation," said Melody. It had burned during the war, and other than the slave house, only the front steps of the plantation, which were made of stone, remained to mark where it had been.

"It's a good thing we can't smell through the mirror," said Emma. "I bet it stinks."

In the mirror, Mouse was waving her hands as though conducting a church choir. And as she waved, visions rose in the air around her. Trees grew, taller and paler than we had ever seen. Melody later told us they were paper birches—she had found a picture in a library book. Mouse was sitting on what seemed to be moss, but there was a low mist covering her knees like a blanket, and we could only see the ground as the mist shifted and swirled. The birches around her glowed in the light of—was it the sun, as pale as the moon, that shone through the gray clouds? The forest seemed to go on in every direction, and it was wet—leaves dripped, and Mouse's eyelashes were beaded with water drops. Then a pale woman stepped out from one of the birches—from behind it or within it, we could not tell, and all the pale women stepped out, and they moved in something that was not a dance, but a pattern, and the hems of their dresses, which were made of the thinnest, most translucent bark, made the mist swirl up in strange patterns. Up it went, like smoke, and suddenly the vision was gone. Mouse sat, curled in a corner, with the rope around her ankle.

"I don't think she learned that from Miss Gray," said Emma.

"What are we going to do?" asked Rose. "We have to do something." And we knew that we had to do something, because we felt in the pit of our stomachs what Rose was feeling: a sick despair.

"Rescue her," said Melody. She looked around at the rest of us, and suddenly we realized that we were going to do exactly that, because Melody was the practical one, and if she had suggested it, then it could be done.

"How?" asked Rose. "We don't even know where she is."

"On our branches," said Justina. "Mirror, show us—slowly, show us the roof. Now the street. Look, it's one of the drying sheds by the old tobacco factory. All we need to do is follow the railroad tracks."

"How can we fly on our branches?" asked Emma. "We'll be seen."

"No, we won't," said Justina. She looked at us, waiting for us to understand, and one by one, as though candles were being lit in a dark room, we knew. "Rose, how long has it been since your mother asked where you spend your afternoons? How long has it been since anyone asked any of us, even Melody? Why has Coralie started doing her afternoon chores? And when Emma burned one of her braids, when we were making butterscotch on the Bunsen burner and Miss Gray came in suddenly and startled us, did anyone notice?" No one had. "I don't think anyone has seen what we've been doing, all summer. We've become like Miss Gray's cats, invisible until you're about to sit on them. I think we could fly through Brickleford on market day and no one would notice."

So we flew through the streets of Ashton, as high as the roofs of the houses, seeing them from the air for the first time. Ashton seemed smaller, from up there, and each of us thought the same thing—I will leave here one day. Only Emma was sorry to think so.

We landed by the shed that the mirror had shown us. One by one, we dismounted from our branches. Justina—we had not known she could be such a good leader—opened the door. It did look like a dungeon of the Inquisition, and smelled just as Emma had expected—the smell of death and rotting meat. Mouse was sitting in her corner, with her arms around her knees and her head down, crying. She did not look up when we opened the door.

"Mouse," said Rose. "We've come to rescue you." It sounded, we realized, both brave and silly.

Mouse looked up. We had never seen her face so dirty. Each tear seemed to have left behind a streak of dirt. "Why?" she asked.

"Because—" said Emma. "Because you're one of us, now."

We could not untie the knot. It was too large, too tight: the rope must once have been wet and shrunk.

"There's a knife, next to the bowl," said Mouse. "I can't reach it from here, the rope won't let me—I tried and tried."

The smell of rotting meat came from that bowl, and it was covered with flies. When Justina had finished cutting the rope from Mouse's ankle—the rest of us were standing as close as we could to the boarded-up window, where the crookedness of the boards let in chinks of light—she said, "I think I'm going to be sick."

The door banged open. "What do you brats think you're doing here?" It was a man, who brought with him a stench worse than rotting meat—the stench of whiskey.

"The drunkard father," whispered Emma. We all stood still, too frightened to move, and from Mouse came a mouse-like whimper.

"You little bitch," he said. "I know you. You're Judge Beaufort's daughter. You know how many times your father's put me in that prison of his? You goddamned Beauforts, sneering down your noses at anyone who isn't as high and all goddamn mighty as you are. Wait until he sees what I'm going to do with you—I'll whip you like a nigger, until your backside is as raw as—as raw meat."

Emma shrieked, a strangled sort of shriek, and dropped her branch.

"You're not a man but a toad," said Justina.

He stared at her, as though she had suddenly appeared in front of his eyes. "What—"

"No, not a man at all," said Rose. "You're a toad, a nasty toad with skin like leather, and you eat flies."

"You don't live here," said Melody. "You live in the swamp by the Picketts' house, where the water is dark and still."

Somewhere, in some other country, where we were still Justina, Rose, Melody, and Emma, instead of witches, we thought, *But we haven't learned transformations yet.*

"That's right," said Emma. "Go home, toad. Go back to the swamp where you belong. You don't belong here."

"Sophie," he said, looking at Mouse. "I'm your father, Sophie." He looked at her as though, for once, asking for something, asking with fear in his eyes.

"You know you are, Papa," she said. "You know you're a toad. I've tried to love you, but you haven't changed. You'll always be a toad in your heart."

"Go home, toad," said Justina. "We don't want you here anymore."

"Yes, go back to your swamp," said Melody. "And I hope Jim Pickett catches you one day, and Mrs. Pickett puts you into her supper pot. The Picketts like toad. They say it tastes like chicken."

Mouse's father, the drunkard, hopped out through the door and away, we assumed in the direction of the swamp. We let out a sigh, together, as though we had been holding our breaths all that time.

We made Mouse a bed in the cottage, on the green sofa. Emma said, "Callie won't let me have any more food. Since the revival came, she says she's found religion, and she's got jewels waiting for her in heaven that are more beautiful than earthly trinkets. She's given me back my rings and necklaces." So Rose stole some bread and jam from the cupboard when Hannah wasn't looking, and Mouse ate bread with jam until she was full. Melody gave her a dress, because the rest of us were too big, although Melody didn't have many dresses of her own. Emma brought soap and water so Mouse could wash her face, and combed her hair. Properly combed, it was as fine and flyaway as milkweed. Before we went home to our suppers, Melody read to her from *The Poetical Works of Keats*, which Emma had taken out of the library for her, while the rest of us curled up on the sofa in tired silence.

"Good night," said Mouse, when we were leaving. "Good night, good night." And because she was one of us now, we knew that she was happy.

The next day, Rose and Melody were punished for taking bread and jam without permission and for losing a perfectly good dress, which Hannah had just darned.

~

"The next lesson," said Miss Gray, "is gaining your heart's desire. For which you will need a potion that includes hearts. Today, I want you to go out and find hearts."

"You don't want us to kill squirrels, or something?" said Emma, incredulously.

"Don't be ridiculous," said Miss Gray. "Have you learned nothing at all this summer? The heart is the center, the essence, of a thing. It is what gives a stone gravity, a bird flight. Killing squirrels, indeed!" She looked at us with as much disgust as on the first day, when we had failed to see ourselves in the mirror. It was not fair—Emma had asked the question, and the scorn was addressed to us all. But when had Miss Gray ever been fair?

So out we went, looking for hearts.

This was what we put into our potions. Into Melody's potion, she put all the plays of Shakespeare, with each mention of the word "heart" underlined in red, and each mention of the word "art" as well, even the art in "What art thou that usurp'st this time of night?"; *The Poetical Works of Keats* with each page cut into hearts; and a butterfly that she had found dead on her windowsill, a Red Admiral. With its wings outstretched, it looked like two hearts, one upside down. And we knew that Justina had been right: we were invisible that summer. Otherwise, Emma would have had to spend her pocket money on library fines. Emma put in the double yolk of an egg she had stolen from under the hens, which she insisted resembled a heart; chocolate bonbons that Callie had shaped into hearts; Cocoanut Kisses that we told her had nothing to do with hearts, but she said that she liked them; and hearts cut out of a Velvet Cake, all stolen from a Ladies' Tea that her mother was giving for the Missionary Society. Rose put in a heart-shaped locket that her mother had given her; her mother's rose perfume, which she said was the heart of the rose (the laboratory smelled of it for days); and water from the icebox that she had laboriously chipped into the shape of a heart. Mouse's potion contained a strange collection of nuts and seeds: acorns; beechnuts, butternuts, and black walnuts; the seeds of milkweed and thistle; locust pods; the cones of hemlock and cypress; and red hips from the wild roses that grew by Slocumb's Bluff. "Well," she said, "Miss Gray did say that the heart is the center. You can't get much more centery than seeds, can you?" Justina's collection was the strangest of all: when Miss Gray asked for her ingredients, she handed Miss Gray a mask shaped like a heart on which she had sewn, so that it was completely covered, the feathers of crows. "The crows gave them to me," she told us later, when we asked her where the feathers had come from, "once I explained what they were for. They seemed to know Miss Gray."

"Nicely done," said Miss Gray. "I think Justina's spell will be the strongest, since she has been the most focused among you, although one can't quite call this a potion, can one? But Emma's and Melody's potions will do quite well, and Mouse, I'll help you with yours."

"And mine?" asked Rose. If she had done something wrong, she wanted to know.

"Yours is complicated," said Miss Gray. "We'll have to wait and see."

⌒

Years later, Emma asked, "Rose, did you ever get your heart's desire?" They were walking in the garden of the house where Emma lived with her husband, the senator. Above them, the maples trees were beginning to turn red and gold. Whenever the wind shook the maple branches, leaves blew down around them.

"That's funny," said Rose, reminding herself not to think of her deadline. This was Emma, whom she hadn't seen in—how long? Her deadline could wait. "I don't think we ever told each other what we wished for. I guess what happened afterward drove it out of our heads."

"I suppose you wanted to fly," said Emma. "I remember—you were obsessed with flying, then."

Rose laughed. "I thought I was so good at keeping it secret!" She stopped and looked out over the lawn, where the shadows of the trees were lengthening. Soon, it would be time to dress for dinner. She worried, again, about her gray merino. Would it do for Rose's party? "No," she said, "I wished that my mother would love me. You remember what she was like, even at the end. What a strange thing to admit, after all these years."

"I wished that I could eat all I wanted and never get fat." Emma absentmindedly pulled a maple leaf from her hair, which was bobbed in the current fashion.

"Well, you got your wish, at least. There's no one in Washington as elegant as Mrs. Balfour." Rose looked at Emma, from her expensively waved hair to her expensively shod feet, in the new heels. "How do you like being a senator's wife?"

Emma let the leaf fall from her fingers. "Has the interview started already?" Rose laughed again, uncomfortably. Nothing is as uncomfortable, her editor had told her, as the truth. Emma continued, and to Rose her voice sounded bitter, almost accusatory, "So did she ever tell you that she loved you?"

How much easier it was, to answer questions instead of asking them. To pretend, for one afternoon, that she was here only as Emma's guest. "No, she never told me. But she did love me, I think, in her own way. It took me a long time to understand that. It wasn't a way I could have understood, as a child."

"Understanding—that's not much of a spell."

Emma sat on a bench beside the ornamental pond, where ornamental fish, red and gold, were darting beneath the fallen leaves. After a moment, Rose sat beside her. She looked at the patterns made by lichen on the ornamental urns, then at the statue of Melpomene, whose name on the pedestal was almost obscured by moss. She did not know how to respond.

"Have you heard from Melody?" asked Emma.

"Not since last spring," said Rose, grateful that Emma had broken the silence. "I don't think she'll ever come back. It's easier in Paris. She says, you know, there are no signs on the bathrooms. But I've brought you a copy of her latest. It's still in my suitcase. I meant to unpack it, but I must be losing my memory. You'll like it—one of the poems is about being a witch. I think that's what she asked for, to be a poet. It's still hard to imagine: Melody, the studious, the obedient one, in Paris cafés with artists and musicians, and girls who dance in beads! Drinking and—did you know? Smoking!"

Emma picked up a piece of gravel and tossed it into the pond, where it splashed like a fish. The sound was almost startling in the still afternoon. "It broke up the group, didn't it? When she left for college. I miss her."

Rose stared up at the leaves overhead, red and gold against the sky. "I think it was broken before that."

"We all paid a price, didn't we?" asked Emma. "Do you remember the advertisement? Reasonable rates. She never charged us, but I think we all paid a price. You—all those years taking care of your mother while she had cancer, when you could have been, I don't know, going to college, getting married, having a life of your own. Melody—she'll never come home. If she did, she wouldn't be a poet, just another colored woman who has to sit at the back of the theater. And me—"

Emma picked up another piece of gravel, then placed it on the bench beside her. "I can't gain weight, you know. No matter what. I've tried. Such a silly problem, but—I don't think James and I will ever have children."

"Oh, Emma!" said Rose. "I'm so sorry." What did her article matter? Emma had been her best friend, so long ago.

"Well, that's the way of the world," said Emma, her voice still bitter. Then suddenly, surprisingly, because this was Emma after all, she wiped her eyes, carefully so as not to smudge her mascara. "You gain and you lose, with every choice you make. That's the way it's always been. But you—" She turned to Rose and smiled, and suddenly she was the old Emma again. "All those years giving sponge baths and making invalid trays, when you barely stepped off the front porch, and now a reporter! Do you remember when we were reporters? Just before we were witches."

"I don't know if the society pages count," said Rose. "Although I suppose everyone has to start somewhere. If only we had stayed reporters! But come to think of it—I really am losing my memory—I have news for you. I've heard of Justina! A friend of mine, a real reporter, who was in Argentina covering the revolution—they're having another one this year—wrote me about an American woman who had married one of the revolutionaries, a man they call—why do revolutionaries always have these sorts of names?—The Mask. They call her *La Serenidad*, and there's a song about her that they play on the radio. He wrote it down for me, but I don't know Spanish."

"Now isn't that Justina all over?" said Emma, laughing. It was the first time, Rose realized, that she had heard her laugh all afternoon. After a pause, during which they sat in companionable silence, Emma continued, "Did you ever hear—"

"No," said Rose. "You?

"No."

It grew dim under the maple trees, and the air grew chill. Emma drew her shawl about her shoulders, and Rose put her hands into her jacket pockets. They sat thinking together, as we had so long ago, when we were children—wondering what had happened to Mouse.

～

Emma heard the news first, at breakfast. Her mother had just said, "Would you like some butter on your toast? Or maybe some jam? You look so nice and thin in that dress. Is it the one Aunt Otway brought from Raleigh?" when Callie came into the morning room and said, "Judge Beaufort, come quick! There's thieves in Ashton. They've gone and murdered Mrs. Balfour, and they'll murder us too, Lord have mercy on our souls!"

"What?" Emma's father rose from the breakfast table. "Who told you this?"

"Mrs. Balfour's Zelia. She stayed just to tell me, then ran on back to help. She's already called Dr. Bartlett, though she says he won't be able to do anything for Mrs. Balfour, poor woman. Blood all over her, Zelia told me, like she sprung a leak. May she rest in the lap of the Lord."

"That's enough. Tell Henry to get Mr. Caldwell and Reverend Hewes, and meet me there." Then he was out the door.

"You haven't finished your boiled egg," said Adeline Beaufort. "Emma? Emma, where are you?"

We watched the events at the Balfour house, the largest house in Ashton, whose white columns leaned precariously left and right, from the top of a tulip poplar, the three of us—Emma, Rose, and Melody. We had looked for Mouse in the cottage, but she was nowhere to be found.

"I heard it all from Coralie," said Melody. "Henry's her sweetheart—at least, one of them. He said the front door was open, and when they went in, they found Mrs. Balfour lying on the parlor floor, with a bullet through her heart. There was blood all over the carpet, and a whole pile of silver, teaspoons and other things, scattered on the floor beside her. They think she heard the thief, then came down with the pistol that General Balfour had used in the war and found him going through the silver. He must have taken it away from her and shot her with it."

"Gruesome," said Emma. "Look, there's the hearse driving up from Pickett's Funeral Parlor."

"And they found Justina in a corner of the parlor, barely breathing, with marks around her neck. They think she must have come down too, and he must have tried to strangle her and left her for dead." Not even our imaginations could picture the scene. Surely death was for people we did not know?

Emma's father came out, with Dr. Bartlett, Reverend Hewes, and Henry. We knew what they were carrying between them: Mrs. Balfour, draped in a black sheet, leaving the house where so many of her ancestors had died with more decorum.

"If he had the pistol, why didn't he just shoot Justina?" asked Rose. "It seems like a lot of trouble, strangling someone. Do you think they'll let us see her?"

"No," said Emma. "Only Zelia can see her. That's what Papa said—she's just too sick. But why don't we look—" and we knew what she was going to say. Why don't we look in the mirror?

The cottage was surrounded by men from the tobacco fields, who had been summoned to form a posse. "Stay away from here, girls," said Judge Beaufort. "That thief's been sleeping in our cottage—can you believe his nerve? We found a blanket and some food, even some books. We think it may be old Sitgreaves, the one with that idiot girl. He hasn't been seen for a while. But it looks like he slept here last night. This time, we'll send him to the prison in Raleigh, and that girl of his should have gone to the asylum long ago. I'll make sure of it, when I find her. But until we catch him, don't you go walking out by yourselves, do you hear?"

We looked at each other in consternation, because—where was Mouse?

"Miss Gray," said Rose. "Let's go talk to Miss Gray."

The roses had fallen from the La Reine and lay in a heap of pink petals on the grass. The garden seemed unusually still. Not even bees moved among the honeysuckle.

"Something's not right," said Emma.

"Nothing's right today," said Rose. "Who wants to knock?" No one volunteered, so she knocked with the brass frog, which was as polished as always. But no one answered. Instead, the door swung open. It had not been locked.

The Randolph house was empty. The sofa in the parlor, where we had eaten with a witch for the first time, the table in the laboratory where we had sat, learning our lessons, all were gone. Even the cats, which had only been partially there, were wholly absent.

"It was all here yesterday," said Melody. "She was going to show us how to make dreams in an eggshell."

"I found something," said Rose. It was a note, in correct Spencerian script, propped on the mantel. It said:

Dear Emma, Rose, and Melody,

Please stop the milk. Don't forget to practice, and don't worry. Sophia and I will take care of each other.

Sincerely, Emily Gray

We looked at each other, and finally Melody said what we were all thinking—"How did she know?" Because it was evident: Miss Gray had known what would happen.

We went to Mrs. Balfour's funeral. Even Melody sat in one of the back pews of the Episcopal Church, beside Hannah. The organist played "Lead,

Kindly Light." We ignored the sermon and stared at the back of Justina's head, in the Balfour pew close to the chancel, and then at her face as she walked up the aisle behind the coffin. She was paler than we had ever seen her, as though she had become a statue of herself. In the churchyard, she watched her grandmother's coffin being lowered into the ground, and when Reverend Hewes said "Dust to dust," she opened her hand and dust fell down, into the grave, on top of the coffin. Then she placed her hand on her mouth and shrieked.

We found her in the privet grove that had been planted around the grave of Emmeline Beaufort, Beloved Wife and Mother. We didn't know what to say.

Justina looked at us with the still, pale face of a statue. She had never looked so beautiful, so like a Balfour. "I shot her," she said. "She tried to strangle me—she said she saw the Devil in my eyes. But I had Grandpa's gun, I'd been carrying it in the pocket of my robe for weeks, and I shot her through the heart." Then she half sat and half fell, at the same time, slowly, until she was sitting on the grass, leaning against the gravestone.

"But the masked man—" said Rose.

"And the silver—" said Emma.

"That was Zelia," she said. She looked at her hands as though she did not know what to do with them. "Zelia scattered the silver before she went to get Dr. Hewes. She told me to lie still, and that there'd been a thief. But there was no thief—only me!"

We were silent, then Melody said, "She must have been going mad for a long time. You could have told us."

We heard the privet shake. "Don't you pester her no more," said Zelia. "*Allons, ma fille*. Your duty here is done." She helped Justina up and put a shawl around her shoulders, then led her away. But just before they left the privet grove, Zelia turned back to us and said, "And don't you forget to stop the milk!"

The next day, as we hid behind an overgrown lilac in the Caldwells' garden, Emma told us that Justina was gone. "To Italy, to find her father, I think. Papa saw her off on the train. Zelia was going with her."

Melody said, "I warned you about eating with witches. First Mouse and then Justina. It's as though they've disappeared off the face of the earth."

"Italy's not off the face of the earth," said Emma.

"It might as well be," said Rose. "And it's all her fault—Miss Gray's. I wish she'd never come to Ashton."

Eventually, when it looked like the thief who had killed Mrs. Balfour, whether or not it was old Sitgreaves, would never be found, we were allowed into the cottage again. The first thing we did was look into the mirror—it was the only mirror we could look in, all three of us, without arousing suspicion. "Show us Justina," we said, and we saw her on the deck of a ship, looking out over the Atlantic, with the wind blowing her hair like a golden flag. But when we said, "Show us Mouse and Miss Gray," all we saw was a road through a forest of birches, with a low mist shifting and swirling beneath the light of a pale sun.

We practiced, at first. But Emma's mother decided it was time for her to come out into Ashton society, so she spent hours having dresses made and choosing cakes. Emma said that the latter made up, in chocolate, for the boredom of the former. And Melody said that she had to prepare for school, although she spent most of her time scribbling on bits of paper that she would not show us. Rose practiced the longest, and for the rest of that summer she could fly out of her bedroom window, which she did whenever she was sent to her room for punishment. But eventually we could no longer talk to birds, or turn gold into pebbles, or see the Battle of Waterloo in a mirror. We realized that we would never be witches. So the next summer, we became detectives.

～

In traditional fairy tales—at least as we know them today—witches are invariably evil and they are usually old and ugly. Since we know those stories so well, this anthology intentionally avoids stories based closely on fairy tales. There are, however, two exceptions. One is Margo Lanagan's "The Goosle." This, from talented newcomer Cory Skerry, is the other. Both involve great cruelty. Skerry's story offers some explanation as to how his "witch" was, perhaps, driven to her savage psychopathic actions.

Those accused of witchcraft in the fifteenth, sixteenth, and seventeenth centuries could seldom be considered insane by modern standards, but their accusers—those who claimed to be bewitched or possessed—may well have suffered from mental disorders. Those who persecuted the alleged witches (and, similarly, conducted the Inquisition or killed those they considered heretics), were, in their day, considered pillars of their faith and community. From our perspective they were sadistic torturers and murderers. Like the woman labeled as a witch in this story, they believed they were doing the "right thing."

The World Is Cruel, My Daughter
Cory Skerry

I still have their eyes in jars, on the shelf in the kitchen. Every morning the beads on my necklace clank together while I fry myself a fishy concoction of duck eggs and marsh tubers. Behind me, light pours in through the large hole in the side of my house and illuminates the staring eyes. They are three colors—blue, brown, and green—and it is the last of these that accuse me while the others stare cattywampus at the floor and ceiling.

I could shake the jar with the green eyes, so they look elsewhere, but I don't.

~

When my daughter was one year old, I loved her for her smile. Anything could tempt her to joy—my own smile, the noises of cooking food, the proximity of the black kitten I gifted her upon her arrival.

What a fool I made of myself, contorting my face and making unladylike sounds. All I needed was another giggle and the game would go on. She couldn't yet ask questions I couldn't answer and was delighted by the information I volunteered. "Kitty," "No, it's hot," and "Boo!" all brought smiles. Even when she disobeyed me, I never struck her. My disappointment was enough to bring her to tears and she would pour herself dry on my bosom before looking up once again with a hopeful smile. Did I forgive her?

Of course I did.

When my daughter was five, I loved her for her eyes. They were the impossible purplish hue of forget-me-nots. We don't have them in the salt marsh where I built our tower. Her eyes told me what she would say before she said it. But sometimes she still surprised me.

I bit my tongue when she asked me why our house had no windows on the bottom floor. She still hadn't conceived of a "door." I knew she would ask some day, but then, on that cool April morning, I wasn't prepared.

"The sea rages in the winter, poppet. We don't have room for her to live with us, do we?"

My daughter giggled and returned to her innocence, but her question haunted me for years, until she was twelve and I loved her for her hair. It hung lustrous as silk, curled at the ends like pumpkin tendrils, glinted like sunlight caressing the sea.

This is when her questions grew children of their own, broods of what-ifs and how-comes. One day it was, "Why haven't you any hair, Mother?" She stroked her own golden locks, which now swept her ankles, as she waited for an answer.

I let my fingers stray up over the gnarled mass of scars that capped my skull, most of it numb, some of it still tingling with ruined nerves if I pressed it, as if it yet burned. "It wasn't as beautiful as yours," I said. "I don't need it."

"Yes, but what did you do with it?" she persisted.

For an instant I regretted having given her a library. I'd selected each book with the intention of keeping her life beautiful. But in choosing only the sweetest tales, I'd inadvertently given her the idea that the world was a beautiful place, one she perhaps would be permitted to explore. Now was my best chance to make it clear to my daughter that this was not so.

"Someone else wanted my hair," I lied, "so she carved it from my head while I slept."

My daughter was horrified, but it didn't stop the questions. "But didn't you awaken?"

"She fed me an herb which forced me to sleep." My daughter had seen me take tea for my aches and accepted this.

And oh, how I bitterly wished I had been unconscious! Sometimes I still wake from nightmares of fire, my robe tangled and spongy with sweat, surprised I'm not held in the flame with the same pitchfork that left the scars across my back. But my daughter only knew of the false deaths in tales in which the princess is revived by a kiss or justice is dealt to wicked stepmothers. Wicked stepmothers, but not witches. There were no witches in *my* daughter's books.

She shook her head. Her sweet blue eyes watered. "But why? Why do something so terrible?"

"We are like the stories in your books," I said. "But other people are not this way; they will value your hair as gold. They'll steal it and leave pain in its place."

To distract her from the books, which she would now doubt and scrutinize, I revealed the fourth floor in the tower.

Until she was eight, my daughter only had the run of the first two floors: the kitchen, scented with bunches of shallots, garlic, and fresh herbs; and the room above wherein the gleaming copper tub and waste chute took up one half and the garden and balcony took up the other. At ten, I allowed her into the library on the third floor, a circular room with an abundance of windows.

The fourth floor, the second-to-last, held a variety of musical instruments. We dusted and shined them. She learned to read a second time. The notes came to her easily, as I'd known they would, and she composed songs in her own spirited voice as often as she played classic tunes on the flute, lute, or harpsichord. The latter I had acquired at great expense, commissioning a man to assemble it inside the room before I stabbed him through the heart and buried his corpse under a driftwood log deep in the marsh. If you sit at the harpsichord and look out the window, you can see gulls and terns perched on the log as you play.

By the time my daughter was fifteen, I loved her for her talents and wit. She sang melodies on the spot, making gentle fun of household tasks or the elderly cat's occasional accidents on the kitchen flagstones. Neither of us begrudged Utney his infirmity; he'd been a loyal companion.

He was her fateful introduction to death.

~

Over the course of fifteen years, the estuary had migrated to the north, leaving the southern marsh more shallow. At the height of summer, our tower now had toes of exposed mud. It was during this summer heat that my daughter's heart was broken.

She put down a dish of broth for the cat, but Utney stayed curled by the fire. Her delicate fingers trailed along his neck, but he didn't lift his head to scratch his chin against her nails.

I held my sobbing daughter, my hands tangled in her golden hair, which now trailed behind her on the floor if she didn't bind it up in loops or braids.

Some children ask for a new pet when the old one passes on, but to my daughter, her cat was a fixture of the world, as irreplaceable as a piece of the tower. If the roof were torn off in a storm, we'd have no roof—likewise, there were no cats in our vegetable garden, no cats come up on our fishing lines, no cats in the bird traps I hung out of the music room windows.

He was the only cat in the world and he was dead.

I'd never seen her blue eyes so raw. They shone with an arterial flow of tears, bruised where blood vessels had burst. I was almost afraid the grief would kill her.

I boiled the carcass and made her a necklace of Utney's bones, whispering that his spirit still lurked there and would love her for all her days. She wore the gift gratefully, but it only quieted her sorrow. In silence, his death still burned her the way my nightmares burned me.

And so I climbed out the window in the night and trudged through four miles of dense sawgrass, marsh bramble, and sucking, salty mud.

There are always unwanted kittens.

~

The boy from whom I got the kitten suggested I choose one of a different color, in case she wanted to separate the memory of her old pet from her new one. He had eyes like my daughter's but lighter, like cornflowers. He refused to look at me any longer than he must. I chose a ginger kitten, with clever eyes and unruly fur.

When the water and mud became very deep on my return journey, I held the kitten over my head. I treated my daughter's gift as carefully as I would have treated her.

I climbed back into the tower with difficulty, the kitten dangling from my mouth the way its own mother might have carried it. And so, with my clothes full of mud and my mouth full of fur, I spilled into the second floor.

I coiled the rope and hid it under the box of brambles I keep for firewood. I scrubbed myself and my clothes. And I said nothing of my journey.

"But where did he come from?" she asked, when I gave her the kitten. One finger tapped the scarred table just ahead of two determined, orange paws.

"We are like the stories," I said, smiling. "We are the only good in the world, and the world appreciates it. It provides for us. He came up in my fishing net."

The next day, my daughter sang again. It was a sad song, an ode to Utney, but beautiful nonetheless. It was the final clue needed by that little blue-eyed bastard to track us. I had made the mistake of mentioning I had a daughter "about your age" who'd lost her cat—and now, of course, he wanted to rut.

I was drying tomatoes and grapes on the balcony, waving a broom at gulls that dared swoop too close, when my daughter's song stopped mid-note.

"Have you named your kitten?" the lusting cur called. The mud I'd tracked through the dry streets of town must have led him to the marsh, his eyes must have led him to the tower, and now his ears had led him to lounge beneath her window.

I imagined him clambering into our world and ripping the lovingly sewn dress from my daughter's nubile form; stabbing her innocence with thrusts of his pimply, adolescent body, tossing her aside, bruised and soaked in seed and sweat and shame. It was why I was there, why I would always be there: so the world couldn't happen to her the way it had happened to me.

To her credit, my daughter didn't speak to the scum—she ran to me, and I met her on the ladder, her forget-me-nots staring wild. "Mother, there's a boy outside!" she said.

"I heard him," I said. "He's after your hair."

"He only asked about my kitten—"

"Quiet! Take Sunshine to the kitchen and stay there until I come for you."

I had never raised my voice to her, and she began to cry. It couldn't be helped; I could soothe her feelings later, after I'd removed the threat.

~

"I only wanted to look at her," he gasped, drooling and coughing as I pulled the knife free. Scarlet life fountained into the morass of human waste that marked the northern face of the tower. This year, the winter storms could feed on his blood with our refuse.

I placed him with the harpsichord builder and the glaziers, but I hated him too much to leave him buried in peace. I hacked apart his body and spread it for the eager gulls. I kept his eyes, because of his final lie. *You'll look at the inside of a cupboard*, I thought.

When I'd finished bathing away the traces of my ordeal, I descended to the kitchen. My daughter crouched by the hearth, red-eyed and nervously stroking Sunshine.

At the time I thought she hadn't seen what transpired, what her mother had done.

But sometimes I wonder.

~

My daughter's sixteenth birthday arrived in the hottest days of summer. When I revealed the attic, the fifth floor of the tower, I expected one of her questions, but not the others.

Windows ringed the room as with the third floor library, every one of them wrought in fantastic rainbows of color. Light streamed in, rays of blue like her eyes, gold like her hair, orange like her growing kitten. The scenes in the windows would have cost me more than I could afford if I had paid the glaziers instead of putting them to rest by the driftwood. Fairies and unicorns, noblemen on a fox hunt, a castle haloed in a striking sunset . . . these I'd commissioned for my daughter. It was a room fit to live a life in.

"Is this—just for me?" she asked. Her eyes shone with the realization of how much I loved her.

"Yes," I said.

And then she ruined it, tore this precious moment apart by asking me if, for her birthday, she could go out into the marsh—into the squelching mud, where we fished only in the turbulent winter to avoid ingesting our own refuse, where frogs and mosquitoes filled stagnant pools with their slimy spawn.

Where I buried the unworthy criminals who would have prevented her paradise.

My ultimate gift wasn't enough for her.

The finality of my answer cracked her belief in my love, and I watched trust bleed out of an innocent heart. I retreated to the kitchen.

Loudly, she wept above in an ocean of colored light, nestled in folds of her silken hair; quietly, I wept below on a hard stool, clutching a jar containing two withered eyes. I stared at those unseeing lumps of flesh and directed my hate at them. The eyes, and the world.

It thirsted for my daughter, but I wouldn't let it hurt her.

~

I take some responsibility for leading Cornflower to the tower, but not Dirt. That foul tom came of his own volition.

I could barely hear my daughter singing, from where I cut shallots in the kitchen, and when she stopped I assumed she was napping again. She'd been sullen those last few weeks, curled in the window seat or reading on her new bed, a hammock strung from the exposed rafters.

I happened to run out of rosemary. I climbed to the balcony, intending to cut some, but at the sound of a male voice, I froze. He was pleading, but I couldn't hear the words clearly. I edged onto the balcony and crouched while I strained to hear their conversation.

"But don't you want my hair?" she asked, doubtful.

The boy laughed, a muddy jackal baying for her blood, but of course she didn't know. "I've got my own, lass. Whyever should I want more?"

"Well, it's golden, and there's an awful lot of it," my daughter said. "Mother says you'd find it valuable."

She must have shown him; he whistled. "Wowee, miss! I could just about climb up on that!"

"You mustn't climb up! Mother would be furious."

"I shall visit again tonight, then, when she sleeps," the arrogant little cockerel promised.

I stomped up the ladder, my anger echoing through the wooden boards of the third floor, the fourth, and then pounding via my fist into the trapdoor of the fifth.

"Daughter!" I called.

Some whispers and a short commotion of bare feet later, she pulled the trapdoor open.

"Are you talking to someone?" I asked.

"No," she quavered. The lie was a fly in cream, piss on snow. Abominable.

I glanced out the window, but the rat had gone. For a moment, I couldn't even breathe, and then I lost my temper. I screamed at her, spit flecking her terrified face, until I collapsed in sobs.

I didn't beat her. I never beat her. She only tripped on her own hair as she backed away from me, and split her brow upon the corner of a table.

My daughter, my perfect, precious, innocent daughter. I made her promise never to speak with strangers again.

"They lie, poppet," I said, smoothing her hair. Tears coursed down both of our cheeks, hot and salty like the stagnant marsh beyond our tower walls. "And their sins are contagious. See how you lied to me today? You've never lied to me before," I said, hoping it was true, sure it was true. "And look what's happened now."

"I'm sorry, Mother," she said, and we embraced, my gnarled, fire-scarred claws stroking her golden silk, her soft hands petting my misshapen baldness.

I was waiting there that night when the boy I thought of as Dirt came back. He never saw me. In the night, I was sure my daughter also was blind to my knife slitting his gullet or scooping out his eyes.

But sometimes, I wonder.

I didn't find out about the third boy until early autumn, when the birds flew away from the marsh and the brambles lost their leaves. My hearing's not what it was and I was prone, especially in the cooling weather, to impromptu naps in my chair by the fire.

One gray morning, while my daughter was safely tucked away in her room, I'd taken my collection from the very back of the bottom cupboard. I met their stupid gazes with smug satisfaction. Insipid blue, conniving brown.

But she was mine again. She adored her cat, perhaps not so much as she'd once adored Utney; she played all her instruments, not just the lyre, and her own voice soared in accompaniment; and she helped me with enthusiasm in the kitchen and garden. Every afternoon we had tea together in the kitchen before she climbed the ladders to the music room while I napped.

I noticed a darkness in her, a hesitance to believe what I said until she'd thought it over, but this I suspected would fade with the removed influence of the village vermin. Her songs, after all, now praised the sun rather than the storm, explored questions of joy and not despair. My favorite was a ballad detailing the playful love of the sleek otters we sometimes glimpsed from our windows.

Rain crawled in from the bay, soaked my tired garden and sluiced dust off of the window panes. It rejuvenated everything but my badly healed bones. It wasn't enough for the townsmen to thrust me into the fire—I was beaten first and bent over a horse trough for their whims. I've always taken the potent marsh skullcap with my tea to dull the pain brought on by inclement weather, but when I uncorked the jar, I found it very low.

Suddenly I understood my daughter's love songs and my frequent naps.

She made my tea.

I switched our cups that day.

⁓

I thought the boy would use the balcony. It was closest to the ground, and the railings provided an anchor for rope. I confirmed it by checking the pumpkin vines where they hung down in a cascade of leafy tendrils. Some of the leaves were bruised.

"I'll save you," I said, to my daughter, or the pumpkins, or myself.

A search of her room turned up no rope, so the boy would have it. Sure enough, he tossed a coil up, and I bent over and knotted it for him, my twisted face hidden behind the yellowed tomato plants and pea trellis.

He spewed lies between breaths as he climbed.

"My father says he'll help build a cottage for us just north of the farm. It won't be as beautiful as your room here—"

That part was true, at least.

"—but we'll be happy. And I asked because you said, but I already knew he'd let you bring Sunshine."

His face popped up over the stone rail, and I stabbed him in the throat.

Hadn't the boy I loved once made those same promises? And hadn't he blamed me when I could save one of his young brothers from the fever but not the other? Hadn't his mother then spit in my eyes and accused me of murder, of witchcraft?

He dribbled blood from the cut, a mere finger's width that leaked as he coughed and swallowed and coughed again. It was nothing then to stomp on the fingers of one hand while I stabbed the other. The lying bastard tumbled down. One of his legs snapped at the wrong angle. Unfortunately, the soft peat saved him from further injury.

Rain stung my scarred head as I dangled over the edge, lowering myself down the rope with even more difficulty than last time. My bones ached, my arms trembled with the effort, but at last my feet sank into the mud.

"Monster," he rasped, and when he coughed, he sprayed red at me from his wound. "You beat her, cage her. Ellis said."

Ellis must have been Dirt's name. That was how this green-eyed turd had come to stalk my daughter—his rat friend's word.

I howled like an animal, and it crumbled into the words, "I love her!"

"No, I love her. You're a witch," he croaked.

He hit me as I crawled onto him, but I didn't feel it, and his wounds weakened him. I knelt astride his chest, pinning his arms down with my knees.

And this time, with one fist wrapped in his black hair, I cut out his eyes before I killed him.

~

I dragged his worthless corpse to the log in the marsh.

I cleaned up and started supper.

And my daughter woke in her chair.

"What time is it?" she asked, stretching.

"It's nearly supper. You've tired yourself playing the flute," I chided. "Perhaps you should go back to the cello for a few days—you won't have to hold it in the air."

She held her breath as she realized the boy had come calling while she slept. Her innocence was only too plain. She supposed she could hide the truth from me.

I thought with great hubris that because she couldn't hide, she also couldn't seek.

For days my daughter still sang love songs, but they became increasingly forlorn. They were no longer of happily-ever-afters, but of unrequited love. The October rain drove me to a drowsy state, all aches and naps and mourning for the sunshine, but not my daughter. A song would no sooner begin than she would change her mind; she would sometimes skip supper because it wasn't to her liking.

Finally, her mood roused her to clean the tower. She started in her room, shining every individual windowpane, dusting the rafters, sweeping away fallen grit while Sunshine pounced at the broom. She oiled the instruments of the music room, categorized and then alphabetized the library. She scrubbed the tub and covered the garden in compost. Then she started in on the kitchen.

While I snored in my chair, she found my collection. I didn't see it, but I can imagine. She would have been repulsed but curious at the blue eyes. She'd never seen a mirror, but I'd told her what color hers were. The brown ones might have given her a clue. And when she found the green ones, she woke me with her screams.

"You killed him! You beast, you killed him!"

I started in my chair, my eyes scanning the room for the intruder before I realized my hysterical daughter was shouting at me. She dropped the glass jar, but she was only kneeling, so it didn't shatter; instead, it simply rolled across the flagstones, the eyeballs searching for her as the jar spun.

She scraped her knees scuttling away from the dusty cupboard, her scrub brush forgotten, her eyes narrowed in revulsion.

"He would have hurt you," I wheedled, tears rolling down my cheeks, but she would hear no excuse.

"He was right. You are a witch!" My daughter began climbing the rungs to the second floor, and by the time I reached the bottom, her young muscles had already ascended the second ladder.

"I'm not! *I'm not!*" I screamed.

Faster than I could follow, she was into her room with the trap door slammed shut. Her feet stomped across the floor, in harmony with her desperate, screaming sobs. I felt her pain in my heart and when glass crashed and tinkled, it somehow felt right.

The trapdoor wouldn't open. I pounded on it for long minutes. Sunshine watched me from behind the legs of the harpsichord, wary of this sudden, loud insanity. In a fury, I descended to the kitchen and snatched the hatchet we used to fit especially large pieces of bramble or driftwood into the kitchen hearth.

The trapdoor was solid, but with relentless chopping, it finally splintered away. I climbed the ladder to see that my daughter had thrown her footstool through the window that depicted a charming castle.

She stared at the hole, her blank, blue eyes swimming red with burst capillaries. Her tongue protruded as dark and swollen as a dead mudskipper, and her soiled dress fluttered in the breeze from the broken window.

My daughter, my sweet Rapunzel, had thrown her hair over the rafter, then braided it tightly around her neck and jumped off one of the hammock braces.

~

I made that hole in the side of the tower, but I don't think I'll fill it with a door. I think I'll let the winter storms in. There's plenty of room in here now, even for the sea.

I moved the green-eyed boy's body, to the stand of stunted trees where I long ago buried my daughter's parents. Rapunzel also sleeps with them, though the necklace that clinks while I make my breakfast is made of her bones. Polished with sand and tears, they look magnificent and feel terrible when I wear them with my woven scarf.

It's lustrous as silk, curls at the ends like pumpkin tendrils, and glints like sunlight caressing the sea.

~

T.A. Pratt's Marla Mason is a modern-day, ass-kicking sorceress who doesn't wear a leather catsuit, doesn't suffer from low self-esteem, doesn't wallow in angst, and is almost always absolutely certain she's right . . . even when she's dead wrong. She's featured in four novels published by Bantam Spectra, a fifth reader-supported novel, a serialized online novella, and several short stories. In this new story, written especially for this anthology, Marla's adventure is enhanced by the author's appreciation of Fritz Leiber and others . . . but mentioning Leiber allows a chance to bring up Conjure Wife, *his 1943 novel based on the premise that all women are practicing witches, a secret kept well-guarded from the husbands they magically assist and protect. The story is told from the point of view of Norman Saylor, a highly rational college professor who discovers his wife, Tansy, is practicing witchcraft. Having spent his career debunking such primitive superstitions, Saylor assumes she is neurotic and convinces her to cease her silliness. Bad things, naturally, start happening. Although it must now be read with the understanding that the book reflects its times,* Conjure Wife *remains a classic of dark fantasy and a must-read of witchcraft fiction. (Already used as the basis for three films, a new movie version was announced in December 2008, but has been "in development" ever since.)*

Ill Met in Ulthar
T.A. Pratt

"His name is Roderick Barrow," Dr. Husch said. "He's what we call 'exothermically delusional.'"

Marla Mason, twenty-two years old and by her own reckoning the deadliest mercenary sorcerer on the east coast, propped her feet up on the doctor's desk. "Good thing he's locked up in the nut hutch, then."

Dr. Husch made a small moue of distaste and shoved Marla's boots off the desk. The doctor looked like a sculpture of a classical nymph that had been brought to life, her hair bound up in a tight bun, and the whole dressed in an impeccably tailored gray suit: lushness tightly contained. "Alas, that's where the 'exothermic' part comes in—his delusions are becoming more and more . . . aggressive."

"I don't know what that means."

"I'll show you." Dr. Husch rose from her desk and led Marla out of the room, down a hospital-clean hallway—which made sense, as they were in a hospital, of sorts. The Blackwing Institute didn't treat diseases of the body, but it contained the diseased in mind—specifically wielders of magic who became a danger to themselves, and others, and occasionally reality. The Institute was funded by prominent sorcerers, who recognized madness as an occupational hazard, and knew they might find themselves in need of treatment some day too.

The corridor was lined with iron doors, some acid-etched with runes of calming or containment. Dr. Husch stopped about halfway down the passage and slid aside a metal panel covering a square eye-level window in one of the barred doors. Light flared out, like someone had lit a strip of magnesium, and Dr. Husch wordlessly handed Marla a pair of sunglasses. Squinting and cursing, Marla pulled on the shades, then looked into the room.

A shape writhed in the air, sinuous and sparking, like a boa constrictor made of lightning instead of flesh. The serpent hovered in the air, and as its jaws snapped open and shut, Marla tried to count its fangs; she gave up after a dozen. The only part of the serpent that *wasn't* made of pure white light was its eyes—they were black pits of absence, but strangely aware. The serpent noticed them, and smashed itself against the door, sparks showering up around it. Marla jumped back, drawing her magical cloak around her. The cloak showed its white side, now, and protected her with healing magics, but with a thought she could reverse it, and make the bruise-purple inner lining switch to the outside. When clothed in the purple, Marla was possessed by vicious battle magics that made her essentially unstoppable— though at the cost of losing some self-control. There were those who said Marla was an amateur, and that only the cloak made her dangerous. The people stupid enough to say that in Marla's presence got their asses kicked, but only after she removed the cloak first, just to prove them wrong. But she was glad to have the cloak on now; there was no such thing as an unfair advantage when you were dealing with flying electric hover-snakes.

Dr. Husch slid the panel over the window shut as the beast continued battering against the door. "Don't worry, it can't get out. The interior of the room is lined with rubber, reinforced by magic. We used to keep a paranoid electrothaumaturge locked up there. There are no electrical outlets or light fixtures, either—when we found the creature in Barrow's room, it had smashed the light bulbs, and was suckling at the outlets like a hamster at a water bottle."

Marla took off the glasses and rubbed her eyes. "What is that thing?"

"Barrow calls it an arc-drake. They live in the haunted mountains called the Lightning Peaks, north of the Sea of Surcease, a vast lake of liquid suffering."

"You sound like the trailer for a bad fantasy movie," Marla said.

"Appropriate, as Barrow was a fantasy writer. Though he wasn't a particularly bad one, especially by the standards of his time. He was a pulp writer, mostly, published alongside the likes of Clifford Simak, Doc Smith, Sprague de Camp, Marsham Craswell—did you ever read much science fiction and fantasy, Marla?"

"Not really. I was too busy smoking and having sex with boys. I was always more interested in this world than in imaginary ones."

Husch sniffed. "As a sorcerer, you should be ashamed. Magic is the act of imposing your will on reality. But without *imagination*, what good is even the strongest will? So what if you can do anything, if you can't think of anything interesting to *do*?"

"I manage to keep myself entertained," Marla said. "But I gotta say, I'm getting a little bored right now. So this Barrow, what, wrote about the arc-drakes in a fantasy story, and then somehow brought one to life?"

"Oh, it's so much worse than that," Dr. Husch said.

~

"We have won through, Lector," Barrow muttered, his eyelids twitching rapidly. "Though our allies and retainers fell, you and I have reached this cursed plain, and now we need only—"

Dr. Husch thumbed off the intercom switch, and Barrow's voice cut off abruptly. Marla leaned against the window, taking in the view on the other side. Barrow's room was small, furnished with a hospital bed and not much else, but it didn't lack for items of interest: A pile of weirdly ridged skulls heaped in one corner. What looked like a lion pelt draped over a chair. Scorch marks on one wall and part of the ceiling. Barrow himself was a white-haired old gent with a wild beard, dressed in a hospital gown, lips moving as he muttered, hands occasionally clenching and unclenching.

"He's been like this for, oh, twenty years," Dr. Husch said. "He suffered a nervous breakdown thirty years ago, was comatose for a decade, and then . . . he began to speak. Since then, he doesn't eat, drink, or eliminate waste, and he doesn't age—as best I can tell, he's sustained by psychic energy. That's when his regular family doctor made some inquiries and had him transferred here, since we're better able to care for . . . unusual cases."

"So he wasn't a sorcerer? Just a writer?"

"As far as we know, he was unaware of his own latent psychic abilities, though the uncontrollable power of his mind may have caused his break-down. His chronic alcoholism might also have been a factor."

"What's he babbling about?"

"That's dialogue," Dr. Husch said. "He seems to be inhabiting an epic fantasy story of his own creation. The only glimpse we *used* to have of that story was the bits of dialogue spoken by his—narrator? Character? Avatar? Barrow is playing the part, *living* the part, of a mighty hero, on a quest to win a great mystical treasure. Delusions of grandeur. But recently he's been . . . *exothermically* delusional. His hallucinations are starting to break through to this world. The skulls of slain goblins, the skinned hide of a manticore—those apports were certainly of clinical interest. But when a *live* arc-drake appeared in his room yesterday . . . I grew more concerned. His dialogue indicates that the goal of his quest is to win a magical Key that will allow him to move between worlds at will."

Marla whistled. "So you think he's in a *real* place?"

Dr. Husch shook her head. "I think he's in an imaginary place, which his psychically powerful mind is *making* real. And if he completes his quest, and breaches the division between reality and the contents of his own mind . . . " Dr. Husch shrugged. "Giants. Demons. Monsters. All of them could come pouring through my Institute. What if the triple suns of his fantasy world appeared in *our* sky? The gravitational consequences alone would be unfathomable."

"Gotcha," Marla said. "So you want me to kill him?"

"I am a *doctor*," Husch said severely. "I want to *cure* him. Bring him back to reality."

"I'm not much good at talk therapy," Marla said. "I'm more of a punch-therapy girl."

"My orderlies are capable of checking Mr. Barrow's vital signs," Husch said, choosing to ignore Marla. "As you may know, they are not human, but homunculi, artificial beings of limited intelligence."

"I bet the poor bastards don't even make minimum wage," Marla said.

"The sorcerers who fund the Institute don't pay me enough to hire employees," Husch said. "So I have to grow them in the basement, in vats. But they get all the lavender seeds and earthworms they can eat. At any rate, the orderlies can go into the room and check on Barrow, being mindless, but no *human* can go near him, not safely. Anyone who enters that room—who comes into contact with the author's psychic field—is pulled *into* Barrow's delusional world. His brother visited once, and we had to bury the poor man out back. Barrow attempts to incorporate anyone who enters his world into his storyline, and let's just say he enjoys slaying the villains they become."

Marla stared at her. "So you want me to go in that room, and get sucked into his fantasy world, and . . . cure him? Like, make him realize his world is imaginary?"

Husch shook her head. "I doubt you could convince him. He's been the hero of that world for *years*. It's more real to him than this world ever was. No, I want you to go into his fantasy world, and make sure his quest *fails*. I want you to be a villain he can't defeat. One theme recurs constantly in his speech—his *destiny*. He is destined to win the Key of Totality, it seems. His fate has been ordained. He's been chosen by the gods. He thinks he's invincible, unstoppable, and *right*. If you defeat him, I think it might be the shock his system needs—a failure, after years of nothing but success, could force him to question his awful certainty. If you can jostle him out of his comfortable place in that world, I might be able to reach him, and bring him back to *this* reality."

"Huh," Marla said. "Why *me*, though? Why not one of the bigtime psychics?"

"I only know of one psychic more powerful than Barrow," Husch said. "And *she's* comatose, too, mentally traumatized and locked up in another room at the Institute. I don't need a psychic, I need a *pragmatist*, a tactician, a fighter—someone who never backs down, never gives up, and never stops. You have a reputation among the sorcerers who fund this Institute. They say you are a formidable operative, and you don't know the meaning of the word 'failure.'"

"Yeah, I must've skipped school the day they taught us that one. It probably doesn't hurt that I'm an independent operator, and nobody will get too upset if you have to bury *me* out back, too, huh?"

"It was a factor," Husch said. "And the fact that you possess a cloak enchanted with battle magics also helps. But mostly, it's because of your will. Everyone says you're pigheaded in the extreme—that an almost complete lack of magical aptitude hasn't stopped you from becoming a formidable sorcerer, because you *want* it badly enough. That gives me hope that you might be able to stand up to the force of Barrow's vision."

"And if I can't—what, do I get stuck there, in half-assed Narnia?"

"If you have not accomplished your goal by morning, or if you show any signs of distress, I will have one of the orderlies drag you out of Barrow's sphere of influence. Just be sure to mention if you're about to be murdered, hmm? I should hear your 'dialogue' as well as Barrow's."

"All right," Marla said. "It's a deal. Assuming you can pay my price?"

"I was told you don't want money . . . "

"Don't need money. My price is you telling me a secret, and teaching me a trick."

"That is acceptable," Dr. Husch said.

"All right," Marla said, and grinned. "I always wanted to be a villain."

～

Barrow of Ulthar wedged the butt of his great spear Ghostreaper into the stony soil of the Plains of Lengue and peered up at the towering heights of the Citadel of Bleeding Glass. He had been born only two leagues from this place, in the kingless kingdom of Ulthar, and his life's journey had taken him across the great seas of the world, through the haunted forests, beneath the stony earth, only to return him here, to the Citadel that had shadowed his boyhood village—the dread fortress he was finally hero enough to brave. The cyclical nature of his journey was further proof he was walking the inescapable path of fate. "My destiny awaits within, Lector," Ulthar rumbled. "Do you have any final advice? What dangers will we face within?"

Lector, the Living Book, was bound onto Barrow's back by chains of silver, iron, and bronze. The mouth gouged into the book's wooden cover spoke in a voice of riffling pages: "There are three Gates: a Gate of Knives, a Gate of Light, and a Gate of Wind. Pass through those, and you will confront the dread Chasm of Flies, which no living man or woman has ever crossed. The Key of Totality awaits, but first you must confront the guardian—"

"What, you're not going to mention me? I'm not enough of a danger for you?"

Barrow crouched, readying his spear. A woman sauntered around one of the skull-shaped boulders—the fossilized remains of giants who'd fallen to the Lengue Fever millennia before—and grinned. She was young, though not especially pretty, and she wore a cloak of rich purple, which shifted like a living shadow around her, as if possessed by its own dark intelligence. "Lector, is this one of the dread witches of the North?"

Before the book could speak, the woman laughed—not a girlish laugh, but a harsh and grating sound. "Nah, I'm from the east coast, Barrow."

The east coast of the Sea of Surcease was home only to the wretched Mirror City, populated by the living reflections of those poor unfortunates who died and subsequently had their mortal remains reflected in glass, their souls reversed into evil and decadence, trapped in mirrored form on this mortal plane. "Mirror witch," Barrow said, raising his spear.

"She is no reflected spirit," Lector said. "She is mortal, but . . . I do not . . . she is not in my index. I do not see her among my manifests. I do not understand—"

"Do you mean to hinder my quest, witch?" Barrow bellowed.

She clapped her hands. "You got it in one, Barrow-boy! Hindering's my business. Right up there with usurping and frustrating. I have to tell you, you look a *lot* better on this side. A tad rugged for my taste, I mean, your *muscles* have muscles, and personally, I like my boys a little leaner—but you're not the dried-up white-haired husk you should be. That's some sweet black magic you've got going on."

Barrow frowned. "I—I have sipped of the waters of the Vital Sea, but not from vanity. Only to restore my strength. My quest has taken longer than the three score years allotted to every man, but it was no foul magic—the Green Goddess herself blessed my undertaking—"

"I can *hear* you capitalizing things. It's really irritating. So this Key we're looking for is up there in that ugly castle, huh? Who'd build a fortress out of volcanic glass? I mean, it's *impressive*, but it's not practical. See you inside?"

"The Key is mine to win," Barrow said. "Be you Mirror Witch or Northern Witch or Graveworm Witch—"

"Always some kind of witch with you, isn't it? Maybe I'm a barbarian warrior like you."

"I am not a barbarian," Barrow said, with great dignity, "though some call me such. It is only that the customs of my village differ from those elsewhere in the world—"

"Those fur boots and the snakeskin pants tell a different story, but whatever. There's a Chasm and a Key and all that good shit waiting for us. Race you."

"No," Barrow said. "We will finish this here. I wield the enchanted spear Ghostreaper. It is a fell instrument, but if you do not stand aside, I will have no choice but to turn its dark magics against you."

"Knock yourself out," the witch said.

"Tell her what fate awaits her, Lector," Barrow said. "I do not believe she understands what I hold in my hands."

"The spear Ghostreaper is tipped with the fang from a murdered god of death," the book said, voice carrying over the cool stillness of the plain, despite the whispered timbre. "When the spear strikes its victim, it does not pierce flesh—it snags the *soul*, tearing the spirit loose while leaving the body a mindless, empty husk. The soul dissolves like fog in the sun, denied any afterlife. This spear brings the death of all deaths, and the empty bodies left behind are pressed into service to follow the spear's wielder, an army of the walking dead."

"I don't see any zombie horde," the witch said. "Are they hiding behind one of these head-bones?" She kicked the gray stone skull of a giant.

"They were all lost in the crossing through the Lightning Peaks," Barrow said. "And I was not sorry to see them go—their silent shuffling is a grim reminder of the dark acts even a hero must undertake to meet his destiny. I would not add your body, however comely it might be, to my retinue. Please, stand aside, or I will have no choice but to thrust my spear at you."

"Ha. Thrust away, then. Good luck ripping out my soul. I think mind-body dualism is bullshit."

Barrow lowered his head briefly, sorrowful but determined, then stepped forward, driving the hungering spear forward.

The witch moved one way—and her cloak moved the other, lifting from her shoulders and taking wing. It was no cloak at all, but a living thing, a creature of hungry shadow, and from within its shroudlike form a dozen red eyes blinked. The cloak flew at Barrow's face, and he gasped, trying to turn his spear thrust against it. The witch stepped in close to him and chopped at his arm with her hand, an expert blow that struck his nerves and made the arm go limp. The point of the spear dropped to the ground, and the witch—

The witch *stomped* on the spear's shaft, snapping it cleanly down close to the spearhead. The hero stood, stunned, looking at the shattered weapon. "The point might be a god's tooth," she whispered in Barrow's ear, "but the shaft's just a piece of wood. Shoddy work."

Barrow knelt to grab the spearhead, but the cloak wrapped its tendrils around his arms and dragged him back. While he struggled against the cloak's soft but unyielding grip, the witch picked up the spearhead, plucked a feather from a pouch at her belt, and swiftly tied the feather around the spear point with a strand of her own hair. She murmured a brief spell of some kind, opened her hand, and the spearhead rose up, up, up into the sky. "Bye, bye, birdie," she said. "That'll just keep flying until it hits the—well, one of the *three* suns up there. Excessive. You'd think with three suns it'd be warmer."

Barrow cried out, and called on the might of his totems—the bear who'd given its fur for his boots, the great serpent who'd given him the skin for his leggings, the wolf who'd provided the leather for his chest-harness. The power of the animals surged through him, and he tore the cloak, ripping great shreds in its fabric. The cloak fluttered away from him, the rends in its body healing instantly as it lowered back onto the witch's shoulders.

"Huh," she said. "I always thought this cloak had a mind of its own."

"You consort with demons!" Barrow shouted, still thrumming with animal energies.

"What, you heard about the incubus? I wouldn't call it 'consorting,' exactly, it was one of those things where we were kind of using each *other*—"

Barrow roared and lunged for her, but she somersaulted away from him. Such acrobatics should have been impossible in a long trailing cloak, but her demonic garment moved out of her way as she rolled. Instead of turning to face him in battle, she *ran*, covering ground in great strides, without even looking back.

"Coward!" he bellowed. "Face me!"

"She's going to the Citadel," Lector whispered from his back. "She's going to get there *first*."

"Fuck me," Barrow of Ulthar said, and ran after her.

The highest towers of the Citadel of Bleeding Glass were jagged onyx, their spires piercing the soft blue belly of the great slumbering sky-goddess, her divine blood running down the fortress's walls to pool on the ground, where malign flowers sprang from the combination of cursed soil watered by divine essence. Barrow thundered up the hill toward the gate, the tall red-petaled flowers turning their heads to watch his approach. Lector jostled hard against his back, and the hero felt every ache and pain of his long journey. The spear Ghostreaper must have lent him magical strength, or else the effects of his last visit to the Vital Sea were beginning to fade—he felt *tired*, at a time when he should be thrumming with power on the cusp of triumph.

The witch was dozens of yards ahead, and the flowers lifted their viney tendrils to block her approach. She shouted out a strange word, presumably an incantation of power—"Deadhead!"—and fireballs bloomed from her outstretched hands, searing the plants and making them scream. The unique stink of charred goddess blood filled the air: the mingled scents of burning sugar and opened entrails. The witch ran through the arching gateway and into the darkness within. No gate or guards prevented entry to the Citadel, for this place did not discourage visitors: it welcomed them, as the lion welcomes its prey.

Barrow hesitated on the threshold, even his legendarily keen eyes unable to pierce the darkness within. "Lector, you must give me counsel. Who is this new foe, and how may I defeat her?"

The Living Book was Barrow's greatest weapon, for it knew all the secrets of the world, and would reveal any mystery . . . if Barrow could only compose the proper question.

"The woman is not mentioned in my codexes or concordances," Lector said. "I cannot tell you how to defeat her."

The hero's heart lurched in his chest. Lector knew the weaknesses of every man and god and beast that had ever lived, or had a semblance of life, and that wisdom had aided most of Barrow's triumphs. "But . . . you know all the truths of the *world* . . . " Barrow paused. "Do you mean she is . . . from outside this world? From another place, some realm of demons? That would explain why she, too, seeks the Key of Totality—perhaps she wants only to return to her rightful home. Witch!" he shouted. "We need not fight! I will gladly open the door to your homeworld, once I have recovered the key!"

She did not answer. Barrow steeled himself for further battle, and stepped through the towering arch.

The darkness within the gate was actually solid, a membrane like the scum on pond water, clammy and vile, but he was through in a moment, wiping ectoplasmic residue from his eyes and looking around for the next inevitable threat. He stood in a vast and gloomy hall filled with jagged columns, not unlike the Temple of the Bile-God in far Paradyll, but vaster by magnitudes. The columns glowed with a reddish inner light.

Something fluttered down from the ceiling toward him, and Barrow drew his hand axe. This was no magical weapon—but well-honed steel and a comfortable grip had a magic of its own. The fluttering thing was the witch's cloak, its red eyes gleaming, its purple-shadowed tendrils reaching out for him. He danced back as it tried to strike him, his axe flashing and tearing a long rent in the cloak's body. But where was the *witch*—

Something wrenched at his back, and he howled as the fine chains cut into his flesh, and the weight of Lector left his back. He spun, but the cloak tried to strangle him, and by the time he'd hacked its tendrils free and sent it fluttering back toward the ceiling, the witch was halfway up a column, perched on an outcropping as casually as Barrow might sit on a fallen log, Lector held open in her lap as she flipped the pages. "So what's the deal with the bleeding sky?" she said.

Before Barrow could curse her, Lector answered—as he would answer any question posed by his holder. "The Citadel is made of eldritch glass, sharp enough to cut even the divine, and so it pierces the belly of the great sky goddess."

"Wait. The sky is somebody's *stomach*? That's . . . it's . . . what?"

"Everyone knows of the goddess," Barrow shouted. "The triple suns are the jewels in her navel! The rains are her sweat! She lays close to her lover, the goddess of the Earth, but they can never touch, for the sins of man keep them forever separated!"

"Sorry, I'm not from around here."

"I know that," Barrow said, and held up his hands in a placating gesture. "Witch—no, warrior—you have proven yourself my equal."

"Equal? Don't flatter yourself. The clothes off my *back* can kick your ass."

Barrow pushed down the rage that seethed within him. "Though you cast away my spear, and stole my book and bosom companion, I would still be your friend. We stand a better chance of winning our way through the Citadel together—"

"You don't get it, Barrel-of-laughs," she said. "You're *done*. Your part of this story is over. Do I have to take away your snake pants next? Leave you naked and tied up for the flowers outside to eat?"

"I have a *destiny*," Barrow began.

"Well *I* don't. But I have a job to do, and that job is keeping you from getting the Key. You're not the hero here. Let me show you something, this chasm thing."

"The Chasm of Flies? But before we can reach that, there are three gates—"

"The Gates are no more," Lector said. "The outsider witch has destroyed them."

Barrow shook his head. "The Gate of Knives? The Gate of Wind? The Gate of Light?"

"Sure," the witch said. "Charm of rust, spell of stillness, tincture of darkness. It's taken me longer to get through airport security than it did for me to rip through those gates. The magic here, seriously, it's weakass shit, and I beat things up for a living. But, anyway, this chasm." She dropped from the column, and Barrow roared and lunged at her, axe in hand.

She stepped around him, graceful as a dancer, and hooked her ankle around his foot as he went by, sending him sprawling, his axe skittering across the smooth black floor.

"Are you done?" she said. Her cloak drifted from the ceiling and settled down around her shoulders again. His face burning in shame, Barrow got to his feet. He left his axe on the floor, afraid of what she might do if he tried to retrieve it. If she attacked, he would fight ferociously, but she was just standing there, looking a little impatient, and even a little bored. Barrow had never before doubted his fate—he *was* a hero, and though the way was long and full of trials, he would win the Key, the greatest magical item in a world full of magic, the item of power no human hand had ever touched before. His allies respected him, and so did his enemies—but this witch from Outside toyed with him and taunted him, and he could not fathom how to strike her down.

So he followed her, through the hall and down a series of winding corridors, past the shattered remnants of the three great Gates, deeper into the red-black heart of the Citadel. *Perhaps this is the part of my journey where I am humbled,* he mused. *Mayhap this witch will show me something important about myself, something to aid me in—*

"The Chasm of Flies," the witch said, shouting to be heard over the horrible buzzing that filled the Citadel, and gesturing at the vast space yawning before them. As wide as the Citadel itself, stretching as far as he could see, the Chasm was a great pit seething and alive with millions upon millions of churning insects, black flies and richly green flies and even the snow-pale flies who carried the Unsleeping Sickness. "Lector," the witch said, patting the Living Book tucked under her arm. "What are those flies feeding on?"

"Heroes," Lector replied, and the witch laughed and laughed.

"I had no idea that's what fly shit smelled like," she said. "But when you multiply one speck of bug poop by about a trillion, I guess it gets noticeable. Whoo. Anyway, check out this spell. I learned it off a bruja when I was living in a really nasty squat last year, there were bugs everywhere. Normally it just clears a room, but I'm pretty sure I can amplify it . . . " She took a deep breath, then shouted, "SHOO, FLIES!"

The insects rose up in their millions, a black and green and white cloud, and revealed below them . . . a mass grave. A great tangle of men and women and the other races capable of heroism—the Grievous Ones with their spiny flesh, the Original Men with their snake's eyes, the amorphous Unshaped—all broken and bloodied and rotting and emptied of their souls, made into nothing but a feast for flies.

"See there?" the witch said. "That's what happens to heroes. It's nothing personal. That's what happens to *everyone*—no one lives forever, and even the gods can bleed. But heroes tend to die unpleasantly, far from home, without any friends."

She slid close to Barrow as he gazed at the bodies, wondering how many of them had famous names, how many had been sung about in stories every bit as loudly as Barrow had heard his own name sung—and, worse, how many of them were not remembered in song or story at all anymore. "But you thought you were special?" she said. "You were going to be the one who *really* made a difference? In your heart of hearts, you thought you were going to be the one that lived forever, didn't you? You're all excited about having a destiny. Big deal. So did *they*. There are enough magical weapons down there to fill a war god's armory, and enough heroic stories to fill even this weird talking infinite book I stole from you. I'm not saying there's never a good reason to do great things, Barrow. But doing it for the sake of *being* a hero is bullshit. I mean, I have just one question—"

The buzzing of the flies suddenly went silent, though the insects themselves continued to bob in the air, and a new voice spoke: "I will ask the questions here." That voice was beautiful, cool, and serene, as was the speaker. She walked across the Chasm on the floating cloud of flies as if their hovering bodies were paving stones, a perfect blonde dressed in little more than three clusters of diamonds that did the minimum necessary to protect her modesty, with a diadem of white gold upon her brow.

Barrow's heart grew lighter when he saw the witch narrow her eyes, her demonic cloak writhing around her body. She didn't like the look of this woman, which meant Barrow *did*.

"I am the Mistress of the Key," the blond enchantress said, standing just a few feet away on a platform of white flies. "You have breached the Gates, and come to the edge of the Chasm, and now, you have the chance to win the Key." She glanced down at the open grave beneath her feet. "Or to join the others who have tried in the past."

Barrow went down on one knee and bowed his head in respect. "Mistress," he said. "I am eager to meet any challenge you care to set."

"So Keymistress," the witch said. "You look a lot like this woman I know. Any chance your last name is 'Husch'? You could be her twin sister."

"I was not of woman born," the Mistress said, her voice as clear as fine crystal. "I have no sister, or mother, or father, or daughters. Do you, too, come to try and win the key?"

"Sure," the witch replied. "So what's the challenge? Mortal combat with Barrow the Barbarian? Staring competition? Or should I just guess what you have in your pocketses?"

"You need only answer my question," the Mistress said. "And if your answer satisfies me, the Key is yours."

The witch snorted. "Let Barrow go first. He's been waiting for this a long time."

The Mistress turned her head to Barrow, and bade him rise. He stood perfectly straight. He had supped with kings, seduced queens, and counted gods among his close friends and dire enemies—but the Mistress seemed like something else again, something greater than the gods, or perhaps merely *apart* from them. "Barrow of Ulthar," she said, "tell me: why do you desire the Key?"

Barrow blinked. He wanted the Key because that was his *quest*; because the swamp witch in his childhood village had seen a vision that he would someday seize it; because the diviner-in-chief for the great Stone King of the Inverted Mountains had declared that Barrow was destined to wield it; because his own dreams were almost nothing anymore but endless wanderings through black hallways filled with locked doors he could not open. He considered coming up with some more elaborate answer, something about breaking the shackles of tyrants, or opening new pathways of opportunity, but he feared the Mistress would sense dissembling or exaggeration. Truth had always served him well, and he would continue to serve truth. "Because it is my destiny," he said. "Because I am the one who has been fated to win the Key, where all others have failed."

The Mistress inclined her head. "And you, Marla Mason of Felport? Why do you desire the key?"

"Where I come from, there's a saying," Marla said, "anyone who *wants* to be president should be disqualified." She nodded at Barrow. "Anyone who thinks he deserves to have the most powerful magical artifact in the world just because it's his *destiny* should never be allowed to get his hands on it. I want it to keep it away from *him*, and people like him, who want power for its own sake."

Barrow took a step back from the edge of the chasm, suddenly dizzy. "But I don't—I don't want it for anything *bad*, it's just—"

"It's just your MacGuffin," Marla said, not unkindly. "You didn't think it through well enough, is all. It's not your fault. You've been telling this story for decades. It's no wonder it's starting to run a little thin. That's always a problem with an ongoing series."

"You have answered well, Marla Mason," the Mistress said. "You may have me."

"What do you mean I may—"

The Mistress leapt up from the flies, and floated toward them. She began to glow, first faintly, then as brightly as the brightest of the triple suns, and then—

She vanished, and a key of shining diamond fell to the floor. Marla Mason knelt and picked it up. "That wasn't so hard," she said. "Then again, I got to skip to the last chapter, which is hardly fair to you."

Barrow licked his lips, eyes fixed on the key. "What will you do with it?"

Marla shrugged. "Open a door." She squinted, then stabbed the key at the air, and gave it a twist. A rectangle outlined in white light appeared in the air, and she tugged the door open. Barrow expected to see something amazing—a heavenly universe, perhaps, or whatever dark pit her demonic cloak hailed from.

Instead, the door just showed a room, with an old white-haired man sleeping in a bed. A woman who looked a bit like the witch Marla Mason was stretched out on the floor in one corner, and through a window, another woman was watching—she wore spectacles, and had a tight blond bun, but she looked *so much* like the Mistress of the Key, who really *was* the Key—

"Want to come in?" Marla said. "See the world?"

Barrow recoiled. What trickery was this? The witch had stolen his *destiny*, and now she offered him a dirty room, an ugly bed, a smeared window, a living artifact transformed into a *nurse*—

"Never!" he shouted, and leapt into the Chasm, to join the other fallen ones. He might die, but he would die a *hero*, which was better than living as nothing but a man.

～

Marla stepped through the door, and immediately rolled over on her side and vomited, which was weird, because she hadn't been *lying* on her side, she'd been walking through a door, except now she was on the floor, and—

"Oh," she croaked. "I woke up in my own body, huh?"

Dr. Husch opened the door, and a doughy orderly hurried in and helped Marla to her feet, then pulled her outside, to the safety of the observation room. "In your hand," Dr. Husch said. "What is that?"

Marla looked down at the crystal key she was holding. "Oh, this, it's—you, I think, he must have seen you at some point, because he sure as hell fantasized about you, or . . . wait." She shook her head. Marla knew she'd just done *something*, gone into a weird fantasy world and said some cold-hearted shit to a crazy man's mental barbarian avatar, but the details were fading fast. "Why can't I remember?"

"It can be difficult to remember dreams," Husch said, plucking the key from Marla's hand. "How much more difficult must it be to remember someone *else's* dream? But you did what you were sent to do. You showed Barrow he is no hero of destiny. You broke the spine of his story, and you took away this key, which is, I think, a rather potent artifact—either great magic he willed into creation, or some existing magic he managed to grasp with his psychic abilities."

"Artifact, huh?" Marla said, plucking at her cloak, which was also an artifact—an object of unknowable age and great magic. An object with *motivations*, however inscrutable they might be to their wielders. For some reason, wearing the cloak was making her skin crawl even more than usual today. Its malign intelligence, always a presence deep in the back of her mind, seemed more active and agitated, now, like a cat who'd spent hours watching squirrels frolic safely behind a pane of glass. "Think we can sell it?"

"I believe I will hold onto this key," Dr. Husch said. "For the very reasons you so neatly articulated while you were unconscious."

Marla waved her hand. "I don't need to know what I say in my sleep. I'm sure it's embarrassing. But . . . why isn't Barrow waking up? Wasn't busting up his delusion supposed to cure him?"

"I don't know," Husch said. "I'd hoped, of course, that he would become lucid when you proved his delusions of grandeur were false—I didn't expect him to be *cured*, but if he could hear me, then therapy might be possible. He's not speaking, though, so I don't know *what* he's experiencing now . . ."

～

Barrow did not die in the pit. He lay among the filth for a while, then began to search the corpses. As the witch said, there *were* magic weapons there, countless ones, and he chose some of the most deadly for himself.

He climbed out of the pit, hauling himself and his implements of war to the Citadel's floor. Lector, the Living Book, rested on the stone, left behind when the witch departed.

"Lector," Barrow croaked. "Old friend. Tell me. Do you know spells to raise the dead, and send this pit of fallen corpses into battle?"

"I do," Lector said.

"This Citadel," Barrow said, licking his lips. "Has it ever been held by a mortal before?"

"It has not," Lector said. "Only by gods."

"Ah," Barrow said, flexing his fingers. "Then I will have to become a god, then."

Lector seldom spoke unprompted, generally limiting himself to answering questions. But he spoke now. "Barrow of Ulthar . . . what are your plans?"

"If I am not a hero," Barrow said, "Then I must be . . . something else. If I do not have a destiny, then I must make a destiny of my *own*. If I cannot unlock all the doors in all the worlds . . . Then I must tear holes in the *walls*. If I cannot *save* the world—"

~

"Then I must *conquer* it," the old writer shouted beyond the glass, and Marla winced. "I will have my revenge!"

"He's gone all Dark Lord on us, hasn't he?" Marla said.

Dr. Husch sighed. "It seems so. His story is taking a darker turn. He's making himself into an anti-hero."

"I can't imagine there's much of a market for stories about *those*," Marla said. "So . . . did we make things worse? Is he going to start *trying* to reach this world now? Are there going to be, I don't know, hordes of orcs and black dragons who breathe napalm and dust storms of living anthrax popping randomly into existence? Aren't you afraid he's going to find another way in, and that he might bring an army next time?"

"Possibly," Dr. Husch said. "Loath as I am to admit defeat, I think it's time to take extreme measures. When therapy fails, sometimes the only solution . . . is isolation. Fortunately, you brought me a key, and keys aren't just used for opening doors—they're also used for *locking* them." She cocked her head, considered the door before her, and slipped the crystal key into the lock. Which was quite a trick, since the key was way too big. Nevertheless, it fit, and Dr. Husch twisted it, resulting in a click as loud as a thundercrack. The door began to change, transforming from beaten-up metal into black volcanic glass. The change crawled up the wall and across the window until the entire room was an unbroken sheet of stone. "There," Husch said. "Locked away." She tucked the key into the pocket of her suit.

Marla whistled. "When you do solitary confinement, you don't fuck around."

"Your payment is due," Dr. Husch said. "A trick and a secret, you said?"

Marla, who'd been staring at her reflection in the black glass, blinked. "Uh, yeah, right. The trick—I wanted to know how you managed to bind up some of the most powerful people you've got here. Agnes Nilsson, Elsie Jarrow, that caliber. From my researches, they should be impossible to hold. Then again, that was before I saw you do *this*."

"It's a rare patient who provides the key to his own security," Husch said. "Barrow is a special case. The bindings on Jarrow and Nilsson are a bit involved, and I've had a trying day, but come back next week, and I'll take you through the sigils and incantations."

"Fair enough. As for the secret—I hear you've been running this place for *decades*, and you don't look a day over twenty-five, no matter how you try to old yourself up with the dowdy hair and clothes and bondage hair. Even if you have one of those spells where you don't age when you're sleeping, that wouldn't account for this kind of youth. So what's the deal?"

Dr. Husch patted Marla on the shoulder. "Oh, Marla. Your mistake is in assuming I'm *human*."

Marla frowned. "Don't tell me you're . . . an artifact in human form?"

"Of course not," Dr. Husch said. "I'm a homunculus, just like the orderlies. Except my creator—he's gone now—made me much smarter than they are, and my tastes go beyond meals of lavender seeds and earthworms. If I were human, I would have been able to go into Barrow's dreams myself, and seen to his therapy directly. Of course I'm not human. Why else would I have hired you, dear?"

Marla frowned. She had a memory of Husch, telling her this *already*—"I am not of woman born"—but, no, that wasn't really *her*, it was Barrow's version of her. The old writer was psychic, so maybe he'd seen into Husch's mind and found her secret, incorporating her true nature as a magical inhuman thing into his fantasy world. If he could see into Husch's mind, then . . .

"Next time, hire someone else," Marla said. "Barrow's bad for my mental health."

∼

That night, Marla stopped by a used book store and pawed through a crate of yellowing old magazines. After half an hour of searching she finally found one with a story by Roderick Barrow, called "Shadow of the Conqueror!"— complete with exclamation point. She paid for the magazine with pocket change.

She read it in her tiny studio apartment south of the river. Barrow wrote a lot like he talked. The last two pages were torn out, but it was pretty clear what was going to happen: the hero would thwart the villain, free the slaves, and get the girl, who was dressed in golden chains and not much else. Nothing in the story really rang any bells, and her memories of the experience in Barrow's mind didn't come any clearer, the details turning to mist whenever she tried to focus on them. Ah, well, screw it. She tossed the magazine into a corner. Who needed fantasy stories, when she had asses to kick and secrets to learn?

~

Later, Marla dreamed of a house of endless black hallways. Every corridor was lined by dozens of doors, some marked with numbers, some with letters, some with runes or mystic sigils. She tried all the doorknobs, but none of them opened—none of them so much as *turned*—and though she pressed her ears to the door, she couldn't hear anything. She just kept walking, until she reached a door made of black volcanic glass, with no knob at all, but something on the other side was *pounding*, and *pounding*, and *pounding*, as if trying to break through—

Marla woke, sweating, and scrambled to the enchanted wardrobe where she kept her white-and-purple cloak. She pulled the garment down and wrapped it around herself, crawling back into bed. Marla didn't like wearing the cloak when she slept—she felt like it tried to communicate with her in her dreams—but even the dark whispers of her artifact would be better than the risk of falling prey to Barrow's psychic grasping. She could all too easily imagine her body left breathing in her bed, but her mind torn out of her body, wriggling on the end of a spear, trapped in a Dark Lord's realm . . .

Her dreams that night were horrible, but they were her own.

~

Neil Gaiman's witch-ghost, Liza, was unfortunately born in 1603, the year King James VI of Scotland also became King James I of England. Witchcraft was not viewed as problematic in Scotland until 1590. Not coincidentally, James had journeyed to Denmark in 1589 to fetch his future wife. In Denmark, a new Christian theory of witchcraft as a demonic pact had led to the persecution of those accused of being witches. A dangerously stormy voyage home convinced James that witchcraft was being used against him. A series of trials and witch hunts began. Although the accused were charged with witchcraft, James was primarily concerned with what he saw as plots to kill him. Still, he considered witchcraft a real threat and even wrote a short book, Dæmonologie, *on the subject in 1597.*

Dæmonologie describes several ways to test for witchcraft. One test was "fleeting" (swimming) a witch: throw her in water and see if she drowned or floated because, as James wrote, "God hath appoynted (for a super-naturall signe of the monstruous impietie of the Witches) that the water shal refuse to receiue them in her bosom, that haue shaken off them the sacred Water of Baptisme, and wilfullie refused the benefite thereof." And thus the dunking Liza refers to in the story.*

The Witch's Headstone
Neil Gaiman

There was a witch buried at the edge of the graveyard; it was common knowledge. Bod had been told to keep away from that corner of the world by Mrs. Owens as far back as he could remember.

"Why?" he asked.

"T'ain't healthy for a living body," said Mrs. Owens. "There's damp down that end of things. It's practically a marsh. You'll catch your death."

Mr. Owens himself was more evasive and less imaginative. "It's not a good place," was all he said.

The graveyard proper ended at the edge of the hill, beneath the old apple tree, with a fence of rust-brown iron railings, each topped with a small, rusting spear-head, but there was a wasteland beyond that, a mass of nettles and weeds, of brambles and autumnal rubbish, and Bod, who was a good boy, on the whole, and obedient, did not push between the railings, but he went down there and looked through. He knew he wasn't being told the whole story, and it irritated him.

Bod went back up the hill, to the abandoned church in the middle of the graveyard, and he waited until it got dark. As twilight edged from grey to purple there was a noise in the spire, like a fluttering of heavy velvet, and Silas left his resting-place in the belfry and clambered headfirst down the spire.

"What's in the far corner of the graveyard?" asked Bod. "Past Harrison Westwood, Baker of this Parish, and his wives, Marion and Joan?"

"Why do you ask?" said his guardian, brushing the dust from his black suit with ivory fingers.

Bod shrugged. "Just wondered."

"It's unconsecrated ground," said Silas. "Do you know what that means?"

"Not really," said Bod.

Silas walked across the path without disturbing a fallen leaf and sat down on the stone bench, beside Bod. "There are those," he said, in his silken voice, "who believe that all land is sacred. That it is sacred before we come to it, and sacred after. But here, in your land, they bless the churches and the ground they set aside to bury people in, to make it holy. But they leave land unconsecrated beside the sacred ground, Potter's Fields to bury the criminals and the suicides or those who were not of the faith."

"So the people buried in the ground on the other side of the fence are bad people?"

Silas raised one perfect eyebrow. "Mm? Oh, not at all. Let's see, it's been a while since I've been down that way. But I don't remember any one particularly evil. Remember, in days gone by you could be hanged for stealing a shilling. And there are always people who find their lives have become so unsupportable they believe the best thing they could do would be to hasten their transition to another plane of existence."

"They kill themselves, you mean?" said Bod. He was about eight years old, wide-eyed and inquisitive, and he was not stupid.

"Indeed."

"Does it work? Are they happier dead?"

Silas grinned so wide and sudden that he showed his fangs. "Sometimes. Mostly, no. It's like the people who believe they'll be happy if they go and live somewhere else, but who learn it doesn't work that way. Wherever you go, you take yourself with you. If you see what I mean."

"Sort of," said Bod.

Silas reached down and ruffled the boy's hair.

Bod said, "What about the witch?"

"Yes. Exactly," said Silas. "Suicides, criminals, and witches. Those who died unshriven." He stood up, a midnight shadow in the twilight. "All this talking," he said, "and I have not even had my breakfast. While you will be late for lessons." In the twilight of the graveyard there was a silent implosion, a flutter of velvet darkness, and Silas was gone.

The moon had begun to rise by the time Bod reached Mr. Pennyworth's mausoleum, and Thomes Pennyworth (*here he lyes in the certainty of the moft glorious refurrection*) was already waiting, and was not in the best of moods.

"You are late," he said.

"Sorry, Mr. Pennyworth."

Pennyworth tutted. The previous week Mr. Pennyworth had been teaching Bod about Elements and Humours, and Bod had kept forgetting which was which. He was expecting a test, but instead Mr. Pennyworth said, "I think it is time to spend a few days on practical matters. Time is passing, after all."

"Is it?" asked Bod.

"I am afraid so, young master Owens. Now, how is your Fading?"

Bod had hoped he would not be asked that question.

"It's all right," he said. "I mean. You know."

"No, Master Owens. I do not know. Why do you not demonstrate for me?"

Bod's heart sank. He took a deep breath and did his best, squinching up his eyes and trying to fade away.

Mr. Pennyworth was not impressed.

"Pah. That's not the kind of thing. Not the kind of thing at all. Slipping and fading, boy, the way of the dead. Slip through shadows. Fade from awareness. Try again."

Bod tried harder.

"You're as plain as the nose on your face," said Mr. Pennyworth. "And your nose is remarkably obvious. As is the rest of your face, young man. As are you. For the sake of all that is holy, empty your mind. Now. You are an empty alleyway. You are a vacant doorway. You are nothing. Eyes will not see you. Minds will not hold you. Where you are is nothing and nobody."

Bod tried again. He closed his eyes and imagined himself fading into the stained stonework of the mausoleum wall, becoming a shadow on the night and nothing more. He sneezed.

"Dreadful," said Mr. Pennyworth, with a sigh. "Quite dreadful. I believe I shall have a word with your guardian about this." He shook his head. "So. The humours. List them."

"Um. Sanguine. Choleric. Phlegmatic. And the other one. Um, Melancholic, I think."

And so it went, until it was time for Grammar and Composition with Miss Letitia Borrows, Spinster of this Parish (*Who Did No Harm to No Man All the Dais of Her Life. Reader, Can You Say Lykewise?*). Bod liked Miss Borrows, and the coziness of her little crypt, and could all-too-easily be led off the subject.

"They say there's a witch in uncons—unconsecrated ground," he said.

"Yes, dear. But you don't want to go over there."

"Why not?"

Miss Borrows smiled the guileless smile of the dead. "They aren't our sort of people," she said.

"But it *is* the graveyard, isn't it? I mean, I'm allowed to go there if I want to?"

"That," said Miss Borrows, "would not he advisable."

Bod was obedient, but curious, and so, when lessons were done for the night, he walked past Harrison Westwood, Baker, and family's memorial, a broken-headed angel, but did not climb down the hill to the Potter's Field. Instead he walked up the side of the hill to where a picnic some thirty years before had left its mark in the shape of a large apple tree.

There were some lessons that Bod had mastered. He had eaten a bellyful of unripe apples, sour and white-pipped, from the tree some years before, and had regretted it for days, his guts cramping and painful while Mistress Owens lectured him on what not to eat. Now he waited until the apples were ripe before eating them and never ate more than two or three a night. He had finished the last of the apples the week before, but he liked the apple tree as a place to think.

He edged up the trunk, to his favorite place in the crook of two branches, and looked down at the Potter's Field below him, a brambly patch of weeds and unmown grass in the moonlight. He wondered whether the witch would be old and iron-toothed and travel in a house on chicken legs, or whether she would be thin and carry a broomstick.

And then he was hungry. He wished he had not devoured all the apples on the tree. That he had left just one . . .

He glanced up, and thought he saw something. He looked once, looked twice to be certain. An apple, red and ripe.

Bod prided himself on his tree-climbing skills. He swung himself up, branch by branch, and imagined he was Silas, swarming smoothly up a sheer brick wall. The apple, the red of it almost black in the moonlight, hung just out of reach. Bod moved slowly forward along the branch, until he was just below the apple. Then he stretched up, and the tips of his fingers touched the perfect apple.

He was never to taste it.

A snap, loud as a hunter's gun, as the branch gave way beneath him.

~

A flash of pain woke him, sharp as ice, the color of slow thunder, down in the weeds that summer's night.

The ground beneath him seemed relatively soft, and oddly warm. He pushed a hand down and felt something like warm fur. He had landed on the grass-pile, where the graveyard's gardener threw the cuttings from the mower, and it had broken his fall. Still, there was a pain in his chest, and his leg hurt as if he had landed on it first, and twisted it.

Bod moaned.

"Hush-a-you-hush-a-boy," said a voice from behind him. "Where did you come from? Dropping like a thunderstone. What way is that to carry on?"

"I was in the apple tree," said Bod.

"Ah. Let me see your leg. Broken like the tree's limb, I'll be bound." Cool fingers prodded his left leg. "Not broken. Twisted, yes, sprained perhaps. You have the Devil's own luck, boy, falling into the compost. 'Tain't the end of the world."

"Oh, good," said Bod. "Hurts, though."

He turned his head, looked up and behind him. She was older than he, but not a grown-up, and she looked neither friendly nor unfriendly. Wary, mostly. She had a face that was intelligent and not even a little bit beautiful.

"I'm Bod," he said.

"The live boy?" she asked.

Bod nodded.

"I thought you must be," she said. "We've heard of you, even over here, in the Potter's Field. What do they call you?"

"Owens," he said. "Nobody Owens. Bod, for short."

"How-de-do, young master Bod."

Bod looked her up and down. She wore a plain white shift. Her hair was mousy and long, and there was something of the goblin in her face—a sideways hint of a smile that seemed to linger, no matter what the rest of her face was doing.

"Were you a suicide?" he asked. "Did you steal a shilling?"

"Never stole nuffink," she said. "Not even a handkerchief. Anyway," she said, pertly, "the suicides is all over there, on the other side of that hawthorn, and the gallows-birds are in the blackberry-patch, both of them. One was a coiner, t'other a highwayman, or so he says, although if you ask me I doubt he was more than a common footpad and nightwalker."

"Ah," said Bod. Then, suspicion forming, tentatively, he said, "They say a witch is buried here."

She nodded. "Drownded and burnded and buried here without as much as a stone to mark the spot."

"You were drowned *and* burned?"

She settled down on the hill of grass-cuttings beside him, and held his throbbing leg with her chilly hands. "They come to my little cottage at dawn, before I'm proper awake, and drags me out onto the Green. 'You're a witch!' they shouts, fat and fresh-scrubbed all pink in the morning, like so many pigwiggins fresh-scrubbed for market day. One by one they gets up beneath the sky and tells of milk gone sour and horses gone lame, and finally Mistress Jemima gets up, the fattest, pinkest, best-scrubbed of them all, and tells how as Solomon Porritt now cuts her dead and instead hangs around the washhouse like a wasp about a honeypot, and it's all my magic, says she, that made him so and the poor young man must be bespelled. So they strap me to the cucking-stool and forces it under the water of the duck-pond, saying if I'm a witch, I'll neither drown nor care, but if I am not a witch, I'll feel it. And Mistress Jemima's father gives them each a silver groat to hold the stool down under the foul green water for a long time, to see if I'd choke on it."

"And did you?"

"Oh yes. Got a lungful of water. It done for me."

"Oh," said Bod. "Then you weren't a witch after all."

The girl fixed him with her beady ghost-eyes and smiled a lopsided smile. She still looked like a goblin, but now she looked like a pretty goblin, and Bod didn't think she would have needed magic to attract Solomon Porritt, not with a smile like that. "What nonsense. Of course I was a witch. They learned that when they untied me from the cucking-stool and stretched me on the green, nine parts dead and all covered with duckweed and stinking pond-muck. I rolled my eyes back in my head, and I cursed each and every one of them there on the village green that morning, that none of them would ever rest easily in a grave. I was surprised at how easily it came, the cursing. Like dancing it was, when your feet pick up the steps of a new measure your ears have never heard and your head don't know, and they dance it till dawn." She stood, and twirled, and kicked, and her bare feet flashed in the moonlight. "That was how I cursed them, with my last gurgling pond-watery breath. And then I expired. They burned my body on the green until I was nothing but blackened charcoal, and they popped me in a hole in the Potter's Field without so much as a headstone to mark my name," and it was only then that she paused, and seemed, for a moment, wistful.

"Are any of them buried in the graveyard, then?" asked Bod.

"Not a one," said the girl, with a twinkle. "The Saturday after they drownded and toasted me, a carpet was delivered to Master Porringer, all the way from London Town, and it was a fine carpet. But it turned out there was more in that carpet than strong wool and good weaving, for it carried the plague in its pattern, and by Monday five of them were coughing blood, and their skins were gone as black as mine when they hauled me from the fire. A week later and it had taken most of the village, and they threw the bodies all promiscuous in a plague pit they dug outside of the town that they filled in after."

"Was everyone in the village killed?"

She shrugged. "Everyone who watched me get drownded and burned. How's your leg now?"

"Better," he said. "Thanks."

Bod stood up, slowly, and limped down from the grass-pile. He leaned against the iron railings. "So were you always a witch?" he asked. "I mean, before you cursed them all?"

"As if it would take witchcraft," she said with a sniff, "to get Solomon Porritt mooning round my cottage."

Which, Bod thought, but did not say, was not actually an answer to the question, not at all.

"What's your name?" he asked.

"Got no headstone," she said, turning down the corners of her mouth. "Might be anybody. Mightn't I?"

"But you must have a name."

"Liza Hempstock, if you please," she said tartly. Then she said, "It's not that much to ask, is it? Something to mark my grave. I'm just down there, see? With nothing but nettles to mark where I rest." And she looked so sad, just for a moment, that Bod wanted to hug her. And then it came to him, as he squeezed between the railings of the fence. He would find Liza Hempstock a headstone, with her name upon it. He would make her smile.

He turned to wave good-bye as he began to clamber up the hill, but she was already gone.

~

There were broken lumps of other people's stones and statues in the graveyard, but, Bod knew, that would have been entirely the wrong sort of thing to bring to the gray-eyed witch in the Potter's Field. It was going to take more than that. He decided not to tell anyone what he was planning, on the not entirely unreasonable basis that they would have told him not to do it.

Over the next few days his mind filled with plans, each more complicated and extravagant than the last. Mr. Pennyworth despaired.

"I do believe," he announced, scratching his dusty moustache, "that you are getting, if anything, worse. You are not Fading. You are *obvious*, boy. You are difficult to miss. If you came to me in company with a purple lion, a green elephant, and a scarlet unicorn astride which was the King of England in his Royal Robes, I do believe that it is you and you alone that people would stare at, dismissing the others as minor irrelevancies."

Bod simply stared at him, and said nothing. He was wondering whether there were special shops in the places where the living people gathered that sold only headstones, and if so how he could go about finding one, and Fading was the least of his problems.

He took advantage of Miss Borrow's willingness to be diverted from the subjects of grammar and composition to the subject of anything else at all to ask her about money—how exactly it worked, how one used it to get things one wanted. Bod had a number of coins he had found over the years (he had learned that the best place to find money was to go, afterwards, to wherever courting couples had used the grass of the graveyard as a place to cuddle and snuggle and kiss and roll about. He would often find metal coins on the ground, in the place where they had been), and he thought perhaps he could finally get some use from them.

"How much would a headstone be?" he asked Miss Borrows.

"In my time," she told him, "they were fifteen guineas. I do not know what they would be today. More, I imagine. Much, much more."

Bod had fifty-three pence. It would not be enough.

It had been four years, almost half a lifetime, since Bod had visited the Indigo Man's tomb. But he still remembered the way. He climbed to the top of the hill, until he was above the whole town, above even the top of the apple tree, above even the steeple of the ruined church, up where the Frobisher Vault stood like a rotten tooth. He slipped down into it, and down and down and still further down, down to the tiny stone steps cut into the center of the hill, and those he descended until he reached the stone chamber at the base of the hill. It was dark in that tomb, dark as a deep mine, but Bod saw as the dead see, and the room gave up its secrets to him.

The Sleer was coiled around the wall of the barrow. It was as he remembered it, all smoky tendrils and hate and greed. This time, however, he was not afraid of it.

FEAR ME, whispered the Sleer. FOR I GUARD THINGS PRECIOUS AND NEVER-LOST.

"I don't fear you," said Bod. "Remember? And I need to take something away from here."

NOTHING EVER LEAVES, came the reply from the coiled thing in the darkness. THE KNIFE, THE BROOCH, THE GOBLET. I GUARD THEM IN THE DARKNESS. I WAIT.

In the center of the room was a slab of rock, and on it they lay: a stone knife, a brooch, and a goblet.

"Pardon me for asking," said Bod. "But was this your grave?"

MASTER SETS US HERE ON THE PLAIN TO GUARD, BURIES OUR SKULLS BENEATH THIS STONE, LEAVES US HERE KNOWING WHAT WE HAVE TO DO. WE GUARDS THE TREASURES UNTIL MASTER COMES BACK.

"I expect that he's forgotten all about you," pointed out Bod. "I'm sure he's been dead himself for ages."

WE ARE THE SLEER. WE GUARD.

Bod wondered just how long ago you had to go back before the deepest tomb inside the hill was on a plain, and he knew it must have been an extremely long time ago. He could feel the Sleer winding its waves of fear around him, like the tendrils of some carnivorous plant. He was beginning to feel cold, and slow, as if he had been bitten in the heart by some arctic viper and it was starting to pump its icy venom through his body.

He took a step forward, so he was standing against the stone slab, and he reached down and closed his fingers around the coldness of the brooch.

HISH! whispered the Sleer. WE GUARDS THAT FOR THE MASTER.

"He won't mind," said Bod. He took a step backward, walking toward the stone steps, avoiding the desiccated remains of people and animals on the floor.

The Sleer writhed angrily, twining around the tiny chamber like ghost-smoke. Then it slowed. IT COMES BACK, said the Sleer, in its tangled triple voice. ALWAYS COMES BACK.

Bod went up the stone steps inside the hill as fast as he could. At one point he imagined that there was something coming after him, but when he broke out of the top, into the Frobisher vault, and he could breathe the cool dawn air, nothing moved or followed.

Bod sat in the open air on the top of the hill and held the brooch. He thought it was all black, at first, but then the sun rose, and he could see that the stone in the center of the black metal was a swirling red. It was the size of a robin's egg, and Bod stared into the stone, wondering if there were things moving in its heart, his eyes and soul deep in the crimson world. If Bod had been smaller, he would have wanted to put it into his mouth.

The stone was held in place by a black metal clasp, by something that looked like claws, with something else crawling around it. The something else looked almost snake-like, but it had too many heads. Bod wondered if that was what the Sleer looked like, in the daylight.

He wandered down the hill, taking all the shortcuts he knew, through the ivy tangle that covered the Bartlebys' family vault (and inside, the sound of the Bartlebys grumbling and readying for sleep) and on and over and through the railings and into the Potter's Field.

He called "Liza! Liza!" and looked around.

"Good morrow, young lummox," said Liza's voice. Bod could not see her, but there was an extra shadow beneath the hawthorn tree, and as he approached it, the shadow resolved itself into something pearlescent and translucent in the early-morning light. Something girl-like. Something gray-eyed. "I should be decently sleeping," she said. "What kind of carrying on is this?"

"Your headstone," he said. "I wanted to know what you want on it."

"My name," she said. "It must have my name on it, with a big E, for Elizabeth, like the old queen that died when I was born, and a big Haitch for Hempstock. More than that I care not, for I did never master my letters."

"What about dates?" asked Bod.

"Willyum the Conker ten sixty-six," she sang, in the whisper of the dawn-wind in the hawthorn bush. "A big E if you please. And a big Haitch."

"Did you have a job?" asked Bod. "I mean, when you weren't being a witch?"

"I done laundry," said the dead girl, and then the morning sunlight flooded the wasteland, and Bod was alone.

It was nine in the morning, when all the world is sleeping. Bod was determined to stay awake. He was, after all, on a mission. He was eight years old, and the world beyond the graveyard held no terrors for him.

Clothes. He would need clothes. His usual dress, of a gray winding-sheet, was, he knew, quite wrong. It was good in the graveyard, the same color as stone and as shadows. But if he was going to dare the world beyond the graveyard walls, he would need to blend in there.

There were some clothes in the crypt beneath the ruined church, but Bod did not want to go there, even in daylight. While Bod was prepared to justify himself to Master and Mistress Owens, he was not about to explain himself to Silas; the very thought of those dark eyes angry, or worse still, disappointed, filled him with shame.

There was a gardener's hut at the far end of the graveyard, a small green building that smelled like motor oil, and in which the old mower sat and rusted, unused, along with an assortment of ancient garden tools. The hut had been abandoned when the last gardener had retired, before Bod was born, and the task of keeping the graveyard had been shared between the council (who sent in a man to cut the grass, once a month from April to September) and local volunteers.

A huge padlock on the door protected the contents of the hut, but Bod had long ago discovered the loose wooden board in the back. Sometimes he would go to the gardener's hut, and sit, and think, when he wanted to be by himself.

As long as he had been going to the hut there had been a brown working-man's jacket hanging on the back of the door, forgotten or abandoned years before, along with a green-stained pair of gardening jeans. The jeans were much too big for him, but he rolled up the cuffs until his feet showed, then he made a belt out of brown garden-twine, and tied it around his waist. There were boots in one corner, and he tried putting them on, but they were so big and encrusted with mud and concrete that he could barely shuffle them, and, if he took a step, the boots remained on the floor of the shed. He pushed the hrough the space in the loose board, squeezed himself out, then he rolled up the sleeves, he decided, it worked quite well. It had pockets, and he thrust his hands into them and felt quite the dandy.

Bod walked down to the main gate of the graveyard and looked out through the bars. A bus rattled past, in the street; there were cars there and noise and shops. Behind him, a cool green shade, overgrown with trees and ivy: home.

His heart pounding, Bod walked out into the world.

⁓

Abanazer Bolger had seen some odd types in his time; if you owned a shop like Abanazer's, you'd see them, too. The shop, in the warren of streets in the Old Town—a little bit antique shop, a little bit junk shop, a little bit pawnbroker's (and not even Abanazer himself was entirely certain which bit was which)—brought odd types and strange people, some of them wanting to buy, some of them needing to sell. Abanazer Bolger traded over the counter, buying and selling, and he did a better trade behind the counter and in the back room, accepting objects that may not have been acquired entirely honestly, and then quietly shifting them on. His business was an iceberg. Only the dusty little shop was visible on the surface. The rest of it was underneath, and that was just how Abanazer Bolger wanted it.

Abanazer Bolger had thick spectacles and a permanent expression of mild distaste, as if he had just realized that the milk in his tea had been on the turn, and he could not get the sour taste of it out of his mouth. The expression served him well when people tried to sell him things. "Honestly," he would tell them, sour-faced, "it's not really worth anything at all. I'll give you what I can, though, as it has sentimental value." You were lucky to get anything like what you thought you wanted from Abanazer Bolger.

A business like Abanazer Bolger's brought in strange people, but the boy who came in that morning was one of the strangest Abanazer could remember in a lifetime of cheating strange people out of their valuables. He looked to be about seven years old, and dressed in his grandfather's clothes. He smelled like a shed. His hair was long and shaggy, and he looked extremely grave. His hands were deep in the pockets of a dusty brown jacket, but even with the hands out of sight, Abanazer could see that something was clutched extremely tightly—protectively—in the boy's right hand.

"Excuse me," said the boy.

"Aye-aye, Sonny-Jim," said Abanazer Bolger warily. *Kids*, he thought. *Either they've nicked something, or they're trying to sell their toys.* Either way, he usually said no. Buy stolen property from a kid, and next thing you knew you'd an enraged adult accusing you of having given little Johnnie or Matilda a tenner for their wedding ring. More trouble than they was worth, kids.

"I need something for a friend of mine," said the boy. "And I thought maybe you could buy something I've got."

"I don't buy stuff from kids," said Abanazer Bolger flatly.

Bod took his hand out of his pocket and put the brooch down on the grimy counter-top. Bolger glanced down at it, then he looked at it. He removed his spectacles, took an eyepiece from the counter-top and screwed it into his eye. He turned on a little light on the counter and examined the brooch through the eyeglass. "Snakestone?" he said to himself, not to the boy. Then he took the eyepiece out, replaced his glasses, and fixed the boy with a sour and suspicious look.

"Where did you get this?" Abanazer Bolger asked.

Bod said, "Do you want to buy it?"

"You stole it. You've nicked this from a museum or somewhere, didn't you?"

"No," said Bod flatly. "Are you going to buy it, or shall I go and find somebody who will?"

Abanazer Bolger's sour mood changed then. Suddenly he was all affability. He smiled broadly. "I'm sorry," he said. "It's just you don't see many pieces like this. Not in a shop like this. Not outside of a museum. But I would certainly like it. Tell you what. Why don't we sit down over tea and biscuits—I've got a packet of chocolate chip cookies in the back room— and decide how much something like this is worth? Eh?"

Bod was relieved that the man was finally being friendly. "I need enough to buy a stone," he said. "A headstone for a friend of mine. Well, she's not really my friend. Just someone I know. I think she helped make my leg better, you see."

Abanazer Bolger, paying little attention to the boy's prattle, led him behind the counter and opened the door to the storeroom, a windowless little space, every inch of which was crammed high with teetering cardboard boxes, each filled with junk. There was a safe in there, in the corner, a big old one. There was a box filled with violins, an accumulation of stuffed dead animals, chairs without seats, books, and prints.

There was a small desk beside the door, and Abanazer Bolger pulled up the only chair and sat down, letting Bod stand. Abanazer rummaged in a drawer, in which Bod could see a half-empty bottle of whisky, and he pulled out an almost-finished packet of chocolate chip cookies, and he offered one to the boy; he turned on the desk-light, looked at the brooch again, the swirls of red and orange in the stone, and he examined the black metal band that encircled it, suppressing a little shiver at the expression on the heads of the snake-things. "This is old," he said. "It's"—*priceless*, he thought—"probably not really worth much, but you never know." Bod's face fell. Abanazer Bolger tried to look reassuring. "I just need to know that it's not stolen, though, before I can give you a penny. Did you take it from your mum's dresser? Nick it from a museum? You can tell me. I'll not get you into trouble. I just need to know."

Bod shook his head. He munched on his cookie.

"Then where did you get it?"

Bod said nothing.

Abanazer Bolger did not want to put down the brooch, but he pushed it across the desk to the boy. "If you can't tell me," he said, "you'd better take it back. There has to be trust on both sides, after all. Nice doing business with you. Sorry it couldn't go any further."

Bod looked worried. Then he said, "I found it in an old grave. But I can't say where." And he stopped, because naked greed and excitement had replaced the friendliness on Abanazer Bolger's face.

"And there's more like this there?"

Bod said, "If you don't want to buy it, I'll find someone else. Thank you for the biscuit."

Bolger said, "You're in a hurry, eh? Mum and Dad waiting for you, I expect?"

The boy shook his head, then wished he had nodded.

"Nobody waiting. Good." Abanazer Bolger closed his hands around the brooch. "Now, you tell me exactly where you found this. Eh?"

"I don't remember," said Bod.

"Too late for that," said Abanazer Bolger. "Suppose you have a little think for a bit about where it came from. Then, when you've thought, we'll have a little chat, and you'll tell me."

He got up and walked out of the room, closing the door behind him. He locked it, with a large metal key.

He opened his hand and looked at the brooch and smiled, hungrily.

There was a ding from the bell above the shop door, to let him know someone had entered, and he looked up, guiltily, but there was nobody there. The door was slightly ajar though, and Bolger pushed it shut, and then for good measure, he turned around the sign in the window, so it said CLOSED. He pushed the bolt closed. Didn't want any busybodies turning up today.

The autumn day had turned from sunny to gray, and a light patter of rain ran down the grubby shop window.

Abanazer Bolger picked up the telephone from the counter and pushed at the buttons with fingers that barely shook.

"Pay-dirt, Tom," he said. "Get over here, soon as you can."

~

Bod realized that he was trapped when he heard the lock turn in the door.

He pulled on the door, but it held fast. He felt stupid for having been lured inside, foolish for not trusting his first impulses, to get as far away from the sour-faced man as possible. He had broken all the rules of the graveyard, and everything had gone wrong. What would Silas say? Or the Owenses? He could feel himself beginning to panic, and he suppressed it, pushing the worry back down inside him. It would all be good. He knew that. Of course, he needed to get out . . .

He examined the room he was trapped in. It was little more than a storeroom with a desk in it. The only entrance was the door.

He opened the desk drawer, finding nothing but small pots of paint (used for brightening up antiques) and a paintbrush. He wondered if he would be able to throw paint in the man's face and blind him for long enough to escape. He opened the top of a pot of paint and dipped in his finger.

"What're you doin'?" asked a voice close to his ear.

"Nothing," said Bod, screwing the top on the paint-pot and dropping it into one of the jacket's enormous pockets.

Liza Hempstock looked at him, unimpressed. "Why are you in here?" she asked. "And who's old bag-of-lard out there?"

"It's his shop. I was trying to sell him something."

"Why?"

"None of your bees-wax."

She sniffed. "Well," she said, "you should get on back to the graveyard."

"I can't. He's locked me in."

" 'Course you can. Just slip through the wall—"

He shook his head. "I can't. I can only do it at home because they gave me the freedom of the graveyard when I was a baby." He looked up at her, under the electric light. It was hard to see her properly, but Bod had spent his life talking to dead people. "Anyway, what are you doing here? What are you doing out from the graveyard? It's daytime. And you're not like Silas. You're meant to stay in the graveyard."

She said, "There's rules for those in graveyards, but not for those as was buried in unhallowed ground. Nobody tells *me* what to do, or where to go." She glared at the door. "I don't like that man," she said. "I'm going to see what he's doing."

A flicker, and Bod was alone in the room once more. He heard a rumble of distant thunder.

In the cluttered darkness of Bolger's Antiquities, Abanazer Bolger looked up suspiciously, certain that someone was watching him, then realized he was being foolish. "The boy's locked in the room," he told himself. "The front door's locked." He was polishing the metal clasp surrounding the snakestone, as gently and as carefully as an archaeologist on a dig, taking off the black and revealing the glittering silver beneath it.

He was beginning to regret calling Tom Hustings over, although Hustings was big and good for scaring people. He was also beginning to regret that he was going to have to sell the brooch when he was done. It was special. The more it glittered under the tiny light on his counter, the more he wanted it to be his, and only his.

There was more where this came from, though. The boy would tell him. The boy would lead him to it . . .

A knocking on the outer door of the shop.

Bolger walked over to the door, peering out into the wet afternoon.

"Hurry up," called Tom Hustings. "It's miserable out here. Dismal. I'm getting soaked."

Bolger unlocked the door, and Tom Hustings pushed his way in, his raincoat and hair dripping. "What's so important that you can't talk about it over the phone, then?"

"Our fortune," said Abanazer Bolger, with his sour face. "That's what."

Hustings took off his raincoat and hung it on the back of the shop-door. "What is it? Something good fell off the back of a lorry?"

"Treasure," said Abanazer Bolger. He took his friend over to the counter, showed him the brooch under the little light.

"It's old, isn't it?"

"From pagan times," said Abanazer. "Before. From Druid times. Before the Romans came. It's called a snakestone. Seen 'em in museums. I've never seen metalwork like that, or one so fine. Must have belonged to a king. The lad who found it says it come from a grave—think of a barrow filled with stuff like this."

"Might be worth doing it legit," said Hustings, thoughtfully. "Declare it as treasure trove. They have to pay us market value for it, and we could make them name it for us. The Hustings-Bolger Bequest."

"Bolger-Hustings," said Abanazer, automatically. Then he said, "There's a few people I know of, people with real money, would pay more than market value, if they could hold it as you are"—for Tom Hustings was fingering the brooch, gently, like a man stroking a kitten—"and there'd be no questions asked." He reached out his hand, and, reluctantly, Tom Hustings passed him the brooch.

And the two men went back and forth on it, weighing the merits and disadvantages of declaring the brooch as a treasure trove or of forcing the boy to show them the treasure, which had grown in their minds to a huge underground cavern filled with precious things, and as they debated Abanazer pulled a bottle of sloe gin from beneath the counter and poured them both a generous tot, "to assist the cerebrations."

Liza was soon bored with their discussions, which went back and forth and around like a whirligig, getting nowhere, and so she went back into the store-room to find Bod standing in the middle of the room with his eyes tightly closed and his fists clenched and his face all screwed up as if he had a toothache, almost purple from holding his breath.

"What you a-doin' of now?" she asked, unimpressed.

He opened his eyes and relaxed. "Trying to Fade," he said.

Liza sniffed. "Try again," she said.

He did, holding his breath even longer this time.

"Stop that," she told him. "Or you'll pop."

Bod took a deep breath and then sighed. "It doesn't work," he said. "Maybe I could hit him with a rock and just run for it." There wasn't a rock, so he picked up a colored-glass paperweight, hefted it in his hand, wondering if he could throw it hard enough to stop Abanazer Bolger in his tracks.

"There's two of them out there now," said Liza. "And if the one don't get you, t'other one will. They say they want to get you to show them where you got the brooch, and then dig up the grave and take the treasure." She shook her head. "Why did you do something as stupid as this anyway? You know the rules about leaving the graveyard. Just asking for trouble, it was."

Bod felt very insignificant, and very foolish. "I wanted to get you a headstone," he admitted, in a small voice. "And I thought it would cost more money. So I was going to sell him the brooch, to buy you one."

She didn't say anything.

"Are you angry?"

She shook her head. "It's the first nice thing any one's done for me in five hundred years," she said, with a hint of a goblin smile. "Why would I be angry?" Then she said, "What do you do, when you try to Fade?"

"What Mr. Pennyworth told me. *'I am an empty doorway, I am a vacant alley, I am nothing. Eyes will not see me, glances slip over me.'* But it never works."

"It's because you're alive," said Liza, with a sniff. "There's stuff as works for us, the dead, who have to fight to be noticed at the best of times, that won't never work for you people."

She hugged herself tightly, moving her body back and forth, as if she was debating something. Then she said, "It's because of me you got into this . . . Come here, Nobody Owens."

He took a step toward her, in that tiny room, and she put her cold hand on his forehead. It felt like a wet silk scarf against his skin.

"Now," she said. "Perhaps I can do a good turn for you."

And with that, she began to mutter to herself, mumbling words that Bod could not make out. Then she said, clear and loud,

"Be hole, be dust, be dream, be wind,
Be night, be dark, be wish, be mind,
Now slip, now slide, now move unseen,
Above, beneath, betwixt, between."

Something huge touched him, brushed him from head to feet, and he shivered. His hair prickled, and his skin was all gooseflesh. Something had changed. "What did you do?" he asked.

"Just gived you a helping hand," she said. "I may be dead, but I'm a dead witch, remember. And we don't forget."

"But—"

"Hush up," she said. "They're coming back."

The key rattled in the storeroom lock. "Now then, chummy," said a voice Bod had not heard clearly before, "I'm sure we're all going to be great friends," and with that Tom Hustings pushed open the door. Then he stood in the doorway looking around, looking puzzled. He was a big, big man, with foxy-red hair and a bottle-red nose. "Here, Abanazer? I thought you said he was in here?"

"I did," said Bolger, from behind him.

"Well, I can't see hide nor hair of him."

Bolger's face appeared behind the ruddy man's, and he peered into the room. "Hiding," he said, staring straight at where Bod was standing. "No use hiding," he announced, loudly. "I can see you there. Come on out."

The two men walked into the little room, and Bod stood stock still between them and thought of Mr. Pennyworth's lessons. He did not react, he did not move. He let the men's glances slide from him without seeing him.

"You're going to wish you'd come out when I called," said Bolger, and he shut the door. "Right," he said to Tom Hustings. "You block the door so he can't get past." And with that he walked around the room, peering behind things and bending awkwardly to look beneath the desk. He walked straight past Bod and opened the cupboard. "Now I see you!" he shouted. "Come out!"

Liza giggled.

"What was that?" asked Tom Hustings, spinning round.

"I didn't hear nothing," said Abanazer Bolger.

Liza giggled again. Then she put her lips together and blew, making a noise that began as a whistling and then sounded like a distant wind. The electric lights in the little room flickered and buzzed. Then they went out.

"Bloody fuses," said Abanazer Bolger. "Come on. This is a waste of time."

The key clicked in the lock, and Liza and Bod were left alone in the room.

~

"He's got away," said Abanazer Bolger. Bod could hear him now, through the door.

"Room like that. There wasn't anywhere he could have been hiding. We'd've seen him if he was."

A pause.

"Here. Tom Hustings. Where's the brooch gone?"

"Mm? That? Here. I was keeping it safe."

"Keeping it safe? In *your* pocket? Funny place to be keeping it safe, if you ask me. More like you were planning to make off with it—like you was planning to keep my brooch for your own."

"Your brooch, Abanazer? *Your* brooch? Our brooch, you mean."

"Ours, indeed. I don't remember you being here when I got it from that boy."

There was another long silence, then Abanazer Bolger said, "Well, look at that, we're almost out of sloe gin—how would you fancy a good Scotch? I've whisky in the back room. You just wait here a moment."

The storeroom door was unlocked, and Abanazer entered, holding a walking-stick and an electric torch, looking even more sour of face than before.

"If you're still in here," he said, in a sour mutter, "don't even think of making a run for it. I've called the police on you, that's what I've done." A rummage in a drawer produced the half-filled bottle of whisky, and then a tiny black bottle. Abanazer poured several drops from the little bottle into the larger, then he pocketed the tiny bottle. "My brooch, and mine alone," he muttered, and followed it with a barked, "Just coming, Tom!"

He glared around the dark room, staring past Bod, then he left the storeroom, carrying the whisky in front of him. He locked the door behind him.

"Here you go," came Abanazer Bolger's voice through the door. "Give us your glass then, Tom. Nice drop of Scotch, put hairs on your chest. Say when."

Silence. "Cheap muck. Aren't you drinking?"

"That sloe gin's gone to my innards. Give it a minute for my stomach to settle . . . " Then, "Here—Tom! What have you done with my brooch?"

"*Your* brooch is it now? Whoa—what did you . . . you put something in my drink, you little grub!"

"What if I did? I could read on your face what you was planning, Tom Hustings. Thief."

And then there was shouting, and several crashes, and loud bangs, as if heavy items of furniture were being overturned . . .

. . . then silence.

Liza said, "Quickly now. Let's get you out of here."

"But the door's locked." He looked at her. "Is there something you can do?"

"Me? I don't have any magics will get you out of a locked room, boy."

Bod crouched and peered out through the keyhole. It was blocked; the key sat in the keyhole. Bod thought, then he smiled momentarily, and it lit his face like the flash of a lightbulb. He pulled a crumpled sheet of newspaper from a packing case, flattened it out as best he could, then pushed it underneath the door, leaving only a corner on his side of the doorway.

"What are you playing at?" asked Liza impatiently.

"I need something like a pencil. Only thinner . . . " he said. "Here we go." And he took a thin paintbrush from the top of the desk and pushed the brushless end into the lock, jiggled it, and pushed some more.

There was a muffled *clunk* as the key was pushed out, as it dropped from the lock onto the newspaper. Bod pulled the paper back under the door, now with the key sitting on it.

Liza laughed, delighted. "That's wit, young man," she said. "That's wisdom."

Bod put the key in the lock, turned it, and pushed open the storeroom door.

There were two men on the floor in the middle of the crowded antique shop. Furniture had indeed fallen; the place was a chaos of wrecked clocks and chairs, and in the midst of it the bulk of Tom Hustings lay, fallen on the smaller figure of Abanazer Bolger. Neither of them was moving.

"Are they dead?" asked Bod.

"No such luck," said Liza.

On the floor beside the men was a brooch of glittering silver; a crimson-orange-banded stone, held in place with claws and with snake-heads, and the expression on the snake-heads was one of triumph and avarice and satisfaction.

Bod dropped the brooch into his pocket, where it sat beside the heavy glass paperweight, the paintbrush, and the little pot of paint.

~

Lightning illuminated the cobbled street.

Bod hurried through the rain through the Old Town, always heading up the hill toward the graveyard. The gray day had become an early night while he was inside the store-room, and it came as no surprise to him when a familiar shadow swirled beneath the streetlamps. Bod hesitated, and a flutter of night-black velvet resolved itself into a man-shape.

Silas stood in front of him, arms folded. He strode forward impatiently.

"Well?" he said.

Bod said, "I'm sorry, Silas."

"I'm disappointed in you, Bod," Silas said, and he shook his head. "I've been looking for you since I woke. You have the smell of trouble all around you. And you know you're not allowed to go out here, into the living world."

"I know. I'm sorry." There was rain on the boy's face, running down like tears.

"First of all, we need to get you back to safety." Silas reached down and enfolded the living child inside his cloak, and Bod felt the ground fall away beneath him.

"Silas," he said.

Silas did not answer.

"I *was* a bit scared," he said. "But I knew you'd come and get me if it got too bad. And Liza was there. She helped a lot."

"Liza?" Silas's voice was sharp.

"The witch. From the Potter's Field."

"And you say she helped you?"

"Yes. She especially helped me with my Fading. I think I can do it now."

Silas grunted. "You can tell me all about it when we're home." And Bod was quiet until they landed beside the church. They went inside, into the empty hall, as the rain redoubled, splashing up from the puddles that covered the ground.

"Tell me everything," he said.

Bod told him everything he could remember about the day. And at the end, Silas shook his head, slowly, thoughtfully.

"Am I in trouble?" asked Bod.

"Nobody Owens," said Silas, "you are indeed in trouble. However, I believe I shall leave it to your foster-parents to administer whatever discipline and reproach they believe to be needed."

And then, in the manner of his kind, Silas was gone.

Bod pulled the jacket up over his head and clambered up the slippery paths to the top of the hill, to the Frobisher vault, and then he went down, and down, and still further down.

He dropped the brooch beside the goblet and the knife.

"Here you go," he said. "All polished up. Looking pretty."

IT COMES BACK, said the Sleer, with satisfaction in its smoke-tendril voice. IT ALWAYS COMES BACK.

～

The night had been long, but it was almost dawn.

Bod was walking, sleepily and a little gingerly, past the final resting-place of Harrison Westwood, Baker of this Parish, and his wives, Marion and Joan, to the Potter's Field. Mr. and Mrs. Owens had died several hundred years before it had been decided that beating children was wrong, and Mr. Owens had, regretfully, that night, done what he saw as his duty, and Bod's bottom stung like anything. Still, the look of worry on Mrs. Owens's face had hurt Bod worse than any beating could have done.

He reached the iron railings that bounded the Potter's Field and slipped between them.

"Hullo?" he called. There was no answer. Not even an extra shadow in the hawthorn bush. "I hope I didn't get you into trouble, too," he said.

Nothing.

He had replaced the jeans in the gardener's hut—he was more comfortable in just his gray winding-sheet—but he had kept the jacket. He liked having the pockets.

When he had gone to the shed to return the jeans, he had taken a small hand-scythe from the wall where it hung, and with it he attacked the nettle-patch in the Potter's Field, sending the nettles flying, slashing and gutting them till there was nothing but stinging stubble on the ground.

From his pocket he took the large glass paperweight, its insides a multitude of bright colors, along with the paint pot and the paintbrush.

He dipped the brush into the paint and carefully painted, in brown paint, on the surface of the paperweight, the letters

E H

and beneath them he wrote

We don't forget

It was almost daylight. Bedtime soon, and it would not be wise for him to be late to bed for some time to come.

He put the paperweight down on the ground that had once been a nettle patch, placed it in the place that he estimated her head would have been, and, pausing only to look at his handiwork for a moment, went through the railings and made his way, rather less gingerly, back up the hill.

"Not bad," said a pert voice from the Potter's Field, behind him. "Not bad at all."

But when he turned to look, there was nobody there.

~

Baba Yaga is a witch from Russian folklore. A thin, ugly old woman, she lives in a forest in a hut that stands on chicken legs and can move about. She flies through the air in a giant mortar using its pestle to steer. She is a witch, but, as Andreas Johns points out in Baba Yaga: The Ambiguous Mother and Witch of the Russian Folktale, *she takes on a number of roles in the tales about her and is not always wicked. She sometimes offers guidance and help, but the act of seeking her out is usually seen as dangerous. Vladimir Yakovlevich Propp has noted her role as a "donor" who must give the hero something needed to complete his quest—whether she wants to or not. Modern English-language authors including Orson Scott Card, Neil Gaiman, Patricia Briggs, Catherynne M. Valente, and Sarah Zettel have used the legendary witch in their fiction. There are a number of books for children featuring Baba Yaga, including* The Flying Witch *(HarperCollins, 2003), a picture book illustrated by Vladimir Vagin and written by the author of this story—Jane Yolen. "Boris Chernevsky's Hands," however, is a very different tale.*

Boris Chernevsky's Hands
Jane Yolen

Boris Chernevsky, son of the Famous Flying Chernevskys and nephew to the galaxy's second greatest juggler, woke up unevenly. That is to say, his left foot and right hand lagged behind in the morning rituals.

Feet over the side of the bed, wiggling the recalcitrant left toes and moving the sluggish right shoulder, Boris thought about his previous night's performance.

"Inept" had been Uncle Misha's kindest criticism. In fact, most of what he had yelled was untranslatable and Boris was glad that his own Russian was as fumbling as his fingers. It had not been a happy evening. He ran his slow hands through his thick blond hair and sighed, wondering—and not for the first time—if he had been adopted as an infant or exchanged *in utero* for a scholar's clone. How else to explain his general awkwardness?

He stood slowly, balancing gingerly because his left foot was now asleep, and practiced a few passes with imaginary *na* clubs. He had made his way to eight in the air and was starting an over-the-shoulder pass, when the clubs slipped and clattered to the floor. Even in his imagination he was a klutz.

His Uncle Misha said it was eye and ear coordination, that the sound of the clubs and the rhythm of their passing were what made the fine juggler. And his father said the same about flying: that one had to hear the trapeze and calculate its swing by both eye and ear. But Boris was not convinced.

"It's in the hands," he said disgustedly, looking down at his five-fingered disasters. They were big-knuckled and grained like wood. He flexed them and could feel the right moving just a fraction slower than the left. "It's all in the hands. What I wouldn't give for a better pair."

"And what *would* you give, Boris Chernevsky?" The accent was Russian, or rather Georgian. Boris looked up, expecting to see his uncle.

There was no one in the trailer.

Boris turned around twice and looked under his bed.

Sometimes the circus little people played tricks, hiding in closets and making sounds like old clothes, singing. Their minds moved in strange ways, and Boris was one of their favorite gulls. He was so easily fooled.

"Would you, for example, give your soul?" The voice was less Georgian, more Siberian now. A touch of Tartar, but low and musical.

"What's a soul?" Boris asked, thinking that adopted children or clones probably weren't allowed any anyway.

"Two centuries ago," the voice said and sighed with what sounded like a Muscovite gurgle, "everyone had a soul and no one wanted to sell. Today everyone is willing to sell, only no one seems to have one."

By this time, Boris had walked completely around the inside of the trailer, examining the underside of chairs, lifting the samovar lid. He was convinced he was beginning to go crazy. "From dropping so many imaginary *na* clubs on my head," he told himself out loud. He sat down on one of the chairs and breathed heavily, his chin resting on his left hand. He didn't yet completely trust his right. After all, he had only been awake and moving for ten minutes.

Something materialized across the table from him. It was a tall, gaunt old woman whose hair looked as if birds might be nesting in it. Nasty birds. With razored talons and beaks permanently stained with blood. He thought he spotted guano in her bushy eyebrows.

"So," the apparition said to him, "*hands* are the topic of our discussion." Her voice, now that she was visible, was no longer melodic but grating, on the edge of a scold.

"Aren't you a bit old for such tricks, Baba?" asked Boris, trying to be both polite and steady at once. His grandmother, may she rest in pieces on the meteorite that had broken up her circus flight to a rim world, had taught him to address old women with respect. "After all, a grandmother should be. . . . "

"Home tending the fire and the children, I suppose." The old woman spat into the corner, raising dust devils. "The centuries roll on and on but the Russian remains the same. The Soviets did wonders to free women up as long as they were young. Old women, we still have the fire and the grandchildren." Her voice began to get louder and higher. *Peh*, she spat again. "Well, I for one, have solved the grandchildren problem."

Boris hastened to reach out and soothe her. All he needed now, on top of last evening's disastrous performance, was to have a screaming battle with some crazy old lady when his Uncle Misha and his parents, the Famous Flying, were asleep in the small rooms on either side of the trailer. "Shh, shhh," he cautioned.

She grabbed at his reaching right hand and held it in an incredibly strong grip. Vised between her two claws, his hand could not move at all. "This, then," she asked rhetorically, "is the offending member?"

He pulled back with all his strength, embarrassment lending him muscles, and managed to snag the hand back. He held it under the table and tried to knead feeling back into the fingers. When he looked up at her, she was smiling at him. It was not a pretty smile.

"Yes," he admitted.

She scraped at a wen on her chin with a long, dirty fingernail. "It *seems* an ordinary enough hand," she said. "Large knuckles. Strong veins. I've known peasants and tsars who would have envied you that hand."

"*Ordinary*," Boris began in a hoarse whisper and stopped. Then, forcing himself to speak, he began again. "Ordinary is the trouble. A juggler has to have *extraordinary* hands. A juggler's hands must be spider web strong, bird's wing quick." He smiled at his metaphors. Perhaps he was a poet-clone.

The old woman leaned back in her chair and stared at a spot somewhere over Boris's head. Her watery blue eyes never wavered. She mumbled something under her breath, then sat forward again. "Come," she said. "I have a closet-full. All you have to do is choose."

"Choose what?" asked Boris.

"*Hands!*" screeched the old woman. "Hands, you idiot. Isn't that what you want?"

"*Boris,*" came his uncle's familiar voice through the thin walls. "*Boris, I need my sleep.*"

"I'll come. I'll come," whispered Boris, just to get rid of the hag. He shooed her out the door with a movement of his hands. As usual, the right was a beat behind the left, even after half a morning.

He hadn't actually meant to go anywhere with her, just maneuver her out of the trailer, but when she leaped down the steps with surprising speed and climbed into a vehicle that looked like a mug with a large china steering rudder sticking out of the middle, his feet stepped forward of their own accord.

He fell down the stairs.

"Perhaps you could use a new pair of feet, too," said the old woman.

Boris stood up and automatically brushed off his clothes, a gesture his hands knew without prompting.

The old woman touched the rudder and the mug moved closer to Boris.

He looked on both sides and under the mug for evidence of its motor. It moved away from him as soundlessly as a hovercraft, but when he stuck his foot under it cautiously, he could feel no telltale movement of the air.

"How do you do that?" he asked.

"Do what?"

"The mug," he said.

"Magic." She made a strange gesture with her hands. "After all, I am Baba Yaga."

The name did not seem to impress Boris who was now on his hands and knees peering under the vehicle.

"Baba Yaga," the old woman repeated as if the name itself were a charm.

"How do you do," Boris murmured, more to the ground than to her.

"You know . . . the witch . . . Russia . . . magic. . . . "

Her voice trailed off. When Boris made no response, she made another motion with her hands, but this time it was an Italian gesture, and not at all nice.

Boris saw the gesture and stood up. After all, the circus was his life. He knew that magic was not real, only a matter of quick hands. "Sure," he said, imitating her last gesture. His right hand clipped his left biceps. He winced.

"Get in!" the old woman shouted.

Boris shrugged. But his politeness was complicated by curiosity. He wanted to see the inside anyway. There had to be an engine somewhere. He hoped she would let him look at it. He was good with circuitry and microchips. In a free world, he could have chosen his occupation. Perhaps he might even have been a computer programmer. But as he was a member of the Famous Flying Chernevsky family, he had no choice. He climbed over the lip of the mug and, to his chagrin, got stuck. The old woman had to pull him the rest of the way.

"You really are a klutz," she said. "Are you sure all you want is hands?"

But Boris was not listening. He was searching the inside of the giant mug. He had just made his third trip around when it took off into the air. In less than a minute, the circus and its ring of bright trailers was only a squiggle on the horizon.

They passed quickly over the metroplexes that jigsawed across the continent and hovered over one of the twenty forest preserves. Baba Yaga pulled on the china rudder, and the mug dropped straight down. Boris fell sideways and clung desperately to the mug's rim. Only a foot above the treetops the mug slowed, wove its way through a complicated pattern of branches, and finally landed in a small clearing.

The old woman hopped nimbly from the flier. Boris followed more slowly.

A large presence loomed to one side of the forest clearing. It seemed to be moving toward them. An enormous bird. Boris thought. He had the impression of talons. Then he looked again. It was not a bird, but a hut, and it was walking.

Boris pointed at it. "Magic?" he asked, his mouth barely shaping the syllables.

"Feet," she answered.

"Feet?" He looked down at his feet, properly encased in Naugahyde. He looked at hers, in pointed-toe lizard skin leather. Then he looked again at the house. It was lumbering toward him on two scaly legs that ended in claws. They looked like giant replicas of the chicken feet that always floated claws-up in his mother's chicken soup. When she wasn't practicing being a Famous Flying, she made her great-great-grandmother's recipes. He preferred her in the air. "Feet," Boris said again, this time feeling slightly sick.

"But the subject is hands," Baba Yaga said. Then she turned from him and strolled over to the hut. They met halfway across the clearing. She greeted it and it gave a half bob as if curtsying, then squatted down. The old woman opened the door and went in.

Boris followed. One part of him was impressed with the special effects, the slow part of him. The fast part was already convinced it was magic.

The house inside was even more unusual than the house outside. It was one big cupboard. Doors and shelves lined every inch of wall space. And each door and cupboard carried a hand-lettered sign. The calligraphy differed from door to door, drawer to drawer, and it took a few minutes before Boris could make out the pattern. But he recognized the lettering from the days when he had helped his Uncle Boris script broadsides for their act. There was irony in the fact that he had always had a good calligraphic hand.

In Roman Bold were "Newts, eye of," "Adder, tongue of," and similar biological ingredients. Then there were botanical drawers in Carolingian Italic: "Thornapple juice," "Amanita," and the like. Along one wall, however, marked in basic Foundational Bold were five large cupboards marked simply: "Heads," "Hands," "Feet," "Ears," "Eyes."

The old woman walked up to that wall and threw open the door marked "Hands."

"There," she said.

Inside, on small wooden stands, were hundreds of pairs of hands. When the light fell on them, they waved dead-white fingers as supple and mindless as worms.

"Which pair do you want to try?" Baba Yaga asked.

Boris stared. "But . . . " he managed at last, "they're miniatures."

"One size fits all," Baba Yaga said. "That's something I learned in the twentieth century." She dragged a pair out of the closet on the tiny stand. Plucking the hands from the stand, she held them in her palm. The hands began to stretch and grow, inching their way to normal size. They remained the color of custard scum.

Boris read the script on the stand to himself. "Lover's hands." He hesitated.

"Try them," the old woman said again, thrusting them at him. Her voice was compelling.

Boris took the left hand between his thumb and forefinger. The hand was as slippery as rubber, and wrinkled as a prune, He pulled it on his left hand, repelled at the feel. Slowly the hand molded itself to his, rearranging its skin over his bones. As Boris watched, the left hand took on the color of new cream, then quickly tanned to a fine, overall, healthy-looking beige. He flexed the fingers and the left hand reached over and stroked his right. At the touch, he felt a stirring of desire that seemed to move sluggishly up his arm, across his shoulder, down his back, and grip his loins. Then the left hand reached over and picked up its mate. Without waiting for a signal from him, it lovingly pulled the right hand on, fitting each finger with infinite care.

As soon as both hands were the same tanned tone, the strong, tapered polished nails with the quarter moons winking up at him, Boris looked over at the witch.

He was surprised to see that she was no longer old but, in fact, only slightly mature with fine bones under a translucent skin. Her blue eyes seemed to appraise him, then offer an invitation. She smiled, her mouth thinned down with desire. His hands preceded him to her side, and then she was in his arms. The hands stroked her wind-tossed hair.

"You have," she breathed into his ear, "a lover's hands."

"Hands!" He suddenly remembered, and with his teeth ripped the right hand off. Underneath were his own remembered big knuckles. He flexed them experimentally. They were wonderfully slow in responding.

The old woman in his arms cackled and repeated, "A lover's hands."

His slow right hand fought with the left, but managed at last to scratch off the outer layer. His left hand felt raw, dry, but comfortingly familiar.

The old woman was still smiling an invitation. She had crooked teeth and large pores. There was a dark moustache on her upper lip.

Boris picked up the discarded hands by the tips of the fingers and held them up before the witch's watery blue eyes. "Not these hands," he said.

She was already reaching into the closet for another pair.

Boris pulled the hands on quickly, glancing only briefly at the label. "Surgeon's hands." They were supple-fingered and moved nervously in the air as if searching for something to do. Finally they hovered over Baba Yaga's forehead. Boris felt as if he had eyes in his fingertips, and suddenly saw the old woman's skin as a map stretched taut across a landscape of muscle and bone. He could sense the subtle traceries of veins and read the directions of the bloodlines. His right hand moved down the bridge of her nose, turned left at the cheek, and descended to her chin. The second finger tapped her wen, and he could hear the faint echo of his knock.

"I could remove that easily," he found himself saying.

The witch pulled the surgeon's hands from him herself. "Leave me my wen. Leave me my own face," she said angrily. "It is the stage setting for my magic. Surgeon's hands indeed."

Remembering the clowns in their make-up, the wire-walkers in their sequined leotards, the ringmaster in his tie and tails—costumes that had not changed over the centuries of circus—Boris had to agree. He looked down again at his own hands. He moved the fingers. The ones on his right hand were still laggards. But for the first time he heard and saw how they moved. He dropped his hands to his sides and beat a tattoo on his outer thighs. Three against two went the rhythm, the left hitting the faster beat. He increased it to seven against five, and smiled. The right would always be slower, he knew that now.

"It's not in the hands," he said.

Baba Yaga looked at him quizzically. Running a hand through her bird's-nest hair and fluffing up her eyebrows, she spoke. But it was Uncle Boris's voice that emerged between her crooked teeth: "Hands are the daughters of the eye and ear."

"How do you do that?" Boris asked.

"Magic," she answered, smiling. She moved her fingers mysteriously, then turned and closed the cupboard doors.

Boris smiled at her back, and moved his own fingers in imitation. Then he went out the door of the house and fell down the steps.

"Maybe you'd like a new pair of feet," the witch called after him. "I have Fred Astaire's. I have John Travolta's. I have Mohammed Ali's." She came out of the house, caught up with Boris, and pulled him to a standing position.

"Were they jugglers?" asked Boris.

"No," Baba Yaga said, shaking her head. "No. But they had soul."

Boris didn't answer. Instead he climbed into the mug and gazed fondly at his hands as the mug took off and headed toward the horizon and home.

～

The women in Silvia Moreno-Garcia's tale inherit their magical powers, but they also pass acquired knowledge of proven spells down through the generations—much as the rest of us pass on family recipes.

Genetic witchcraft or witches as a separate species is a popular—and varied—fantasy trope. L. Frank Baum's witches of Oz were born as such, and chose to be either good or evil. On the Bewitched *television series, Samantha's family were all witches and "warlocks." The Sanderson sisters are sibling witches in the film* Hocus Pocus *(1993). In both the book by Alice Hoffman (1966) and movie (1996)* Practical Magic, *the "craft" is passed down through generations of Owens women. The sisters on the television series,* Charmed, *are descended from a powerful line of good witches. Kelley Armstrong's The Otherworld books have both an all-female witch breed and an all-male sorcerer one. Amelia Atwater-Rhodes' novels feature a female-only species of witches. Witches in Philip Pullman's His Dark Materials trilogy are a female race who mate with human men; their daughters are witches, but not their sons. Witches in Kim Harrison's The Hollows novels are not human. J.K. Rowling's wizarding world is based on those with inherited magical abilities living among mundane magicless muggles.*

Bloodlines
Silvia Moreno-Garcia

Elena flipped the picture of San Antonio de Padua on its head and placed thirteen coins before him. She split a coconut, bathed it in perfume and whispered his name. When neither worked, she phoned Mario. Five minutes later she was yelling at the receiver. My mother was shaking her head.

"She should have given him her menstrual blood to drink. Now there's no way she'll bind him. He's out of love."

"But they've had fights before. He'll come back to beg her forgiveness before next week," I said, and wished it true even though my wishes don't count.

"Not this time."

"Maybe there's something you could do."

"Ha," my mother said.

The screaming stopped. Elena stomped through the living room and went to her room, slamming the door so hard San Antonio's portrait fell to the ground and cracked.

~

Come morning, cousin Elena's door was open. She stood before her vanity, applying lipstick and humming. She looked especially nice that day, long lustrous hair combed back and high-heeled boots showing off her legs. Elena was the prettiest woman in town, and she knew it.

My whole family was filled with beautiful women. Black-and-white photographs, old Polaroids, and even painted portraits testified to a lineage that gave way to the most ravishing beauties in the region. It also gave the women magic and an explosive temper. That temper had driven my great-grandmother to insanity, made my grandmother shoot her husband, and caused my Aunt Magdalena to stab her boyfriend three times. They got back together after each one of those times, but, nevertheless, a stabbing is a stabbing.

I had no beauty and little talent for magic. My mother assured me I was a late bloomer. I didn't believe her.

Short, fat, and pimpled, with hair that never stayed in place and crooked teeth decorated with braces: I was potato bug ugly. Like most bugs, I was in constant danger of being squashed. My cousins did not like me, abhorred the genetic joke that I was, and went to play hand-clapping games by themselves. My schoolmates did not know spells, but didn't enjoy my company either. My only two friends were Paco and Fernando. The only reason they walked me home some afternoons was so they could ogle my cousin when she danced through the living room wearing her leather mini-skirts.

It sucked because Paco was a nice boy with dimples and a good laugh. He always looked through me, like I was the Transparent Woman, you know, like that anatomical plastic model I put together the year before.

The people who really looked at me were my cousins Jacinta and Elena. Jacinta was born with a bad eye and the others teased her about it. Her father was of our lineage, which meant she was destined for the maquilas: magic can't go through the male bloodline. If you couldn't spin magic, you'd have to bend over a sewing machine and make pants for a few pesos an hour.

Even worse for Jacinta, she was a bastard and we couldn't recognize her as one of the bloodline. My mother had taken pity on her but when she turned sixteen we'd chase her out of the house.

With such low prospects, it made sense that Jacinta would keep me company. It was more difficult to understand why Elena stomached my presence, since she was one of the brujas chicas. I think she enjoyed having me run around, doing her errands, crushing beetles for the spells, kneeling in the dirt to pick glass that could be made into bracelets. I was never going to be an important witch, but I made a decent assistant.

Plus I could read Latin, German, and French, a feat Elena never achieved. She relied on spells passed through oral tradition, but I liked to pore over the old books and flip through my great-grandmother's grimoire. It gave me a thrill to excel at one thing, even if I could only muster weak spells.

"You going out?" I asked.

"Just heading downtown. I got to do some shopping. I'll be back before supper."

"Can I go with you? I want to watch a movie."

"Some other time," Elena said flashing me a smile and putting down her lipstick.

"But if you're heading there anyway . . . "

The smile turned sour.

"Another time."

I knew better than to push, so I looked for Jacinta. I found her playing behind the house. She was drawing with chalk on the wall, copying the symbols I traced over the bricks. Her marks had no power, so it was a waste of time for her to bother making circles and crosses. But she did it anyway to imitate me.

"Want to ride to the movie theatre on your bicycle?" I asked.

"It's hot outside," she said.

It's always hot. At least the movie theatre had air conditioning. Inside our house we only had the fans.

"Come on," I said. "You got money for the ticket?"

"Yeah," she muttered.

"Then let's ride."

"Why doesn't Elena take us in the truck?"

"Elena's gone."

"Okay, but I'm hungry."

I sat behind Jacinta while she pedaled. She didn't let me pedal. I didn't blame her; she was afraid I'd damage the old bike. It was the only thing her shit father had left her before he hitched a ride to Guadalajara three years before.

We ate gaznates and watched a movie about aliens and then this lady killed them with guns and stuff. It was all right.

When we went out I saw Paco walking down the street, hand in hand with Patricia Espinoza. My heart took a tumble. I thought about cousin Elena, and how she must feel like she's the Transparent Woman now that Mario doesn't return her calls.

~

For her birthday, my mother took Elena to eat at the Chinese restaurant with the tank full of carp. Jacinta and some of my other cousins came along with assorted uncles and aunts.

Jacinta and I looked at the carps tapping our fingers against the glass, while the rest of our family was lost in conversation. They were so busy toasting, making jokes and chatting between themselves that none of them saw Mario and his new girlfriend walk in.

I did. Jacinta noticed and she also stared in their direction.

Slowly, everyone at our table turned their heads and the laughter stopped. Cousin Elena, who was holding her chopsticks in the air, watched the merriment die and her face grew pale. Finally, she turned.

She looked at Mario. Mario looked at her.

Mario stepped out of the restaurant, girlfriend in tow.

I thought Mario was an okay guy, even after he dumped Elena. I owed him one for that time he didn't tell my mom I was sipping booze and smoking dope behind the factory with Jacinta. And overall, well, I thought he was harmless and charming despite his flaws.

But right then, I thought he was an ass for shuffling out like that with a fresh piece of arm candy, just weeks after breaking it off with my cousin.

I'm sure Elena thought the same. Her hand remained suspended in mid-air. Suddenly, she crushed her chopsticks with a flick of her fingers.

The tank behind us exploded, shards of glass flying through the air, water splashing our feet, dribbling across the red and gold carpets. The carp flopped on their bellies. Dying fish mouthed for air.

On an impulse, I grabbed one and rushed to the bathroom. I tossed it into the toilet.

I closed my eyes and wished it would live.

It twitched, then floated up to the surface.

Our magic can never mend broken hearts, nor give life. Spells are for taking, for subduing, and stealing. Even if I could cast stronger magic, it would have never worked.

~

Grandma rarely visited us. She lived down the coast in an old white house that oversaw the beach. There she sat and watched the waves while she strung seashells together and made necklaces. Her eyes were not sharp anymore and her spells had weakened, but she made her necklaces and loaded them with magic nevertheless.

One wonders why having the power to weave a necklace of death, she once bothered shooting her husband.

Maybe it was more enjoyable that way.

They've got a bad streak, all of the witches in the family.

Anyway, Grandma came that afternoon, looking like a hermit crab loaded under the weight of her long gray hair and her years. Jacinta and I saw her walk in. We pressed our backs against the wall, hiding in the shadows.

We could hear the fan spinning in the living room. Soon we heard grandmother's steady voice.

Cousin Elena tried to interrupt and there was a slap that echoed throughout the house. Elena might be one of the four brujas chicas, but she was no match for Grandmother.

I know what Elena did was wrong. We don't flash our gifts in public. In the old days, back when the family was still living in Europe, princes and kings hired our kind to cast spells for them. An invitation would arrive and a contract drawn up. An infinite number of rules governed family behavior, including the day when a spell could be cast, as well as the materials employed.

Things changed. Guns and cannons made spells with chicken bones archaic. The families sold their services to lower bidders: first merchants, then common folk. The spells, like the families, had lost their effectiveness, but when you are paying only a few coins even a mediocre spell will do.

Eventually the families traded Spain for the unknown coasts of America, and like other mercenaries before them, washed up on Veracruz. A few of them went south, off to Argentina and Brazil. Most spread through Mexico.

The luster and weight of the old customs had been lost, but rules remained. Key among them: do not show your magic in public. Spells are intimate things, sewn in private parlors among female relatives.

The slaps continued. Cousin Elena sobbed.

I couldn't bear to hear her crying and I rushed to the living room door, ready to yell at grandmother. Jacinta pinched my arm and pulled me back.

"Don't," she said. "That's grownup stuff."

I didn't care what it was. But my valiant rescue was no longer necessary. The door swung open and out walked cousin Elena. She did not look at us.

~

Elena played her radio. She kept the door to her room locked. I knew she was stuffing a dead lizard with ashes.

I knew Elena would blame Mario for grandmother's tongue lashing and the spectacle at the restaurant, even though he had no direct part in either incident. But I hadn't thought she'd go so far until I saw her catch the lizard using an empty marmalade jar.

"Well, what's the worse thing that could happen?" Jacinta asked.

"Death. Someone should warn him," I said.

"Someone would be stupid."

"Someone would be a coward."

"She could just give him boils on his ass or something," Jacinta said. "Maybe she's not even going to try something real bad."

"You think so?"

Jacinta shrugged. Elena was not going to be content with a mild spell. I would have been, but the power in me was weak; my blood was thin. Elena was a different thing altogether. Elena would kill an ant with a bullet instead of swatting it with a newspaper. She'd nuke it.

I rode the bus all the way across town to the colonia where the cars are shiny and there's no broken glass bottles on the walls surrounding the houses. Mario's house was a huge, two-bedroom concrete monster. I felt intimidated just ringing the bell.

The maid let me in and I waited in the game room, which had an enormous TV. It had been fun when Mario invited me and Elena over to watch the TV. He even invited Jacinta one time too.

I felt absolutely rotten when he walked in and smiled at me. On the one hand I was thinking about Elena. On the other well . . . shit, I didn't want him dead.

"Hey, how's it going?"

"It's going fine," I said.

He nodded. I guessed he was wondering what I was doing in his house. I didn't have time to waste, so I just let it out.

"You've got to get back together with Elena."

"Um, says who?" he asked me, frowning.

"Look, you simply got to. She really misses you and, you know . . . hey, Mario, you know about my family, right?"

"What, exactly?"

"You know . . . the thing," I muttered. I didn't want to say witchcraft. We never said it outright to outsiders. Oh, sure. People could whisper all they wanted, but none of the women at the maquilas who bought charms to punish their cheating husbands or get back at the greasy foreman making them work two extra hours said the word "witches."

Sometimes the adventurous ones, the women who came from the city in their fancy cars, called us "the ladies." Anything more than that was trouble.

Mario stared at me like he had no idea what I was referring to. I wondered if he really was that thick-headed to haven't realized Elena was a witch. Maybe he just wanted to believe it wasn't true. Who knows?

"Mario, Elena's going to get back at you if you don't ask her to forgive you and take you back," I said.

"Yeah?" He rolled his eyes. "Did she put you up to this?"

"No! She'd get really mad if she knew."

"It's sweet of you to worry about Elena and me, but we're through. We're not going to go out together again. Besides, I'm seeing someone else."

"You and your girlfriend should get a cruz de caravaca and hang it on a red string," I told him.

"Oh, Lourdes, the stuff you say."

A long time ago during the Revolution, a woman in my family transformed her cheating lover into a chair. Three witches made the man who tried to rape one of them fall off a cliff. An aunt turned into a ball of fire at night and sat on the roof of a farm, cooing for the man who had shot her brother to come out.

This was the kind of outcome Mario would face. You didn't toy with the family. You especially didn't toy with the women. There were new witches and warlocks roaming the north of Mexico, doing work for the drug dealers and the polleros, killing each other and squabbling constantly. They didn't mess with us. They knew to steer clear. Mess with the Arietas and you risk your skin.

Mario humiliated Elena. He'd gone out with her for a year and then he dumped her without ceremony. But Elena wasn't like the girls at the maquila, sewing blue jeans and shirts; she could sew spells. She could take a needle and black thread and sew a lizard's belly shut. Elena wasn't going to show restraint. She was seething mad and I knew she would kill Mario and his girlfriend.

She was a bruja chica, after all.

"Mario, I'm warning you because overall you're an okay guy and I owe you one," I said, thinking about the time he didn't tattle on me and putting my hands in my pockets. "Elena's got a temper and she's really pissed at you. She really, really loved you, do you know that? Other girls, they'll cry it off. Elena will get even. When Elena gets even, you better be afraid. You get it?"

Mario did not answer. He only frowned but I could tell he finally understood.

"Take care," I said.

By the time I got back it was dark. Jacinta was waiting with sweaty palms behind the house.

"You took a long time to come home," she said.

"I went far."

"How far?"

"Mmmmm."

"Did you go to see Mario?"

I fiddled with my plastic watch.

"Hey," said Jacinta. "You went, didn't you?"

"Yeah."

"Are you dumb?"

"Cut it out," I said.

"Elena's going to go apeshit."

It was true. What the hell, I'd already fucked it up so there was no point in moping. I kicked a rock and nodded at Jacinta.

"Damn," Jacinta whispered and bit her lip. "Maybe if we stick together the next few days she won't dare to hurt you."

"Yeah, I don't know about it."

"Or, if she tries to hit you and stuff, I'll go run and get your mom."

It didn't make me feel any better to think about running behind my mom's skirts to avoid Elena's wrath because then I'd have to confess I'd gone to see Mario. I'd get a good lesson from my grandmother for that. Not only had I discussed family business with an outsider, I'd put a man's safety before my cousin's quest for justice.

Don't get in a witch's path. Especially if you are the weaker witch. If you do, be prepared to face her. That's one of the first things you learn in my family.

～

Two days later, when Jacinta and I were reading comic books, sprawled on the hallway floor to keep our bellies cold, I knew I was screwed the moment I heard the click of Elena's high-heeled shoes.

I stood up as she walked down the hallway. Better to face her than to run. She'd catch me and it would be even worse.

"You little traitor," she said, jabbing a finger at my chest. "You told him. That lousy coward's left town with his bitch of a girlfriend."

At last Mario had grown a brain. That was nice. On the other hand, Elena was glaring at me.

"Elena, come on," I said, not even pretending innocence. "You can't just toss a maleficio into the air like that."

"Says who? Mario lied to me."

"What did the girl ever do to you?"

"Oh, so it's that whore that matters instead of me," she said, raising her eyebrows.

Jacinta glanced at me, then back at Elena, not knowing whether to hide or stay.

"No. It's . . . Elena, it's not fair. It's not right."

"Who the hell do you think you are?"

Elena's nails were long, lacquered and red. She raised them and scratched my cheek, making me wince. Oh, she was pissed.

"I'm going to cast such a spell on you," she said. "I'm going to make your fucking teeth fall out."

"Come on."

She opened her purse and took out the dried lizard, pressing it against my face.

"Lourdes," she whispered to the lizard and I shivered. "Lourdes, Lourdes."

I'd never done a maleficio before, but I'd read about it enough times to recognize it and damn, the lizard reeked of concentrated rage and power.

"Don't hurt her!" Jacinta screamed. She gave Elena such a shove that she tripped and fell to the floor.

Jacinta and I froze. We watched in horror as Elena lifted her head, blood pouring from her nose and tears in her eyes.

Elena wouldn't have really hurt me, direct bloodline connecting us and all. But that shove had altered the balance. If she had been pissed before, now she was furious. If she had meant to take revenge on me, now she was aiming for Jacinta. Poor little Jacinta who wasn't even real family; just the bastard daughter of one of the men.

Elena stood up, the lizard cupped in her left hand. She looked like an illustration in one of the old books, a scary convolution of dark, rigid lines.

"One," she muttered, wiping the blood from her nose with her right hand.

There had been a spell next to the illustration. It made me squint when I poured over the letters and tremble because it was not only a maleficio, it was my great-grandmother's maleficio. They said it was the kind of spell that drove her insane.

"I'm sorry," Jacinta said.

Elena pulled at a thread holding the lizard's belly close. "Two."

"I said I'm sorry. I'm really sorry!"

"Three."

Elena pulled at another thread. Jacinta was trembling all over and her bad eye, always darting in the wrong direction, had gone white.

I kept thinking of the letters in the book: black on white. Spidery writing extending to the margins and the words so knitted they seemed to flip in my head; turned white upon black, searing the world around me.

"Four," Elena whispered and a thread of saliva leaked from the corner of Jacinta's mouth. "Fi—"

Elena gasped. She choked and began to cough. She bent down, pressed her hands against her belly and opened her mouth into an O, spitting a long, black thread. The thread fell onto the floor, pooling at her feet.

The words poured from my mouth, loud and blazing white, like the chalk marks on the walls.

That's the last thing I remember. My mother said she found Elena on her knees and me standing next to her. It took three of the women to stop me from killing Elena.

Which I suppose proves two things: my mother was right about the late blooming, and don't get in a witch's path. Especially if you are the weaker witch.

～

Grandmother came into the city to see me afterwards and she nodded her head and gave me her blessing. It was all very odd, considering how happy everyone was and how much I'd hurt Elena.

As soon as I could I slipped out of the house.

I found Jacinta behind it, drawing stars in the dirt with a stick.

"What's up?" I said.

"Nothing," she muttered and kept on with her drawing.

I watched her trace row upon row of stars.

"You want to read a comic book with me?"

"No."

I scratched my head. "Nothing's going to change, you know."

"It is going to change," she said soberly.

Well, yeah. But I didn't want to say it just like that. Now I would get invited to all the gatherings and I'd never have to set a foot in a maquila, not even to sell spells because there'd be better places to hawk my stuff. I could even hex Patricia and twist Paco's dreams until he asked me to be his girlfriend.

"You're going to be just like Elena."

"No, I'm not," I protested.

Jacinta gave me a harsh look that made me feel like a cheat.

"Fine, crap," I said erasing one of the stars with the sole of my shoe. "Look, maybe I will be like Elena . . ."

"And I'll work at the factory and you'll never talk to me anymore."

"No . . . look, it doesn't matter. This whole bruja chica thing, it's inconsequential."

"Only it's not."

She returned to her pattern of stars, head bowed. At this pace, she'd draw the entire night sky behind our house.

My mouth felt dry and my skin was cold. It wasn't inconsequential and I already felt different. There was a feeling in the pit of my stomach that was half ache and half bliss.

"I'm always going to watch your back," I said. "You'll always watch mine."

Jacinta did not look convinced. She raised her head a fraction, like a deer peering through the trees.

"You sure about that?"

"Yeah."

"Even if we're not bloodline?"

"We *are* bloodline," I told her.

Jacinta smiled real big. She let me ride her bicycle that night while she sat in the back, holding on tight as I circled her mantle of stars.

∼

"The Way Wind" is set in author Andre Norton's Witch World universe. In this alternate universe magic is performed (at first) only by female virgins; sex deprives a witch of her powers.

In much witchcraft lore, witches are involved with sex—love spells, magic worked to invoke or deny fertility or virility. Since the female witch was often an empowered single woman, in many cultures she was also seen as sexually alluring or intentionally seductive. By the Middle Ages, Western European Christianity equated witchcraft with serving Satan, an inversion of serving God. Sex, frowned upon by Christianity in general, was the Devil's turf, so witches were assumed to be lascivious. Witches supposedly sealed their deals with the Devil by copulating with him and frequently participating in orgies.

Still, the equation of virginity—or at least a life not dominated by love for a man—with magical power also has a place in witch mythos. Spinsters learn witchcraft in Mary Norton's The Magic Bed-Knob *(1943), on which the 1971 Disney movie* Bedknobs and Broomsticks *was based. Elizabeth Burton's* Miss Carter and the Ifrit *(1945) has a similar theme. Gillian Holroyd in the 1958 film (and 1950 play)* Bell, Book, and Candle *sacrifices her magic for love. In Alice Hoffman's* Practical Magic *(and in the movie based on it) the sacrifice for loving a witch takes a different turn: if a woman of the witchly Owens family finds true love with a man, he is destined to die tragically.*

The Way Wind
Andre Norton

The crumbling walled fortress and the dreary, ragged town, which had woven a ragged skirt about it during long years, stood at the end of the Way Pass. It was named l'Estal, which in a language older than legend, had a double meaning—First and Last.

For it was the first dwelling of men at the end of Way Pass along which any traffic from the west must come. And it was also the end of a long, coiling snake of a road stretching eastward and downward to Klem, which long ago it had been designed to guard. There could have been another name for that straggle of drear buildings also—End of Hope.

For generations now it had been a place of exile. Those sent from Klem had been men and women outlawed for one reason or another. The scribe whose pen had been a key used too freely, the officer who was too ambitious—or at times, too conscientious—the rebel, the misfit, those sometimes fleeing the law or ruler's whim, they came hither.

There was no returning, for a geas had been set on the coil road, and those of lowland blood coming up it might only travel one way—never to return. There had been countless attempts, of course. But whatever mage had set that barrier had indeed been one of power, for the spell did not dwindle with the years as magic often did.

Through the Way Pass there came only a trickle of travelers, sometimes not more than three or four in a season. None of them lingered in l'Estal; there was that about the place which was like a dank cloud, and its people were grim of face, meager of livelihood.

Over the years they had managed to scrape a living, tilling small scraps of fields they terraced along the slopes, raising lean goats and small runtish sheep, hunting, burrowing into the rock of the heights to bring out stores of ore.

The latter was transported once a year to a certain bend in the descending road, and there traded for supplies they could not otherwise raise—salt, pigs of iron, a few items of what was luxury to them. Then it was also that the Castellan of the fort would receive the pouch bearing the royal arms containing, ever the same, orders. And now and again there would be another exile to be sent aloft.

The trickle of travelers from the west were mostly merchants, dealers in a small way, too poor to make the long journey by sea to the port of Klem itself. They were hunters with pelts, drovers of straggles of lean mountain cattle or sheep. Small, dark people who grunted rasping words in trade language, kept to themselves, and finished their business as soon as possible.

Of the Klemish exiles, none took the westward road. If there was a geas set upon that also, no one spoke of such. It was simply accepted that for them there was only one place to be longed for, dreamed of, hopelessly remembered—and that lay always eastward.

There had been many generations of exiles, and their children had known no other place; yet to them l'Estal was not a home but a prison of sorts, and the tales told of the eastern land made of that a paradise forbidden, changed out of all knowledge of what it had been or was.

Still there was always one point of interest that stirred the western gate sentries each year—and that was the Way Wind. At the very beginning of spring, which came slowly and harshly in these gaunt uplands, a wind blew strongly from west to east, souring the pass, carrying with it strange scents. It might last a single day; it might blow so for three or four.

And by chance, it always brought with it one of the western travelers, as if it pulled them on into the line of the pass and drew them forward. Thus, in a place where there was so little of the new and strange, the Way Wind farers were a matter of wager, and often time not only, the armsmen at the gate but their officers and their women gathered, along with townspeople, when they heard the outer horn blast, which signaled that the wind herded a traveler to them.

This day there were four who stood on the parapet of the inner wall, not closely together as if they were united in their company, but rather each a little apart. The oldest of that company, a man who had allowed the hood of his cloak to fall back so the wind lifted tufts of steel gray hair, had the paler face of one who kept much indoors. Yet there was a strength in his features, a gleam of eye which had not been defeated, nor ever would. At the throat of his cloak was the harp badge of a bard. Osono he had named himself ten years before when he had accompanied the east traders back from their rendezvous. And by that name he was accepted, eagerly by the Castellan and those of his household.

Next to him, holding her own thick cloak tightly about her as if she feared the wind might divest her of it, was the Lady Almadis, she who had been born to the Castellan's lady after their arrival here. Her clothing was as coarse as that of any townswoman on the streets below, and the hands that held to that cloak were sun-browned. There was a steady look to her, as if she had fitted herself to the grim husk housing her.

A pace or so behind her was a second man. Unlike the other two he had no cloak, but rather dressed in mail and leather, sword-armed. But his head was bare also as he cradled a pitted helm on one hip. His features were gaunt, thinned, bitter, his mouth a mere line above a stubborn jaw—Urgell, who had once been a mercenary and now served as swordsmaster in the fortress.

The fourth was strange even in that company, for she was a broad-girthed woman, red of face, thick of shoulder. Her cloak was a matter of patched strips, as if she had been forced to sew together the remains of several such in order to cover her. A fringe of yellow-white hair showed under the edge of a cap covering her head. For all the poverty of her appearance, Forina had a good position in the town, for she was the keeper of the only inn, and any the Way Wind brought would come to her for shelter.

"What is your wager, my lady?" Osono's trained bard's voice easily overreached the whistle of the wind.

Almadis laughed, a hard-edged sound which lacked any softening of humor.

"I, sir bard? Since my last two wind wagers were so speedily proved wrong, I have learned caution. This year I make no speculation; thus I shall not be disappointed again. Think me over-timid of my purse if you will."

Osono glanced at her. She was not looking toward him but rather down the wind road. "Lady," he returned, "I think you are over-timid in nothing."

After a moment she laughed again. "Bard, life in l'Estal makes for dull acceptance—perhaps that gives root to timidity."

"There is the priest." The observation from the mercenary cut through their exchange. He had moved forward, as if drawn by some force beyond his own understanding, to look down at the cluster of townspeople and guards by the gate.

"Thunur," Osono nodded. "Yes, that crow is well on the hop. Though if he tries to deliver his message to either herdsman or trader, he will not get the better of them. Shut-mouthed they are, and to all of them I think we are Dark-shadowed—they would listen no more to one of us than to the bark of a chained hound."

Urgell had put his hand to the edge of the parapet wall, and now his mail and leather gauntlet grated on the stone there. Chained hound, Almadis thought, proper term not only for such as this man, but perhaps for all of them. But then a Bard was trained in apt word choice.

"That is one as makes trouble—" Forina had come forward also on the other side of the soldier. "He has a tongue as bitter as var, and he uses it to dip into many pots. It would be well to keep an eye on him."

Urgell turned his head quickly. "What stir has he tried to set, goodwife?"

"More than one. Ask Vill Blacksmith what a pother made his sister sharp-tongue him. Ask of Tatwin why three of those snot-nosed brats he strives to beat learning into no longer come to his bidding, ask Solasten why she was pelted with market dung. Ask me why the doors of the Hafted Stone are now barred to him. A troublemaker he is, and this is a place where we need no one to heat old quarrels and pot new ones!"

"If he is a brawler, speak to the guard," Osono suggested. "But I think he is perhaps something even more to be watched—"

"What may that be?" The bard had all their attention now, but it was Almadis who asked that question.

"A fanatic, my lady. One so obsessed with his own beliefs that he is like a smoldering torch ready to be put to a straw heap. We have not an easy life here; there were many old hatreds, despairs, and these can be gathered up to fuel a new fire. Ten years ago, one of his nature arose in Salanika—there was such a bloodletting thereafter as the plains had not seen since the days of Black Gorn. It took full two seasons to quench that fire, and some brands still smoldering may have been scattered to blaze again—"

"Such a one as Thunur, you think?" Almadis demanded. "L'Estal has answers to such—have we not?" The bitterness in her voice was plain. "What are we all but outlaws, and we can exist only as we hold together." She did not turn her head, but she loosed one hand from her cloak hold and motioned to that dark, ill-fortuned spread of age-hardened timbers which surmounted the wall of the shorter tower. "That has borne fruit many times over."

"He has a following," Urgell said, "but he and they are under eye. If he tries aught with the western travelers, he will be in a cell within an hour. We want no trouble with them."

Certainly they could afford no trouble with the few who came the western road. Such wayfarers were their only real link with a world which was not overshadowed by the walls about them and the past which had brought them here.

The gray-robed priest had indeed been roughly jostled away from the gate. He was making small hops, for he was a short man, trying to see over the crowd before him the nature of the wayfarer who was now well within sight.

"It—it is a child!" Almadis was shaken out of her composure and came with a single step to stand beside the mercenary. "A child—! But what fate has brought her here?"

The wayfarer was slight, her bundle of travel cloak huddled about her as if it were intended for a much larger and stouter wearer. Hood folds had fallen back on her shoulders, and they saw hair that the wind had pulled from braids to fly in wisps about her face. She was remarkably fair of skin for a wilderness traveler, and her hair was very fair, though streaked here and there by a darker strand closer to the gleam of red-gold.

There was no mistaking, however, the youth of that slight body and those composed features. She walked confidently, and at her shoulder bobbed the head of a hill pony, still so thick with winter hair that it was like an ambling mound of fur.

Bulging panniers rode on either side of a packsaddle. And that was surrounded in the middle by what looked to be a basket half covered by a lid.

Contrary to all who made this perilous way through the high mountains, the girl carried no visible weapons except a stout staff which had been crudely hacked from some sapling, stubs of branches yet to be marked along its length. This was topped, however, with a bunch of flowers and leaves, massed together. Nor did any of them look wilted; rather it would seem they had just been plucked, though there were yet no flowers to be found in the upper reaches where reluctant patches of snow could be sighted.

"Who—what—?" Almadis was snapped out of her boredom, of that weariness which overshadowed her days and nights.

As the girl came to the gate, there was a sudden change. The Way Wind died; there was an odd kind of silence as if they all waited for something, they did not know what.

So complete was that silence that the sound Osono uttered startled them all.

"Who—what—?" Almadis turned upon the bard almost fiercely.

He shook his head slowly. "Lady, I have seen many things in my time, and have heard of countless more. There is said to be—somewhere in the western lands—those who are one with the land in a way that none of our blood can ever hope to be—"

The sentries at the gate seemed disinclined to ask any questions. In fact they had fallen back, and with them the townspeople withdrew to allow her a way path. In their doing so, Thunur won to the front rank and stood, his head stretched a little forward on his lank neck, staring at her, his teeth showing a little.

Almadis turned swiftly but Osono matched her, even extending his wrist in a courtly fashion to give her dignity. Forina, closest to the stairway, was already lumbering down, and behind them Urgell seemed as eager to catch a closer sight of this most unusual wayfarer.

They gained the portion of street just in time to witness Thunur's up-flung arm, hear his speech delivered with such force as to send spittle flying.

"Witchery! Here comes witchery! See the demon who is riding in such state!"

The crowd shrunk back even more as there was a stir to that half-covered basket on the top of the pony pack.

"Fool!" Forina's voice arose in the kind of roar she used to subdue a taproom scuffle. For so large a woman she moved very fast, and now she was halfway between the slavering priest and the girl, who watched them both serenely as if she had no cause to suspect that she was unwelcome.

"Fool! That is but a cat—"

The rust-yellow head with pricked ears had arisen yet farther from within its traveling basket, and green eyes surveyed them all with the same unconcern as that of the girl.

But such a cat. One of those pricked ears was black, and as the cat arose higher in its riding basket, they could see that there was a black patch on its chest. There was such a certain cockiness about it, an air of vast self-confidence, that Almadis laughed; and that was a laugh that had no edge of harshness.

Her laugh was quickly swallowed up by a chuckle from Osono, and a moment later there sounded no less than a full-lunged bellow from Vill Blacksmith.

The girl was smiling openly at them all as if they were greeting her with the best of goodwill.

"I am Meg, dealing in herbs and seeds, good folk. These traveling companions of mine are Kaska and Mors—"

The hair-concealed head of the pony nodded as if it perfectly understood the formalities of introduction, but Kaska merely opened a well-fanged mouth in a bored yawn.

Now the sergeant of the guard appeared to have recovered from the surprise that had gripped them all. He dropped his pike in a form of barrier and looked at the girl.

"Mistress, you are from—?" he demanded gruffly.

"From Westlea, guardsman. And I am one who trades—herbs—seeds."

Almadis blinked. The girl had moved her staff a fraction. That bouquet of tightly packed flowers which had looked so fresh from above now presented another aspect. The color was still there but faded—these were dried flowers surely, yet they preserved more of their once life than any she had ever seen.

"There be toll," the pike had lowered in the sergeant's hold. "'Tis a matter of four coppers, and there be a second taking for a market stall."

Meg nodded briskly. Her hand groped beneath her cloak and came forth again to spill out four dulled rounds of metal into his hand.

Those who had gathered there had begun to shift away. Since this stranger the wind had brought was going to set up in the marketplace, there would be plenty of time to inspect her—though she was indeed something new. None of her kind of merchant had entered l'Estal before in the memories of all.

Only Thunur held his place until the sergeant, seemingly unaware that he was close behind him, swung back the pike and the priest had to skip quickly aside to escape a thud from that weapon. He was scowling at the girl, and his mouth opened as if to deliver some other accusation when Urgell took a hand in the matter.

"Off with you, crow! You stand in the lady's way!"

Now the priest swung around with a snarl, and his narrowed eyes surveyed Almadis and the bard. There was a glint of red rage in that stare. But he turned indeed and pushed through the last of the thinning crowd, to vanish down one of the more narrow alleys.

"Mistress," the mercenary spoke directly to the young traveler. "If that fluttering carrion eater makes you trouble, speak up—his voice is not one we have a liking for."

Meg surveyed him as one who wished to set a face in memory. "Armsman," she inclined her head, "I think that here I have little to fear, but for your courtesy I give you thanks."

To Almadis's surprise, she saw Urgell flush and then he moved swiftly, leaving as abruptly as the priest had done.

"You'll be wantin' shelter," Forina said. "I keep the Hafted Stone—it be the trade inn."

Again Meg favored the speaker with one of those long looks, and then she smiled. "Goodwife, what you have to offer we shall gladly accept. It has been a long road and Mors is wearied. Our greatest burden has been his—sure foot and clever trail head that he has."

She reached out to lace fingers in the puff of long hair on the pony's neck. He gave another vigorous nod and snorted.

"If you have spices—or meadowsweet for linens—?" Almadis had an odd feeling that she did not want this girl to disappear. A new face in l'Estal was always to be hoped for, and this wayfarer was so different. She had kept stealing glances at the bouquet on the staff. It seemed so real, as if, at times, it had the power of taking on the freshness it had had when each of those blossoms had been plucked.

"Your flowers, Herbgatherer, what art gives the dried the seeming of life?"

"It is an art, my lady, an ancient one of my own people. In here"—Meg drew her hand down the side of one of those bulging panniers—"I have others. They be part of my trade stock. Also scents such as your meadowsweet—"

"Then surely I shall be seeing you again, Herbgatherer," Almadis said. "A good rest to you and your companions."

"My lady, such wishes are seeds for greater things—"

"As are ill wishes!" Osono said. "Do some of your wares come perhaps from Farlea?"

Meg turned now that measuring look to the bard.

"Farlea is sung of, sir bard. If it ever existed, that was many times ago. No, I do not aspire to the arts of the Fair Ones, only to such knowledge as any herbwife can know, if she seeks always to learn more."

Now it was her turn to move away, following Forina. Kaska had settled down again in her basket until only those mismatched tips of ears showed. But there were those who had been in the crowd at the gate who trailed the girl at a distance as if they did not want to lose sight of her for some reason.

"Farlea, Osono? I think with that question you may have displeased our herbwife," Almadis said slowly. "You are a storer of legends; which do you touch on now?"

He was frowning. "On the veriest wisp of an old one, my lady. There was a tale of a youth who followed my own calling, though he was of a roving bent. He vanished for a time, and then he returned hollow-eyed and wasted, saying that he sought something he had lost, or rather had thrown away through some foolishness, and that his fate was harsh because of that. He had been offered a way into a land of peace and rare beauty, and thereafter he sang always of Farlea. But he withered and died before the year was done, eaten up by his sorrow."

"But what makes you think of Farlea when you look upon this herbwife?" Almadis persisted.

"Those flowers on her staff—fresh plucked." His frown grew deeper.

"So I, too, thought when first I saw them. But no, they are rather very cleverly dried so that they are preserved with all their color, and I think their scent. Surely I smelled roses when she held them out a little. That is an art worth the knowing. We have no gardens here—the rose walk gives but a handful of blooms, and those are quickly gone. To have a bouquet of such ever to hand"—her voice trailed off wistfully and then she added—"yes, such could even fight the grim aging of these walls. I must go to the market when she sets up her stall."

Meg did set up her stall on the following day. From the market mistress she rented the three stools and a board to balance on two of them, to form the humblest of displays. Mathe, who oversaw the trading place, watched the girl's sure moves in adjusting the plank to show her wares. He lingered even a fraction longer, though it was a busy day, to see her unpack bundles of dried herbs, their fragrance even able to be scented over the mixed odors, few of them pleasant, which were a part of market day.

There were packets also of yellowish, fine-woven cloth which gave forth even more intensified perfumes, and small, corner-wrapped bits of thin parchment such as were for the keeping of seeds. While in the very middle of that board was given honored place to that same bunch of flowers as had crowned Meg's trail staff.

Kaska's basket was set on the pavement behind the rude table. And Mors stood behind. The cat made no attempt to get out of her basket, but she was sitting well up in it surveying all about her with manifest interest.

Two small figures moved cautiously toward the stall. Beneath the grimed skin and the much-patched clothing, one face was the exact match of the other. Between them strutted a goat, each of his proud curl of horns clasped by a little, rough-skinned hand.

They proceeded slowly, darting glances to either side as if they were scouts in enemy territory. Only the goat was at ease, apparently confident in his ability to handle any situation which might arise.

"You—Tay—Tod—take that four-legged abomination out of here!" A man arose from the stoop behind one of the neighboring stalls and waved his arms.

The goat gave voice in a way which suggested that he was making a profane answer to that, and refused to answer to the force dragging at him from either side. The boys cowered, but it was apparent they had no idea of deserting their four-legged companion to run for cover.

Meg was on her feet also, smiling as if the two small herds and their beast were the most promising of customers. When her neighbor came from behind his own stall table, a thick stick in his hand, she waved him back.

"No harm, goodman," she said. "This beast but seeks what is a delicacy for his kind. Which he shall be freely given." She selected a stalk wrapped loosely around with its own withered leaves and held it out to the goat. For a moment he regarded her and then, with the neat dexterity of one who had done this many times before, he tongued the proffered bit of dried stuff and drew it into his mouth, nodding his head up and down, as if to signify his approval, with a vigor to near shake free the grip of his two companions.

The other tradesman stared, his upraised club falling slowly to his side. But there was a wariness in his look when he shifted his glance toward Meg, then he withdrew behind his own table, as if he wished some barrier against a threat he did not truly understand.

However, Meg paid no attention to him. Rather now, she reached behind her and brought out a coarse napkin from which she unrolled thick slices of bread with green-veined cheese between—the food she had brought for her nooning.

Two pair of small eyes fastened upon that, as she broke the larger of the portion in half, holding it out to the boys. Though they did not entirely loose their hold on the goat's horns, their other hands shot out to snatch what she held, cramming it into their mouths as if they feared that it might be demanded back.

"Tay—Tod." She spoke the names the man had spoken.

The one to her right gave a gulp that left him choking, but his twin was the quicker to answer. "I be Tod, lady—this be Tay."

"And your friend—" Meg nodded gravely to the goat, as if indeed the beast were a person of two-legged consequence.

"He be Nid!" There was pride in that answer such as a liege man might show in naming his lord.

"Well met, Tod, Tay, and Nid," Meg nodded gravely. "I am Meg, and here are my friends, Kaska and Mors." The cat only stared, but the pony uttered a soft neigh.

A valiant swallow had carried the food down, and Tay was able to speak:

"Lacy-torn"—he gestured toward the bouquet of dried flowers—"But too cold now—" He shook his head.

"Lacy-torn," Meg repeated with a note of approval in her voice, "and hearts-ease, serenity, and love-light Kings-silver, Red-rose, Gold-for-luck, Sorrows end, Hope-in-the-sun—maiden's love and knight's honor, yes." The old country names came singingly from her as if she voiced some bard's verse.

"Bright—" Tod said before he stuffed his mouth with another huge bit.

"You see them bright?" Meg's head was cocked little to one side. "That is well, very well. Now, younglings, would you give me some service? My good Mors needs some hay for his nooning, and we had too much to carry from the inn to bear that also. Can you bring me such? Here is the copper for Mistress Forina."

"Nid—" began Tod hesitantly.

"Nid will bide here, and there will be no trouble." There was complete assurance in her answer.

Tod took the proffered coin and with his twin shot off across the marketplace. Meg turned to the man who had warned off the boys and the goat.

"Of whose household are those two, if you please, goodman?"

He snorted. "Household? None would own such as those two. Oh, they make themselves useful as herds. They be the only ones as can handle beast Nid," he shot a baneful glance at the goat. "Three of a kind they be, stealing from stalls and making trouble."

"They are but children."

The man flushed, there was that he could read in her voice and eyes which he did not like.

"There are a number such. We had the green-sick here three seasons agone, herbwife. Many died, and there were fireless hearths left. Mistress Forina, she gives them leftovers and lets them sleep in the hay at the stable. More fool she; they are a plaguey lot." He turned away abruptly as a woman approached his stall, and to have done with Meg's questions.

The goat had shifted to one side and touched noses with Mors. Kaska gave a fastidious warn-off hiss just as a thin man in a shabby cloak paused before Meg's narrow table.

He was eyeing the flowers.

"I thought them real." He spoke as if to himself.

"Real, they are, good sir. But this is what you wish—for your daughter." Meg's hand was already on a small packet. "Steep it in apple ale, and let her have it each morning before she breaks her fast."

"But—herbwife—you did not ask me—I did not tell—"

"You saw," Meg answered slowly and firmly, as one might speak to a child learning its letters, "and I am a healer. We all have gifts, good sir. Even as you have yours. Out of love of learning, you have striven hard and given much—"

Never taking his eyes from hers, he fumbled in the pouch at his belt and brought out a coin.

"Herbwife, I know not what you are—but there is good in what you do, of that I am sure. Just as"—his eyes had dropped as if against his will to the flowers and he gave a start—"just as those are real! Yet it is out of season, and some I have not seen for long. For such grew once in a garden eastward where I can no longer go. I thank you."

Meg was busy with the bouquet, freeing from its tight swathering a spike of violet-red flower. As she held it up, it did in truth seem to be fresh plucked.

"This for your hearth-home, scholar. May it bring you some ease of heart for not all memories are ill ones."

He seemed unable for a moment or two to realize that she meant it. And when he took it between two fingers, he was smiling.

"Lady, how can one thank—"

Meg shook her head. "Thanks are worth the more when passed along. You had one who has given much, scholar—therefore to you shall be given in turn. Remember this well"—and there was force in those three words.

It was almost as if he were so bemused by the flowers that he did not hear her. For he did not say one word in farewell as he turned away from her stall.

Those shadows awakened in the afternoon from the walls about the market square were growing longer when Almadis came. As usual Osono was at her side, and behind her Urgell. Though she had been free of l'Estal since childhood, taking no maids with her, it was insisted that she ever have some guard. And usually the armsmaster took that duty upon himself.

There were feuds brought into l'Estal, for men of power arose and fell in the lowlands, and sometimes a triumphant enemy suffered the same fate as his former victim. Lord Jules had been a mighty ruler of a quarter of Klem before his enemies had brought him down. His lordship became this single mountain hold, instead of leading armies he rode with patrols to keep the boundaries against the outlaws of the western heights; his palace was this maze of ancient cold and crooked walls, and warrens of rooms. But he was still remembered and feared, and there were those who would reach him even if they must do so through his only child.

So Urgell went armed, and Almadis carried in her sleeve a knife with which she was well trained. There was a sword also sheathed by Osono's side, though as a bard he supposedly had safe conduct wherever he might go. Might go—that was no longer true—there was only l'Estal. No man or woman asked of another what had brought one to exile here, so Almadis did not know the past tale of either of the men pacing with her now, but that they were of honor and trust she was sure, and she welcomed their company accordingly.

Meg's stall had been a popular one this day. Most of those coming to buy had been dealt with briskly, but there were some with whom she spoke with authority, and twice more she had drawn flowers from that amazing bouquet and given them to the amazement of those with whom she dealt. So it had been with Vill Blacksmith, who had come seeking a herb known to be helpful against a burn such as his young apprentice had suffered. He went off with not only his purchase, but a sprig of knight's honor gold-bright in the hand of his bonnet. And there was Brydan the embroideress, who wished a wash for aching eyes, and received also a full-blown heart's-ease, purple and gold as a fine lady's gem when she fastened it to the breast of her worn gray gown.

Oddly enough it seemed that, though Meg plundered her bouquet so from time to time, it did not appear to shrink in size. Her neighbor began to watch her more closely, and his frown became a sharp crease between his eyes. Now and again his own hand arose to caress a certain dark-holed stone which hung from a dingy string about his throat, and once he muttered under his breath while he fingered it.

He was the first to sight Almadis and her companions, and his frown became a sickly kind of smile, though there was no reason to believe the Castellan's daughter would be interested in his withered roots of vegetables, the last remaining from the winter stores.

Indeed she crossed the market as one with a definite mission in mind, heading straight to Meg's stand.

"Goodwill to you, herbwife," she said. "I trust that trade has been brisk for you. We have but very few here who follow such a calling."

Meg did not curtsey, but smiled as one who greets an old friend.

"Indeed, lady, this is a fair market, and I have been well suited in bargaining. We spoke of meadowsweet for the freshening before times—"

"Lad's Love—dove's wings"—Osono paid no attention to the women, his was all for the bouquet—"Star fast—"

"Falcon feather!" Urgell's much harsher voice cut across the smooth tones of the bard.

"You are well learned, good sirs," Meg returned, and her hand hovered over the bouquet. "Those are names not common in these parts."

Osono's gaze might be aimed at the flowers, but yet it was as if he saw beyond them something else—as might grow in a meadow under that full, warm sun, which never even in summer seemed to reach into these stark heights.

Meg's fingers plucked and brought forth a stem on which swung two white blooms, star-pointed. She held that out to the bard, and he accepted it as one in a dream. Then she snapped thumb and forefinger together with more vigor and freed a narrow leaf, oddly colored so that it indeed resembled a feather.

"For you also, warrior." And her words held something of an order, as if to make sure he would not refuse. Then she spoke to Almadis:

"Meadowsweet, yes." She swept up a bundle of leaves and wrapped them expertly in a small cloth. "But something else also, is it not so?"

"Red-rose," Almadis said slowly. "My mother strove to grow a bush, but this land is too sere to nurture it. Red-rose—"

The flower Meg handed her was not full opened yet, and when Almadis held it close to her, she could smell a perfume so delicate that she could hardly believe such could come into the grayness that was l'Estal.

"Herbwife," she leaned a little forward, "who are you?"

"Meg, my lady, a dealer—a friend—"

Almadis nodded. "Yes, of a certainty that."

She brought out her purse. "For the meadowsweet"—she laid down one of the coins.

"Just so," Meg agreed. "For the meadowsweet."

Osono was fumbling at his own purse with one hand, the other carefully cupping the starflower. Then he caught Meg's eye, and flushed. Instead he bowed as he might to the lady of some great hall where he had been night's singer. "My thanks to you—herbwife."

Urgell's bow was not so low or polished, but there was a lightening of his harsh features. "And mine also, mistress—your gifts have a value beyond price."

There were others who sought the herb dealer after the castle's lady had departed. But few of them were favored with a gift of bloom. Perhaps six in all bore away a leaf or flower, but still the bouquet appeared to grow no smaller. When Meg, in the beginning twilight, gathered up her wares and repacked them, two small figures appeared.

Behind them still ambled their horned and bewiskered companion. For the second time Nid touched noses with Mors, who was hardly taller than he. And Kaska voiced a small hiss.

"Help you, mistress?" Tay shuffled a bare foot back and forth in the straw which strewed the market square in marketing days.

"But of course. Many hands make light of work." Meg swung one of her cord-tied bundles to the boy, and he hurried to fit it into the panniers, which his brother had already placed on Mors.

"You are not out with the herds, youngling?" she added as she picked up the last of her supplies, that bouquet.

Tod hung his head. "They will not have Nid now—he fought with Whrit, and they say he has too bad a temper—that any of his get are not wanted. They—set the dogs on us and Nid savaged two, so—so they talk now of—" He gulped and his brother continued:

"They talk of killing him, mistress."

"But he is yours?"

Both small faces turned toward hers, and there was a fierce determination in the chorus of their answer.

"Before times, he was herd leader, mistress. When Lan, our brother, was herder. But"—now their voices faltered—"Lan died of the green-sick. And the herd went to Finus—they said as how Lan had told him so—that we were too young. And Finus—he said as how there was much owed him by Lan, and that he had the rights. Only Nid would come with us, and he stayed. But—" Tod stopped as if to catch breath, however Tad's words gushed on:

"They won't let us to the pasture anymore. Finus, he lives in our house and says it is his."

"What have you then as shelter?" asked Meg quietly. She was holding the flowers close to her, beneath her chin, as if she breathed in for some purpose the faint scents.

"Inn mistress Forina—she lets us in the stable—but they say that Nid is bad for the horses."

"Not for this one," Meg nodded to Mors. "Let he and Nid bed down together, and we shall see what can be done."

They made a small procession of their own out of the marketplace. Meg carried the flowers and humped Kaska's basket up on one hip with the familiar gesture of a countrywoman bearing burdens. Mors trotted after her, no leading rein to draw him on, and he was matched by the goat, the two forming a guard, one to each side.

There were those who watched them go, narrow-eyed and sour of face. It would seem that just as there were those who had been drawn to the stall during that day, so also there were those who shunned it. Now a darker shadow moved forward to stand beside the stall which had neighbored Meg's.

"You have kept eye on her, goodman?" it hissed a question.

"I have, priest. There is that about her which is not natural right enough. She is weaving spells, even as a noxious spider weaves a web. Already she has touched some here—"

"Those being?" The voice was hot, near exulting.

Now the stall keeper spoke names, and those names were oddly companioned—lady, bard, soldier, smith, scholar, needlewoman, a laborer in from one of the scanty hill farms, a gate sentry off duty, a washer-woman, the wife of a merchant and her daughter—

And with the speaking of each name, Thunur nodded his head. "You have done well, Danler, very well. Continue to watch here, and I shall search elsewhere. We shall bring down this slut who deals with the Dark yet! You are a worthy son of GORT, the Ever-Mighty."

~

Within the keep the ways were dark and damp as always. Though in some of the halls there were dank and moldy tapestries on the walls, no one had made any attempt to renew them, to bring any hint of color into those somber quarters. Even candles seemed here to have their halos of dim light circumscribed so that they could not reveal too much of any way.

Almadis tugged at her heavy-trained skirt with an impatient hand. She had but little time, and this was a way which had not been trodden for long. She could remember well her last visit here, when rage at all the world had seemed to so heat her, she had felt none of the chill thrown off by the walls. The loss of her mother had weighed both heart and spirit.

Now the pallid light of her candle picked out the outline of the door she sought. But she had to set that on the floor and use both hands in order to force open the barrier, which damp had near sealed beyond her efforts.

Then she was in, candle aloft, looking about. No one had cared—there had probably been no one here since last she left. Yet the mustiness was still tinged with a hint of incense. The room was small, its floor covered with the rotting remnants of what had once been whortle reeds, which trodden upon, gave back sweet scent.

There was a single window, shuttered tight, a bar dropped firmly in place to hold it so. Beneath that stood a boxlike fixture which might be an altar.

That was shrouded with thick dust, a dust which clouded the round of once-polished mirror set there, gathered about the bases of three candlesticks.

For a long moment Almadis merely stood and looked at that altar and its furnishings. She had turned her back on what this stood for, told herself that there was nothing here beyond what she could see, touch, that to believe in more was folly—a child's folly. Yet her mother—

Slowly Almadis moved forward. There were still half-consumed candles in those sticks, grimed, a little lopsided. She used the one she carried to touch the wicks of those into life. Then, suddenly, she jerked her long scarf from about her shoulders, and, in spite of its fine embroidery, she used it to dust the mirror free, dropping its grime-clogged stuff to the floor when she had done.

Lastly she turned to the window. Straining, she worked free the bar, threw back the shutter, opened the room to the night, in spite of the wind which wove about this small side tower.

For so long it had not mattered what rode the sky; this night it did. And what was rising now was the full moon in all its brilliance and glory. Almadis returned to the altar. She could not remember the forms. Those other times she had merely repeated words her mother had uttered without regard for their meaning. There were only scraps which she could assemble now.

But she stationed herself before that mirror, leaning forward a little, her hands placed flat on either side. On its tarnished surface she could see reflected the light of the three candles—but nothing else. There was no representation of her own face—the once-burnished plate was too dim.

Nor had she that learning which could bring it alive. Yet she had been drawn here and knew that this had meaning, a meaning she dared not deny.

Tucked in the lacing of her bodice was that rose Meg had given her. Dried it might be—with great skill—yet it seemed to have just been plucked from a bush such as her mother had striven to keep alive.

The girl moistened her lips.

"One In Three," she began falteringly. "She who rules the skies, She who is maiden, wife, and elder in turn, She who answers the cries of her daughters in distress, who reaches to touch a land and bring it into fruitfulness, She who knows what truly lies within the heart—"

Almadis's voice trailed into silence. What right had she to ask for anything in this forsaken place, return to a faith she had said held no meaning?

There was certainly another shadow of something on the mirror—growing stronger. It was—the rose!

Almadis gasped, for a moment she felt light-headed, that only her hold on the altar kept her upright.

"Lady"—her voice was the thinnest of whispers—"Lady who was, and always will be—give me forgiveness. Your messenger—she must be one of your heart held—Lady, I am not fit—"

She raised her hands to that flower caught in her lacing. Yet something would not let her loosen it as she wished, to leave it as an offering here.

Instead there was the sweetness of the rose about her, as if each candle breathed forth its fragrance. She looked down—that flower which had been yet half a bud was now open.

Quickly, almost feverishly in her haste, Almadis reached again for the altar. There had been something else left there long ago. The dust had concealed it, but she found it— Her fingers caught the coil of a chain, and she held it up, from it swung a pendant—the flat oval of silver (but the silver was not tarnished black as it should have been) on it, in small, raised, milky white gems, the three symbols of the Lady in Her waxing, Her full life, Her waning.

It seemed to Almadis that the candlelight no longer was the illumination of that chamber, rather the moon itself shone within, brighter than she could remember it. She raised the chain, bowed her head a fraction, slipped those links over it, allowing the moon gem-set pendant to fall upon her breast. Then she did as she remembered her mother had always done, tucked it into hiding beneath her bodice, so that now the pendant rested between her breasts just under the rose. Though it did not carry the chill of metal to her flesh, it was rather warm, as if it had but been passed from one who had the right to wear it to another.

Now she gathered courage to speak again.

"Lady, you know what will be asked of me, and what is in me. I cannot walk my father's way—and he will be angry. Give me the strength and courage to remain myself in the face of such anger—though I know that by his beliefs he means me only well."

She leaned forward then, a kind of resolution manifest in her movements, to blow out the three candles. But she made no move to bar away the moonlight before she picked up her journey candle to leave the room.

~

Though it was day without, the guardroom was grimly dusk within.

"Three of them we took," a brawny man in a rust-marked mail coat said to one of his fellows. He jerked a thumb at a rolled ball of hide. "Over the gate to the west, he says."

The older man he addressed grunted. "We do things here by my Lord Jules's ordering."

"Don't be so free with words like that hereabouts, Ruddy," cautioned the other. "Our Knight-Captain has long ears—"

"Or more than one pair of them," retorted Ruddy. "We've got us more trouble than just a bunch of lousy sheep raiders, Jonas. While you've been out a-ridin', there's a stew boilin' here."

The bigger man leaned on the edge of the table,

"Thunur, I'm thinkin'. That one came at dawn light a-brayin' somethin' about a witch. He's a big mouth, always yappin'."

"To some purpose, Jonas, there's more an' more listen to him. An' you know well what happened below when those yellin' 'GORT, come down' broke loose."

"Gods," snorted the city sergeant. "We be those all gods have forgot. Perhaps just as well, there was always a pother o' trouble below when priests stuck their claws into affairs. There are those here who are like t' stir if the right spoon is thrust into the pot, too. Thunur is gettin' him a followin'—Let him get enough to listen an' we'll be out with pikes, an' you'll remember outlaw hunting as somethin' as a day's good ramble."

"Well, I could do with a ramble—over to the Hafted Stone to wet m' gullet an' then to barracks an' m'bunk. His Honor is late—"

"Right good reason." A younger man turned from the group of his fellows by the door and leered. "Hear as how it was all to be fixed up for our Knight-Captain—wed and bed the lord's daughter—make sure that he is firm in the saddle for the time when m'lord don't take to ridin' anymore. They have a big feastin' tonight just to settle the matter, don't they?"

There was no time for an answer. Those by the door parted swiftly to allow another to enter. He was unhelmed, but wore mail, and over that a surcoat patterned with a snarling wolf head. His dark hair was cropped after the fashion of one who wore a helm much, and it was sleeked above a high forehead. The seam of a scar twisted one corner of his mouth, so that he seemed to sneer at the world around.

He was young for all of that, and once must have been handsome. His narrow beak of a nose gave him now the look of some bird of prey, an impression his sharp yellowish eyes did nothing to lighten. Otger, Knight-Captain under the Castellan, was no man to be taken lightly either in war or council. Now he stalked past the men who crowded back to give him room, as if they were invisible, even Jonas pulled away quickly as his commander fronted Ruddy face-to-face.

"There is trouble, Town Sergeant?"

Ruddy had straightened. His face was as impassive as that of a puppet soldier.

"Sir, no more than ever. Th' priest of GORT is brayin' again. Some are beginnin' to listen. This mornin' he came here—"

"So!" Otger turned his head but a fraction. "Dismissed to the courtyard."

They were quick to go. Only Jonas and Ruddy remained. The Knight regarded them with the hooded eyes of a predator biding time.

"He is still here?"

"Sir, he spilled forth such blather that I thought it best you hear. He speaks of those above him in a manner which is not fit."

Otger moved past him, seated himself on the single chair behind the table, as a giver of justice might install himself in court. His hand went to his cheek, the fingers tracing his scar. Jonas edged backward another step. That was always a trouble sign. Young as Otger was, he had gained such influence here as to be served swiftly.

It was the Castellan who had advanced him swiftly—and in a way, who could blame Lord Jules? The years spun by only too swiftly, and a man aged with them. The lord had no son—but there was a daughter. One wedding her would surely rule here. Those of the east plains would take no notice, if all was done properly, and there had been no exile of high blood now since Otger himself had ridden in as a gold-eyed youth five seasons back.

"Bring the priest," he ordered now. And Jonas went to fetch Thunur.

The man did not cringe as he came. Instead, he was bold at this fronting, his head up, and eyes blazing with the fire of the rage that always burned in him.

"I hear you wish to see me," Otger's gaze swept the fellow from head to foot and back again. Just so had he looked two days before at that wounded outlaw they had taken.

"Witchery, Sir Knight. Foul witchery has come by the Way Wind into l'Estal. It must be routed out. Already it has ensorcelled many—many, Sir Knight. Among them"—Thunur paused for a moment to make his next statement more portentous, "The Lady Almadis—"

"And who is this dealer in witchery?" Otger's voice was very calm. Ruddy hitched one shoulder. This priest would soon learn his lesson by all the signs.

Thus encouraged, Thunur spoke his tale, so swiftly that spittle accompanied the words he spewed forth. He ended with the listing of those who had borne away tokens of Meg's giving. And at the saying of some of those names, Otger's eyes narrowed a fraction.

"It is laid upon all true men and women to deal with witches as GORT has deemed right—with fire. This—this sluttish whore, and those brutes she brought with her—they must be slain; and those whom she has entoiled must be reasoned with—'less they too are tainted past cleansing."

"You name some who are above you, priest. Tongues that wag too freely can be cut from jaws. I would advise you to take heed of the need of silence for now—"

"For now?" Thunur repeated slowly.

"For now." Otger arose. "You seem to have an eye for such matters. Out with you to use that eye, but not the tongue, mind you!"

Thunur blinked. And then he turned and went. But Otger spoke to Ruddy. "Have the patrol keep an eye to that one. I have seen his like before—they can be well used if they are handled rightly, but if they are not under rein, they are useless and must be removed."

~

The market was alive. Though some of the sellers noted that there were more men at arms making their ways leisurely among the booths. However, since the border patrol had just returned, that might be expected.

Again Meg had taken her place, Mors behind her and Kaska's basket carefully out of the way. Her bouquet centered her table board. But those who came to look over her stock this day did not seem to note it particularly, nor did she all the morning lose any bloom from it for gifting.

Tod and Tay came by just before the nooning bell and brought her a basket Forina had promised. This time Nid walked behind them, his heavy-horned head swinging from side to side, as if he wished to keep a close eye on all about.

Just as he stepped up to exchange polite nose taps with Mors, one of the guards halted before Meg's display. He had the weather-roughened and darkened skin of a man who had spent many years around and about, and there was a small emblem caught fast in the mail shirt he wore that marked his rank.

"Fair day to you, herbwife." He studied her, and then his eyes dropped to her wares. "You have Ill-bane, I see."

"You see and you wonder, Guard Sergeant? Why?"

She took up the bundle of leaves. "It stands against evil, does it not—ill of body, ill of mind. What do they say of it? That if those of dark purpose strive to touch it, they are like to find a brand laid across their rash fingers."

"You know what they say of you, then?"

Meg smiled. "They say many things of me, Guard Sergeant Ruddy. It depends upon who says it. I have already been called witch—"

"And that does not alarm you?"

"Guard Sergeant Ruddy, when you are summoned to some duty, would any words from those not your officers turn you aside?"

"Duty—" he repeated. "Herbwife, I tell you that you may well have a right to fear."

"Fear and duty often ride comrades. But fear is the shadow and duty the substance. Look you"—she had laid down the bundle of leaves, turned her hand palm-up to show the unmarked flesh, and carried that gesture on so that as his eyes followed they touched the bouquet.

"Rowan leaf and berry," he said.

"Such as grow in hedgerows elsewhere." Meg pulled out the stem to show a pair of prick-defended leaves, a trefoil of berries.

Slowly he reached out and took it from her.

"Watch with care, herbwife." He did not tuck her gift into full sight as had the others who had taken such, but rather closed his fist tightly upon it and thrust that into his belt pouch.

~

Almadis stood by the window. One could catch a small sight of the market square from this vista. But she could not sight Meg's stall. She was stiff with anger, and yet she must watch her speech. It might be that she was caught at last, yet she could not bring herself to believe that.

"He rode in," she tried to keep her words even in tone, not make them such as could be used against her. "And with him he brought heads—heads of men! He would plant those as warnings! Warnings!"

"Against raiders, outlaws. They only understand such." That answering voice held weariness. "Their raids grow bolder—oftener. The land we hold, which supplies us with food, with that very robe you are wearing, cannot yield what we need when it is constantly under raid. Now, with the upper snows fast-going, we shall have them down upon us more and more. I know not what presses them these past few seasons, but they have grown bolder and bolder. We lost a farm to fire and sword—Otger collected payment. They deal in blood, thus we must also."

Almadis turned. "He is a man of blood," she said flatly.

"He holds the peace. You call him man of blood—well, and that he is in another way also. We are of ancient family, daughter—thrown aside though we may be. Rank weds with rank. Otger is the son of a House near equal to our own. Whom you wed will rule here afterward; he must be one born to such heritage. There is no one else."

She came to stand before her father where he sat in his high-back chair. And she was suddenly startled, then afraid. Somehow—somehow he had aged—and she had not seen it happening! He had always remained to her, until this hour, the strong leader l'Estal needed. He was old and to the old came death.

So for the moment she temporized. "Father, grant me a little more time. I cannot find it in me to like Otger—give me a little time." Her fingers were at her breast pressing against the hidden pendant, caressing the rose which still held both color and fragrance.

"Where got you that flower, Almadis?" There was a sharpness in his tone now.

Swiftly she told him of Meg, brought by the Way Wind, and of her stall in the market.

"I have heard a tale of witchery," he returned.

"Witchery? Do some then listen to that mad priest?" Almadis was disturbed. "She came with the Way Wind—from the west—she brings herbs such as we cannot grow—for the soothing of minds and bodies. She is but a girl, hardly more than a child. There is no evil in her!"

"Daughter, we are a people shunned, broken from our roots. There is shame, pain, anger eating at many of us. Such feelings are not easily put aside. And in some they take another form, seeking one upon whom blame may be thrown, one who may be made, after a fashion, to pay for all that which has caused us ill. Eyes have seen, ears have heard, lips reported—there are those who cry, witchery, yes. And very quickly such rumors can turn to action. This Meg may be a harmless trader—she may be the cause of an uprising. There is the ancient law for the westerners, one which we seldom invoke but which I turn to now—not only for the sake of town peace but for her safety also. This is the third day in the market—by sundown—"

Almadis swallowed back the protest she would have cried out. That her father spoke so seriously meant that indeed there might be forces brewing who might take fire in l'Estal. But on sudden impulse, she did say:

"Let me be the one to tell her so. I would not have her think that I have been unmindful of her gift." Once more she touched the rose.

"So be it. Also let it be that you think carefully on what else I have said to you. Time does not wait. I would have matters settled for your own good and for my duty."

So once more Almadis went down to the market and with her, without her asking, but rather as if they understood her unhappiness about this matter, there came Osono and Urgell. She noted in surprise that the bard had his harp case riding on his shoulder, as if he were on the way to some feast, and that Urgell went full armed.

It was midday, and Almadis looked about her somewhat puzzled for the usual crowd of those in the market, whether they came to buy and sell, or merely to spend time, was a small one. The man whose stall had neighbored Meg's was gone, and there were other empty spaces. Also there was a strange feeling which she could not quite put name to.

Ruddy, the guard sergeant, backed by two of his men, were pacing slowly along the rows of stalls. Now Urgell came a step forward so that he was at Almadis's right hand. His head was up, and he glanced right and left. Osono shifted the harp case a little, pulling loose his cloak so that the girl caught sight of his weapon, a span of tempered blade between a dagger and a sword in length.

If there had been a falling away of the crowd, that was not so apparent about the stall where Meg was busied as she had been since she first came into l'Estal. But those who had drifted toward her were a very mixed lot. Almadis recognized the tall bulk of the smith, and near shoulder to him was Tatwin, the scholar, his arm about the shoulders of a slight girl whose pale face suggested illness not yet past, while by her skirts trotted a small shaggy dog with purpose which seemed even more sustained than that of the two it accompanied.

There was also, somewhat to Almadis's surprise, Forina of the inn, and behind her wide bulk of body came Tod and Tay, once more grasping the horns of Nid with the suggestion about them that they were not going to lose touch with that four-footed warrior.

Others, too, a shambling-footed laborer from the farmlands, with one hand to the rope halter of a drooping-headed horse that might have drawn far too many carts or plows through weary seasons.

Just as they gathered, so did others in the marketplace draw apart. That feeling of menace which had been but a faint touch when Almadis trod out on this cobbled square grew.

There was movement in the alleyways, the streets, which led into that square. Others were appearing there who did not venture out into the sunlight.

Urgell's hand was at sword hilt. Almadis quickened pace to reach Meg's stall.

"Go! Oh, go quickly!" she burst out. "I do not know what comes, but there is evil rising here. Go while you can!"

Meg had not spread out her bundles of herbs. Now she looked to the Castellan's daughter and nodded. She picked up her staff and set to the crown of it the bouquet of flowers. The twins suddenly loosed their hold on Nid and pushed behind the board of the stall, shifting the panniers to Mors's back. Meg stooped and caught up the basket in which Kaska rode, settled it firmly within her arm crook.

"Witch—get the witch!" The scream arose from one of the alley mouths.

In a moment, Vill was beside Urgell, and Almadis saw that he carried with him his great hammer. Osono had shifted his harp well back on his shoulder to give him room for weapon play. There were others, too, who moved to join that line between Meg and the sulkers in the streets and alleys.

"To the gate," Almadis said. "If you bide with me, they will not dare to touch you!" She hoped that was true. But to make sure that these who threatened knew who and what she was and the protection she could offer, she pushed back her cloak hood that her face might be readily seen.

"To the gate," Ruddy appeared with his armsmen, added the authority of his own to the would-be defenders.

They retreated, all of them, bard, mercenary, smith, sergeant forming a rear guard. Only before the gate there were others—

A line of men drawn up, men who had been hardened by the riding of the borders, Otger's chosen. Before them stood the knight-captain himself.

"My lady," he said as they halted in confusion. "This is no place for you."

Almadis's hand went to Meg's arm. "Sir, if you come to give protection, that is well. But this much I shall do for myself, see an innocent woman free of any wrong—"

"You give me no choice then—" He snapped his fingers, and his men moved in, he a stride ahead plainly aiming to reach Almadis himself.

"Sir Knight," Almadis's hand was on her breast, and under it the moon token was warm. "I come not at your demand or that of any man, thank the Lady, save at a wish which is my own."

Otger's twisted mouth was a grimace of hate, and he lunged.

Only—

From the staff Meg held, there blazed a burst of rainbow-hued light. Otger and those with him cried out, raising their hands to their eyes and stumbled back. From behind Almadis and Meg moved Mors and Nid and the ancient horse, whose head was now raised, and those three pushed in among the guard, shouldering aside men who wavered and flailed out blindly.

Then Almadis was at the gate, and her hands were raised to the bar there. Beside her was the scholar, and with more force than either of them came Forina. So did the barrier to the freedom without fall. And they came out into the crisp wind without the walls, the very momentum of their efforts carrying them into the mouth of the Way Wind road.

There were cries behind them, and the screeching of voices, harsh and hurting. Almadis looked behind. All their strangely constituted party had won through the gates, the rear guard walking backward. Urgell and Osono had both drawn steel, and the smith held his hammer at ready. There were improvised clubs, a dagger or two, Ruddy's pike, but none were bloodied. Urgell and Ruddy, the smith beside them, slammed the gates fast.

Almadis could still hear the shouting of Otger, knew that they had perhaps only moments before they would be overwhelmed by those who were ready for a hunt.

Meg swung up her staff. There was no wide burst of light this time—rather a ray as straight as a sword blade. It crisscrossed the air before them, leaving behind a shimmer of light the width of the road, near as high as the wall behind them.

As she lowered her staff, she raised her other hand in salute to that shimmer, as if there waited behind it someone or thing she held in honor.

Then she spoke, and, though she did not shout, her words cried easily over the clamor behind them.

"Here is the Gate of Touching. The choice now lies with you all. There will be no hindrance for those going forward. And if you would go back, you shall find those behind will accept you again as you are.

"Those who come four-footed are comrades—the choice being theirs also. For what lies beyond accepts all life of equal worth. The comradeship of heart is enough.

"The choice is yours, so mote it be!"

She stood a little aside to give room, and Tod and Tay, laying hands once more to Nid's horns, went into the light. Behind them, his hand on the old horse's neck, the laborer trod, head up and firmly. Almadis stood beside Meg and watched them pass. None of them looked to her or Meg, it was as if they were drawn to something so great they had no longer only any knowledge of themselves, only of it.

At last there were those of the rear guard. Osono and Vill did not glance toward her. But Urgell, whose sword was once more within its sheath, dropped behind. Somehow her gaze was willed to meet his. The leaf Meg had given him was set in his battered helm as a plume, the plume that a leader might wear to some victory.

Almadis stirred. She stepped forward, to lay her hand on the one he held out to her as if they would tread some formal pattern which was long woven into being.

Meg steadied Kaska's basket on her hip, and looked up to the glimmer as Castellan's daughter and mercenary disappeared.

"Is it well-done, Lady?"

"It is well-done, dear daughter. So mote it be!"

With staff and basket held steady, Meg went forward, and when she passed the gate of light it vanished. The Way lay open once again to the scouring of the wind.

~

Madeleine L'Engle's witch woman seems to have several familiars: two cats (one black, one white), a leopard, and, most unusually—especially since the story is set in the American Deep South—a camel. The concept of a witch's familiar depends on one's idea of witchcraft. To medieval Christians sure witches were the Devil's minions, the familiar was an imp or low-level demon that assumed the form of an animal (or even a human) and assisted in magic-making. Others consider them spirits or supernatural beings that helped a witch. There is also some English and Scottish folkloric evidence that links fairies with familiars. Familiars are also credited in some lore with supernatural powers of their own— including the ability to take human shape—and provided the witch with companionship. Cats, dogs, toads, mice, and owls were the most common forms for familiars in Western culture. The black cat has become the stereotypical witch's familiar and, consequently, accrued various superstitions concerning bad luck. Two famous modern feline familiars include Gillian Holroyd's Siamese cat/familiar Pyewacket in Bell, Book, and Candle *(whose name dates back to at least the seventeenth century) and Salem Saberhagen, the talking black cat from the comic book and TV series* Sabrina, the Teenage Witch.

Poor Little Saturday
Madeleine L'Engle

The witch woman lived in a deserted, boarded-up plantation house, and nobody knew about her but me. Nobody in the nosy little town in south Georgia where I lived when I was a boy knew that if you walked down the dusty main street to where the post office ended it and then turned left and followed that road a piece until you got to the rusty iron gates of the drive to the plantation house, you could find goings-on would make your eyes pop out. It was just luck that I found out. Or maybe it wasn't luck at all. Maybe the witch woman wanted me to find out because of Alexandra. But now I wish I hadn't, because the witch woman and Alexandra are gone forever and it's much worse than if I'd never known them.

Nobody'd lived in the plantation house since the Civil War when Colonel Londermaine was killed and Alexandra Londermaine, his beautiful young wife, hung herself on the chandelier in the ballroom. A while before I was born some northerners bought it, but after a few years they stopped coming and people said it was because the house was haunted. Every few years a gang of boys or men would set out to explore the house but nobody ever found anything, and it was so well boarded up it was hard to force an entrance, so by and by the town lost interest in it. No one climbed the wall and wandered around the grounds except me.

I used to go there often during the summer because I had bad spells of malaria when sometimes I couldn't bear to lie on the iron bedstead in my room with the flies buzzing around my face, or out on the hammock on the porch with the screams and laughter of the other kids as they played, torturing my ears. My aching head made it impossible for me to read, and I would drag myself down the road, scuffling my bare, sun-burned toes in the dust, wearing the tattered straw hat that was supposed to protect me from the heat of the sun, shivering and sweating by turns. Sometimes it would seem hours before I got to the iron gates near which the brick wall was lowest. Often I would have to lie panting on the tall, prickly grass for minutes until I gathered strength to scale the wall and drop down on the other side.

But once inside the grounds it seemed cooler. One funny thing about my chills was that I didn't seem to shiver nearly as much when I could keep cool as I did at home where even the walls and the floors, if you touched them, were hot. The grounds were filled with live oaks that had grown up unchecked everywhere and afforded an almost continuous green shade. The ground was covered with ferns that were soft and cool to lie on, and when I flung myself down on my back and looked up, the roof of leaves was so thick that sometimes I couldn't see the sky at all. The sun that managed to filter through lost its bright, pitiless glare and came in soft yellow shafts that didn't burn you when they touched you.

~

One afternoon, a scorcher early in September, which is usually our hottest month (and by then you're fagged out by the heat, anyhow), I set out for the plantation. The heat lay coiled and shimmering on the road. When you looked at anything through it, it was like looking through a defective pane of glass. The dirt road was so hot that it burned even through my calloused feet, and as I walked clouds of dust rose in front of me and mixed with the shimmying of the heat. I thought I'd never make the plantation. Sweat was running into my eyes, but it was cold sweat, and I was shivering so that my teeth chattered as I walked. When I managed finally to fling myself down on my soft green bed of ferns inside the grounds, I was seized with one of the worst chills I'd ever had in spite of the fact that my mother had given me an extra dose of quinine that morning and some 666 Malaria Medicine to boot. I shut my eyes tight and clutched the ferns with my hands and teeth to wait until the chill had passed, when I heard a soft voice call:

"Boy."

I thought at first I was delirious, because sometimes I got light-headed when my bad attacks came on; only then I remembered that when I was delirious I didn't know it; all the strange things I saw and heard seemed perfectly natural. So when the voice said, "Boy," again, as soft and clear as the mockingbird at sunrise, I opened my eyes.

Kneeling near me on the ferns was a girl. She must have been about a year younger than I. I was almost sixteen so I guess she was fourteen or fifteen. She was dressed in a blue and white gingham dress; her face was very pale, but the kind of paleness that's supposed to be, not the sickly pale kind that was like mine showing even under the tan. Her eyes were big and very blue. Her hair was dark brown and she wore it parted in the middle in two heavy braids that were swinging in front of her shoulders as she peered into my face.

"You don't feel well, do you?" she asked. There was no trace of concern or worry in her voice. Just scientific interest.

I shook my head. "No," I whispered, almost afraid that if I talked she would vanish, because I had never seen anyone here before, and I thought that maybe I was dying because I felt so awful, and I thought maybe that gave me the power to see the ghost. But the girl in blue and white checked gingham seemed, as I watched her, to be good flesh and blood.

"You'd better come with me," she said. "She'll make you all right."

"Who's she?"

"Oh—just Her," she said.

My chill had begun to recede by then, so when she got up off her knees, I scrambled up, too. When she stood up her dress showed a white ruffled petticoat underneath it, and bits of green moss had left patterns on her knees and I didn't think that would happen to the knees of a ghost, so I followed her as she led the way toward the house. She did not go up the sagging, half-rotted steps that led to the veranda, about whose white pillars wisteria vines climbed in wild profusion, but went around to the side of the house where there were slanting doors to a cellar. The sun and rain had long since blistered and washed off the paint, but the doors looked clean and were free of the bits of bark from the eucalyptus tree that leaned nearby and that had dropped its bits of dusty peel on either side; so I knew that these cellar stairs must frequently be used.

The girl opened the cellar doors. "You go down first," she said. I went down the cellar steps, which were stone and cool against my bare feet. As she followed me she closed the cellar doors after her and as I reached the bottom of the stairs we were in pitch darkness. I began to be very frightened until her soft voice came out of the black.

"Boy, where are you?"

"Right here."

"You'd better take my hand. You might stumble."

We reached out and found each other's hands in the darkness. Her fingers were long and cool and they closed firmly around mine. She moved with authority as though she knew her way with the familiarity born of custom.

"Poor Sat's all in the dark," she said, "but he likes it that way. He likes to sleep for weeks at a time. Sometimes he snores awfully. Sat, darling!" she called gently. A soft, bubbly, blowing sound came in answer, and she laughed happily. "Oh, Sat, you are sweet!" she said, and the bubbly sound came again. Then the girl pulled at my hand and we came out into a huge and dusty kitchen. Iron skillets, pots, and pans were still hanging on either side of the huge stove, and there was a rolling pin and a bowl of flour on the marble-topped table in the middle of the room. The girl took a lighted candle off the shelf.

"I'm going to make cookies," she said as she saw me looking at the flour and the rolling pin. She slipped her hand out of mine. "Come along." She began to walk more rapidly. We left the kitchen, crossed the hall, went through the dining room, its old mahogany table thick with dust, although sheets covered the pictures on the walls. Then we went into the ballroom. The mirrors lining the walls were spotted and discolored; against one wall was a single delicate gold chair, its seat cushioned with pale rose and silver woven silk; it seemed extraordinarily well preserved. From the ceiling hung the huge chandelier from which Alexandra Londermaine had hung herself, its prisms catching and breaking up into a hundred colors the flickering of the candle and the few shafts of light that managed to slide in through the boarded-up windows. As we crossed the ballroom, the girl began to dance by herself, gracefully, lightly, so that her full, blue and white checked gingham skirts flew out around her. She looked at herself with pleasure in the old mirrors as she danced, the candle flaring and guttering in her right hand.

"You've stopped shaking. Now what will I tell Her?" she said as we started to climb the broad mahogany staircase. It was very dark so she took my hand again, and before we had reached the top of the stairs I obliged her by being seized by another chill. She felt my trembling fingers with satisfaction. "Oh, you've started again. That's good." She slid open one of the huge double doors at the head of the stairs.

As I looked in to what once must have been Colonel Londermaine's study, I thought that surely what I saw was a scene in a dream or a vision in delirium. Seated at the huge table in the center of the room was the most extraordinary woman I had ever seen. I felt that she must be very beautiful, although she would never have fulfilled any of the standards of beauty set by our town. Even though she was seated, I felt that she must be immensely tall. Piled up on the table in front of her were several huge volumes, and her finger was marking the place in the open one in front of her, but she was not reading. She was leaning back in the carved chair, her head resting against a piece of blue and gold embroidered silk that was flung across the chair back, one hand gently stroking a fawn that lay sleeping in her lap. Her eyes were closed and somehow I couldn't imagine what color they would be. It wouldn't have surprised me if they had been shining amber or the deep purple of her velvet robe. She had a great quantity of hair, the color of mahogany in firelight, which was cut quite short and seemed to be blown wildly about her head like flame. Under her closed eyes were deep shadows, and lines of pain were about her mouth. Otherwise there were no marks of age on her face but I would not have been surprised to learn that she was any age in the world—a hundred or twenty-five. Her mouth was large and mobile, and she was singing something in a deep, rich voice. Two cats, one black, one white, were coiled up, each on a book, and as we opened the doors a leopard stood up quietly beside her but did not snarl or move. It simply stood there and waited, watching us.

The girl nudged me and held her finger to her lips to warn me to be quiet, but I would not have spoken—could not, anyhow, my teeth were chattering so from my chill, which I had completely forgotten, so fascinated was I by this woman sitting back with her head against the embroidered silk, soft, deep sounds coming out of her throat. At last these sounds resolved themselves into words, and we listened to her as she sang. The cats slept indifferently, but the leopard listened, too:

> "I sit high in my ivory tower,
> The heavy curtains drawn.
> I've many a strange and lustrous flower,
> A leopard and a fawn
> Together sleeping by my chair
> And strange birds softly winging,
> And ever pleasant to my ear
> Twelve maidens' voices singing.
> Here is my magic maps' array,
> My mystic circle's flame.
> With symbol's art He lets me play,
> The unknown my domain,
> And as I sit here in my dream
> I see myself awake,
> Hearing a torn and bloody scream,
> Feeling my castle shake . . . "

Her song wasn't finished but she opened her eyes and looked at us. Now that his mistress knew we were here, the leopard seemed ready to spring and devour me at one gulp, but she put her hand on his sapphire-studded collar to restrain him.

"Well, Alexandra," she said, "whom have we here?"

The girl, who still held my hand in her long, cool fingers, answered, "It's a boy."

"So I see. Where did you find him?"

The voice sent shivers up and down my spine.

"In the fern bed. He was shaking. See? He's shaking now. Is he having a fit?" Alexandra's voice was filled with pleased interest.

"Come here, boy," the woman said.

As I didn't move, Alexandra gave me a push, and I advanced slowly. As I came near, the woman pulled one of the leopard's ears gently, saying, "Lie down, Thammuz." The beast obeyed, flinging itself at her feet. She held her hand out to me as I approached the table, If Alexandra's fingers felt firm and cool, hers had the strength of the ocean and the coolness of jade. She looked at me for a long time and I saw that her eyes were deep blue, much bluer than Alexandra's, so dark as to be almost black. When she spoke again her voice was warm and tender: "You're burning up with fever. One of the malaria bugs?" I nodded. "Well, we'll fix that for you."

When she stood and put the sleeping fawn down by the leopard, she was not as tall as I had expected her to be; nevertheless she gave an impression of great height. Several of the bookshelves in one corner were emptied of books and filled with various shaped bottles and retorts. Nearby was a large skeleton. There was an acid-stained washbasin, too; that whole section of the room looked like part of a chemist's or physicist's laboratory. She selected from among the bottles a small, amber-colored one and poured a drop of the liquid it contained into a glass of water. As the drop hit the water, there was a loud hiss and clouds of dense smoke arose. When they had drifted away, she handed the glass to me and said, "Drink. Drink, my boy!"

My hand was trembling so that I could scarcely hold the glass. Seeing this, she took it from me and held it to my lips.

"What is it?" I asked.

"Drink it," she said, pressing the rim of the glass against my teeth. On the first swallow I started to choke and would have pushed the stuff away, but she forced the rest of the burning liquid down my throat. My whole body felt on fire. I felt flame flickering in every vein, and the room and everything in it swirled around. When I had regained my equilibrium to a certain extent, I managed to gasp out again, "What is it?"

She smiled and answered,

"Nine peacocks' hearts, four bats' tongues,
A pinch of moon dust, and a hummingbird's lungs."

Then I asked a question I would never have dared ask if it hadn't been that I was still half drunk from the potion I had swallowed. "Are you a witch?"

She smiled again and answered, "I make it my profession."

Since she hadn't struck me down with a flash of lightning, I went on. "Do you ride a broomstick?"

This time she laughed. "I can when I like."

"Is it—is it very hard?"

"Rather like a bucking bronco at first, but I've always been a good horsewoman, and now I can manage very nicely. I've finally progressed to sidesaddle, though I still feel safer astride. I always rode my horse astride.

Still, the best witches ride sidesaddle, so . . . Now run along home. Alexandra has lessons to study and I must work. Can you hold your tongue or must I make you forget?"

"I can hold my tongue."

She looked at me and her eyes burnt into me like the potion she had given me to drink, "Yes, I think you can," she said. "Come back tomorrow if you like. Thammuz will show you out."

The leopard rose and led the way to the door. As I hesitated, unwilling to tear myself away, it came back and pulled gently but firmly on my trouser leg.

"Good-bye, boy," the witch woman said. "And you won't have any more chills and fever."

"Good-bye," I answered. I didn't say thank you. I didn't say good-bye to Alexandra. I followed the leopard out.

~

She let me come every day. I think she must have been lonely. After all, I was the only thing there with a life apart from hers. And in the long run the only reason I have had a life of my own is because of her. I am as much a creation of the witch woman's as Thammuz the leopard was, or the two cats, Ashtaroth and Orus. (It wasn't until many years after the last day I saw the witch woman that I learned that those were the names of the fallen angels.)

She did cure my malaria, too. My parents and the townspeople thought that I had outgrown it. I grew angry when they talked about it so lightly and wanted to tell them that it was the witch woman, but I knew that if ever I breathed a word about her I would be eternally damned. Mama thought we should write a testimonial letter to the 666 Malaria Medicine people, and maybe they'd send us a couple of dollars.

Alexandra and I became very good friends. She was a strange, aloof creature. She liked me to watch her while she danced alone in the ballroom or played on an imaginary harp—though sometimes I fancied I could hear the music. One day she took me into the drawing room and uncovered a portrait that was hung between two of the long, boarded-up windows. Then she stepped back and held her candle high so as to throw the best light on the picture. It might have been a picture of Alexandra herself, or Alexandra as she might be in five years.

"That's my mother," she said. "Alexandra Londermaine."

As far as I knew from the tales that went about town, Alexandra Londermaine had given birth to only one child, and that stillborn, before she had hung herself on the chandelier in the ballroom—and anyhow, any child of hers would have been this Alexandra's mother or grandmother. But I didn't say anything, because when Alexandra got angry she became ferocious like one of the cats and was given to leaping on me, scratching and biting. I looked at the portrait long and silently.

"You see, she has on a ring like mine," Alexandra said, holding out her left hand, on the fourth finger of which was the most beautiful sapphire and diamond ring I had ever seen—or rather, that I could ever have imagined, for it was a ring apart from any owned by even the most wealthy of the townsfolk. Then I realized that Alexandra had brought me in here and unveiled the portrait simply that she might show me the ring to better advantage, for she had never worn a ring before.

"Where did you get it?"

"Oh, She got it for me last night."

"Alexandra," I asked suddenly, "how long have you been here?"

"Oh, awhile."

"But how long?"

"Oh, I don't remember."

"But you must remember."

"I don't. I just came—like Poor Sat."

"Who's Poor Sat?" I asked, thinking for the first time of whoever it was that had made the gentle bubbly noises at Alexandra the day she found me in the fern bed.

"Why, we've never shown you Sat, have we!" she exclaimed. "I'm sure it's all right, but we'd better ask Her first."

So we went to the witch woman's room and knocked. Thammuz pulled the door open with his strong teeth and the witch woman looked up from some sort of experiment she was making with test tubes and retorts. The fawn, as usual, lay sleeping near her feet. "Well?" she said.

"Is it all right if I take him to see Poor Little Saturday?" Alexandra asked her.

"Yes, I suppose so," she answered. "But no teasing." And she turned her back to us and bent again over her test tubes as Thammuz nosed us out of the room.

We went down to the cellar. Alexandra lit a lamp and took me back to the corner farthest from the doors, where there was a stall. In the stall was a two-humped camel. I couldn't help laughing as I looked at him because he grinned at Alexandra so foolishly, displaying all his huge buckteeth and blowing bubbles through them.

"She said we weren't to tease him," Alexandra said severely, rubbing her cheek against the preposterous splotchy hair that seemed to be coming out, leaving bald pink spots of skin on his long nose.

"But what—" I started.

"She rides him sometimes." Alexandra held out her hand while he nuzzled against it, scratching his rubbery lips against the diamond and sapphire of her ring. "Mostly She talks to him. She says he is very wise. He goes up to Her room sometimes and they talk and talk. I can't understand a word they say. She says it's Hindustani and Arabic. Sometimes I can remember little bits of it, like: *iderow*, *sorcabatcha*, and *anna bibed bech*. She says I can learn to speak with them when I finish learning French and Greek."

Poor Little Saturday was rolling his eyes in delight as Alexandra scratched behind his ears. "Why is he called Poor Little Saturday?" I asked.

Alexandra spoke with a ring of pride in her voice. "I named him. She let me."

"But why did you name him that?"

"Because he came last winter on the Saturday that was the shortest day of the year, and it rained all day so it got light later and dark earlier than it would have if it had been nice, so it really didn't have as much of itself as it should, and I felt so sorry for it I thought maybe it would feel better if we named him after it. . . . She thought it was a nice name!" She turned on me suddenly.

"Oh, it is! It's a fine name!" I said quickly, smiling to myself as I realized how much greater was this compassion of Alexandra's for a day than any she might have for a human being. "How did She get him?" I asked.

"Oh, he just came."

"What do you mean?"

"She wanted him so he came. From the desert."

"He *walked*?"

"Yes. And swam part of the way. She met him at the beach and flew him here on the broomstick. You should have seen him. He was still all wet and looked so funny. She gave him hot coffee with things in it."

"What things?"

"Oh, just things."

Then the witch woman's voice came from behind us. "Well, children?"

It was the first time I had seen her out of her room. Thammuz was at her right heel, the fawn at her left. The cats, Ashtaroth and Orus, had evidently stayed upstairs. "Would you like to ride Saturday?" she asked me.

Speechless, I nodded. She put her hand against the wall and a portion of it slid down into the earth so that Poor Little Saturday was free to go out. "She's sweet, isn't she?" the witch woman asked me, looking affectionately at the strange, bumpy-kneed, splay-footed creature. "Her grandmother was very good to me in Egypt once. Besides, I love camel's milk."

"But Alexandra said she was a he!" I exclaimed.

"Alexandra's the kind of woman to whom all animals are he except cats, and all cats are she. As a matter of fact, Ashtaroth and Orus are she, but it wouldn't make any difference to Alexandra if they weren't. Go on out, Saturday. Come on!"

Saturday backed out, bumping her bulging knees and ankles against her stall, and stood under a live oak tree. "Down," the witch woman said. Saturday leered at me and didn't move. "Down, *sorcabatcha!*" the witch woman commanded, and Saturday obediently got down on her knees. I clambered up onto her, and before I had managed to get at all settled she rose with such a jerky motion that I knocked my chin against her front hump and nearly bit my tongue off. Round and round Saturday danced while I clung wildly to her front hump and the witch woman and Alexandra rolled on the ground with laughter. I felt as though I were on a very unseaworthy vessel on the high seas, and it wasn't long before I felt violently seasick as Saturday pranced among the live oak trees, sneezing delicately.

At last the witch woman called out, "Enough!" and Saturday stopped in her traces, nearly throwing me, and knelt laboriously. "It was mean to tease you," the witch woman said, pulling my nose gently. "You may come sit in my room with me for a while if you like."

There was nothing I liked better than to sit in the witch woman's room and to watch her while she studied from her books, worked out strange-looking mathematical problems, argued with the zodiac, or conducted complicated experiments with her test tubes and retorts, sometimes filling the room with sulphurous odors or flooding it with red or blue light. Only once was I afraid of her, and that was when she danced with the skeleton in the corner. She had the room flooded with a strange red glow, and I almost thought I could see the flesh covering the bones of the skeleton as they danced together like lovers. I think she had forgotten that I was sitting there, half hidden in the wing chair, because when they had finished dancing and the skeleton stood in the corner again, his bones shining and polished, devoid of any living trappings, she stood with her forehead against one of the deep red velvet curtains that covered the boarded-up windows and tears streamed down her cheeks. Then she went back to her test tubes and worked feverishly. She never alluded to the incident and neither did I.

As winter drew on she let me spend more and more time in the room. Once I gathered up courage enough to ask her about herself, but I got precious little satisfaction.

"Well, then, are you maybe one of the northerners who bought the place?"

"Let's leave it at that, boy. We'll say that's who I am. Did you know that my skeleton was old Colonel Londermaine? Not so old, as a matter of fact; he was only thirty-seven when he was killed at the battle of Bunker Hill—or am I getting him confused with his great-grandfather, Rudolph Londermaine? Anyhow he was only thirty-seven, and a fine figure of a man, and Alexandra only thirty when she hung herself for love of him on the chandelier in the ballroom. Did you know that the fat man with the red mustache has been trying to cheat your father? His cow will give sour milk for seven days. Run along now and talk to Alexandra. She's lonely."

When the winter had turned to spring and the camellias and azaleas and Cape Jessamine had given way to the more lush blooms of early May, I kissed Alexandra for the first time, very clumsily. The next evening when I managed to get away from the chores at home and hurried out to the plantation, she gave me her sapphire and diamond ring, which she had strung for me on a narrow bit of turquoise satin.

"It will keep us both safe," she said, "if you wear it always. And then when we're older we can get married and you can give it back to me. Only you mustn't let anyone see it, ever, ever, or She'd be very angry."

I was afraid to take the ring but when I demurred Alexandra grew furious and started kicking and biting and I had to give in.

Summer was almost over before my father discovered the ring hanging about my neck. I fought like a witch boy to keep him from pulling out the narrow ribbon and seeing the ring, and indeed the ring seemed to give me added strength, and I had grown, in any case, much stronger during the winter than I had ever been in my life. But my father was still stronger than I, and he pulled it out. He looked at it in dead silence for a moment and then the storm broke. That was the famous Londermaine ring that had disappeared the night Alexandra Londermaine hung herself. That ring was worth a fortune. Where had I got it?

No one believed me when I said I had found it in the grounds near the house—I chose the grounds because I didn't want anybody to think I had been in the house or indeed that I was able to get in. I don't know why they didn't believe me; it still seems quite logical to me that I might have found it buried among the ferns.

It had been a long, dull year, and the men of the town were all bored. They took me and forced me to swallow quantities of corn liquor until I didn't know what I was saying or doing. When they had finished with me, I didn't even manage to reach home before I was violently sick and then I was in my mother's arms and she was weeping over me. It was morning before I was able to slip away to the plantation house. I ran pounding up the mahogany stairs to the witch woman's room and opened the heavy sliding doors without knocking. She stood in the center of the room in her purple robe, her arms around Alexandra, who was weeping bitterly. Overnight the room had completely changed. The skeleton of Colonel Londermaine was gone, and books filled the shelves in the corner of the room that had been her laboratory. Cobwebs were everywhere, and broken glass lay on the floor; dust was inches thick on her worktable. There was no sign of Thammuz, Ashtaroth or Orus, or the fawn, but four birds were flying about her, beating their wings against her hair.

She did not look at me or in any way acknowledge my presence. Her arm about Alexandra, she led her out of the room and to the drawing room where the portrait hung. The birds followed, flying around and around them. Alexandra had stopped weeping now. Her face was very proud and pale, and if she saw me miserably trailing behind them she gave no notice. When the witch woman stood in front of the portrait the sheet fell from it. She raised her arm; there was a great cloud of smoke; the smell of sulphur filled my nostrils, and when the smoke was gone, Alexandra was gone, too. Only the portrait was there, the fourth finger of the left hand now bearing no ring. The witch woman raised her hand again and the sheet lifted itself up and covered the portrait. Then she went, with the birds, slowly back to what had once been her room, and still I tailed after, frightened as I had never been before in my life, or have been since.

She stood without moving in the center of the room for a long time. At last she turned and spoke to me.

"Well, boy, where is the ring?"

"They have it."

"They made you drunk, didn't they?"

"Yes."

"I was afraid something like this would happen when I gave Alexandra the ring. But it doesn't matter. . . . I'm tired. . . . " She drew her hand wearily across her forehead.

"Did I—did I tell them everything?"

"You did."

"I—I didn't know."

"1 know you didn't know, boy."

"Do you hate me now?"

"No, boy, I don't hate you."

"Do you have to go away?"

"Yes."

I bowed my head, "I'm so sorry. . . . "

She smiled slightly. "The sands of time . . . cities crumble and rise and will crumble again and breath dies down and blows once more . . . "

~

The birds flew madly about her head, pulling at her hair, calling into her ears. Downstairs we could hear a loud pounding, and then the crack of boards being pulled away from a window.

"Go, boy," she said to me. I stood rooted, motionless, unable to move. "Go!" she commanded, giving me a mighty push so that I stumbled out of the room. They were waiting for me by the cellar doors and caught me as I climbed out. I had to stand there and watch when they came out with her. But it wasn't the witch woman, my witch woman. It was their idea of a witch woman, someone thousands of years old, a disheveled old creature in rusty black, with long wisps of gray hair, a hooked nose, and four wiry black hairs springing out of the mole on her chin. Behind her flew the four birds, and suddenly they went up, up, into the sky, directly in the path of the sun until they were lost in its burning glare.

Two of the men stood holding her tightly, although she wasn't struggling but standing there, very quiet, while the others searched the house, searched it in vain. Then as a group of them went down into the cellar I remembered, and by a flicker of the old light in the witch woman's eyes I could see that she remembered, too. Poor Little Saturday had been forgotten. Out she came, prancing absurdly up the cellar steps, her rubbery lips stretched back over her gigantic teeth, her eyes bulging with terror. When she saw the witch woman, her lord and master, held captive by two dirty, insensitive men, she let out a shriek and began to kick and lunge wildly, biting, screaming with the blood-curdling, heart-rending screams that only a camel can make. One of the men fell to the ground, holding a leg in which the bone had snapped from one of Saturday's kicks. The others scattered in terror, leaving the witch woman standing on the veranda supporting herself by clinging to one of the huge wisteria vines that curled around the columns. Saturday clambered up onto the veranda and knelt while she flung herself between the two humps. Then off they ran, Saturday still screaming, her knees knocking together, the ground shaking as she pounded along. Down from the sun plummeted the four birds and flew after them.

Up and down I danced, waving my arms, shouting wildly until Saturday and the witch woman and the birds were lost in a cloud of dust, while the man with the broken leg lay moaning on the ground beside me.

~

Nancy Holder's witches fly on jets as well as brooms. Supernatural flight (also known as transvection) on a broomstick is one of the most common attributes of witches. The classic witch's broom is a bundle of twigs or straw tied around a central pole—a besom or besom broom. From the fifteenth century on, it was thought that witches applied a magical ointment to themselves or the broomstick in order to fly. Flying, however, was a point of some contention among serious demonologists of the day. Some felt witches flew only in spirit, not in body, or that the salve contained hallucinogenic ingredients that made witches think they were flying.

Nowadays, thanks to J.K. Rowling, we know that flying broomsticks have come a long way—at least in fantasy. In her wizarding world there is a wide range of broomsticks—from the family-friendly reliable Bluebottle model to Harry Potter's state-of-the-art, Quidditch-winning Firebolt. Still, even the Firebolt is a direct descendent of the medieval besom: its tail is described (in Harry Potter and the Prisoner of Azkaban*) as being made of "perfectly smooth, streamlined birch twigs." In the movie version the twigs aren't even smooth or streamlined; it looks quite besom-like.*

The Only Way to Fly
Nancy Holder

Jessamyne was either gazing out the window or dozing when Drucilla's scratchy Cockney twang pierced her right eardrum.

"Blimey!" Drucilla cried. "The movie's *Bell, Book and Candle*. Oh, isn't that just too right?"

"How nice," Jessamyne said mildly. Her own accent, very Received Standard, very prim and proper, rang as condescending, though she didn't mean it to be.

"Oh, and we're 'aving eye of newt for tea!"

That got Jessamyne's interest. How many years since she'd tasted that delicacy? Of course she knew the answer: Since she had married Michael

Wood. From that point on, everything had fallen away, everything had changed, more drastically than she could have imagined.

"'Course it's airline food," Drucilla said speculatively. There seemed to be a bit of the old Romany line in her high cheekbones and hooked nose, the wart on the end of her chin. She gave a tug on the brim of her steepled hat (Jessamyne had put her own, newly purchased, in the overhead bin shortly after takeoff, finding the size and weight of it uncomfortable) and looked every part the witch she was.

Jessamyne was not so lucky. After all the time she had lived undercover, it was difficult to "let it all hang out," as the kids used to say. The kids of the last century, at any rate. If one looked into a mirror—or, in this case, the window over the ice-coated wing of a large silver jetliner—one saw a rather pleasant, plump old lady with a dumpling face, square glasses perched on the tip of her nose, and gray hair pulled back in a bun. Not the stuff of nightmares.

She sighed wistfully. Not even the stuff of a second, startled glance.

"I wonder if it's fresh," Drucilla went on. She wrinkled up her fabulous nose and pulled back her lips, showing awe-inspiring jagged yellow teeth. "No doubt they'll zap it." She laughed at her double entendre and pantomimed enchanting an object with a magic wand. "Not 'abracadabra' zap. I mean microwave."

"Yes." Jessamyne settled back in her seat and thought about taking out her knitting. Michael had loved to watch her knit as they sat by the fire. But everyone else here would probably cackle at her; witches did not knit, not even those on the brink of retirement.

She surveyed the others. Pointed hats, a few white ruffled bonnets on the really old witches. Some wore buttons they had purchased at the airport gift shop: I SURVIVED THE INQUISITION, OLD WITCHES NEVER DIE, THEY JUST LOSE THEIR MAGIC. I ♥ BLACK CATS. They were chatting and laughing, milling in the aisles, waving at ancient friends now reunited with them—in short, having a high old time.

Jessamyne only dimly remembered a few of their faces. Along with everything else, she had given up attending Sabbats and Samhains. All Hallows' Eve found her handing out candy to little mortals. And how many times had she hidden her tears from Michael on the various Friday the Thirteenths, remembering all the fun she used to have? Curdling milk, backing up chimneys—ah, those had been good days!

And now those days were nothing more than memories. Michael was gone the way of all mortal men, and she, old before her time, was on her way to the Royal Home for English Witches in Kent. Gathered with some other British war brides—those wars ranging from the French and Indian War, the Revolutionary War, the War Between the States, and so forth—she was going home.

But could it be that she and she alone was the only witch who had stopped using her powers to please her husband? Surely not; there had been an American television series about that very thing. *Bewitched*. She had watched it not so much for amusement as for instruction, and had found it soothing on those days when it just didn't make much sense not to launch her husband to the top of his profession, conjure up expensive cars and beautiful clothes and gems for herself, and keep them both young-looking as long as possible. *No, no, no*, he had insisted. And, because she loved him, she had obeyed him.

Now, her powers fading both with disuse and with age—though she was only three hundred and twelve years old—she wondered if she had done the right thing.

"Miss, miss!" Drucilla cried, waving her hand in the air. "Miss!"

"Yes, ma'am?" A flight attendant bustled over. Oh, fabulous creature. She wore a short, tight black dress draped over her bosom and a heavy necklace of jet shaped into a bat. Her black hair fell to the small of her back. Jessamyne's hair had been black. At first she had had to bleach it gray to match Michael's as he aged (so rapidly!) but very quickly it began to lighten and to dull. It would take powerful restorative magic to blacken it now. That, or a visit to a beauty parlor. How they would laugh at her for that.

"The newt, is it fresh?"

The stewardess smiled kindly. "I'm afraid not, ma'am. But we do have a nice dessert of floating toad."

"Oh, bloody good!" Drucilla clapped her hands together. "Jessamyne, isn't that wonderful?"

Jessamyne winced. She had never fallen into the American habit of calling perfect strangers by their first names. But they were all wearing name tags emblazoned with HELLO, MY NAME IS and their names printed in thick red ink. (It was supposed to look like blood, but it didn't. It didn't smell like blood, either, so what was the point?)

"Oh, yes, yummy toads for all you nice ladies," the beautiful young attendant went on, including Jessamyne in her smile. Jessamyne had a dismal image of someone in a nurse's cap and dress saying exactly the same thing in one or two days' time.

She shifted uncomfortably. Perhaps this was all a big mistake. She had thought that returning to the Sisterhood would be a wonderful thing. Her thirst for coven life had gone unquenched for over sixty years, and the idea of spending her last century or so with rooms and rooms of other aged witches had been nothing less than an oasis to her. But was it a mirage? As she looked around at the humped old ladies, she thought, *Am I like that? How did it happen so soon?*

As the kids of today also said: *Use it or lose it.*

"More Bloody Marys!" an old crone shouted three rows away.

The stewardess smiled again at them both and said, "Anything you ladies need, y'all just let me know." She had a slight Texas twang. Michael had had relatives in Texas.

Oh, Michael. She pushed the recline button on her seat and closed her eyes, allowing his image to enter her mind's eye even though it still hurt. She remembered when she had first seen him, fresh from battle—he had conquered the beach in Normandy! She was visiting a cousin in the London hospital, a warlock once removed who had insisted on doing his bit for Britain, and had actually been wounded. (No one knew how that had happened! There had been a few jokes about his patrimony—the milkman, the mailman, the Grand Inquisitor, and so on, but he had taken them all with good grace.)

Michael had lain in his hospital cot, so dashing and heroic, his arm in a sling, his vivid blue eyes shining from beneath his bandaged forehead. The attraction had been so intense, so complete, that Jessamyne simply assumed he was a warlock friend of her cousin out to enchant her. Imagine her dismay when she learned that he was mortal. Her family's fury when she had married him and announced they were moving back to America. How it had hurt to leave them all!

The homesickness. And then, Michael's edict: No Witchcraft. None. Not even for protection. He would not have it. And if she would not agree to it, he would send her flying back to England.

"In an airplane," he had added firmly.

Alone, perplexed, homesick, and desperately in love, she had agreed.

At first, it had been terrible for her. The laborious chores, done by her instead of familiars and enchanted household appliances, the endless sameness of mortal life. Watching herself age, and doing nothing about it. But worst of all, feeling her powers weaken from lack of use.

But what could she do? If she did otherwise, she would lose Michael's love. And that was a power she had no ability to withstand. So perhaps he had been a warlock after all. At the least, a demon lover.

She managed a wistful smile. Drucilla misread it, saying, "Isn't it wonderful, how they're taking care of us?"

"Oh, yes, quite," Jessamyne said. Taking care of us. That's what Michael had said when he had laid down the law: *I want to take care of you, Jessie. It makes me feel like a man.*

How puzzled she had been, and how confused. But she had permitted it, even perhaps growing to like it.

She thought of the brochure for the Home: *Three meals a day to tuck into! Your own room with a lovely view of the Kentish countryside. Our staff on hand twenty-four hours a day to anticipate your every need.*

Her every need. She didn't suppose they would let her fly Aphrodite, her trusty broom, but she had brought her nonetheless. She barely knew how to ride anymore, had fallen off last night when she'd tried to take one last turn around the small Connecticut village where she had lived with Michael. They would probably pack Aphrodite away somewhere where she would be "safe."

"No!" she cried. She clapped her hands. "This is a terrible mistake! What are we doing?"

Drucilla stared at her goggle-eyed. "Jessamyne?"

"You've forgotten," Jessamyne said. "You don't remember the glory. The wonder. Think for a moment. Think of riding the moon! Riding the night wind! Think how splendid! How free, how marvelous!" She squeezed Drucilla's biceps. "Remember it!"

"What?"

"Or will you go off to the airy coffin in Kent with everyone waiting on you?"

"Coffin? Coffin?" Drucilla echoed, distressed. "I thought we were going to a pensioners' home!"

"Let's get out, go, before it's too late," Jessamyne told her fiercely. She raised her voice and called, "Aphrodite!" There was a rumbling beneath their feet.

Then parts of the floor whooshed up toward the ceiling, as Aphrodite flew into the compartment and hovered beside Jessamyne. The flight attendant hurried toward the broom, repairing the floor with a wave of her hand as she said, "I'm sorry, ma'am, but all brooms must be safely stowed in the baggage compartment."

"Move, move," Jessamyne hissed at Drucilla, who got out of her seat and took a few steps down the aisle, out of the way.

Jessamyne grabbed Aphrodite by the handle. The broom nickered in her grasp. "Gone!" she shouted, pointing at the nearest window. It shattered instantly. Wind howled around them, the suction pulled at everything in the plane.

"Madam!" the stewardess remonstrated, raising her hands to repair the damage.

Jessamyne hopped on Aphrodite and shot through the window. A few loose pieces of straw were caught in the window as it sealed up again.

And then she was outside the plane in the icy night, the howling blackness, with a half moon overhead. At first she faltered, plummeting a thousand feet downward, but she felt the blood move in her veins again, felt the magic circulating again.

"Aieee, hee-hee-hee-hee!" she shrieked, speeding to catch up with the plane. She flew, she soared, she turned in huge circles. Aphrodite reared and pranced beneath her hands. The old broom was overjoyed to be back among the stars.

Through ice clouds she flew until she was beside the large jet. Hundreds of witches peering at her, some in shock, some with tears in their eyes. A few were cheering. To those she called, "Come on!"

Suddenly a dozen windows popped and a dozen witches flew out. A dozen more, and more. Soon there were a hundred. They coursed behind Jessamyne, shrieking and cackling, calling to the others in the plane.

"Freedom!" shouted an aged witch with wispy green hair.

"A new coven!" another cried.

"A new queen!"

They looked admiringly at Jessamyne. "Let's ride, sisters!" she cried, with her fist above her head. "And as the Dark Brother is my witness, we'll never eat oatmeal ever!"

"Aye!" they all cried as one, even all the very old witches who could barely stay astride their brooms.

"To England! And Spain! And Japan! To curdle milk and make two-headed calves!" Jessamyne grinned and jerked her head toward the jet. "And to terrify old ladies who have forgotten how to live!"

"Aye!" came the shout all around her like a thunderclap. With Jessamyne at their head, they screamed into the night, flying as witches were meant to fly to their dying day . . . and as all wise witches do!

Ceren, in Richard Park's story, is considered to be young for a "wise woman," but she soon shows she is wise not only beyond her own years but beyond the "wisdom" she was taught. Although there were male healers, women were, in most cultures, the ones who took care of the sick or injured. Knowledge of healing properties of various plants and herbs was often passed down from the females of one generation to the next. Possession of what we now view as simple knowledge could improve chances for survival. Although the role of hygiene and germs were not fully understood, ancient Romans cleaned wounds with vinegar and Roman surgeons boiled their instruments before use. Ceren knows to look for a fleck of rusty blade left in Kinan's wound—doubtlessly saving him from gangrene. Arousing someone with a minor head trauma to consciousness by releasing ammonia from a "pungent blend" of herbs and cider, triggers an inhalation reflex that alters the pattern of breathing, and improves respiratory flow and alertness.

Some folk healers employed "magical" incantations along with their remedies. As Christian influence grew in Europe, such "spells" had to be separated from the physical cures, or replaced with prayers. And, since the Church taught that God sent illness as a punishment, the very act of healing could be viewed as countering His will.

Skin Deep
Richard Parks

The hardest part of Ceren's day was simply deciding what skin to put on in the morning. Making an informed decision required that she have a clear view of her entire day, and who other than a prisoner in a dungeon or a stone statue on a pedestal had that particular luxury?

Ceren went into her Gran's storeroom where the skins were kept. She still thought of the storeroom as her grandmother's, just as the small cottage in the woods and the one sheep and a milk goat in the pen out back belonged to her Gran as well. Ceren still felt as if she was just borrowing the lot, even though she had been on her own for two full seasons of the sixteen she had lived. Yet she still felt like a usurper, even though she herself had buried her grandmother under the cedar tree and there were no other relatives to make a claim. She especially felt that way about the skins, since Gran herself hadn't owned those, at least to Ceren's way of thinking. Borrowed, one and all.

They lay on a series of broad, flat shelves in the storeroom, covered with muslin to keep the dust off, neatly arranged just as a carpenter would organize his tools, all close to hand and suited for the purpose. Here was the one her Gran had always called the Oaf—not very bright, but large and strong and useful when there were large loads to be shifted or firewood to cut. There was the Tinker—slight and small, but very clever with his hands and good at making and mending. On the next highest shelf was the Soldier. Ceren had only worn him once, when the Red Company had been hired to raid the northern borders and all the farmers kept their axes and haying forks near to hand. She didn't like wearing him. He had seen horrible things, done as much, and the shell remembered, and thus so did she. She wore him for two days, but by the third she decided she'd rather take her chances with the raiders. The Soldier was for imminent threats and no other.

The skin on the highest shelf she had never worn at all. Never even seen it without its translucent covering of muslin, though now that Gran was gone there was nothing to prevent her. That skin frightened Ceren even more than The Soldier did. Gran had told her that at most she would wear the skin once or twice in her life, that she would know why when the time came. Otherwise, best not to look at it or think about it too much. Ceren didn't understand what her Gran was talking about, and that frightened her most of all because the old woman had flatly refused to explain or even mention the matter again. But there lay the skin on its high shelf. Sleeping, supposedly. That's what they all were supposed to do when not needed, but Ceren wasn't so sure about this one. It wasn't sleeping, she was certain. It was waiting for the day when Ceren would be compelled to put it on and become someone else, someone she had never been before.

It'll be worse than the Soldier, she thought. *Has to be, for Gran to be so leery of it.*

The day her grandmother had spoken of was not here yet, since Ceren felt no compulsion to find the stepstool and reach the mysterious skin on the high shelf. Today was a work day, and so today there was no guessing to be done. Ceren slipped out of her thin shift and hung it on a peg. Then she slipped the muslin coverlet off of the Oaf. She had need of his strength this fine morning. She could have even used that strength to get the skin of its shelf in the first place, but for the moment she had to make do with what she had. She used both hands and finally pulled it down.

Like cowhide, the skin was heavier than it looked. Unlike cowhide, it still bore an uncanny resemblance to the person who had once owned it, only with empty eye sockets now and a face and form much flatter than originally made, or so Ceren imagined. Gran never said where any particular skin came from; Ceren wasn't sure that the old woman even knew.

"They once belonged to someone else. Now they belong to us, our rightful property. I also came into a wash basin, a hammer, a saw and a fine, sharp chisel when my own mam died, and I didn't ask where they came from. Your mam would have got them, had she lived, but she wouldn't wonder about those things and neither should you."

Ceren had changed the subject then because her Gran had that little glow in her good eye that told anyone with sense that they were messing around in a place that shouldn't be messed around in. Ceren, whatever her faults, had sense.

It took all of her strength, but Ceren managed to hold up the skin as she breathed softly on that special spot on the back of its neck that Gran had showed her. The skin split open, crown to crack, and Ceren stepped into it like she'd step into a dancing gown—if she'd had such a thing or a maid or friend to lace up the back when she was done.

Next came the uncomfortable part. Ceren always tried not to think about it too much, but she didn't believe she would ever get used to it, even if she lived to be as old as Gran did before she died. First Ceren was aware of being in what felt like a leather cloak way too large for her. That feeling lasted for only a moment before the cloak felt as it it was shrinking in on her, but she knew it must have been herself getting . . . well, *stretchy*, since the Oaf was a big man, and soon so was she. Her small breasts flattened as if someone was pushing them, her torso thickened, her legs got longer and then there was this clumsy, uncomfortable *thing* between them. She felt her new mouth and eyes slip into place. When it was all over, she felt a mile high, and for the first dizzying seconds she was afraid that she might fall. Now she could clearly see the covering of muslin over the topmost skin on its shelf. She looked away, closed her eyes.

The uncomfortable part wasn't quite over; there was one final bit when Ceren was no longer completely Ceren. There was someone else present in her head, someone else's thoughts and memories to contend with. Fortunately the Oaf hadn't been particularly keen on thought, and so there wasn't as much to deal with.

The Soldier hadn't been quite so easy. Ceren tried not to remember.

"Time to go to work," she said aloud in a voice much lower than her own, and the part of her that wasn't Ceren at all but now served her understood.

She was never sure how much of what followed was her direction or the Oaf's understanding. Ceren knew the job that needed doing—a dead tree had fallen across the spring-fed brook that brought water to her animals and had diverted most of it into a nearby gully. That tree would have to be cleared, but while Ceren rightly thought of the axe and the saw, it was the Oaf who added the iron bar from her meager store of tools and set off toward the spring, whistling a tune that Ceren did not know, nor would it have mattered much if she *did* know, as she had never had the knack of whistling. Ceren was content to listen as she—or rather *they*—set out on the path to the head of the spring.

Ceren's small cottage nestled into the base of a high ridge in the foothills of the Pinetop Mountains. The artesian spring gave clear cold water year round, or at least it did before the tree dammed up the brook. Now the brook was down to a trickle, and the goat especially had been eyeing her reprovingly for the last two mornings as she milked it.

The Oaf had been right about the iron bar. It was a large old tree, more dried-out than rotten. Even with her new strength, it took Ceren a good bit of the morning with the axe and saw and then a bit more of that same morning with the iron bar and a large rock for a fulcrum to shift the tree trunk out of the brook. She moved a few stones to reinforce the banks and then it was finally done. The brook flowed freely again.

The Oaf cupped his calloused hands and drank from the small pool that formed beneath the spring. Ceren knew he wanted to sit down on a section of the removed log and rest, but Ceren noticed a plume of smoke from the other side of the ridge and gave in to curiosity. The ridge was steep, but spindly oak saplings and a few older trees grew along most of the slope, and she made her borrowed body climb up to the top using the trees for handholds.

My own skin is better suited for this climb, she thought, but the Oaf, though not nearly so nimble as Ceren's own lithe frame, finally managed to scramble to the top.

Someone was clearing a field along the north-south road in the next valley. Ceren recognized the signs: a section of woodland with its trees cut, waste fires for the wood that couldn't be reused, a pair of oxen to help pull the stumps. She counted three men working and one woman. The farmhouse was already well under way. Ceren sighed. She wasn't happy about other people being so close; her family's distrust of any and all others was bred deep. Yet most of the land along the road this far from the village of Endby was unclaimed, the farm did not infringe on her own holdings, and at least they were on the *other* side of the ridge, so she wouldn't even have to see them if she didn't want to.

Ceren had just started to turn away to make the climb back down before she noticed one lone figure making its way down the road. It was difficult at the distance, but Ceren was fairly sure that he was one of the men from the new homestead.

Doubtless headed toward the village on some errand or other.

Ceren watched for a while just to be sure and soon realized the wisdom of caution. The ridge sloped downward farther east just before it met the road. To her considerable surprise, when the man passed the treeline he did not continue on the road but rather stepped off onto the path leading to her own cottage. She swore softly, though through the Oaf's lips it came out rather more loud than she intended. Ceren hurried her borrowed form back down the ridge to the path from the spring, but despite her hurry, the stranger was no more than ten paces from her when she emerged into the clearing.

"Hullo there," said the stranger.

Ceren got her first good look at the man. He was wearing his work clothes, old but well-mended. He was young, with fair hair escaping from the cloth he'd tied around his head against the sun, and skin tanned from a life spent mainly outside. She judged him not more than a year or so older than she herself. Well-formed, or at least to the extent that Ceren could tell about such things. There weren't that many young men in the village to compare to, most were away on the surrounding farms, and those who were present always looked at her askance when she went into town, if they looked at her at all. It used to upset her, but Ceren's grandmother had been completely untroubled by this.

"Of course they look away. You're a witch, girl, the daughter of a witch and the granddaughter of a witch, the same as me. They're afraid of you, and if you know what's what, you'll make sure they stay that way."

The memory passed in a flash, and for a moment Ceren didn't know what to do. The stranger just looked at her then repeated, "Hullo? Can you hear me?"

Ceren spoke through her borrowed mouth and tried to keep her tone under control. The Oaf had a tendency to bellow like a bull if not held in check. "Hello. I'm sorry I was . . . thinking about something. What do you want?"

"I'm looking for the Wise Woman of Endby. I was told she lived here. Is this your home, then?"

"The Wise Woman is dead, and of course this isn't my home. I just do some work for her granddaughter who lives here now," Ceren/Oaf said.

"So I was given to understand, but is her granddaughter not a . . . not of the trade?"

Ceren nearly smiled with her borrowed face in spite of herself. The stranger's phrasing was almost tactful. Obviously he wanted something. But what? She finally noticed the stained bandage on the young man's right forearm, mostly covered by the sleeve of his shirt. Obviously, he needed mending. That was something Ceren could do even without a borrowed skin.

"She is," Ceren said. "If you'll wait out here, I'll go fetch her."

By this point Ceren was used to her borrowed form, but she still almost banged her head on the cottage's low door when she went inside. She made her way quickly to the storeroom and tapped the back of her neck three times with her left hand.

"Done with ye, off with ye!"

The skin split up the back again like the skin of a snake and sloughed off, leaving Ceren standing naked, dazed, and confused for several moments before she came fully to herself again. She quickly pulled her clothes back on and then took just as much time as she needed to arrange the Oaf back on his shelf and cover him with muslin until the next time he'd be needed.

When she emerged from the cottage, blinking in the sunlight, the young man, who had taken a seat on a stump, got to his feet. He had pulled the cloth from his head like a gentleman removing his cap in the presence of a lady. For a moment Ceren just stared at him, but she remembered her tongue soon enough.

"My hired man said I'm needed out here. I'm Ceren, Aydden Shinlock's granddaughter. Who are you?"

"My name's Kinan Baleson. My family is working a new holding just beyond the ridge there," he said, pointing at the ridge where Ceren-oaf had stood just a short time before. "I need your help."

"That's as may be. What ails you?"

"It's this . . . " he said, pulling back the sleeve covering the bandage on his right forearm.

Just as Ceren had surmised, he'd injured himself while clearing land at the new croft, slipped and gouged his arm on the teeth of a bow saw. "My ma did what she knew to do, but she says it's getting poisoned. She said to give you this . . . " He held out a silver penny. "We don't have a lot of money, but if this isn't enough, we have eggs, and we'll have some mutton come fall."

"Unless the hurt is greater than I think, it'll do."

Ceren took the coin and then grasped his hand to hold the arm steady and immediately realized the young man was blushing and she almost did the same.

Why is he doing that? I'm no simpering village maid.

She concentrated on the arm to cover her own confusion and began to unwrap the bandage, but before she'd even begun she knew that Kinan's mother had the right of it. The drainage from the wound was a sickly yellow, but to her relief it had not yet gone green. If that had happened, the choice would have been his arm or his life.

"Should have come to me sooner," Ceren said, "with all proper respect to your mother."

"She tried to make me come yesterday," Kinan said gruffly, "but there's so much to do—"

"Which would be managed better with two arms than one," Ceren said, planting a single seed of fear the way her Gran had taught her. In this case Ceren could see the wisdom of it. Better a little fear in the present than a lifetime disadvantage. "Hold still now."

Kinan did as he was told. Ceren finished unwrapping the bandage and pulled it away to get a good look at the wound. The gash was about two inches long, but narrow and surprisingly clean-edged, considering what had made it. The cut started a hand's width past his wrist, almost neatly centered in the top of the forearm. A little deep but not a lot more than a scratch, relatively speaking. Yet the area around the cut had turned an angry shade of red, and yellowish pus continued to ooze from the wound.

"Sit down on that stump. I'll be back in a moment."

Ceren picked up her water bucket, went to the stream and pulled up a good measure of cold, clear water. Before she returned to Kinan, she went back into her cottage and brought out of her healer's box, a simple pine chest where her Gran had kept her more precious herbs and tools. While most everything else in her life felt borrowed, Ceren considered that this box belonged to *her*. She had earned it. Both by assisting her Gran in her healer's work for years and by being naturally good at that work. Ceren inherited the box, inherited in a way that didn't seem to apply to the rest of the things around her.

Especially the skins.

Ceren carefully washed out the gash as Kinan gritted his teeth, which Ceren judged he did more from anticipation than actual added pain. A wound of this sort had its own level of pain which nothing Ceren had done—yet—was going to change. Once the wound was cleaned out, she leaned close and sniffed it.

"I can't imagine it smells like posies," Kinan said, forcing a smile.

"I'm more interested in *what* it smells like, not how pleasant it is." Ceren wondered for a moment why she was bothering to explain, since her Gran had been very adamant on the subject of secrets: "Best that no one knows how we do what we do. Little seems marvelous, once you know the secret." And it was important for reputation that all seem marvelous; Ceren saw the wisdom in that as well.

Even so, Ceren found it easy to talk to Kinan, she who barely had reason to speak three words in a fortnight. "My Gran taught me what scents to look for in a wound. A little like iron for blood, sickly-sweet for an inflamed cut like this one. Yet there's something . . . ah. You said you cut yourself on a saw? Fine new saw or old, battered saw?"

He sighed. "Everything we have is old and battered, but serves well enough."

"Yes, this saw has served you pretty well indeed. There's something in there that smells more like iron than even blood does. Unless I miss my guess, your saw left a piece of itself behind and is poisoning the wound. That's why your arm isn't healing properly."

He frowned. "You're saying you can smell iron?"

"Of course. Can't you?"

"Not at all. That's amazing."

Ceren almost blushed again. *So much for Gran's ideas about secrets,* Ceren thought. *Or at least that one.*

Ceren reached into her box and pulled out a bronze razor, which she proceeded to polish on a leather strop. Kinan eyed the blade warily, and Ceren nodded. "Yes, this is going to hurt. Just so you know."

Kinan flinched as Ceren gently opened the edges of the wound with her thumbs. More pus appeared and she rinsed that away as well. She judged the direction the sawblade had cut from and looked closer. A black speck was wedged deep into the wound's upper end. Now that she had found the culprit, it only took a couple of cuts with the razor to free the piece of broken sawblade. Kinan grunted once but otherwise bore the pain well enough and kept still even when new blood started to flow. Ceren held the fragment up on the edge of her bloody razor for Kinan to see before flicking it away into the bushes. She then washed the wound one more time and bound it again with a fresh strip of linen.

"Considering what you're likely to do with that arm, I really should stitch it," she said. "And it's going to bleed for a bit as things are. Let it, that'll help wash out the poison. If you'll be careful and wash the cut yourself at least once a day—clean, clear water, mind, not the muck from your stock pond—you should get to keep the arm."

"We have our own well now," Kinan said. "I'll heed what you say. I'm in your debt."

She shook her head. "You paid, so we're square. But mind what I said about washing."

Kinan thanked her again and left. Ceren watched him walk back down the path toward the road. After a moment she realized that she was, in fact, watching him long past the point where it was reasonable to do so. She sighed and then went to clean her razor in the cold stream.

~

That night Ceren dreamed that she walked hand in hand with Kinan through a golden field of barley, the grain ready to harvest. Yet no sooner had Kinan taken her in his arms than there stood his family: the brothers whom Ceren saw that day from the ridge, a mother and father with vague, misty faces.

"Stay away from that witch! She's evil!" they all said, speaking with one voice.

"There's nothing wrong with me!" Ceren said, but she didn't believe it. She knew there was. Those in the dream knew it too. Kinan turned his back on her and walked away with his family as the barley turned to briars and stones around a deep, still pool of water.

"You can't do it alone, you know. Your Gran knew. How do you think you got here?"

Ceren looked around, saw no one. "Where are you?"

"Look in the pond."

Ceren looked into the water but saw only her own reflection. It took her several moments to realize that it was not her reflection at all. Her hair was long, curly, and black, not the pale straw color it should have been. Her eyes were large and dark, her rosy-red lips perfectly formed. Ceren looked into the face of the most beautiful girl she had ever seen, and the sight was almost too painful to bear. "That's not me."

"No, but it could be. If you want."

When Ceren opened her eyes again, she had her own face once more, but the other girl's reflection stood beside her on the bank of the pool, wearing golden hoops in her ears and dressed like a gypsy princess. Ceren couldn't resist a sideways glance, but of course there was no one else there.

"Dreams lie," Ceren said. "My Gran told me that."

"This one is true enough and you know it. Even if Kinan was interested, what do you think his family would say if he came courting a witch?"

"He's not going to court me. I'd toss him out on his ear if he did. What a notion."

"Liar."

Ceren's hands balled into fists. "I just met him! He's not even that handsome."

The girl's laugh was almost like music. "What's that got to do with anything? He's young, he's strong, he has a touch of gentleness about him, despite his hard life. And he's not a fool. Are you?"

"Be quiet!"

The strange girl's reflection sighed, and ripples spread over the pond. "I never cared much for your Gran, but I will say this: she was always clear on what she wanted and never feared to go after it, too. So. She's dead and now you're the Mistress here. Tell me you don't want him. Make me believe you, and I'll go away."

"How do you know me? Who are you?"

"I've known you all your life, just as you know who I am."

Ceren did know. Just as she knew how she felt about Kinan and how strongly she tried not to feel anything at all.

"The topmost shelf. That's you."

"No, there is no one there. What remains is little more than a memory, but it is a memory that can serve you in this, as the memory of the Oaf and the Soldier and the Tinker cannot. What remains is merely a tool. Your Gran understood that. Use me, as she did."

"No!"

"Mark me—you will." The ripples faded along with her voice and reflection, but just before she awoke, Ceren gazed into the pool once last time and saw nothing at all.

~

For the next few months Ceren kept herself too busy to think about either Kinan or what lay on the topmost shelf. It was easy enough. There was always something that needed doing around her croft and a fairly steady stream of villagers and farmers from the surrounding countryside.

After her grandmother was cold and buried, Ceren had worried about whether the people who had come to her Gran would come to her now, she being little more than a girl and not the Wise Woman of Endby, who always wore her Gran's face so far as Ceren was concerned: ancient, bent, hook-nosed and glaring, while Ceren was none of those things except, now and then, glaring. But she needn't have worried. A Wise Woman was always needed where more than a few folk gathered, and as long as there was someone to fill the role, there were always people willing to let her. Ceren knew she would grow into the part, in time. Besides, "Wise Woman" was them being polite; she knew what they called her behind her back. Such rubbish had never bothered her grandmother. Ceren couldn't quite say the same.

One day it will seem perfectly natural, she thought, but the prospect didn't exactly fill her with joy. Fear and secrecy were the witch's stock in trade, just as her Gran had always said. She had no right to complain if other, less pleasant things came with them.

Ceren had just doled out the herb bundle that would rid a silly village girl of her "problem" when she heard an alarm bell clanging from the village itself. The girl mumbled her thanks and hurried away. Ceren looked south toward Endby but saw nothing out of the ordinary. When she looked back north it was a different story.

Smoke.

Not Kinan's home, she realized with more relief than she cared to admit; this was further west. Still, too close, to all of them. Ceren didn't hesitate. She didn't think of all the other things so much smoke in the sky might mean. She knew what the smoke meant, just as her Gran would have known. She went to the storeroom and put on the Soldier, because it was the only thing she knew to do.

The face and form of the Soldier remembered, so Ceren did too. There was no time to worry about what she did not want to see; it was all there, just as she'd left it the last time she had worn his skin, but now there was too much else that needed remembering.

Too far from the Serpent Road for this to be the main body. Most likely foragers.

This was what the Soldier knew, and so Ceren knew it, too. After a moment's reflection, the Soldier took one long knife from the cutlery rack and placed it in his belt. Ceren had expected him to take the felling axe, but now she understood why he didn't—too long in the handle and heavy in the blade to swing accurately at anything other than a target that wasn't moving. A short, balanced hatchet would have been better for their purpose, but there was none.

The Soldier trotted up the path toward the ridge, not hurrying, saving their strength. They passed the spring and scrambled up the ridge, and from that height the flames to the west were easy to see. Neither Ceren nor the Soldier knew which farm lay to the west, but they both knew there was one, or had been. The foragers would be spreading out from the Serpent Road; it was likely that they didn't know the north road—little more than a cart path—or the village of Endby even existed, but it looked like one group was going to find it if they kept moving east.

How many?

That was a question that needed to be answered and quickly. From the ridge the Soldier simply noted that a group of farmers had arranged themselves at the western border of their field, armed with little more than pitchforks and clubs. Ceren noted that Kinan and his father and his two brothers were about to get themselves killed, and there was nothing she could do about it.

They mean to keep the raiders from burning the field! thought Ceren.

Foolish, thought the memory of the Soldier, *they'd be better served to save what they could and make for the village.* Ceren couldn't disagree, since she knew the same could be said for herself. Yet here she was. She tried not to dwell on that or why her first instinct had been to don the Soldier. She thought instead of how hard the Balesons had worked to get their farm going. And how hard it would have been for them to let it all be destroyed.

The Soldier's thoughts closed in after that, so Ceren didn't understand at first why they turned left along the ridge rather than descending to stand with Kinan's family, but she knew better than to interfere. He was in his element, just as she was not. The Soldier kept low and moved quickly, using the trees and bushes that grew thick on the ridge as cover. Soon they left the bramble hedge that marked the edge of the Baleson farm. About three bowshots from the boundary, the ridge curved away south. They peered out of the thicket at the bend. There was still no sign of the foragers.

"Maybe they've stopped."

The Soldier's thought was immediate and emphatic. *Not enough time. They're not finished.*

Ceren and the Soldier found a way to descend and, once they were on level ground again, slipped away quickly into the trees. Ceren realized that they were approaching the burning farmhouse by a circular route, keeping to the cover of the woods. They heard a woman scream—and then silence.

They found a vantage point and looked out in time to see a man tying the straps of his leather brigandine back into place. He was lightly armored otherwise, but well armed. A bow and quiver lay propped against a nearby railing. The body of a man and a child lay nearby. A woman lay on the ground at the raider's feet, unmoving, her clothing in disarray and even at their distance they could see the blood. It took Ceren a moment to realize that the sword that she'd thought stuck into the ground was actually pinning the woman's body to the earth. She felt her gorge rising, but the Soldier merely judged the distance and scanned the rest of the scene. The farmhouse was still burning well, though the flames were showing signs of having passed their peak. Another moment and the roof came crashing down in a shower of embers.

Unmounted auxillaries with one scout. We have a chance, thought the Soldier.

Kill him, she thought in her anger.

The Soldier remained cold as a winter stream. *Not yet.*

The memory contained in the Soldier forced her to look toward the east. She saw four more men armed and armored similarly to the one lagging behind, but only the straggler had a bow. For some reason this seemed to please the Soldier. The other four carried bundles over their shoulders, apparently the spoils of the farm.

"You said there was another farm this way," shouted one of them. "We need to hit it and then return before nightfall if we're to be ready to move at daybreak. We haven't got time for your dallying."

"I'm almost done," said the first, "but this baggage has befouled my good blade. I'll catch up when I've cleaned it."

One of them swore, but they didn't wait. The other four disappeared into the trees, heading toward Kinan's farm. Ceren still felt sick but now there an even greater sense of urgency.

Kill him!

Soon.

They kept out of sight. They didn't move until the man had carefully wiped his sword on the dead woman's torn dress and sheathed the blade, then reclaimed his bow and quiver. The Soldier moved quickly and quietly, keeping to the trees at the edge of the woods, Ceren little more than a spectator behind borrowed eyes.

The Soldier caught the scout from behind before he had taken six steps into the trees. The scout managed only a muffled grunt as the Soldier clamped his hand over the man's mouth and neatly slashed his throat. The raider's blood flowed over their arms, but the Soldier didn't release their grip until the man went limp. They took the sword and the bow and quiver, but that was all.

The armor?

No time.

Ceren felt a little foolish for asking the question in the first place, and the reason was part of why she so feared to wear the Soldier's skin—she was starting to think like the Soldier. Like he had to think to serve his function. She knew why they left the armor, just as she knew why they did not follow the raiders along the same path, even though it was the most direct route. They took their course a little to the right, to place themselves just south of where the raiders would have to pass the barrier. At this point Ceren wasn't certain if this was the Soldier's direction or hers, but she knew they did not want to place the farmers directly in front of the raiders, not when arrows were about to fly.

They found a gap in the bramble thicket bordering the field, but the raiders had already emerged and were a good thirty paces into the field, moving directly to where Kinan stood with his father and brothers. Their numbers were matched, but that was all. It was hay fork and club against sword and spear, the difference being that those who held the sword and spear knew how to use them for this particular form of work.

Kinan, his family . . . They'll be slaughtered!

The first arrow was already nocked, but the Soldier did not draw. Not yet. Ceren again knew why, and she hated it. The raiders were still too close. Fire now and they'd probably get one of them, but then the three left would charge their position. The Soldier was waiting for advantage; a longer shot versus time to aim and fire. Ceren understood the tactical necessity, just as she understood that it might get one or more of Kinan's family killed. She let the Soldier wait until she could stand it no longer.

Now.

The closest raider went down screaming in pain with an arrow in his thigh. At first Ceren thought it was a bad shot, but then realized the Soldier had hit exactly what he aimed at. He wanted the raider incapacitated but calling attention to himself. The distraction worked. The raiders hesitated and turned toward their fallen companion. The Soldier's second arrow hit the next-closest raider high in the chest. He went down with barely more than a gasp.

This was the Soldier's purpose, and he was serving it well. Ceren felt the Soldier's satisfaction, and she felt sick as she realized that it wasn't just satisfaction that he felt. The Soldier was enjoying himself, and thus so was she, no matter how much she did not wish to, no matter how much she had wanted to see the raiders die.

Let them charge us now, Ceren thought, but it didn't work out that way. The raiders charged the farmers. Ceren didn't know if they meant to cut down Kinan's family or merely get *past* them to use them as cover, but now the odds were two to one in the farmers' favor. One farmer went down; Ceren couldn't tell who because the Soldier had already tossed the bow aside, and they ran full speed toward the fighting, borrowed sword drawn. The man on the ground made a feeble cut at him as he raced past, and the Soldier split the man's skull with barely a pause, but by the time they reached the farmers, it was all over. Kinan was down on the ground, a gash in his forehead.

Somehow Ceren knew it would be Kinan. She felt cold, almost numb at the sight of him.

The raiders were dead. The farmers were still furiously clubbing the bodies when Ceren in her Soldier skin reached them. The farmers eyed the Soldier warily.

"Who are you?" Kinan's father asked without lowering his club.

"The Wise Woman sent me," the Soldier said, sheathing the sword as he spoke. "She saw the smoke."

Ceren saw the look in the older man's eyes. Relief, certainly, but fear as well. One more debt. Ceren shook her head, and of course the Soldier did the same. "She figured they'd be at her steading next. Best to stop them here. What about the boy?"

They were all still breathing hard; Ceren wasn't even sure they'd noticed that Kinan was down, but then they were all clustering about him. Ceren shoved her way down to Kinan's side in her borrowed skin.

It was a glancing blow, and that was probably the only reason Kinan was still breathing. Even so, it was a nasty gash, Kinan was unconscious, and they could not rouse him.

"We should take him to the Wise Woman," one of the brothers said, but Ceren had the Soldier shake his head for her.

"No. Until we know how bad his hurt is you shouldn't move him any farther than needs must. Lift him gently and put him in his bed. Clean and bandage the cut, and I'll fetch the Wise Woman to you."

The father looked toward the barrier. "What if there are more of them?"

The Soldier shook his head without any help from Ceren. "Keep watch, but I doubt there will be. It was a foraging party. There's an army on a quick march south, and the king will have to deal with that if he can, but auxiliaries? It's likely no one will even miss these bastards."

The farmers looked doubtful, but they did as the Soldier directed. Ceren watched them carry Kinan off, then quickly turned back toward her own home.

She shed the Soldier's skin with relief, but she was nearly stumbling with exhaustion. Even so, she managed to carry her box of medicines up the road to Kinan's farm. It was his mother that greeted her this time.

Ceren had never met the woman before, but she could see Kinan in the older woman's eyes. Most of the rest of his looks he got from his father. She frowned when Ceren appeared, but she seemed to be puzzled, not disapproving.

"Kinan said you were young. I didn't realize how young."

"My Gran trained me well," Ceren said, a little defensively. "I can help him."

The woman shook her head. "That's not what I meant. You already have helped him, so I hope you can again. He hasn't moved since they brought him in. My name is Liea, by the way. Thank you for coming," she said, and sounded as if she meant it.

Ceren found herself blushing a little. She couldn't remember the last time anyone had said thank-you to her and seemed sincere rather than grudging. Except Kinan.

"I'm Ceren. I don't know if your son told you or not. . . . I trust no more raiders have been seen?"

The woman shook her head. "Not here, though we've heard rumors of attacks further south. The men are out burying the carcasses in a deep hole."

"Then maybe we won't see more of them again."

Liea shrugged. "Even if the army is beaten, likely some like them will come this way again, and likely be even more hungry and desperate in the bargain. We heard what they did to the steading west of us."

Ceren only hoped that they hadn't seen it as well, as she had. Liea took her to where Kinan had been put to bed. It wasn't a large room, and clearly he shared it with his brothers. Ceren found him lying pale and still under a quilt. His breathing was regular and strong; the head wound had stopped bleeding and she removed the bandage, noting with approval that it had been cleaned out properly, doubtless Liea's doing. Now it was easy to see that the cut had not gone clear through to the skull, though it hadn't missed by much. Still, Kinan's continued unconsciousness was not a good sign, and the longer it lasted, the worse the portents.

Liea stood nearby watching. Her eyes were moist and her lower lip trembled. Ceren believed she knew how the woman felt, at least a little. She took a needle and thread from her box and calmly proceeded to sew up the gash. She noted with approval that Liea turned away only once, on the first pass of the needle.

"These stitches will need to come out, but probably not before a fortnight. Just cut one side under the knot and pull. It'll sting him, but no more than that."

Liea looked as if she was ready to collapse where she stood. She put her hand against the lintel for support. "You . . . you think he will live?"

"The next few minutes should tell. Would you like to help me?"

Ceren mixed a pungent blend of herbs with a few drops of apple cider supplied by Liea. She then had the older woman hold Kinan's head while she soaked a bit of linen in the mixture and held it under Kinan's nose. "I'd try not to breathe for a few moments, if I were you."

While Ceren and Liea both held their breath, Kinan inhaled the scent at full strength. In a moment his eyelids fluttered and then his eyes opened wide and tears started to flow. He sat upright in the bed despite Liea's best efforts. "What is that damn stench?"

"Your salvation," Ceren said calmly. She took the rag and stuffed it in an earthenware bottle with a tight cork to seal it. After she closed the lid of the box the scent began to fade immediately. Liea already had her arms around her son, who didn't seem to understand what all the fuss was about.

"I'm fine, Ma. My head hurts, but that's all . . . Wait, what happened to—"

"Your father and your brothers are all fine, as are you. Mostly thanks to this young woman here," Liea said. "Ceren, I don't know where you found that man you sent to help us, but we are in your debt for that as well. I don't know how we can repay you."

Debt. Well, yes. That was how it worked. Gran had always said as much. You use your skills and make other people pay for them. It was no different from being a cobbler and a blacksmith. Except that it was different. A cobbler could make a gift of shoes or a blacksmith an ironwork, to a friend. What witch—yes, that was the word; Gran spoke it if no one else would— gave her skills away? Who would trust such a gift? Ceren's weariness caught up with her all at once. She rose with difficulty.

"Can we discuss that later? I think I need to go home . . . "

Liea looked her up and down. "I think we both need to sit for a moment and have a taste of that hard cider first—without the herbs. Then I'll have Kyne or Beras make sure you get home safe."

～

"She was worried about me. She was nice to me."

As Ceren lay in her Gran's bed trying to sleep, she examined the thought and wondered if what she thought was concern in Liea's eyes was something else.

Child, everyone acts nice and respectful when they want something or when they owe you, Gran said. *You think we wear a false skin? Feh. Everyone drops the mask as soon as they get what they want. You don't owe them courtesy or aught else.* Ceren remembered. She was still remembering when she finally fell asleep, and heard the voice again.

"Your Gran knew better."

"Go away," Ceren said.

"I can't. Neither can you. We're stuck here, each in our own way. Or do you still think Kinan or his family will welcome you with open arms? Fool, if you want Kinan, you'll have to take him. Your Gran knew. Your Gran always got what she wanted. Or who she wanted."

That was a subject Ceren definitely did not want to hear about, but the message had already come through. "I collect what I need, but I take what I want, and that's what makes me a true witch. Is that it?"

"It's what your Gran taught you, and she taught you well. Don't deny what you are."

"What if I don't want to be like that?" Ceren heard faint laughter. "Then you 'be' alone and you 'be' nothing. Stop talking rubbish and use the right tool for the purpose. It'll get easier as time passes. You'll see. Your Gran did. Use me, as she did."

"If I'm a witch, then don't tell me what I must do!"

More laughter. Ceren remembered the sound of it in her head when she finally awoke, even more so than the sound arrows made when they struck human flesh and the image of what a man looked like split from crown to chin by a broadsword. The sun was streaming in from a dusty window. Ceren blinked. How long had she slept? The sun was already high and the morning half gone, at least, and she was famished. Ceren didn't bother to dress properly. First she visited the privy, then washed her face and hands in cold water from the stream. After that she stumbled to the larder and found some hard bread and cheese.

"What do you plan, then? A courtesy call on the boy's family?"

Ceren pinched herself just the once to verify that she wasn't dreaming, but she hadn't really thought so in the first place. Ceren addressed the person who was not there. "Haunting my dreams was bad enough. Are you going to talk to me while I'm awake too?"

"Someone needs to, but no. Your Gran said you would know when the time came, and this is how you know. It is time, Ceren. Put me on."

"Why?"

"So that you may achieve your heart's desire, of course."

Ceren closed her eyes briefly and then spoke to nothing again. "Very well."

The shelf was high. She needed a stool to stand on when she pulled down the long wrapped bundle that rested there. She barely glanced at it, but what she did see confirmed what she had long believed. In a moment the new skin was settling around her. She felt her legs lengthen, her small breasts swell and reshape as she surged up to fit the appearance she now wore.

As always, there was more to it than appearance. As with the Oaf, and the Soldier, and the Tinker, now she wore another person's memories. Only this time Ceren did not keep her own thoughts and memories tight and protected. She did not fight the new memories, as she tried to do with the Soldier. She took them as far as they would go, all the while she looked in the mirror.

She wasn't merely pretty. She had a face and form that would stop any man dead in his tracks. Ceren was now the reflection of the girl in the pond.

Didn't I tell you? The Girl sounded a bit smug. *You know what life was like for me. What it can be for you. All you need do is take what you want.*

Ceren nodded. "You're beyond beautiful. Was that why that man drowned you in the pond?"

She felt the laughter. She wondered if she was the one laughing, but the reflection looking back at her was sad and solemn. Her own reflection, somewhere hidden beneath a borrowed skin. *So you've seen that as well. Some men will destroy what they cannot possess, and I chose poorly. What of it? Neither Kinan nor his brothers are like that.*

"I know."

All you need do is show yourself to him as you are now, and he is yours.

Ceren shook her head. "No. I show your face to him and he is yours."

A frown now showing in the mirror that was none of Ceren. *It is the same thing, and he is your heart's desire!*

"No. I merely want him. I even think I like him. If there's more to the matter, then time alone will tell. You never understood my heart's desire. Maybe because it took me so long to understand it myself." She tapped the back of her neck three times. "Off with ye, done with ye!"

The skin split as it must, but it did not release her quickly or easily. The Girl was fighting her. Ceren thought she understood why. She pulled off one arm like a too-tight glove and then another, but the torso refused to budge.

"Does the servant question the mistress? Let me go."

You can't do it without me, without us! You're ugly, you're worthless . . .

"Let me go," Ceren said calmly. "Or I'll cut you off." And just to show that she was serious, Ceren went to her herb box and took out the bronze razor. She had already started a new cut down the side when the skin finally relented. In a thrice Ceren had the Girl wrapped carefully back on her shelf.

The voice was still there, taunting her. *You'll be back. You need me to gain your heart's desire. If it's not Kinan, then another! You're plain at best, hideous at worst. You'll never achieve it on your own.*

Ceren almost giggled. "I didn't understand. All this time I thought the skins were tools and we the purpose. Now I know it's the other way around. I am the instrument, just as Gran was before me. You, the Oaf, the Tinker, the Soldier . . . You who died ages ago, and yet still live through us. You are the purpose. We serve you."

You still do. And will.

"Why?"

Because only we can give you what you want.

Ceren shook her head. "You still don't understand. You already have, at least in part."

What are you talking about?

"I've always felt like one living in a borrowed house, with borrowed strengths, borrowed skills, but I thought it was because of Gran. It wasn't. It was because of *you*."

Fool! The raiders will return or bandits or village boys too drunk to know who they're forcing! You will fall in love. A heavy tree will fall. You can't do this on your own. You need us.

"No," Ceren said. "I need to find out what belongs to me and what does not. You gave me that last part, but now I have to find the rest. That is my true heart's desire."

Ceren left the storeroom and latched it behind her. Then, upon consideration, she slowly and painfully pushed her Gran's heavy worktable to block the door.

Setting fire to her Gran's cottage was the easy part. Watching it burn was harder. Listening to the four voices screaming in her head was hardest of all, but she bore it. She heard the pounding from inside as the flames rose, tried not to think of what supposedly had no volition, no independent action, and yet still pounded against a blocked door. Ceren led her sheep and her goat to a grassy spot a safe distance away, where they grazed in apparent indifference as the cottage and pen alike burned.

Her Gran had never taught Ceren any prayers. She tried to imagine what a prayer must be like, and she said that one as the voices in her head rose into a combined scream of anguish that she could not shut out.

"Go to your rest, and take your memories with you."

She didn't think the prayer would work. Some of the memories were hers now, and she knew that was never going to change. She wasn't sure she wanted it to.

The roof finally collapsed, and just for a moment Ceren thought she saw four columns of ash and smoke rise separately from the fire to spiral away into the sky before all blended in flame and smoke as the embers rained down.

Kinan found her sitting there, on the stump, as the cottage smoldered. He looked a little pale, but he came down the path at a trot and was only a little out breath when he reached her. "We saw the smoke. Ceren, are you all right?"

She wondered if he really wanted to know. She wondered if now was the time to find out. "I should ask you the same. You shouldn't be out of bed," Ceren said, not looking at him. "My home burned down," she said, finally stating the obvious. "Such things happen."

"I'm sorry," Kinan said. "But I'm glad you're all right. Have you lost everything?"

She considered the question for a moment. "Once I would have thought so. Now I think I have lost very little." She looked at him. "I'm going to need a place to stay, but where can I go? I have a goat and a sheep and my medicines . . . I have skills. I'm not ugly, and I'm not useless!" That last part came out in a bit of a rush, and Ceren blinked to keep tears at bay. She only partly succeeded.

Kinan smiled then, though he sounded puzzled. "Who ever said you were?"

Ceren considered that for a moment too. "Nobody."

Kinan just sighed and held out his hand. "You'll stay with us, of course. We'll find room. Let's go talk to Ma; we'll come back for your animals later."

Ceren hesitated. "A witch in your house? What will your father say?"

Kinan didn't even blink. "My father is a wise man. He may grumble or he may not, but in the end he'll say what Ma says, and that's why we're going to her first. We owe you . . . I owe you."

Ceren decided she didn't mind hearing those words so much. Coming from Kinan, they didn't sound like an accusation. Besides, Ceren understood debts. They could start there; Ceren didn't mind. Just so long as they could start somewhere. She took Kinan's offered hand and he helped her to rise.

Kinan then carried Ceren's medicine box as he escorted her, understanding or not, down the road in search of her heart's desire.

～

Dr. Sarah Martin, Cynthia Ward's modern physician who realizes there is power in old "superstitions," uses a very ancient form of spellcraft: knots. The tying and untying of knots to either bind or release energy is often found in magic-making. Love spells—some dating back to the ancient Egyptians and Greeks—often involved knots. Some thought pregnancy could be prevented with the tying of magical knots; untying them restored fertility. Sailors, particularly those from Scotland and Scandinavia, believed knots could control the winds. Three magical knots in a rope (or sometime fabric) "tied up" the wind. When the wind was needed, one untied a single knot for a gentle breeze, two for stronger wind, and all three brought on gales.

The Robbery
Cynthia Ward

Sarah Martin unlocked the front door of her tract house and stood staring: the kitchen door had been broken open. She'd been burglarized. Again. A month after she'd bought this house in a "safe suburban neighborhood," someone had broken in when she'd gone to Chicago for the weekend. They hadn't taken anything except the coins on her nightstand, but still she had felt furious and violated.

This time Sarah had told no one she was going away except her neighbors, the Armstrongs: a friendly, nervous blond housewife named Trisha and her pompous lawyer husband, Carmichael. They'd known about her previous break-in, and they'd agreed not to tell anyone she was going away. They wouldn't have told anyone. Except, Sarah suddenly realized, their son.

She'd never met the boy, but when she'd invited the Armstrongs to dinner, Carmichael had boasted at length about his only son, Thomas. About what a great athlete and terrific quarterback, what an over-achieving student and well-behaved Christian his son was. Because Thomas was so good, Carmichael Armstrong had bought his son a Corvette and, if Thomas didn't get a full scholarship, he would pay his son's way through college and law school. "I had to drive a dangerous junk car and pay for my education with lousy back-breaking labor," Carmichael had told Sarah over dinner. "Why should my son suffer through some low-paying menial job when he doesn't have to?" Sarah had said nothing, though she'd been angry at Carmichael's scornful dismissal of labor—all her relatives back East worked hard jobs, lobstering, logging, driving trucks, waiting tables, and they deserved respect. Sarah had held her tongue and, remembering the brawny, sullen youth she'd seen working on the sports car in the Armstrongs' driveway, she had thought that Thomas would benefit enormously from working like every college-bound teenager she'd ever known—including herself.

But they seemed to do things differently in the Midwest. Especially when the kid was the star quarterback of the high school football team.

She'd lived here a year now, and Sarah still couldn't believe how *big* football was in the Midwest. God, the high school teams played in stadiums of NFL dimensions! Some schools in eastern Maine couldn't even afford football. The boys played soccer, and often the spectators didn't have a bench to sit on.

Sarah Martin realized she was still standing in her doorway, staring into space. Shaking off her stunned reverie, she reached down and picked up the rope that had lain alongside the inner sill of her front door. The rope was slightly longer than the doorsill, and tied along its length in four complex knots. Sarah stepped into the house, closed the door, and untied every knot in the rope. She went to each window, removing the ropes from their sills and undoing their knots. Then she went to the half-open kitchen door that opened into her tiny back yard. The doorjamb had been splintered by blows to the latch and deadbolt. Hammered open by someone strong, just like last time. Sarah looked down. The knotted rope had been slightly disturbed. She picked up the rope but did not touch the four knots.

The utility drawer was open and in disarray, but nothing appeared to be missing. Sarah dropped the lengths of rope in the drawer. *Had it worked?*

She called the police.

While moving through the house she'd noticed that she hadn't lost any big-ticket items; she still had the stereo, the TV and VCR, the CDs and videocassettes, the computer and printer. When she hung up the phone, she checked her medicine cabinet and her yanked-open closets and drawers. The thief had gone through her jewelry box but taken nothing—had busted open her strongbox but ignored her stock certificate for the private medical clinic where she worked; however, he had taken the silver dollar her father had given to her before he'd died.

Sarah's fists clenched with rage.

He'd gone through her underwear drawer. He hadn't done anything except search for money, but she still couldn't bear the knowledge that he'd fingered her panties and bras. She emptied the drawer in the laundry basket.

Two officers and one detective arrived in response to her call. The uniforms dusted for fingerprints. The plainclothesman asked questions and Sarah answered.

Then she said, "Detective Adams, can I tell you something in private?"

"Pete," he said. "Sure."

She stepped into her home office and Pete Adams followed. She closed the door and spoke softly: "I've only been gone two nights. And I'm a doctor, so I keep weird hours. Someone who knows my movements did this. It was a neighborhood kid."

"Definitely," Adams said. "This has all the earmarks of a juvenile perpetrator. Ninety percent of these crude B-and-Es are committed by kids looking for money."

"I'll bet," Sarah said. "Pete, I know my neighbors' son broke in here."

"He's under eighteen?" Adams asked. Sarah nodded. "A juvenile. If he has a record, we can bring him in."

"*What?*" Sarah cried. "Under those conditions, no juvenile thief could *get* a record!"

"I'm sorry, I was unclear. If we lift fingerprints that match a convicted juvenile's prints, we can make an arrest. But we can't go and fingerprint a juvenile without a record purely on your say-so. We'll question your neighbors—if someone else witnessed the crime and recognized the perpetrator, or gives a description matching your neighbor's kid, then we can bring him in. But a hunch isn't enough, Dr. Martin."

"Christ," Sarah said. "I *know* it's the son of my neighbors across the street. I asked them to keep an eye on my place and not to tell anyone I was gone. I know their son did it. I know he did *both* break-ins here. The thief is Thomas Armstrong."

"Thomas Armstrong!" Adams exclaimed. "The star quarterback of the Lincolnville Eagles. Ma'am, no one will believe the biggest celebrity in town broke into your place."

Sarah's eyes narrowed and her mouth opened.

"Oh, I believe you, Dr. Martin," Adams said. "Thomas is a spoiled, swell-headed brat. I think he's broken into some other houses on this street. But you keep your suspicion to yourself. Telling anyone else won't do anything but make you enemies. Anyway, it is possible Thomas didn't break into your house this time. Yesterday he woke up in such terrible pain he could hardly move. His parents took him to the hospital. He's developed such a bad case of arthritis the doctors can't *believe* it. They can't do anything except give him tests and pills and a wheelchair. They can't even figure out how it developed so fast."

"My God," Sarah said. "I've never heard of such a thing!"

"No? And you're a GP. Jesus!"

When the police left, Sarah went across the street. Carmichael Armstrong was at the law office where he was a junior partner, but his wife, Trisha, was home, taking care of their son. Sarah told Trisha how sorry she was to hear about Thomas's illness, and asked if she could speak to him; she was a general practitioner, maybe she could think of something that might help. It was a long shot, but surely worth trying. . . .

"Of course!" Trisha said, nodding several times. She looked more nervous than ever, and seemed brittle; Sarah guessed another blow would shatter her. Sarah suppressed a sigh. She liked Trisha. "Please, Sarah, come in—this way."

The Armstrongs' house was laid out exactly like Sarah's. Sarah hated suburban housing, but she couldn't afford anything old enough to possess individuality.

"His room . . ." Trisha pointed to an open door. One of the two bedrooms, Sarah knew from her own tract house.

"I think it would be best if I spoke to Thomas alone."

"Oh, of course." Trisha drifted away.

Sarah closed the door and turned around to see a riot of color; the bedroom walls were covered with glossy posters of NFL stars. Sarah didn't know their names, but she recognized the logos of the Chicago Bears, the Denver Broncos, the San Francisco 49ers.

Thomas wore a Minnesota Vikings jersey. He sat rigidly in a wheelchair. His face was even more sullen than Sarah remembered.

"What do you want?" he demanded. "Did you come to *pity* me? You can't help me, Dr. Martin. The experts said *nobody* can help me." His voice rose, harsh with rage. "You doctors are all useless bastards!"

"I understand your frustration," Sarah said, glancing over the powerfully built, utterly motionless body. "But sometimes a clear conscience can work wonders, Thomas." She kept her voice calm. "While I was away, you broke into my house. If you apologize and return the silver dollar you stole, I will forgive you and you may feel better."

"You lying bitch!" Thomas's tone was furious, but his voice was soft. "I didn't break into your house!" His voice rose: "Get *out!*"

Sarah stepped out of his bedroom and softly closed the door. She saw Trisha rushing toward her. She apologized for disturbing Thomas, and said, "If there's anything I can do, Trisha, please don't hesitate to ask."

"You're so kind, Sarah," Trisha said.

Back in her house, Sarah took the knotted rope out of the utility drawer. She'd learned how to tie a knot practically in infancy; her father and grandfather had been fishermen, in the days when fishermen made their own nets. But the foreign trawlers stripped New England's ocean waters, and most of Maine's fishermen were driven ashore, or turned, like her father and grandfather, to lobstering. Sarah heard tales of the old days on Dad's or Grampa's knee, and she heard that there was power in the knots a fisherman tied: power to summon the fish, to summon a wind fair or foul, to summon trouble for a troublemaker. When she grew older, Sarah realized no amount of knots could regenerate the schools of fish captured in miles-long nets; she realized her father and grandfather were superstitious old men embroidering tales of past glory.

She studied science, she was going to be a doctor; she knew better.

But when someone broke into her new house, Dr. Martin found herself feeling vulnerable. Unable to afford installation of an alarm system on top of her mortgage and medical school loan payments, she thought about buying a dog. But she worked such long, odd hours, it would be cruel neglect. So she found herself thinking about what her father and grandfather had told her. Dad and Grampa were dead. She called her grandmother, said she was just curious about it—couldn't quite remember what she'd heard when she was a kid, you know how that goes, Gram . . .

"Oh, ayuh, there's power in knots," Grandma said in her age-weakened voice, "if someone's troubling you, granddaughter."

"That's just it, Gram," Sarah had said, dropping the pretense of idle curiosity. She'd listened carefully to everything her grandmother had told her.

Sarah looked at the rope in her hand, the rope that had caught the unwelcome intruder without his noticing; she looked at the four knots, one for each of the intruder's limbs. If she untied the knots, she would unbind the intruder's arms and legs, free him from crippling agony.

Her grandmother had told her the best thing to do would be to tie a slipknot. Make a noose. But Sarah was a doctor. She worked to save lives, not end them. All she wanted to do was stop the thief from breaking in.

The idea of causing such pain was disturbing enough. But this pain could be stopped. Death could not be reversed.

But if the crippling pain were stopped, it was clear Sarah would be right back where she started.

Sarah sealed the knotted rope in a Ziploc bag. She took her trowel out of the utility drawer and went through the broken door into her back yard. She struck the earth of her tiny flower bed with angry blows of the trowel. She buried the rope.

She would give the boy one more chance. Perhaps another week of pain like ground glass in his joints and he would confess, return the coin, and allow her to heal him.

If not?

She had sworn an oath: she was a member of society with special obligations to *all* her fellow human beings. Thomas was like a disease that, if not stopped, would worsen and adversely affect—no, *infect* the lives of many more.

Sarah returned to the kitchen and rinsed her trowel off in the sink. She dried it and replaced it in the drawer, hoping she would soon need it again.

But if Thomas did not wish to be cured, the rope would remain buried, the bag would corrode, the hemp would rot, the knots dissolve without unbinding. Thomas Armstrong would remain crippled for as long as he lived.

~

Demeter Alcmedi is a modern witch—but she's not young and sexy. Her granddaughter, Persephone, is the sexy younger one. At the start of Linda Robertson's Circle series, Demeter—Nana—has just begun sharing her granddaughter's home. Our story is a "prequel" and explains, for the first time, how Nana gets booted out of the retirement center before moving in with Seph.

The Alcmedis, although their witchcraft is fictional, follow the same code as many modern practitioners of the Wiccan religion, the Rede, which states: "An it harm none, do what ye will." Since the Rede (the word means "advice" or "counsel" and is related to the German Rat and Swedish råd) is open to interpretation, individuals must decide what it means in their own lives and specific situations. It gives one the freedom to act, as long as one minimizes harm to oneself and others and takes responsibility for the outcome. You'll have to decide for yourself if Demeter adheres to the Rede in this tale.

Marlboros and Magic
Linda Robertson

"You know why I'm here." Persephone Alcmedi fixed her grandmother with a hard stare.

Demeter Alcmedi—Seph called her Nana—dug a cigarette case from the pocket of her white Capri pants. "Yep." She put a Marlboro to her lips, flicked the lighter.

Seph leaned against the brick wall of the Woodhaven Retirement Community's patio assessing the woman who had raised her. Under her scrutiny, Nana molded her wrinkled face into a stern expression that dared Seph to admonish her. She tapped the toe of her untied size-four tennis shoe—untied because her feet were swollen—in an intentional display of impatience.

Nana's silvery bee-hive hairdo surmounted her head in mound closer to a football helmet than a crown. As she crossed her thick upper arms under her breasts her tummy rounded even more. Nana's hips swelled in a generous third curve, producing an undeniable snowman shape. The plus-size tunic with big red cabbage roses did nothing to disguise it.

Seph knew Nana was a resourceful, fierce, polar bear of an old woman. Her grandmother's icy practicality and arctic wit were also dominant traits. The heat from the chain-smoked cigarettes must be the only thing preventing the elderly woman from freezing solid.

Those little tubes of tobacco were also the reason Seph was here visiting Nana at the Woodhaven Retirement Community on this late-September Friday. "Do you need me to buy you some of those smoking cessation patches?"

"No."

"Nicotine gum?"

Nana repeated belligerently, "No."

Seph paused then threw in another option. "Should I hire a hypnotist?"

Nana's arms dropped to her sides in exasperation. "Now shit, Persephone."

"What?"

" 'What' yourself."

"You could stop any time you want." Seph made a decidedly magical hand gesture. "Cast a spell."

With a defiant lift of her chin, Nana looked away.

But Seph knew how to push her buttons. "The addiction tougher than you are?"

Nana stamped her foot. "I. Want. To. Smoke." She took another hit, blew the gray results into the air. "I like it. I like what it does. And since I'm paying mightily for the privilege of living in this dressed-up nursing home—"

"It's *not* a nursing home!" They'd had this discussion a dozen times since Nana moved into Woodhaven four months before.

Nana harumphed. "Polish a turd, it's still a turd." She punctuated the last few words by pointing her cigarette for each.

Persephone crossed her arms in a fine, if far more slender, copy of Nana's former pose.

"I should be allowed to smoke *whenever* and *wherever* I want."

"You knew the rules when you moved in here. You agreed. You signed a paper."

Nana smirked. "That's exactly what Mr. Loudcrier said to me yesterday." She mimicked a puppet talking with her free hand. "Blah blah blah."

278 – Linda Robertson

Persephone knew the name. He was the CEO of Woodhaven. She hadn't been impressed by the self-aggrandizing ass, but he was in charge and had to enforce the rules. "They have the right to evict you if you don't stop, and trust me, *he* will." She pushed away from the wall. "Then where are you going to go?"

Nana didn't answer.

"You better think about that before you light up again." She left Nana with that thought and walked to her car without looking back.

~

Demeter snorted as the Toyota Avalon drove away, but Seph was right. Due to a fire-safety clause, that peckerhead of a CEO *could* authorize an eviction.

Maybe I'd give a damn if I liked it here, but I don't.

A pair of women whose faces were in danger of being mistaken for prunes were on their way in from a stroll. Their terribly thinning hair was kept very short, tightly permed, and dyed coal black.

Looks ridiculous. Like pubic hair all over their heads.

She brought the Marlboro up.

Due to a sound amplification spell that was centered around her ears, she heard one of them whisper, "That one's a rule-breaker. I don't like her."

That was how most of the residents here reacted to her. Antipathy and avoidance.

Demeter blew out the smoke so they'd both have to walk through it as they entered the building. If they did evict her, she sure wouldn't miss any of these wrinkled old biddies in their golf shorts, plastic visors, and Velcro-fastened footwear.

Their dislike of her wasn't even because she was a witch. They didn't realize she was one.

Witches had come out of the proverbial broom closet twenty years before when the rest of the "other-than-humans" did. It hadn't been easy. Her generation in particular had had a difficult time dealing with the new world. Most simply gave in to their fears. As they aged, those fears deepened.

Older humans had a tendency to not adapt to *any* new notion as readily as younger folks.

And prejudices ripened until they were rotten on the vine.

Still, it wasn't bigotry working against Demeter, it was her aura. Demeter's aura had developed a static edge a long time ago. Having lived her life regularly utilizing universal energies, this "fringe" served as both a buffer and a conduit, depending on her magical intentions. It was a blessing in that it made magic easier, but it was also a curse as her aura felt *off* to mundane humans.

After moving into Woodhaven the feeling of unease attached to her aura made it impossible for her to find friends.

It wasn't simply the other residents' aversion to her that made her unhappy, though. This place couldn't be *home*. Inside, everywhere she looked she saw a walker, an oxygen tank, or ears stuffed with hearing aids. Certain halls reeked of antiseptic and piss. Outside, there was no energy in the ground. The whole facility felt barren and aged. It felt like death.

Holding the cigarette out in front of her, she stared at it, watching the smoke waft and grow thin until it completely disappeared.

She was supposed to be with her peers here, with people who moved at her pace and with whom she had common interests. "Bullshit," she muttered to herself.

She couldn't just wait here for her life to dissipate like that wisp of smoke.

She wouldn't.

She had to get out of here.

But her condo was sold. Seph had pegged it. *I have nowhere to go.*

The nearby doors opened again and, too late, she jerked her hand behind her back to hide the cigarette. A short man in a dark suit exited— Mr. Longcrier. He was only in his late forties, but the paunch, glasses, and receding hairline added a decade. She thought his exterior was a fitting punishment for the hours he'd spent waxing poetic about his own arguably great deeds.

He gave her a stern, reproachful glare as he passed. He'd seen the cigarette.

She smiled sweetly. *Got us old timers by the shorthairs, don't you? Got us trapped 'cause our families don't want us. Enjoy your lunch, you bombastic asshole.*

Her conscience told her to listen to Seph and make the best of her situation.

But in her heart, she didn't want to be here. She couldn't make the best of it.

Or could she?

Could she make this place *better*? Could she make *it* suit *her*?

She crushed what little was left of the Marlboro against the wall. *They can't afford to throw us all out. If everyone wanted the right to smoke on the premises, I bet we could get the rules changed.*

With an admittedly devious idea forming, she shuffled back inside and punched the button for the elevator. She tapped her toe until the *ding* signaled arrival and the doors slid open.

A trio of residents stood inside the elevator. Seeing her, they tried to exit the elevator without making eye contact.

Gushingly, Demeter said, "Oh, Diane! I was just looking for you," as she blocked them all with her bulk.

"Me?"

"And you too, Patty and Dean." Demeter ignored their obvious suspicion and linked arms with Patty and Diane keeping them in the elevator. "Third floor, if you would, Dean."

"But we were just—"

"Now, now. I've decided to have a party."

Not taking no for an answer, she towed them to her apartment and insisted they make themselves comfy at her dining table. She quickly served them crackers, smoked sausage, and Colby cheese, with orders for Dean to do the slicing honors.

"I'll be right back," she said cheerily. Demeter paused to nonchalantly set her cigarette case on the table and smile at her company before proceeding into the kitchen.

While her apprehensive guests stacked meat and cheese on crackers, they whispered back and forth about how to politely make a hasty exit. With her sound amplification spell a constant, Demeter could hear every word, even when the aggressive side of the usually quiet and meek Patty showed through. "That woman is strange and gives me the heebie-jeebies," she whispered. "I say we knock her over the head and run before she does something . . . evil."

Friends or not, however, Demeter was sure that politeness would keep her guests deliberating for a few more minutes—more than enough time to get her spell together.

Demeter removed a clear glass saucer from the kitchen cupboard, followed by a strongly scented black pillar candle, and a Baggie of gray sand. After pouring a neat circle of sand on the saucer's edge, she placed the candle in the center.

Next, she selected a bottle of thunder water—water collected during a thunderstorm and then blessed in a ritual to enhance the potency—and poured the water into the saucer until it reached the gray sand.

Finally, she took a vial of Dragon's Blood essential oil and mixed drops of the oil and water in a shot glass. Dragon's Blood bore a powerful scent and it gave serious *oomph* to any spell. Considering the size and scope of the Woodhaven Retirement Community, she added more Dragon's Blood . . . and a few drops more for good measure.

After dipping her finger into the mixture, she rubbed it on the candle whispering,

"Dragon's Blood on candle black
Draw forth their urge to smoke
Thunder water on and under
Infuse this candle as I invoke!"

Finished dressing the candle, she quickly whispered her way through the words of a ritual. When she mentally drew the circle for this spell-casting, she closed her eyes and envisioned the entire grounds of the Woodhaven Retirement Community. She lit the wick with a lighter from her pocket.

"All who live here are enticed,
From the top floor to the bottom.
React and share now as I say
Smoke 'em if you got 'em."

Demeter carried her saucer from the kitchen to her still-open front door. Fanning the scent of the candle into the hall, she chanted the last line nine times. "So mote it be." She placed the saucer in front of a return air vent, knowing it would get sucked into the ventilation and spread throughout the building.

When she reappeared at the table, her three guests had fallen silent. One by one, their gazes fell to the case she'd left on the table.

Nana reached out, reclaimed it, and opened it. Withdrawing a Marlboro, she placed it between smiling lips and lit it up. "Anybody else want one?"

Within minutes, the four of them sat at the table and each had a cigarette in hand. Demeter's room was hazy with ribbons of smoke.

"I never smoked in my life—until now," Patty said, taking an awkward draw on the filter.

Go on, Patty. It'll work against those heebie-jeebies.

Diane giggled. "Seriously? Never even tried it?"

"Can't you tell by the way she's doing it?" Dean asked.

In answer to Diane, Patty shook her head side-to-side, then her face fell into a worried expression. Her color changed as if she was blushing, but more green than red.

Demeter stood and hurriedly grabbed a small garbage can and handed it to Patty.

"What's this for?" As soon as she finished speaking, Patty started heaving up chunks of cracker, sausage, and Colby.

Demeter's cigarette was pinched in the corner of her mouth as she spoke. "That." *How's that for doing something evil?* She reached out and nonchalantly lifted her cigarette case, slipping it back into her pocket.

Just then, in the hall, someone screamed.

Demeter eased away from her guests and shuffled toward the door. Just as she opened it, a wrinkly, giggling old man streaked past—wearing only his black nylon socks.

If not for the ability of paper to adhere to something slightly damp, Demeter's cigarette would have fallen from her lips.

In a frail voice Diane asked, "Was that Emmet Johnson?"

"I think so." *What the hell is he doing?* Demeter blinked repeatedly, having stopped in her tracks. Patty continued to heave and vomit behind her. Another scream resounded as she stepped into the hall. She gazed in the direction the naked man had taken. With the Marlboro once more firmly between her lips, she frowned at his jiggling pasty-white ass as he strutted onward, his arms open wide and his laughter echoing.

Emmet was a doddering and dirty-minded old fool, but he'd never done anything like this. She wondered what might have brought it on.

Then the smell hit her: burning rope.

Incredulous, she whispered, "Weed?"

Demeter started walking toward Emmet's room. She had to make a turn near the elevators. Peering through his open door, she looked across the room, gaze stopping on the coffee table on which sat a strangely shaped, blown-glass vase. No, not a vase . . . it was one of those pot-smoking things. What were they called? *Bongs.*

With an angry frown, she entered the apartment. Next to the bong there was a plastic pill bottle. Demeter picked it up, read the label, and learned that Emmet had a prescription for medicinal marijuana.

"Well, I'll be damned." She knew Emmet had glaucoma; she hadn't known he smoked pot to treat it.

From behind the closed door of the room on the opposite side of the hall, she detected a boisterous round of laughter. With a twitch of her finger she adjusted the spell that allowed her to amplify sound. She replaced the bottle and left Emmet's room to listen at the other resident's door. She could make out three distinct voices whispering and giggling.

Could they be smoking weed too? She reached down and turned the knob slowly, then opened the door just enough to peek in.

Inside, the two old women she'd seen earlier returning from their stroll were sitting on either side of Gerald Clampet, the third floor's not-so-secret Viagra dealer. This room also smelled of burnt rope and rings of smoke billowed around them. One of the ladies put her hand on Gerald's chest and puckered up. He leaned into her.

"No, Gerald, kiss me first!" The other woman grabbed his chin and turned him toward her.

"No, me, Gerald!" The first let her hand fall to his crotch.

Demeter shut the door in disgust and backed five shuffling steps away from it.

Smoke 'em if you got 'em.

She snorted.

I didn't know there were any folks here who had medicinal pot.

She was still staring at that door, trying to figure out what to do when screams sounded again. She spun to see Emmet Johnson's "Johnson" flopping this way and that as he strutted back toward his apartment.

"Demeter!" His arms spread wide in greeting.

"Damn it, Emmet, where are your pants?"

"In my room, of course."

"Put them on before one of the nurses sees you!" With all the dour humorlessness of a cross school marm, Demeter jabbed the air to point Emmet toward his door. This was not what she'd wanted to happen. Not at all.

"Help me get my pants on, babe?"

"Get your ass in there and keep it there, you dirty old man!" Demeter grabbed him by the arm and shepherded him over his threshold. "And put your damn pants on." She shut his door with a bang and headed down the hall as fast as her waddling steps could carry her.

She leaned against it, panting. *I have to redo the spell. I have to re-word it to specify tobacco and not marijuana. What rhymes with tobacco besides whacko? What about marijuana? Hmmm . . . share-a-sauna? Neither would*

284 – Linda Robertson

make a good spell rhyme. Cannabis? Man-abyss? She groaned again as she made the turn at the elevators—and stopped dead in her tracks.

"What in Hell . . . " she mumbled.

Lost in her own thoughts she hadn't noticed the music, but as she made the turn it was impossible to ignore Sly and the Family Stone's "I Wanna Take You Higher" or the throng of people filling the third floor hall. Most were dressed as they always were, but some had dug out tie-dyed shirts. A few had donned black turtlenecks and berets.

Just then, the elevator *ding*ed. She twisted around as it opened, and two women she recognized as first floor residents maneuvered their wheelchairs from the elevator. "I haven't heard this song in ages," one said to the other.

Demeter backed away to let them pass. She had enough to deal with. She couldn't let more people get to third floor. She hurried to the elevator, kicked her tennis shoe off, and shoved the toe into the track of the doors, wedging it deep. She watched the doors roll almost shut, then pop open again.

Satisfied, she pressed through the crowd, advancing toward her apartment. She heard snippets of conversations, mentions of anti-materialism and Dali paintings, of Pink Floyd and Bob Dylan. Some man incredulously asked another, "You've never read Aldous Huxley's *The Doors of Perception*?"

She narrowly avoided getting slapped as Emmet Johnson, now wearing pants—but only pants, threw his arms wide and declared, "Hell, Irene, I was wading shirtless in the Reflecting Pool in D.C. at the 1970 Honor America Day Smoke-In!"

A few feet from her door, she encountered Diane and Dean. Patty stood between them with her fingers clamped on a half-smoked joint. There was a lazy look of bliss on her face.

Diane asked, "Don't you feel better now?"

"Oh yeah. I sure do," Patty said slowly, drawing out the word *do*. "I Scooby-doobie-doo."

"It always helps with nausea," Dean said. "I used to smoke it when I took chemo."

"It always made your mouth dry, though," Diane added. "And you were always so hungry." She noticed Demeter. "Oh *there* you are. We wondered where you ran off to. Your party idea was fantastic! How did you get the whole floor involved?" Her arms lifted as she spoke and she started dancing. Was that The Twist? A moment later she stumbled and sidestepped. There was the sound of a clattering dish as she plopped down on the floor.

Patty burst out laughing.

"Are you okay?" Dean stepped forward.

"Yes, just help me up!"

Dean wrestled her onto her feet. She turned to see what she had bumped. "Who put a candle in the hall?"

The bottom of Diane's shirt was on fire.

Demeter rushed forward and began smacking Diane's rump to put out the flame.

Diane shrieked. Dean grabbed Demeter by the arm. He jerked her backwards. "What do you think you're doing?"

Demeter pointed at the flames.

Dean bellowed and started smacking his wife's behind. "Hold still! Hold still!"

Patty remained motionless the whole time, shoulders jumping in mute laughter.

The shouting caught the attention of those nearby. Curious heads turned and, except for the music—which had changed to "Everyday People"—silence settled into the hall.

Demeter threw her arms up and shouted. "This party is over. All of you go back to your apartments!"

Patty wedged the joint in the corner of her mouth and put her hands on Demeter's shoulders. "Go to *your* room, you old bat. We're having fun." She shoved Demeter so hard she backpedaled over the threshold.

Demeter stood in her living room, stunned, as her three former guests traipsed merrily down the hall.

It's my spell. It's running amok.

She thought back over her wording. "Smoke 'em if you got 'em," was, to her, not only clever but a good way to get around the rules of magic. A practitioner was never to cause harm to or to interfere with the free will of another person. She had assumed that if there were other smokers on the premises they would not harm themselves further, nor would this interfere with their free will as they were already smokers.

Sharing was fair game, too, as people would only accept the offered cigarette if they were inclined to do so under normal circumstances.

But she *had* purposely placed the tempting cigarettes in front of the people she'd dragged to her room. Patty had admitted she wasn't a smoker. Even so, Demeter had encouraged her and allowed her to try. She'd even been elated when the woman had tried them and gotten sick—though that had more to do with a vengeful urge over the "evil" comment.

But Demeter had messed with people's free will.

Independence of thought was not something to take lightly. Ever. The repercussions tended to be of an unexpected nature. Such as quiet, meek Patty—whose mean side had been confined to verbal bitterness—suddenly manifesting physical aggression.

Demeter returned to the hall and scooped up the plate and candle and hurried back to her kitchen with it. Diane had squashed the candle, but she could work with it. She could either break the spell and start over—not as likely to work with the effect so riotously underway, or she could weave in a modification to the one in progress.

The latter was a trickier enterprise, but the right choice given the circumstances.

Working on her spell rhyme, she wrote down the words then scribbled them out only to rewrite until she had:

By the consummate grace
Of frog and garter snake
This new beginning is in motion.
Banished by birch
My spell is purged
And now rewritten with this potion:
Three ounces of reddest wine,
Sticky sap of greenest pine.
Mix and mingle, stirring nine times nine.
Purest drop of morning dew,
Ground up leaves of sacred yew.

She needed a statement of redirection. Considering rhymes for words like *narcotic* and *psychedelic*, her thoughts were interrupted when someone in the hall shouted, "Hey! Who's hungry?"

There was an overwhelmingly positive response. Every apartment had its own kitchen, so the thought of them going to their rooms was a welcome one. But the raised voice wasn't finished. "Let's all go to Grumbellies!"

That was the name of the facility's small deli-type restaurant that made sandwiches, salads, and soups. It was on the first floor near the front entrance and the administrative offices—the last place she wanted this crowd to go.

Leaving her spell components on the counter, she headed into the hall once more. Half the crowd was gone already, having filed into the stairwell while those few with wheelchairs, walkers, or oxygen tanks on rolling carts waited for the next elevator. An elderly man was holding Demeter's shoe and examining it. "How in the world does someone step out of their sneaker in the gap of the elevator doors and leave it?"

Demeter snatched it from his grip. "Wouldn't you like to know." She inelegantly replaced it on her foot and shuffle-stomped away, ramming herself into what was left of the crowd. They were funneling into the stairwell.

On a day when she'd already made at least one bad call, this definitely had to be the second. A deep tiredness settled over her after only a few steps. Her knees were aching by the time she had descended half a flight. Something was grinding in one joint. Clutching the rail with white-knuckled hands, she took each step slower than the last. Around her, others objected to her pace and complained they were going to miss something as they scurried around her.

Sweat had beaded on her brow by the time she reached the second floor landing. She wanted a cigarette more than she'd *ever* wanted one in her whole life, but she had to get to the cafeteria. She had to break this up before Mr. Loudcrier returned from his lunch.

Just one more flight of stairs. Just twelve steps and you're done.

Twelve steps. Like a Twelve-Step program. Demeter knew the program from a volunteer experience long ago when . . . Now was not the time to dwell on past history, but using her knowledge for the present . . .

Pausing on the first step, she whispered, "I admit that my spell was selfish, and that I am powerless over tobacco. My spell, such as it is, has become the proverbial turd in the punchbowl." On the second step, she said, "I have come to believe that a power greater than myself will restore the bunch of buffoons I live with to their usual amount of sanity." She hesitated on that step, adding, " . . . and granted, they weren't all equally blessed to start with."

On the third step, she mumbled, "I've made a decision to turn my spell casting and my cigarette smoking over to the care of my patron Goddesses: Hestia, Artemis, and Athena."

On the fourth, she hesitated to count the steps she'd taken before saying, "I will make a searching and fearless moral inventory of myself as soon as I get this bullshit fixed. Five—" another step—"I admit to no other human being the exact nature of my wrongs—the Goddesses already know what I've done and we don't need to keep harping on and on about it." And another. "Six, I am entirely ready to have my Goddesses or any willing deity remove all the defects from my aching knees, and the sooner the better."

She groaned in pain, rubbed her knees and proceeded. "Seven, I . . . humbly . . . ask that my shortcomings be ignored by that peckerhead Mr. Loudcrier and that my witchery is not revealed to him. Eight, I will make a list of the persons involved in this malarkey today—no, wait. I'll just use the directory—but I will make amends to them all by baking up a batch of oatmeal cookies bespelled to make them forget the whole damn incident. Nine . . . ouch, ouch, ouch . . . I will make that recipe and that spell as benign and sweet as possible, except where there are diabetics who would be harmed by the sugar. Oh Hell, ten—two to go—I'll continue to take personal inventory and when, I mean *if*, if I am out of line again, I'll promptly conduct corrective measures, even if I have to . . . apologize." Demeter made a face that had more to do with the word *apologize* than the pain in her knees.

"Eleven, through prayer and meditation I'll improve my conscious contact with my Goddesses, praying for knowledge and the good sense not to create such a whacko circumstance for myself ever again. Twelve— Goddess thank you it's the last—I have had a spiritual awakening as the result of the suffering I've endured coming down these arduous, bone-grinding, pain-in-the-ass steps. Let it be my penance for screwing things up so royally and I will carry this message—well a shorter and plainer version to my Alzheimer-ed and aged peers—that they might practice these principles in all our affairs."

She drew an equal-armed cross in the air. "So mote it be."

Opening the door from the stairwell, she heard squeals of laughter and delight and was nearly run over when two men zipped past, pushing ladies in wheelchairs.

Along with cheering and applause from the cafeteria, someone shouted, "George and Imogene are the winners of the wheelchair race!"

There were many people here. More than just the third floor.

Damn it. That spell was *for the whole facility. The ventilation system here must be better than I thought.*

As she digested the scene, she saw two of the nurse's aides sharing a joint near the front doors. It surprised her, but that surprise turned to horror and dread as she saw Mr. Longcrier walk in behind them.

He stopped dead, sniffed, and his usually pale face turned beet red. He demanded of the aides, "What do you think you're doing?"

Their eyes widened and they shared a long look before turning to face the overflowing cafeteria and gesturing. That forced Mr. Longcrier take in the entire scene. Nearly every resident in the facility was mingling in the entry, the first floor hall, and the eating area.

As his presence caused the white noise of hundreds of elderly voices to fall silent, it became obvious that somewhere nearby there was an eight-track playing. Donna Summer's sultry voice crooned out the orgasmic sounds of "Love to Love You Baby" making the *in flagrante delicto* moment even more awkward.

All movement ceased, except for Mr. Longcrier's mouth, which slowly fell open. He seemed incapable of any sound.

Demeter watched him suffer through his thought process, trying to make sense of the panorama before him and having no clue how to react to the geriatric merrymaking. She could practically read the words going through his mind by the shifting of his expressions. Disbelief to identification and back to disbelief, on to denial, again to disbelief, to over-the-shoulder glancing and concern—probably stemming from legal ramifications should the state inspectors show up now—to irritation that finally settled on anger. His hands clenched at his sides.

Demeter shuffled forward. "It's my fault," she said quietly.

Those around her gasped and spun to look at her.

"What?" Mr. Longcrier asked. His voice was a taut rope about to snap.

His anger pissed her off; he wasn't the only one who was irate. This all started because she was unhappy here. Demeter let her wrath start bubbling up as she lumbered up to him. By the time she reached him, her irritation was a geyser of sarcasm and obscenities. "I said, 'It's my fault,' you horse's ass. But if you weren't such a rump-hole none of this bullshit would have happened in the first place."

"Wh-what did you call me?" Shaking with rage his fingers unclenched. He reached into the breast pocket of his sports coat and produced a small note pad and pen. He began writing.

Demeter watched him scribble and rolled her eyes. "Expletive doesn't have an *A*."

Mr. Longcrier's fingers curled tighter and she heard the plastic casing of his pen crack. "I am the Chief Executive Officer of this facility and as such I deserve your respect, Ms. Alcmedi. I work very hard to—" He paused for the slightest second and took a deep breath to calm himself. He then continued, "—to ensure that this community is rigidly maintained and that the grounds are beautiful. I make sure the best care is offered to each and every resident here, and offered in such a manner that none of you feel your dignity is impugned. My high standards have made this facility the envy of comparable facilities across the nation. My rigid standards have raised the bar, and all of you benefit as I not only produced the beauty in which you reside, but I ensure that the staff all endeavor to maintain it." By the time his speech was complete, he had made eye contact with many of the residents behind Demeter in the cafeteria. His gaze hardened when it came to rest on her again.

Demeter blinked at his absurd, propaganda laden tirade. "Does it hurt your back to kiss your own ass like that?"

"All of you must disperse," he said, ignoring her. "According to the fire code only sixty-eight persons may occupy the cafeteria at one time." At the last he focused on Demeter. "You. Come to my office."

He turned on his heel, grabbed the nurse's aides by the shoulders and growled, "Get your wits about you, see these people to their apartments, and I *might* forget what I saw you doing when I walked in." He stormed off towards the main offices.

Demeter shuffled along at her best pace. Mr. Longcrier's secretary, a prim middle-aged woman in a high-collar blouse, stood stiffly behind the reception desk. She openly glared at Demeter when she passed.

The CEO waited impatiently at his office door, but before he could shut it, the secretary said, "Mr. Longcrier. You should see this first."

He stepped to the secretary's desk as Demeter planted herself in the same seat she'd sat in when she'd been called in for her formal reprimand after being caught smoking on the premises for the fifth time. He'd lectured her about the health risks of smoking and of second-hand smoke, then nattered on and on about the dangers of fires started by smoking—both interior and exterior—before presenting her with an official document stating she was "hereby duly warned" that the next occurrence of smoking on-site would end with her official eviction.

Like a high school principal threatening to expel me.

When Mr. Loudcrier entered, he slammed the door behind him and settled at his desk. Leaning forward, he assumed an interested pose and kept his hands on the blotter, his fingertips touching. "So what did you do that makes the . . . grouping . . . out there your fault?"

She considered admitting she was a witch and that she'd performed spellwork that brought it about. But that would only give him fuel for an anti-witch policy and she didn't want that.

Still, she had said she was to blame. "I incited them."

"How?" The corner of his eye twitched.

She picked at the edge of her cabbage rose shirt. "I just . . . riled them up. There are more smokers here than you seem to be aware of."

"But *how* did you rile and incite them, Ms. Alcmedi?"

The tone he used said more than his actual words. In an instant, Demeter switched from meekly plucking a thread to staring coldly across the desk. He knew. She couldn't guess how, but she was certain he did. "How do you think I did it?"

His palms pressed together until he was squeezing his own hands white as if he were about to break into the most fervent of prayers. His voice dropped to a vehement whisper. "I know what you did."

"How?"

"How do you think?" he mocked.

It hit her: video cameras in the hall. The secretary had checked the video and played it for Loudcrier. They had seen her put the candle and saucer in the hall and saying the spell. It wasn't much of a leap to surmise she was a witch. A broad smile spread across her face. "Good. That saves us both the trouble of dancing around the truth."

"Sorry. I don't dance."

"I'd have smashed your toes anyway."

"Is that a threat, Ms. Alcmedi?"

She didn't answer. This was her best shot. "I want an on-site smoking area."

"That will not be happening."

"There are obviously enough smokers among us that you should consider it."

"Woodhaven is a non-smoking community. That is locked into our insurance policy and it keeps our costs down. Changing it would mean higher fees for all residents. No one wants an increase."

Demeter sat back in her chair. "So you're saying that what residents want is irrelevant. Some bureaucratic bean-counter rules us by the law of the profit margin?"

"Yes. I am that bean counter." Smugness claimed his face. "You're free to live elsewhere."

"But—"

"No buts." He opened a desk drawer and pulled out a file, removed a sheet of paper. "I'm evicting you, Ms. Alcmedi."

292 – Linda Robertson

"That's ridiculous. You can't kick me out because I want a smoking area."

"You were smoking on premises earlier. I saw you. You had, previously, been formally, duly, and legally warned."

He was right. Demeter couldn't deny it.

Mr. Loudcrier snatched a pen from the cup on his desk corner. He did not answer, but simply began filling in the blanks.

Where will I go? How much time do I have to make arrangements? I don't even have a good suitcase. "You know . . . someday Mr. Loudcrier you'll be old and people half your age, determined to make a profit, will have authority over your environment. Maybe then you'll understand."

He didn't even look up.

Demeter reached into her pocket and pulled out her cigarette case. She carefully removed one and lit up.

"You cannot smoke in here."

"Just fill out your damn form, sunshine."

He slammed the pen on his desk. "You can*not* smoke in here!" At his shout, the secretary rushed into the doorway.

Demeter looked from Loudcrier to the secretary and back. The fact that her remark was ignored but her lighting up wasn't made her wonder why. "Aren't you going to finish filling out my eviction, Mr. Loudcrier?"

Just as his fingers curled to grasp the pen, Demeter wiggled her fingers and the pen squirmed away from him. Confused, he grabbed at it again, but this time it rolled away and lifted into the air. Mr. Loudcrier gasped and pushed away from his desk. His mouth worked like a mute puppet as the pen continued to write in the blanks.

The secretary crossed herself. "You're a witch!"

"You bet your sweet stenography pad, I'm a witch." *Didn't they already know that?* Demeter focused on Mr. Loudcrier again. "What did she show you before you came in?"

"Video footage of you placing a candle on the floor in the hall—which is a direct fire violation." His face somehow got paler. "That . . . that was a spell. That's how this is your fault!"

Pissed off that she'd needlessly outted herself, Demeter snarled, "No shit, Sherlock." Demeter took another drag on her Marlboro. She had one last ploy. "You might want to reconsider evicting me and just build a smoking area. I mean, unless you want this to turn into an ugly witch discrimination lawsuit."

Mr. Loudcrier's eyes darted back and forth as he thought.

Demeter sat back, crossed her legs, and blew smoke in his direction again.

The CEO suddenly stilled. He shot a look at his secretary, nodded, pushed his glasses up his nose and smoothed his receding hair. He faced Demeter squarely. "No. I will not reconsider." He grabbed a new pen and jerked the paper away from the hovering pen. He signed.

Demeter's mouth fell open. "Huh?"

He turned the paper and pushed it across the desk to her. "Unless you want my video footage released and elderly witches to be shown to be belligerent and dangerous firebugs, you'll sign by the X."

She glared at him and stuck her cigarette between her lips before holding out her open hand. The floating pen crashed into her palm and she adjusted it into her grip.

She scanned the eviction form. *I have to leave.*

Knowing she was losing this battle of the wills with Mr. Loudcrier hurt more than that thought. In fact, the idea of not having a choice in leaving here actually felt . . . good. As for her future residence . . . well, she had to trust the Goddesses. And she would fix the spell before she left. She'd promised. Besides, no one deserved to have a naked Emmet Johnson inflicted on them, not even her soon-to-be-former mundane neighbors.

Demeter signed.

Without a word she stood and walked toward the door. The secretary moved out of her way just as Demeter blew a smoke ring in her face.

Demeter shuffled a pair of steps, then spun back ready to say a nasty farewell to the secretary but, hearing an odd rustling noise from the office, she said nothing. Instead, she stepped back to the doorway and peeked in, watching as Mr. Loudcrier pulled the backing off of a small sticker, shoved his sleeve up, and slapped the sticker onto his arm.

Nicotine patch.

Demeter laughed out loud.

∼

The piece of "crystal" Mrs. Garcia gives to the young baseball fan in Leslie What's story is not really made of crystalline rock. But magic is said to make use of "intent" when the real item is missing, so perhaps glass can be effectively magical if it needs to be. Crystals, gemstones, semiprecious stones, and even more common stones are traditionally thought to possess powers or metaphysical energy that can be tapped in various ways. The wearing of amulets or jewelry decorated with stones or gems has been practiced throughout history to ward off evil, for protection, healing, or fertility. Some stones are even considered unlucky and to be avoided. Stones can also be used in divination— lithomancy. Most of us are familiar with the "crystal balls"—also known as shew stones—used by stereotypical "gypsy" fortune tellers. Crystal-gazing (crystallomancy or spheromancy) is actually a form of scrying—a way of "seeing" the past, present, or future by looking into a crystal ball, a bowl or body of liquid (hydromancy), or other reflective surface.

Magic Carpets
Leslie What

The Santa Ana winds arrived, whipped into frenzy by a spirit with the power to fold hot air inside wind. I lay beside my big sister Pammy in the backyard, feeling the dry breeze tickle the backs of my legs. My skin itched where the crop top had exposed a four-inch band of belly to dead grass. I sat up to scratch and Pammy sat up, too. She tugged her shirt down, as if to cover the welts Daddy had raised that morning, then reached to pull the sports page from beneath her transistor radio.

"What time is the game?" I asked. We hadn't had a radio or a team back home, but in Los Angeles we had both.

Pammy checked her watch. "Now," she said.

A wind blew, thick and breathy like a child learning to whistle. I watched a leaf fall from one of our two avocado trees and circle in the air, stirred by the wind's hand. Pammy let go of the paper and it skimmed twenty feet along the grass before landing on the chain-link cyclone fence that divided the back of our property from the neighbor's.

"I better get it," Pammy said, "before it flies into Mrs. Garcia's yard." Daddy had warned us just that morning to stay away from Mrs. Garcia, " . . . that witch next door. Stay away from her and her devil magic," he'd said, but if it hadn't been magic, he would have found another reason to keep us to our yard.

Pammy found his superstitions funny. I couldn't help looking past the fence to Mrs. Garcia's back door, wondering why she had been nice to us all summer, awfully nice for someone who wasn't even a blood relative. I didn't want to trust her. Maybe Daddy was right. Maybe Mrs. Garcia was a witch.

Pammy stood and slipped her tanned feet into her rubber thongs. She smoothed the wrinkles from her shorts and walked to the fence to ply away the newspaper. She crumpled the paper into a ball, which she threw at me. I straightened my arms to bat it away, but the wind changed, and the paper floated past me.

Pammy pointed to the leaves and paper scraps littering the lawn. "Daddy will be happy the wind is keeping us busy," she said. "Won't be able to do nothing today except clean up this mess."

I was twelve and didn't mind the yard. But Pammy was almost seventeen and for her, things were different. "If it wasn't for this radio," she said, "I'd go crazy."

"It wouldn't hurt to rake the yard while we listen to the game," I said, wanting to get it over with.

Pammy winced as she rubbed a yellowing bruise above her elbow. "We might as well wait till the winds stop," she said. She stuck out her tongue at our peeling stucco house. "Sometimes I wish Daddy was dead."

"You don't really mean that," I said. Daddy wouldn't be home for another hour, but I worried Pammy's wish might be carried on the wind to the slaughterhouse where he worked. Daddy had learned the butcher's trade during the Korean war, but now he hated his job, said the work was fit for idiots.

"Maybe I don't," Pammy said, "but I do wish things were different." She slumped to the ground and positioned her legs out in front to catch the sun. "Well, I'm turning on the radio before we miss any more."

We listened to the radio voice. "There's talk Maury Wills may break Ty Cobb's record of ninety-six stolen bases." Hearing Maury's name made me

296 – Leslie What

smile. Pammy noticed this and grinned, her lipstick forming pink lines along the creases of her lips.

I strained to hear above the static. "Turn it up," I said; she took her sweet time to do that. A boy had given the transistor radio to Pammy, but she'd told Daddy that she'd won it at school.

Mama called out from the house. "You girls in the yard?" She opened the screen door and stepped onto the patio. She sipped her whiskey from one of the two crystal wedding glasses that had survived our move to California. "I'm going to take my nap," Mama said, "unless you need something." Her matted hair was the color of unbaked red clay and her brown polka-dot dress was wrinkled, discolored under her arms.

"We're okay," Pammy said. "Go on to sleep."

Mama yawned. "Look at this yard," she said in a lazy drawl. "It's those avocado trees, stealing life itself right from the ground, bearing the Devil's fruit. No wonder I can't start my garden."

"You won't need no garden when those avocados ripen," I said. "We'll be eating them for the rest of the year." I didn't tell Mama I'd already tried the green fruit, even though it was still sour and hard and had given me a bad stomachache.

"You girls clean up before your Daddy gets home," Mama said. "And stay in the yard."

"We always do," said Pammy, and Mama went inside.

"Koufax comes out of his windup . . . and the throw . . . is . . . strike three . . . and the Giants are down after scoring one run. We'll come back with the top of the order, starting with number thirty, Maury Wills, leading off for the Los Angeles Dodgers." The announcer made me listen by stringing out his words and letting his excitement show at the end of every sentence. He sounded thrilled even when I knew he was disappointed, even when the Dodgers were losing. "Vince Gully really loves baseball," I said.

"It's Vin," Pammy said, shaking her head. "Vin Scully."

"Vin?" I asked, feeling my jaw drop. "Vin?"

Pammy smirked. "You probably agree Wills is gonna break Ty Cobb's record," she said.

"You bet," I said. "Maury Wills is the fastest man in baseball."

"Mrs. Garcia says he's a Negro," Pammy said.

"I don't believe it," I said. I looked down, not wanting to meet her glance. "Not that it makes any difference."

"It'd make some difference if Daddy was to see your diary," Pammy said. She pulled up a handful of brown grass, held her palm upward and spread her fingers to let the grass fall through. "Maury Wills," she said in a false high voice that mimicked mine. "Running. Stretching out his hand to touch . . . the base beyond reach. What's that, a haiku?"

"Pammy! You said you'd stay out of my diary," I said. I plucked some grass to throw toward her, but the wind blew the grass back toward me. "Maury Wills is a great athlete," I said, knowing Daddy wouldn't care if he was the President. There were people we weren't supposed to talk to, weren't supposed to think about, people my parents seemed afraid of because they were different. "How would Mrs. Garcia know if he was a Negro, anyway?"

"Maybe she's got a television," Pammy said, and I felt stupid because I hadn't even thought about that.

In a little while Mrs. Garcia came into her yard—just as she did every afternoon—to water her rose garden. "Hello girls," she called.

Pammy waved. "Our fairy godmother, at last," she whispered.

I looked through the chain-link fence into her yard, alive with color. Mrs. Garcia wore an orange flowered sundress. Her black hair was swept into a knot sprayed stiff enough to keep it from coming undone in the wind. She always looked magazine-model perfect, like someone make-believe. "How's your mother feeling today?" she asked.

I wanted to say, "She's fine," but Pammy said, "She's gone back to sleep," before I could get my words out. Sometimes I wondered at Pammy, telling all our troubles to a stranger.

"It's not right," said Mrs. Garcia, fingering a crystal necklace that made the sunlight dance along her skin. "You girls need to get out of that yard." She bent to smell her roses. "How are my Beauties?" she said. "How's Mr. Lincoln? And Silver Jubilee? Irish Gold? First Prize? And Honor?"

"Ground ball through the hole and into center and Wills is on with a base hit," said the radio.

Mrs. Garcia started the faucet and held her thumb in front of her hose. A whisper of spray flew over the back fence and landed on my arms. I watched her fret over her flowers like they were something precious, not just backyard shrubs. "They get thirsty in this wind," she said. "So, who's winning?"

The winds shifted direction and suddenly, I caught the sweet scent of roses. The fragrance cut straight through the heat to make my nostrils tingle. It was early on in the game so I said, "The Dodgers are behind, but they'll make it up."

"I'm sure they will," said Mrs. Garcia. "Would you girls like a soda?"

I looked at Pammy, suddenly afraid. "Thank you very much," Pammy said. "We're very thirsty."

Mrs. Garcia smiled. She set the hose down on the grass and hurried into her house. She came out with two opened Coke bottles and made her way to the fence. She stood on her tiptoes and handed the sodas over to Pammy.

Pammy started sipping hers right away, but I held onto to mine, afraid to drink.

"There he goes . . . and the throw . . . *is* . . . in time . . . and Wills is caught at second."

I could not stop the sigh that made me sound so young.

"I'm sorry," said Mrs. Garcia.

"It's okay," I said. "They'll make it up." For the first time all day I felt as if I might break down, and I said without thinking, "Maybe you could stop by for iced tea, sometime." I was sorry the moment I had spoken.

"That would be nice," said Mrs. Garcia.

Pammy strained to hit me with her elbow and her crop top split along the side seam. She stuck two fingers in the hole and frowned. "Well, isn't this just great," she said.

" . . . a high fly to center and Davis is going back. Back, back, back, to the wall . . . and it's gone. One run in and here comes Mays. And the Giants lead it three to one."

Mrs. Garcia stopped watering to listen. "Don't worry, girls. They'll make it up."

"Too bad Wills got caught at second," Pammy said.

I stared at my feet, tan except where the straps had carved out a pale upside-down V. "Too bad," I said, but something inside me felt wrong, worried that it was a terrible omen for the fastest man in baseball to be thrown out.

~

The winds blew hard that night. My bedroom faced the back yard and I was awakened by the noise of something walking on the roof. I crept from my room through the hallway to the door. I stepped out to the patio and into a warm breeze that pressed a dry kiss against my skin. The moon was low; streamers of light peeked through the tree branches. One avocado fell onto the roof, followed by another.

The wind blew around me, above me, over my ears, and down my neck, and in and out of the spaces between my toes. I felt warmth under my feet and knew it was truly the very breath of the Devil. Leaves hovered in the sky like hummingbirds. I heard an echo in the canyon and imagined that the canyon was Chavez Ravine, the Dodgers' new stadium.

I leaned forward and felt the wind hold me in an unnatural tilt. I could fly, I thought, with the Santa Ana winds lifting me into the air. I ran to the chain-link fence and back to the patio, then tried running from one side of the yard to the other, but I couldn't gather enough speed to take off.

I knew now that I was in the presence of magic, and I did not want that magic to end. "Never," I said aloud, as I plucked an eyelash and let it fly away into the night because Mama used to say that wishing on eyelashes made things come true.

In a while I went back to my room. I pulled my diary from its new place under the mattress and started another in a series of imaginary correspondences. "Dear Maury," I wrote, and when that didn't sound right, I changed it to "Dear Maurice." I chewed the end of my pencil and thought. "I will show you how to fly," I wrote, "and maybe you could teach me how to run."

~

After breakfast, Pammy and I dressed and put on our thongs to go out into the yard. The air smelled of eucalyptus, a medicinal scent, only faintly distasteful. We saw hundreds, maybe even thousands of avocados on the ground, shiny skins, bumpy and green. Our yard had never looked so alive. I pretended money had fallen from heaven as I skipped through the yard, kicking avocados out of my way. "Fastball," I said, and threw one at Pammy, barely missing her. She grabbed an avocado and beaned me on my head.

That made me cry, which brought Daddy out. He hadn't finished eating and his yellow paper napkin was tucked inside his collar. He glared at Pammy with his concrete-gray eyes. A wad of toilet tissue covered a red spot on his chin.

"What do you think you're doing?" he said. "I've got to get to work. I can't be bothered with you." He looked at the yard. "What's happened here?" he said.

"It's the wind, Daddy," Pammy said, using the haughty tone she'd recently adopted.

"You making fun of me, girl?" he asked. "You think I don't know that?" He narrowed his eyes. "What's that on your face?" he said. Pammy reached up to wipe away her lipstick. "I know you been using my razor," he said. "Who you showing off for, Pammy? You think I don't know what goes on here when I'm gone to work?"

"All the girls my age shave," Pammy said. "Wear makeup, too."

"You hear that?" Daddy said to no one. "What a place Los Angeles turned out to be." He threw his napkin to the ground and stormed over close enough to grab Pammy's hair. He shook her head back and forth.

Daddy swatted her belly, then switched to the small of her back. Pammy cried out as he smacked her cheek. He raised his hand again. If Mama was there, she would have told him, "Not in the face." That was what Mama always said since reading about the child whose face was paralyzed by a slap to the head. But Mama wasn't there, she was inside, still asleep.

Pammy cried out, "I can't see. Stop it, Daddy!"

Daddy held her chin in one hand and lifted his other hand to hit her.

I yelled, "Not in the face! Not in the face!" He was breaking our family rule, one that even Mama believed.

"You shut up," he said. "This is none of your concern."

"I can't see, Daddy!" Pammy said. She was bawling.

I felt scared. I was the one who had wished for the winds to continue and now our yard was ankle-deep in debris and Pammy was getting a beating. I should have been more careful after Maury Wills was caught at second.

"Stop," I said. "Please, Daddy. Not in the face."

Daddy stopped and stared at me.

"You telling me what to do?" he asked.

"No, Daddy," I said. I hoped it wasn't too late to save Pammy. "Hit me instead," I said, thankful when he walked my way because I thought I could take anything.

At that moment I understood what it meant to see things crystal clear. The winds trickled to a breeze while the fury in Daddy grew. The air was clean and I saw the world as it was, with all the haze stripped away. Daddy raised his hand to strike my backside and I knew all at once that he wasn't even mad at me. Daddy didn't care who he was hitting. Just knowing that made me feel strong, because I loved him and I wanted him to love me. I let my body take the beating while my thoughts floated up with the leaves, tiny magic carpets on the wind.

After a while Daddy stopped and rubbed his hands together. He said, "You girls stay in the yard, now. I don't want any boys coming to the house."

"Yes, Daddy," I said in a whisper. I didn't know why Daddy was so afraid of boys. Pammy knew, but she wouldn't tell me.

"And clean up this mess," Daddy said. He left us to go to the job he hated.

Pammy held her hand against her face. She blinked hard. "I'm okay," she said. It was already hot outside, but she was shivering. "Why did you do that for me? Why'd you take my punishment?"

"I couldn't watch," I said. "Anyway, it really don't hurt that bad, so long as you don't keep your mind on it."

Then we heard Mrs. Garcia call, "Good morning," from her yard. There was an urgent questioning in her voice and I froze, not knowing how long she'd been there. Pammy bowed her head.

"Everything okay?" asked Mrs. Garcia. She fingered her crystal necklace.

"Just fine," Pammy answered, but there was a hard edge to her voice.

"You're sure?" Mrs. Garcia said. She stood just on the other side of the fence and slipped her fingers through the wire. "You'll tell me if there's anything I can do."

"We're fine," said Pammy, her voice breaking.

Mrs. Garcia narrowed her eyes and I knew she didn't believe that we were fine. After a while she said, "Look at all those avocados. What a waste." She shook her head. "What a waste," she said again, but she was looking at Pammy and not the avocados. "Must be fifty dollars worth, at least. Maybe it's time you girls got out of that yard. At the same time, you might as well try to make some money."

Pammy made her way toward the fence. "Will you help us?" she asked, and Mrs. Garcia agreed.

"Don't worry anymore," she said. "I'll do whatever you need. Let me bring some orange crates for the avocados."

"I don't think we should do this," I said. "We're not supposed to leave the back yard."

Pammy gave a sideways glance to me. She rubbed her cheek and I saw how the redness had given her a look of defiance. "Daddy will never know," Pammy said, "unless you tell him."

~

Mrs. Garcia set up a card table and two folding chairs on the sidewalk. Pammy and I each filled a crate full of avocados. We carried the crates to the table and sat facing the street. Mrs. Garcia left us, saying she'd tack up a sign announcing our sale on the street corner.

"We shouldn't be doing this," I said. I had to go to the bathroom, but didn't want to leave my sister alone.

"Go on and tell Mama, if you're so worried."

"I'm not worried," I said, looking back at the house.

After a few minutes a battered green station wagon pulled up and a young Mexican boy with smooth skin and shiny black hair stepped from the car. His car keys jingled from his pinkie. He walked close to Pammy's side of the table.

"Good morning, young ladies," he said. His shirt was open to the second button; a few curly hairs poked through. He tipped his blue baseball hat as he nodded his head.

Pammy smiled. "Good morning," she said. "Are you interested in any avocados?"

He kneeled beside the table and set his elbow down, near Pammy's tanned arm. "How much you want?" he asked.

"Twenty for one dollar," Pammy answered without lowering her gaze.

The boy pursed his brown lips and pushed out his breath. "You drive a hard bargain," he said, "but I'll pay you five dollars for the two boxes."

"What will you do with them all?" Pammy asked.

"My father's restaurant," he said. "They'll ripen and we'll freeze what we don't use right away." He handed the five-dollar bill to Pammy. I saw her red cheeks blush even darker as he folded his hand over hers.

He walked over to open the back of his station wagon. "Help me empty them into my car," he said to Pammy.

A hot wind blew against my chest. I tried to say, "No," but the wind had sucked away my breath.

Pammy put her arms around one crate to pick it up. The boy walked close and pressed his hip against hers. They carried one crate to the station wagon, balanced it on the edge of the car door until the boy tipped the crate on its end and let the fruit roll out. They did the same with the other crate.

"May I have a glass of water?" he asked, tipping his head toward me.

Pammy ordered, "Go on. Get him something."

"No," I said. "I won't do it."

"You'd better," she said, "or I'll tell Daddy about your diary."

"Go ahead," I said, but she gave me such a look that I said, "Okay. I'll get it." I ran through the front yard to the house, flung the door open, and ran to the kitchen. I picked up Mama's dirty glass from next to the sink. I didn't worry that it was too nice a glass for a Mexican to use and that I'd get in trouble, should my parents find out what I had done. I filled the glass with water, and ran back outside.

The boy was sitting in my chair beside Pammy, his arm over her shoulder, his head bent close to hers. I hurried to him. "Here's your drink," I said, thrusting the glass forward. The water splashed on the table. The boy licked his lips and said, "Thanks."

Pammy was hiding something from me, something big. I looked down the street toward the intersection Daddy would turn from when he came home from work.

After a while, the boy said, "I should get going." He set the glass on the edge of the folding table, stood up and pushed me out of his way to walk to his car. He pulled away from the curb.

I punched Pammy's arm, and the motion set the table rocking. The water glass tipped and rolled to the edge of the table. I reached out, but I couldn't grab it in time, and the glass fell to the ground—Mama's crystal—shattering into rainbows.

I collected the shards and stacked them in a pile on Mrs. Garcia's table. I couldn't speak for a long time, but finally I said, "Didn't you notice that boy was Mexican?"

"I noticed," Pammy said, and she was smiling. "I think he likes me."

"No, he doesn't," I said. It was clear that Pammy already knew this boy and I sensed that what Daddy was afraid of happening was going to happen to Pammy, soon. "We're going to be in really big trouble," I said.

"Not me," said Pammy. She picked up an empty crate and headed for the back yard to pack more avocados. I hurried after her. "You promised you'd take my punishments from now on," Pammy said. "I'm not ever gonna get in any trouble again."

~

In a while, Mrs. Garcia came out to check on us. She saw the broken crystal, now a pile of rainbows, on her table and put her hand on my shoulder. She leaned close enough to whisper and before I knew it, she had her arms around me and was hugging me tight. I didn't mean to do it, but in a few seconds I was also hugging her. "Don't worry. Things will turn out okay," she said. "You must believe that."

Mrs. Garcia gathered up the broken crystal and dropped the shards into her purse. She handed me one nearly round piece. "Keep this," she whispered, "and don't ever lose it. When you look through crystal, you can see the different facets of the world. Whenever you can't bear to live in one of those facets, I want you to look through your crystal and find another. And then I want you to take a step and go into that world."

304 – Leslie What

She left, but came back in an hour with an unbroken crystal glass in her purse. "Here," she said, "good as new. Go on. Put this in the kitchen where it belongs."

When I looked through the crystal glass I saw one place where the glass was dull, a circle where no rainbows formed. I hid my tiny piece of crystal in my shorts pocket, but still felt its warmth through the fabric. When I pulled out the crystal I saw the sun's reflection, red like the edge of fire.

~

The last of the windfall fruit began to ripen by the end of the week. Pammy warmed a can of cream of mushroom soup for lunch, but I was hungry again by late afternoon. I picked up an avocado and felt its bumpy skin, then pushed in with my thumbs to check the softness. I found one I wanted and dug my nail into the skin. I peeled back a raspy slice that tickled me like a cat's tongue. The avocado was wet, lush and smooth, the Devil's fruit. I put my lips to the hole I had made and stuck my tongue inside to lap up the fruit.

"Is there a game today?" Mrs. Garcia said when she came into her yard.

"Starts in five minutes," said Pammy.

"I'm going out," Mrs. Garcia said, looking at Pammy. She cleared her throat. "Is there anything else you need?"

I started to say, "No, thank you," but Pammy answered, "Yes. There is something," before I could speak.

Mrs. Garcia nodded and stared at us both for a minute before leaving.

I gripped my hands into fists. "What are you up to?" I asked.

Pammy ignored me and painted on a fresh coat of lipstick. She turned away, and looked back toward the house.

Something bad was going to happen, but I didn't know if it would happen to Pammy—or to Maury—or to me.

The game started. We listened to the top half of an inning that was over one, two, three. Then commercials, then the bottom half of the inning.

"Maury Wills steps out onto the plate. And the first pitch is high and inside. Ball one."

I heard Pammy say, "Hello."

I turned and saw the Mexican boy in the side yard.

Pammy stood and took a step toward him. "We have to hurry," she said. "I have money."

"The throw is low and Wills checks his swing. Marichal doesn't believe it and asks for a ruling. Did Wills hold up in time? . . . Ball two!"

"Get away," I said. "Our mother is home, inside!"

Pammy took another step toward the boy.

"I won't take your punishment," I said to her. "You're on your own for this."

"Next pitch is in the dirt! Unbelievable. Marichal is wild. Bailey goes over to calm him down. Two pitches into the inning and he's already out of control. The next pitch . . . and it's high. Wills is on with a walk!"

"Don't go," I said, but Pammy shrugged me off.

"Keep the radio," she said. "I'll come back for you soon as I can." The boy held her hand and together, they walked through the side yard, then disappeared from view.

My throat began to close and I sat stunned, afraid to stay, afraid to move. With no one out, Wills was certain to steal second. I broke into a cold sweat and tasted something sour twisting in my stomach. I stopped myself from breathing, because I was afraid my breath would blow a bad omen from my yard to Chavez Ravine, and Wills would be thrown out. The Devil only knew what would happen then.

"Marichal comes out of his stretch and throws and Wills is off and running. . . . "

Breezes gathered from all directions. Then from nowhere a gust blew strong enough to knock the radio over on its side. I moved to right the radio. "Please don't get caught," I prayed, but I didn't know who I was praying for—Pammy or Maury Wills. The winds pressed against my back and forced me upright, pushed me toward the side yard, then into the front. My neighborhood was a ghost town, with papers and loose garbage rolling along the empty street. There wasn't a soul anywhere, no birds, no barking, the only noise I heard was of freeway traffic in the distance. I found myself running along the sidewalk away from our house toward the intersection. I pulled the crystal from my pocket and held it up. As I stared through the glass, my world became many.

Winds gusted and hot breath rushed under my heels, lifting me out of my thongs and into the air. I raised my arms and looked upward, praying I'd see heaven and not the Devil. The sky was so bright it stung my eyes. When I looked down, I saw my neighborhood had become a quilt of color, alive except for one small patch of brown.

I gripped the crystal tight and tried to imagine what Maury Wills was really like, but the man I pictured was all a blur, as if he were running past me.

Mrs. Garcia had told me not to worry and for the first time, I started to believe her. The most important thing was that Pammy had gotten free and Mrs. Garcia had given me the magic to get away when I needed to. I felt strong enough to face whatever was about to happen.

The Santa Anas carried me on a carpet of air that raced above the city to Chavez Ravine and the fastest man in baseball. Below, the road meandered up the dry hill, asphalt shiny as glass. I floated over the ridge of a stadium shaped like a broken bowl, where inside, a thousand fans stood screaming. Something streaked across the brilliant green of the diamond and I looked down—just in time—to see number thirty, Maury Wills, slide free into second.

~

Leah Bobet writes of a modern-day witch whose roots lie in the idea of the "herbwoman." Although similar to the "cunning folk" tradition, this concept of witchcraft grows more from seeds planted by fantasists than history or superstition. According to Jennifer A. Heise, this witch-type made her fictional appearance in the early 1970s with the rise of feminism and the development of female roles in fantasy, a time that also saw a surge in the number of women reading and writing fantasy. During the same era, there was renewed interest in herbal medicine; getting "back to the land" and a distrust of "establishment medicine" were in vogue. As Heise points out, this interest was at least partially related to a justifiable backlash against science-based medicine in the women's movement. (The abysmal state of female health care in the 1960s has been well documented.) "Natural" cures provided by knowledgeable women—whether set in fantasy worlds, supernatural versions of our past, or modern times—became a frequent genre trope.

The Ground Whereon She Stands
Leah Bobet

Alice sent me flowers. I didn't realize until midmorning, when I walked through the hallway into the kitchen and greening stems twisted and crushed under bare feet. Then I looked back, and saw the petals shading the carpet, pulping on the grout. They didn't like tiles. I backtracked, and there were daisies rooted in the shower drain. They smelled like the second day of spring.

"Oh, Alice," I said to the flowers, and instead of grinning or crying put the coffee on the stove.

After the third cup, two cream, two sugar, I closed the laptop and went up the road to Idaho.

I lived in the last house with electricity before the Canadian border. Alice's house was past mine, up on a rise where the red oaks shrank to larch and bristly sumac. There was only one trail there, an old logging track wide enough for her asthmatic red old truck. She clipped the branches clean when they battered at the windows in the summertime.

It was close enough to walk, but not without hiking boots. By the time I reached the turnoff Russian sage nosed through the eyelets, fighting my shoelaces for sunlight.

Alice was in the back garden, coaxing a ripe heirloom tomato off its heavy stem. Idaho had three gardens: the back was the farm garden, stands of tomato plants and curling cucumber standing sentry between fat and heavy lettuces, patches of collard greens, toddler-fat corn, potatoes. There were four kinds of potatoes. "Well, it's Idaho," she'd said diffidently last summer when I'd first had the tour. Her hands were in the pockets of her dirt-stained jeans, head down and looking just away. She'd been smiling.

She was humming now, a folksong in time with the pull and roll of vegetable flesh. I shifted my feet; I didn't want the sage rooting down in her beds. Its leaves rustled and rubbed against each other, and the noise brought her head up. She smiled again when she saw me, that crooked half-wince which was the closest she ever got.

"Hi," I said, and tripped over a fragrant stand of fresh-bloomed lavender flowers.

Her mouth opened, shaped a syllable. "Let's get you inside."

The light in the farmhouse was orchard-light, coming from the east. Alice shed her ballcap with one hand and settled me in a chair, a carved wooden one that might have come from the Heritage Festival down in Newfane. I picked my way through the brush toward the laces, snapping off green branches as they hardened into wood.

The boots came off in tangles. I worked both feet free and wiggled my toes. They smelled sweet, and sharp, and green.

Alice came back in with scrubbed-clean hands, dirt still hiding under a fingernail. She took my right foot in her palms. "Russian sage," she said mildly. "Good for fevers."

Her hand was cool. The sweaty muscle in the peak of my arch relaxed against it. This close I could smell her shampoo, sharp with tea tree oil and vinegar. "It started growing this morning. There's daffodils in the shower."

I looked out the window instead of down at her, to spare myself the sight of it. It didn't matter. I caught the motion; the line of her mouth pressing together and her head turning down. "Someone put a spell on you," she said, perfectly even.

Because you're mine, my head filled in. Someone. Of course, Alice. I eased my foot away.

She looked up, no change in her face but the oh-so-white whites of her eyes. "Could take a few days," she muttered.

"Mmhmm," I replied. She knew full well I was rotating into town next week.

"Come take these down with me," she asked, barely a question. Eglantine spilled from between my toes onto her polished wood floor. The prickles tugged skin along with it. She winced watching, and I felt cruel.

"All right," I said. I crushed the opening petals when I stood.

∽

We sat side by side on the tailgate at the side of 147 with the sign out, and watched the tourists roar along the highway. LOCAL GROWN, it announced. BEST VEGGIES IN CALEDONIA COUNTY! I had painted it in bright blue and yellow at the end of last autumn. Alice coaxed taut and sweet early squash out of soil the farmers had left for dead, but she was clumsy with things like advertising. I swung my legs back and forth over the muddy shoulder and felt the traffic wind blow, golden dandelions fading and sporing from the creased soles of my feet.

There was no wireless signal here; it was barely a rest stop, just a collection of picnic tables and parking spots where the brush had been hacked away. I rested the laptop on my thighs, half-open against the summer sunshine glare.

Alice watched me from the edges of her eyes, in the way the old men called Indian. "Gonna need a few things."

I clicked the laptop shut.

"To take off the spell," she said. Cars pulled off the highway: sleek family sedans. A thick and sleepy blonde ducked out from a Honda's passenger seat and lit up a cigarette.

"Gonna find out who's enchanting me?" A trio of children tumbled from the Honda's backseat, the oldest dark-haired and pouting, her two little brothers pinching with sly and sloppy grins. I watched them, watched her Indian-style.

"Don't have 'em all in the garden. Have to look around."

The dandelions dropped to the pitted asphalt, their stems baking hot and sweet. Hissing marigolds and daisies sprung up in their place.

"So you're not going to find out." I shifted onto one thigh and turned to look her in the face. She had long, sharp lines in her cheeks, a straight nose. The kind of straightnesses you wanted to touch, which would maybe send the message: give it up. I've known for months. "Have to start sleeping with a rowan cross."

Her hands clasped in her lap, long and strong and dirty. She swallowed, soft.

"Mama," the youngest boy's voice rose over the traffic. "Apricots."

I hadn't seen a flick of the fingers, a whisper of words, anything she could have charmed to turn the kid's head our way. Luck; I bit down on a sigh and swung my legs again. Just a damned coincidence.

"Saved by the bell," I muttered, and the surprise on her face held me over until the kids came barreling across the lot.

They took the apricots, and some new potatoes, red peppers, strawberries, and mint besides. "Good for the stomach," Alice told the stringy-haired blonde, who up close looked too young for three school-age children.

"I get carsick," she winced, looking like she wished the dirt would swallow her. Wondering how Alice had smelled her sour stomach, no doubt, with her breath covered in the smell of cigarettes. Cringing at the touch of a stranger's attention on her for one flat minute.

I turned away.

The little girl was standing by the back tire of the truck, watching her shouting, bouncing brothers. "There's flowers on your feet," she informed me, mild. Her own feet were encased in plastic sandals.

"So there are," I replied.

"Are you magic?"

"No," I told her. "Just enchanted."

Alice plucked a daisy from my toes and tucked it behind the little girl's ear, her hands as careful as with her carrots.

When I got home the daffodils were blooming, and Alice had said not a word more. Butterflies nested along the kitchen counter, following the train and twist of flowering mint. I eased them off and into the air with the hem of my shirt. My mother taught me young about touching butterfly's wings: so delicate the valleys of your skin would strip their scales away.

They fluttered through the open windows into the growing evening, while I tapped and cropped away at the job manual for next summer's crop of state park guides. They tickled my toes, drifting to the floor, attracted by my sweat and the scent of roses. I walked like a sworn Jain monk across my sea-green kitchen tiles, placing every toe gently to avoid crushing living wings. Tiger lilies seeded in my wake, pushing uselessly at the solid floors.

I had brushed my teeth with Alice's homemade mint toothpaste and tucked into sheets scented with her lavender before I remembered my hiking boots, still at Idaho, abandoned for the tingle of her hands upon my skin.

~

She woke me late morning from butterfly dreams, with the sun coming hard through the window. "Lisbet?" the leaves said, sawing one on the other like cricket legs. They smelled rich: sunlight on soft, hot veins, life churning and spreading into the summer skies. The smell of Alice's skin, I thought, and shivered.

"Oh gods, Lizzie—"

A branch snapped. I opened an eye.

There were flowers in my mattress, curling around the springs. Ivy had strangled my alarm clock sometime before eight-forty-five a.m., and all around me, opening, were roses, roses.

And above them Alice, hands twisting in each other like drowning worms.

"G'morning," I told her, and her hands stilled.

"I'll fix the door," she blurted, and reached out for the woody tangle around the nightstand. Ivy curled around her finger. She pulled her hand back.

"You broke in?" I mumbled, still half-asleep and pollen-drunk. There were no break-ins this far up, by the border. Everyone was neighbors here. I still locked my door come nightfall.

"You didn't answer the door," she said breathily, windy enough that I opened my other eye. Her mouth was twisted, not a wince, but pained like I'd never seen before. "It looked like a bier," she said, and dropped into my wicker chair.

"Let—" I tugged with one leg "—let me make you some coffee."

The rose-roots caressed my calf and ankle and held on fast.

"Oh," I said, and my heart sped up to panicking.

"Shh," Alice said, one hand flat on my forehead, cool and a little damp and smelling sharp like tea tree. "Breathe for me, that's right, that's good—"

She parted the roses with her pocketknife, murmuring an apology for every pruned-out life. Blossoms drifted down the comforter to the floor, parting and bruising on the hand-knotted rug that covered wood that stayed cold even in summertime. "Stay still for me," she soothed. The knife blade touched my outer thigh.

I breathed.

The shade peeled off my legs like a long morning, inching down to full noon. When I felt the sun on my ankles Alice said, "Okay, up," and thrust arms under my armpits, rolled and lifted and I was standing on the battered old rug. Underfoot was satin; underfoot were petals, ankle-high, delicate. Like walking on butterfly wings.

I stared at my rose-grown bedsheets, split with thorns and staining deepest red. My chest stuttered again. "Coffee," I said, pressing a hand against my breastbone, and fled into the kitchen.

I leaned over the coffeepot and breathed it in, real, until the steam was too hot. Alice was in the doorway when I looked up. My old Christy Moore tour T-shirt hung over her arm. She held it out with a face red as roses, eyes fast on the floor where my trail of desperate bud blooms scrabbled, sent out roots, and died. I took it and slipped it on over goose-pimpled skin.

"We go up into the woods today," she said when I was decent. My hiking boots were toes-to-the-wall by the kitchen door.

"I have to have this manual done for when I rotate in—"

My right leg tickled. *Butterflies*, I thought, and looked down at a thin trail of blood. Thorn-scratched. The gouge looked like a cat's-claw, or a woman's. "Today," she said fixedly, and took my broom to the aborted flowers.

The daffodils were gone from the shower drain. In their place grew a cluster of impatiens, touch-me-not, a bright raspberry-puff of a bloom whose name I didn't know. I washed my hair thoroughly. The shampoo poisoned them on its way to the septic tank.

The bedroom was clean of roses when I tiptoed in to dress. The mattress was stripped, spring-marks and sweat stains laid open. I looked away from it and thought about shorts, underwear. A T-shirt not the color of roses.

"I couldn't find spare sheets," Alice said when I crept back into the kitchen. The dead buds had vanished, and there was toast on a plate in the centre of my table, a bowl of sectioned oranges. Shipped in from Florida: something that'd never see the inside of Alice's fridge. She hadn't touched them. Her hands were clean and scratched raw where they cradled the chipped old mug.

"I don't have any," I said, and poured myself some coffee. She'd laid out a teaspoon for me: two cream, two sugar. My hand had stopped shaking. That was good.

The corners of her mouth firmed. I watched her around my coffee. There'd be sheets on my doorstep by nightfall.

I laced up my hiking boots when the breakfast was gone. The leather was scratched where the sage had groped along sole and arch for live earth. "All right," I said to Alice, looked up at her seated at the table.

She looked away.

"We go up," she said.

I closed my broken-lock door behind us. We went up.

～

There were honeybees in the woods above Idaho. They made the stepping treacherous as butterflies, gathered in my bootprints to roll in virgin pollen. "Wild swarm," Alice volunteered. The sun was hot on my back. She shaded her eyes to watch me. Her face reflected ruddy sunlight; I couldn't see if she was smiling. "Jailbreak from an apiary down in the valley."

"What if I was allergic to beestings?" I put another foot down, narrowly missing a flash of yellow.

"I'd save you." Diffident. Not a speck of feeling.

Perhaps I was making up the whole thing.

There was no path this far onto the mountain. Instead I walked in Alice's footsteps, around prickly tree-branches and their slender young. Crushed leaves from last autumn's fall muffled her light tread, my heavy. The branches leaned in to touch my hair. Alice put a rough hand on bark, and they stilled.

"Don't mind 'em," she said, and led deeper on. Plucked a stem of grass here, a fingernail of bark there.

We stopped in front of a blossoming brush tree, all flat green leaves and straggling yellow flowers. The bees bobbed around it giddily, dancing buzzing maypole steps between the forking branches. "Here," she said. Tugged out a bucket, and handed it over. It was a kid's bucket, the kind they sell at beachside stalls with little plastic shovels attached. It was blue; the appliquéd white daisies were scratched halfway off. "Halfway full."

"What's this?" I ran my right hand along the branch. Stringy yellow flowers crumpled into my cupped left palm.

"Witch hazel," Alice said, and for the first time ever I saw her crooked-tooth grin.

She came back with wild raspberries; we ate them when the bucket was half full, leaned against the deer-nibbled bark of a knotty old birch. The tickle between my toes was lazy strawberry vine, rambling curled across the busy earth. Alice reached down and plucked a ripening berry.

"It'll taste like feet," I warned.

She popped it in her mouth. It felt like being kissed. I breathed out, soft, and she heard it; I saw her sit up straighter, out of the corner of my eye.

I looked up at her.

She looked away.

We emerged from the woods with the sun falling, thick light moving slantwise through the muttering trees. "How long before it's fixed?" I asked.

"Soon," she murmured, a caress of the hair. And Idaho rose from the horizons, its gardens spread out before us like the breeding ground of stars.

The stove was cold in Idaho. It was chilly, even with the rugs and woven tapestries, the seam-free joints of the floor, the double-leaded windows that blurred the view of the stars. Northern mountain summer: a breath of strawberry-wind across the cheeks, and then leaves falling before you knew it. I sat at the kitchen table and Alice stirred up the fire. The chimney was older than the rest of the house; it leaked. Alice's furniture smelled of loam and old maple smoke.

She made up two plates—apricots and sage cheddar, her own brown bread—and we ate quiet as the night crept in. When the moon came through the window Alice got up, padded barefoot to the door for her water pail, and went out to the pump. "Time to start," she said as she came back in. "Need the big pot."

Alice had deep cabinets. I opened them by firelight, one and then the next, feeling for the lip of a pot bigger than the others. When I brushed it my hand tingled. The room was warm; its lip was hot like hearthlight. I reached in and tugged it out, short unmuscular jerks. It was prickly black iron, weathered down on the rim.

"You have a witch pot," I said, half-smiling. She didn't reply.

I rested it on my belly and levered it up to the stove. The weight bore on my stomach like I imagined children did from the other way in: steady and thick. Warm. It clanked when it cleared the edge of the stovetop.

In the bottom, snagged on the iron, was a single rose petal.

I put the pot down on the stove. I went back to the table. I sat.

Alice poured her bucket of water in and wicked the petal into the fire. It had dried out in the cupboard, in the bottom of the forever-warm pot. It burned fast. She stirred something into the water with a stained-smooth wooden spoon. It rang out seconds against the rim of the pot.

"Pass me the witch hazel?" she said. Didn't look up. I sat. Something rough pushed through a hole in my battered socks and snaked into the world. I didn't care to identify it.

"Lisbet?" she said, and turned her head.

"It was you." I leaned my head on my knuckles. I couldn't look at her. "I knew, okay?"

The wood-on-iron sound stopped. After the shifts of the woodstove, the house was as silent as winter.

"There's only one hedgewoman in the next three towns. People'd talk if there were more. They talk about you at the post office." I closed my hands tight so the nails pinched my palms. I was babbling. Stupid. Angry.

She put the spoon down. It clanked on the cloudy glass rest. "Yeah," she said soft.

"That's all you have to say?" I got to my feet, and pain pierced the skin of the arches. I was standing on briars. They had scored the soft polished wood of Alice's floor. "I *know*. I know you did this, and I got a good idea why, and that's all you have to say to me."

She gripped the edge of the counter.

I walked clock-steady over to her and turned her right around. "Usually you kiss a girl. Or you ask her up for dinner."

She let go of the counter easily. Boneless, like a toddler.

"Or you take her out to a movie. Or if you don't like movies you send her—" and my voice failed. I came down on my heels onto thorns. Flowers.

"So you know why." Her head was down. Her shoulders hunched. She muttered like a beaten child.

"Tell me why."

A pause. "Not gonna—" Her hair was too short to hide behind: a utilitarian woodsman's cut. The way her chin shrunk into her chest, it hadn't been once. It had been long and dusty blond like beehives.

"Tell me."

"—if you know—"

The joints of my fingers were aching. "*Just say it.*"

Alice opened her mouth. A cough.

A river of flowers poured onto the floor.

I yanked my hands back, swearing. Roses spilled over them between us, scraping breasts and belly, digging thorns into my sleeves. I shook, and they clung, dragged me back, rooted down into the rug. The blooms were thick, sick scarlet. The smell was a slick in the back of the mouth. "The hell—"

She opened her mouth. Closed it. And then bent over, heaving, and choked.

"Alice!"

A thorn curled under her front tooth. She twitched her lips a little. In the firelight, I couldn't tell if they were blue.

The thorns tore when I pushed through them: legs, arms, chest. One step and blood dribbled down between my breasts. Two, and it tingled at my knees. Her lips were blue. Up close I could see it. Her eyes were big and emptying out.

"Breathe for me," I whispered, and heard the rattle of leaves in her throat.

I thrust my hands into the thorns and pulled.

They came out bloody. Hers, and mine. They came out rooting and squeezing: I threw them to the floor and the roots died blind. I pulled until I had the last of them and checked her heartbeat, the color of the delicate skin beneath her eyes. State Parks employees got mandatory first aid training—even the ones who just wrote and set the manuals.

Her heart was pounding. Her lips were dry and purpled. I couldn't feel breath.

"Breathe for me," I told her. No answer.

I laid a hand on her chest. Laid her back on the floor she'd joined herself, hardwood, stained with roses. My bloody hands stained her shirt.

Pinched her nose, touched her lips to mine. Began to breathe.

∿

I swept the petals into a clear compost bag when it was over. Red rose, and white rose, and rue.

∿

The roses scratched her throat. The rue was poison—not to be taken orally. Dr. James looked down Alice's throat with his pointed penlight and scraped down low in Alice's mouth with a tongue depressor, and put her on a liquid diet until the bloody scratches healed. "No rough food," he told her and me, her nearest neighbor. "No shouting. Nothing acidic. Lukewarm soup, not hot."

Alice pressed her mouth shut. Alice turned away.

The doctor packed his cracked black bag and I saw him to the door. "You'll make sure she takes it careful." A statement, not a question. A sprig of sharp goldenrod scratched at my right arch. I kept both feet planted.

"I'll come up afternoons. Maybe Mrs. Nguyen—"

"She won't otherwise," he interrupted, and looked down his blob of a nose at me. I looked away. My face felt warm. A lone white violet vined around my ankle and hid.

"I'll make sure," I said, small, and he nodded and let himself out.

I watched him drive down the trail from Idaho and then went back inside.

Alice leaned against the kitchen counter, solid butcher's-block wood she'd cured and fitted herself. Her hands were clasped in front of her mouth. I couldn't see her eyes.

"Doctor gave me these for you." Ibuprofen. Household medicine anywhere but Idaho, where Alice didn't let chemical things. "He said one every four hours, when it hurts." I set the bottle down before her, clumsy. The doctor'd bandaged my hands up fat with gauze.

Alice swept the ibuprofen bottle into a drawer and took out ginger for tea.

"He said no hot liquids—" I protested. Not very well. My voice was sympathy-raw and too thin to be strong or firm.

"Goodnight," she whispered, hoarse. Rose-stricken.

~

There was a hedge grew up around Idaho that night, lavender and rose-teeth and rue. I found it in the morning with a Tupperware of white bean soup under one arm and pressed cough drops in a bag on the other, with the soles of my scratched-up boots sprouting bright pink eglantine and filling in Alice's reclaimed path. There'd been no sheets on my doorstep this morning. I'd slept wrapped in the winter storm blanket on the cool kitchen floor. I woke to a halo of mayfly weeds, withering into compost, laying down soil for an army of spiky green aloe.

I touched a finger to the twining growth, and it hissed at the thought of blood.

I went back down the mountain.

The second day there was a message on my phone from Mrs. Nguyen, down in town. Alice hadn't come for her baskets, she said, in her odd mix of late-learned English and the drawn-out local accent. Could her neighbah go up the mountain and look in?

The hedge had sprouted purple lobelia overnight. They weren't used to the thin air. They died, outside-in, as they opened. Their corpses blanketed the dirt.

"I don't do this," I told the hedge, soft. "I have a manual to finish in five days. I have a boss and a job."

The hedge spat withering blossoms.

My teeth clacked together; a muscle in my cheek started to hurt. "Nuh-uh," I said. "You want something of me, you *ask* it. I'm not gonna hurt you

318 – Leah Bobet

for it. I'm not . . . whoever that was," and bit my cheek at the thought. "But I won't be—" I rolled words around in my mouth, looked for the one whose taste matched foul "—herded."

My footprints filled with cactus on the way down the trail. I only looked back the once.

~

Two days before I was to rotate in, Alice sent me a letter.

No stamp: she wouldn't have mailed it, not in our little town with its one post office and one whitewashed wood church. Both run by Mrs. Jeffrey Mays—that was how she styled herself, Missus Jeffrey—who would surely comment to the pastor on crazy old Alice sending handwritten letters to the Forestry woman up the highway. Hand*made* letters: the paper was textured and soft, speckled with flower petals and the twisting skeleton of a stem. I almost placed a toe on it to see if it would grow.

Inside was a sachet: soft fabric and pungent, full of smells and sweet and strange that made my eyes water. "Green," I whispered to myself. It didn't smell like grass, or forests, or gardens. It smelled *green.*

This'll do it, the letter said, in Alice's angular hand. The perfect loops trembled. Not unpracticed; just seldom used. *Steep it into tea. I'm sorry.*

"Drink me," I murmured, and coughed a laugh. Cupped the sachet in my hands and imagined it staining them green, streaks the color of sunlight on maple leaves that would never wash away. She was sorry.

There was a lot of magic here, in the tucked-away hills by the Canadian border. No way of knowing if this was a love spell, or a hate spell, or one to strip the flowers away from the ground whereon I stood.

"Oh, Alice," I whispered, and put the kettle upon the stove.

I drank it when it cooled. It tasted like the forest in midsummer.

The flowers fell out like cancer, shriveling away and fading into dust that coated the kitchen tiles. When it was done I flexed my feet, felt the muscles. They looked naked. A bare few days, and I'd grown used to the scent of roses.

The aloe was blooming in the kitchen floor. A butterfly hovered around one of the blossoms. I could pot them. There was a potter halfway to the city who threw solid pots for plants. She sold them by the roadside, painted Indian colors. Tourists bought them wrapped in newspaper fifty miles before the clattering painted sign on Alice's parked red truck. There was a market for growing things here, in the hills. They bloomed better. As if by magic.

I teased the daffodils from the shower drain and put them into water. They'd stood up against the onslaught of chemical soap and synthetic shampoo. I bundled them into a bouquet and brought them when I locked the house up for my week in the city office.

Perhaps on my way down, into the smoke and asphalt, I'd drop them off at Idaho.

∼

Don Webb's story is, ultimately, about fear and hatred of anyone who is perceived as "different": race, gender, creed . . . so many reasons we devise to destroy our fellow humans. But his witch, Barbara, is of particular interest because she challenges our ideas of "good witch/ bad witch" and exposes how shallow our own beliefs may be. There are certainly those who do believe in a God who is opposed by Satan, but one wonders how many of the residents of this small fictional Wisconsin town actually believe in either. Of those who do, theologically they would believe witches must be in league with the Devil and use their powers to harm people and property. Yet Barbara not only has done no harm, she has done considerable good. And popular culture now tends to side with the witch rather than condemn her.

So, the question arises: Is the following scenario unlikely? Or do we still fear "the other" on such a primal level that we instinctually destroy rather than think? Don't worry. Merely offering food for thought. There will be no quiz at the end of the book.

Afterward
Don Webb

After twenty-four years of working for Wisconsin Data Systems, Barbara made her first tactical error. She revealed that she was on the side of Darkness to someone she'd known for seven years. She was fired within a week, then there were the harassing phone calls and she began hearing things outside her house at night, and woke to find foul things written on the sidewalk in front of her house.

It had happened like this:

The boss had had yet another bad idea, he wanted to remove all horizontal communications between fellow workers. No one would talk about the Project save to him. He didn't like innovation, "self empowerment," or "total quality culture." He had dismissed them jokingly as "Tools of the devil" not knowing how right he was. No one, of course, would stand up to him.

Except Barbara.

Barbara had the work record and the smarts and the "Question Authority" button. She should have risen far on the management ladder, but she liked what she was doing—she liked writing code. She was good at it and she believed that the answer to life's questions was to find a job that provided endless pleasurable challenges.

The meeting went as everybody hoped it would.

Barbara called the plan "Bullshit."

Then a polite and detailed logical analysis showed why the plan would not only stifle creativity, but cost money, slow production, absorb the boss's time and otherwise disrupt the company. The boss had almost begged her to stop when she reached her fourteenth point.

He retreated as he always did, saying it had been a proposal, an experiment, and that he had merely wanted feedback.

After he left the room, some people giggled.

Robert Hiker followed Barbara back to her cubicle. They made small talk while various folk drifted by to thank her for standing up to the boss (as always).

Then Robert said, "Do you get what you want with the boss because you're good with people or because you're a witch?"

Barbara laughed, "Isn't 'good with people' and 'witchcraft' the same thing?"

"No, I mean it. I mean we all know you're a witch."

"What do you mean?"

"Oh we've noticed that you pick up certain stones, that you make teas when anybody is sick, that anybody you really don't like isn't real lucky. It's okay because we know that you're a white witch."

"You mean some goddess-worshiping woman who takes her clothes off a lot and dances under the moon? I suppose that's all quite beautiful and everything, but that's hardly me."

"But you are a witch."

"Robert, you've known me for seven years, been to my house, taken me to the movies, would have made a pass at me if you weren't scared of your wife. You know I'm the one who helped you through your bad flu last year. You've borrowed money from me."

"What's your point?"

"I am wondering out loud if I can trust you. Trust you as a friend and trust you to think rather than spasm-off in knee jerk reactions."

"Sure. You can trust me."

"You know," Barbara said, "I think I can. I am witch, a Black Witch. I am on the side of the Prince of Darkness."

"You can't be serious, you're the nicest person I know."

"Think about it, Robert. I always stand up to the boss. Does that sound more like Lucifer or Michael? When someone's sick I don't pray for help, I do things. I don't call upon God as male or female, I am working to be as God. Lucifer is my role model, the rebel against cosmic injustice."

"Do you drink blood or something?"

"No, Robert, I don't drink blood, do black masses, or anything else the tabloids might ascribe to me. You know me, remember?"

"Yeah, I guess I know you."

He backed out of her cubicle and she knew she had blown it. She figured he was bright enough: she had taught him C++, she had made potato salad for his birthday (he loved potato salad). Maybe it was just the shock. At least he wouldn't blab it around the office. It wasn't exactly the kind of thing that made office gossip.

She hoped.

She was wrong.

It was in their eyes the next day. All of the forces that keep stupidity the ruling paradigm of the Earth: fear, loathing, forced humor. By the end of the day, she knew that her work place of twenty-four years had turned on her. People didn't drop by her cubicle to chat, no one asked her to lunch. When people had to hand her things they kept their bodies as far away from her as they could. The boss had called in and taken her keys away from her. He said it was a new company policy that only he could have keys to the office.

She had felt this kind of hatred before from male chauvinists. She knew that time could cure it, but she didn't know if she had time.

She worked harder than ever, kept her tone bright and cheery, tried to get people alone so she could talk with them.

There was some goofy movie about a Satanic cult on Thursday night TV. On Friday she was fired.

The putative reason was bad performance on a project about six months ago. The project hadn't shipped on time, but that had been the boss's fault. She had had good performance reviews for twenty-four years. The security guard helped clean out her desk.

She could get more work, but she would have to move. Her gloomy garden with its dark ivy and green moss would be gone. The owl who frequented the twisted old oak would be gone. If she moved to a big city there would be too much light pollution for her beloved telescope. Oh and the packing! Hundreds of books on everything.

Her phone rang a couple of times in the night, but when she picked it up there was no one there. This might be scarier than she imagined.

She thought of her mother, who used to be scared at night after her father had died. Mom was scared if someone called her at night, she wouldn't leave the house at night, and sometimes she thought there might be someone in the dark rooms at the front of the house.

She wouldn't let herself be like Mom. She wished she knew some protective magic. But like all true magicians she did her magic in the plain simple way of the world. She wanted protection, so she had moved to a small town with a low crime rate. She wanted work that was just stimulating, so she made herself indispensable for a small company. Over the years she had more of a hand in determining company policy than some of the people on the board of directors.

She could cast a spell over everybody so they would forget and forgive— but it would take a vast amount of work, and she would have to keep it going all the time, and besides she didn't like casting spells that interfered with the free will of others. It wasn't the path of spiritual rebellion.

She would hire a headhunter and flog her resumes in bigger cities, she had enough to live on comfortably in the meantime. Her mother had suffered through the Depression and so she had a fear of poverty.

In the next week, Sharon, an old friend from the office called and wanted to talk to her about "it."

They had dinner in a diner in the next town.

Sharon wanted her to know that she was still her friend.

Hard to know how to answer a statement that is both brave and cowardly, loving and pathetic.

"What's it like?" asked Sharon.

"You mean," said Barbara, "are there Sabats and do I get to fuck demons, and fly on broomsticks?"

"Well, that's kind of silly, but yeah that's what I mean."

"No, it's not like that at all. It is quiet and philosophical. I just realized over the years that I'm on the side of the rebels. Everyone's on Superman's side, you know. He's got better lighting and all these powers. I was always on Lex Luthor's side. He's just a human, but by his own hard work becomes something better than himself. That's what's life's about. Well, I did fuck a demon once, but that was years later."

The raw heat of that memory possessed her, she hoped Sharon would ask about it, but when no questions came she realized that Sharon had thought she was joking.

"Were you born that way?" asked Sharon, "I mean—evil?"

"What evil thing have I done?"

"Well, you're a Satanist."

"I can repeat the query."

"What about demons?"

"After years of rebellion I became aware of them. It's like being on a battlefield. Even a foot soldier like me knows that there's tanks and planes and bigger firepower. I am part of the cosmic struggle to be free."

"Do you have powers?"

"All humans have powers. Here."

Barbara put her hands briefly on Sharon's head. Sharon purred and put her head back.

"Tell me what you see," whispered Barbara.

"I see the stars of the night sky. They're different colors—did you know that stars are different colors?—and I am rising towards them. And I hear singing, 'To me the white nights, to you the gray days, to me the crows and toads, to you salvation and the promise, to me the Fall and the moon and neon lights, to you milk, to me venom, to me, to me, to me.'"

Barbara took her hand away from Sharon's forehead.

"That," said Barbara, "is the infernal choir."

They ate dessert and Sharon promised to see her again real soon.

Two days later someone had written BURN THE FUCKING WITCH on the sidewalk outside of her house.

Barbara knew of few other practitioners of the Black Arts. There were some groups, and a few individuals, but they had their own agenda. She doubted that they would be of much help. She could sue for religious discrimination, she supposed, but since she was alone in her practice it was an unlikely suit. She might want to keep that option open, though, she would call an attorney as soon as she moved out of town.

She washed her sidewalk. Washed it three times, it seemed so dirty to her. When she was bent over scrubbing it, someone drove by and threw an apple core onto the middle of her back. Threw it hard.

She jumped up and saw the blue Mustang wheeling around the corner. It was the boss's two teenaged sons.

She yelled a word, a word that she had sensed that the demon troops used in their battles with the self-righteous ones. In human languages it would have been "Stop!" but the language of demons is much more operative.

The car stopped, the engine died, and the teenagers peeled out of it like pop bottle rockets on the Fourth of July. She went inside and called the police complaining that there was a car blocking traffic on Maple Street.

The next couple of nights were quiet, and she thought she had scared them off. She got a good call from the headhunter on a job in Houston, Texas and she made airline reservations for three days later.

Houston? She could live in Houston—big city, no telescope, but there was a giant butterfly house and she could drive out to bathe in the warm Gulf of Mexico anytime she wanted. There was probably a poetry group there too. She had been promising herself for a long time to learn the art of poetry. Things were looking up. Perhaps her magic had caused the crisis as a way of getting her out of the nest. The Prince of Darkness doesn't like satisfaction. Faust, she recalled, lost his contract when he was satisfied. Satisfaction was for the forces of Light in their static heaven. Houston? Yes, she could do Houston.

That night someone dumped about twenty gallons of raw sewage on her front porch.

Barbara packed her bags and got ready to move into the local motel.

"Sorry, ma'am, we're remodeling, we've got no rooms."

She didn't see any remodeling going on. She drove home. She could stick it out, what's the worst that they could do? It wasn't Salem for God's sake.

Barbara figured the local moving company might not be the best either, so she talked to the one in a nearby town. She'd seen their sign the night Sharon had taken her to Big Eddy's. She decided that she was going to move to Houston, job or no job. If she stayed here, she'd wind up using her powers to hurt the panicked sheep. After she left, the move of claiming power would be gone from the office. It would be just like God's hierarchy—all communication lines straight up to him. No decisions, no use of free will. She would have lost her battle for freedom, which meant in the cosmic sense a tiny loss for the side of the Devil. She wondered if she should invoke him and tell him about it.

It was probably too small a thing to care about, and besides her fight wasn't over yet. There was no doubt a battlefield waiting for her in Houston—some petty tyrant to lead rebellions against—some mock-up of the heavenly bureaucracy to test her powers on.

But on the other hand, maybe he needed to know. So she lit a candle and she poured her heart out to the Archetype of Human Consciousness, the force always seeking to be free.

They came for her the next night. She knew it was going to be bad about seven in the evening. The sun had set and darkness was beginning to pool up in the low places of the Earth. The birds that graced dark skies were beginning to sing, and with her heightened senses she had felt that tiny shudder the earth gives just as she is falling asleep. The plane would take her away tomorrow, but she doubted it would be that easy.

She called for a pizza. The phone was dead. She looked out her front window. Someone had parked across her driveway with a Ford Bronco. There were a lot of cars in the neighborhood.

What had suddenly made them so fearful?

Had they had a cow that went dry, or couldn't get it up after having a few too many beers, or maybe their gamble in the stock market hadn't worked so well . . .

Maybe it was watching movies on TV till they were good and scared—and then calling each other until the wee hours of the morning. Or maybe it was something they had always longed to do. Mankind has a great hatred for anyone who is different. Race, gender, creed. All good excuses to kill.

But not, thought Barbara, to die for.

When it got good and dark, she could hear them gathering on the lawn. She saw lights.

Torches.

Oh good, this really was a movie ending.

They began banging on her door about nine.

She opened the door, wearing a see-through black silk dress, a little too tight, that ended just above the knees. It was all she wearing, let them see what they were about to waste. Not a bad looking broad for forty-five.

Robert grabbed her by her right arm.

They had put a stake in the middle of the yard and piled firewood around it, as she had foreseen in her magical working the night before.

Robert pulled her toward it, she could not smell the roses she grew, not even the sweet tuberoses that usually enchanted the night. She could smell gasoline. She pulled her arm from his, but kept walking toward the stake.

"Do I get a final speech before you roast me?"

Some yelled, "No!" and others, "Yes!" and so she knew that she could speak since they were too weak-willed to stop her.

"I have lived among you for twenty-four years. I don't see a face here that I haven't spent pleasurable time with. I have fought for the right, when all of you have fought for inertia. I led the fight against the city council when they wanted to take away our parks, I have fought for every cause that furthers human freedom. And tonight if your pitiful fire were to take me before God's great judgment seat, I would look Him right in the eye and say, '*Non Serviam*—I will not serve!' Now watch!"

She said a magical word and she flew about twenty feet into the sky. Then she returned.

"See? I can escape. But I won't. I have other battles to fight, and bigger battlefields to fight on. Go ahead, put me to the torch. Remember the night you burned your village's freedom fighter."

For awhile they were afraid of her, but their dull-eyed anger flared and they put the fire beneath her.

She died screaming at first, then suddenly she seemed to be gone from the flames—at least some said so, quietly, years later.

The fire went out and a great cloud of ash blew up and it got in the townsfolk hair, or stained their foreheads, or their hands and arms. Some were stained on their cheeks and others their lips or teeth. They found that when they went home, they couldn't scrub it off.

They all stayed in the next day, scrubbing their flesh, bleaching their hair, or polishing their teeth. They washed and they remembered her screams and they remembered the good she had done and they washed. And they washed.

Then the next day they took to avoiding one another on the streets. It was a little embarrassing to meet people in daylight after the burning. There was a run on scarves, big hats, and trench coats. The motel was genuinely full of one half of the town's married couples, who found the idea of looking at (or being looked at by) the stained spouse too painful.

The tattoo parlor did a lively business afterwards, but the ash stain would show up through the new tattoo after about a month.

They moved away from the town after that, hiding themselves in big cities and going out only at night in scarves and hats and long coats.

You may have seen one of them in your city. They will occasionally look up and see a bit of ash floating in the air—maybe from a wholesome suburban chimney—maybe from a fire that the homeless have made in a barrel. They'll be looking at the ash, like a feather from a black angel's wing, and they'll run.

Sometimes they scream.

〜

Ursula K. Le Guin is now a living legend. But before the Earthsea Trilogy, The Left Hand of Darkness, The Lathe of Heaven, *the awards and the honors . . . it all started with her first published story—this 1962 tale that combines time travel, Paris, the quest for knowledge, and a male practitioner of magic. It's also the only story in this collection with a man who might be termed a witch.*

The etymology of the word witch *in English is rather complicated (and, for some, controversial), but the word seems to have originally applied to both men and women. By 1601, however, terms like* men-witches *or* he-witch *were being used, so* witch *was taking on a primarily feminine meaning. In modern English,* wizard *(originally meaning "philosopher, sage" with the "magical power" connotation beginning around 1550) and* warlock *(the base word* wærloga *primarily meant "oath-breaker"; the "-ck" ending a "male witch" meaning emerging from Scottish in the 1560s) are now commonly used for "male witch" in fiction and film.*

April in Paris
Ursula K. Le Guin

Professor Barry Pennywither sat in a cold, shadowy garret and stared at the table in front of him, on which lay a book and a breadcrust. The bread had been his dinner, the book had been his lifework. Both were dry. Dr. Pennywither sighed, and then shivered. Though the lower-floor apartments of the old house were quite elegant, the heat was turned off on April 1st, come what may; it was now April second, and sleeting. If Dr. Pennywither raised his head a little he could see from his window the two square towers of Notre Dame de Paris, vague and soaring in the dusk, almost near enough to touch: for the Island of Saint-Louis, where he lived, is like a little barge being towed downstream behind the Island of the City, where Notre Dame stands. But he did not raise his head. He was too cold.

The great towers sank into darkness. Dr. Pennywither sank into gloom. He stared with loathing at his book. It had won him a year in Paris—publish or perish, said the Dean of Faculties, and he had published, and been rewarded with a year's leave from teaching, without pay. Munson College could not afford to pay unteaching teachers. So on his scraped-up savings he had come back to Paris, to live again as a student in a garret, to read fifteenth-century manuscripts at the Library, to see the chestnuts flower along the avenues. But it hadn't worked. He was forty, too old for lonely garrets. The sleet would blight the budding chestnut flowers. And he was sick of his work. Who cared about his theory, the Pennywither Theory, concerning the mysterious disappearance of the poet François Villon in 1463? Nobody. For after all his Theory about poor Villon, the greatest juvenile delinquent of all time, was only a theory and could never be proved, not across the gulf of five hundred years. Nothing could be proved. And besides, what did it matter if Villon died on Montfaucon gallows or (as Pennywither thought) in a Lyons brothel on the way to Italy? Nobody cared. Nobody else loved Villon enough. Nobody loved Dr. Pennywither, either; not even Dr. Pennywither. Why should he? An unsocial, unmarried, underpaid pedant, sitting here alone in an unheated attic in an unrestored tenement trying to write another unreadable book. "I'm unrealistic," he said aloud with another sigh and another shiver. He got up and took the blanket off his bed, wrapped himself in it, sat down thus bundled at the table, and tried to light a Gauloise Bleue. His lighter snapped vainly. He sighed once more, got up, fetched a can of vile-smelling French lighter fluid, sat down, rewrapped his cocoon, filled the lighter, and snapped it. The fluid had spilled around a good bit. The lighter lit, so did Dr. Pennywither, from the wrists down. "Oh hell!" he cried, blue flames leaping from his knuckles, and jumped up batting his arms wildly, shouting "Hell!" and raging against Destiny. Nothing ever went right. What was the use? It was then 8:12 on the night of April 2nd, 1961.

A man sat hunched at a table in a cold, high room. Through the window behind him the two square towers of Notre Dame loomed in the spring dusk. In front of him on the table lay a hunk of cheese and a huge, iron-latched, handwritten book. The book was called (in Latin) *On the Primacy of the Element Fire over the Other Three Elements*. Its author stared at it with loathing. Nearby on a small iron stove a small alembic simmered. Jehan Lenoir mechanically inched his chair nearer the stove now and then, for warmth, but his thoughts were on deeper problems. "Hell!" he said finally (in Late Mediaeval French), slammed the book shut, and got up. What if his theory was wrong? What if water were the primal element? How could you prove these things? There must he some way—some method—so that one could be sure, absolutely sure, of one single fact! But each fact led into others, a monstrous tangle, and the Authorities conflicted, and anyway no one would read his book, not even the wretched pedants at the Sorbonne. They smelled heresy. What was the use? What good this life spent in poverty and alone, when he had learned nothing, merely guessed and theorized? He strode about the garret, raging, and then stood still. "All right!" he said to Destiny. "Very good! You've given me nothing, so I'll take what I want!" He went to one of the stacks of books that covered most of the floor-space, yanked out a bottom volume (scarring the leather and bruising his knuckles when the overlying folios avalanched), slapped it on the table and began to study one page of it. Then, still with a set cold look of rebellion, he got things ready: sulfur, silver, chalk. . . . Though the room was dusty and littered, his little workbench was neatly and handily arranged. He was soon ready. Then he paused. "This is ridiculous," he muttered, glancing out the window into the darkness where now one could only guess at the two square towers. A watchman passed below calling out the hour, eight o'clock of a cold clear night. It was so still he could hear the lapping of the Seine. He shrugged, frowned, took up the chalk and drew a neat pentagram on the floor near his table, then took up the book and began to read in a clear but self-conscious voice: "*Haere, haere, audi me . . .* " It was a long spell, and mostly nonsense. His voice sank. He stood bored and embarrassed. He hurried through the last words, shut the book, and then fell backwards against the door, gap-mouthed, staring at the enormous, shapeless figure that stood within the pentagram, lit only by the blue flicker of its waving, fiery claws.

~

Barry Pennywither finally got control of himself and put out the fire by burying his hands in the folds of the blanket wrapped around him. Unburned but upset, he sat down again. He looked at his book. Then he stared at it. It was no longer thin and gray and titled *The Last Years of Villon: An Investigation of Possibilities*. It was thick and brown and titled *Incantatoria Magna*. On his table? A priceless manuscript dating from 1407 of which the only extant undamaged copy was in the Ambrosian Library in Milan? He looked slowly around. His mouth dropped slowly open. He observed a stove, a chemist's workbench, two or three dozen heaps of unbelievable leatherbound books, the window, the door. His window, his door. But crouching against his door was a little creature, black and shapeless, from which came a dry rattling sound.

Barry Pennywither was not a very brave man, but he was rational. He thought he had lost his mind, and so he said quite steadily, "Are you the Devil?"

The creature shuddered and rattled.

Experimentally, with a glance at invisible Notre Dame, the professor made the sign of the Cross.

At this the creature twitched; not a flinch, a twitch. Then it said something, feebly, but in perfectly good English—no, in perfectly good French—no, in rather odd French: "*Mais vous estes de Dieu,*" it said.

Barry got up and peered at it. "Who are you?" he demanded, and it lifted up a quite human face and answered meekly, "Jehan Lenoir."

"What are you doing in my room?"

There was a pause. Lenoir got up from his knees and stood straight, all five foot two of him. "This is *my* room," he said at last, though very politely.

Barry looked around at the books and alembics. There was another pause. "Then how did I get here?"

"I brought you."

"Are you a doctor?"

Lenoir nodded, with pride. His whole air had changed. "Yes, I'm a doctor," he said. "Yes, I brought you here. If Nature will yield me no knowledge, then I can conquer Nature herself, I can work a miracle! To the Devil with science, then. I was a scientist—" he glared at Barry. "No longer! They call me a fool, a heretic, well by God I'm worse! I'm a sorcerer, a black magician, Jehan the Black! Magic works, does it? Then science is a waste of time. Ha!" he said, but he did not really look triumphant. "I wish it hadn't worked," he said more quietly, pacing up and down between folios.

"So do I," said the guest.

"Who are you?" Lenoir looked up challengingly at Barry, though there was nearly a foot difference in their heights.

"Barry A. Pennywither. I'm a professor of French at Munson College, Indiana, on leave in Paris to pursue my studies of Late Mediaeval Fr—" He stopped. He had just realized what kind of accent Lenoir had. "What year is this? What century? Please, Dr. Lenoir—" The Frenchman looked confused. The meanings of words change, as well as their pronunciations. "Who rules this country?" Barry shouted.

Lenoir gave a shrug, a French shrug (some things never change), "Louis is king," he said. "Louis the Eleventh. The dirty old spider."

They stood staring at each other like wooden Indians for some time. Lenoir spoke first. "Then you're a man?"

"Yes. Look, Lenoir, I think you—your spell—you must have muffed it a bit."

"Evidently," said the alchemist. "Are you French?"

"No."

"Are you English?" Lenoir glared. "Are you a filthy Goddam?"

"No. No. I'm from America. I'm from the—from your future. From the twentieth century AD." Barry blushed. It sounded silly, and he was a modest man. But he knew this was no illusion. The room he stood in, his room, was new. Not five centuries old. Unswept, but new. And the copy of Albertus Magnus by his knee was new, bound in soft supple calfskin, the gold lettering gleaming. And there stood Lenoir in his black gown, not in costume, at home . . .

"Please sit down, sir," Lenoir was saying. And he added, with the fine though absent courtesy of the poor scholar, "Are you tired from the journey? I have bread and cheese, if you'll honor me by sharing it."

They sat at the table munching bread and cheese. At first Lenoir tried to explain why he had tried black magic. "I was fed up," he said. "Fed up! I've slaved in solitude since I was twenty, for what? For knowledge. To learn some of Nature's secrets. They are not to be learned." He drove his knife half an inch into the table, and Barry jumped. Lenoir was a thin little fellow, but evidently a passionate one. It was a fine face, though pale and lean: intelligent, alert, vivid. Barry was reminded of the face of a famous atomic physicist, seen in newspaper pictures up until 1953. Somehow this likeness prompted him to say, "Some are, Lenoir; we've learned a good bit, here and there . . . "

"What?" said the alchemist, skeptical but curious.

"Well, I'm no scientist—"

"Can you make gold?" He grinned as he asked.

"No, I don't think so, but they do make diamonds."

"How?"

"Carbon-coal, you know—under great heat and pressure, I believe. Coal and diamond are both carbon, you know, the same element."

"Element?"

"Now as I say, I'm no—"

"Which is the primal element?" Lenoir shouted, his eyes fiery, the knife poised in his hand.

"There are about a hundred elements," Barry said coldly, hiding his alarm.

Two hours later, having squeezed out of Barry every dribble of the remnants of his college chemistry course, Lenoir rushed out into the night and reappeared shortly with a bottle. "O my master," he cried, "to think I offered you only bread and cheese!" It was a pleasant burgundy, vintage 1477, a good year. After they had drunk a glass together Lenoir said, "If somehow 1 could repay you . . . "

"You can. Do you know the name of the poet François Villon?"

"Yes," Lenoir said with some surprise, "but he wrote only French trash, you know, not in Latin."

"Do you know how or when he died?"

"Oh, yes; hanged at Montfaucon here in '64 or '65, with a crew of no-goods like himself. Why?"

Two hours later the bottle was dry, their throats were dry, and the watchman had called three o'clock of a cold clear morning. "Jehan, I'm worn out," Barry said, "you'd better send me back." The alchemist was too polite, too grateful, and perhaps also too tired to argue. Barry stood stiffly inside the pentagram, a tall bony figure muffled in a brown blanket, smoking a Gauloise Bleue. "*Adieu*," Lenoir said sadly. "*Au revoir*," Barry replied. Lenoir began to read the spell backwards. The candle flickered, his voice softened. "*Me audi, haere, haere*," he read, sighed, and looked up. The pentagram was empty. The candle flickered. "But I learned so little!" Lenoir cried out to the empty room. Then he beat the open book with his fists and said, "And a friend like that—a real friend—" He smoked one of the cigarettes Barry had left him—he had taken to tobacco at once. He slept, sitting at his table, for a couple of hours. When he woke he brooded a while, relit his candle, smoked the other cigarette, then opened the *Incantatoria* and began to read aloud: "Haere, haere . . . "

"Oh, thank God," Barry said, stepping quickly out of the pentagram and grasping Lenoir's hand. "Listen, I got back there—this room, this same room, Jehan! but old, horribly old, and empty, you weren't there—I thought, my God, what have I done? I'd sell my soul to get back there, to him—What can I do with what I've learned? Who'll believe it? How can I prove it? And who the Devil could I tell it to anyhow? Who cares? I couldn't sleep, I sat and cried for an hour—"

"Will you stay?"

"Yes. Look, I brought these—in case you did invoke me." Sheepishly he exhibited eight packs of Gauloises, several books, and a gold watch. "It might fetch a price," he explained. "I knew paper francs wouldn't do much good."

At sight of the printed books Lenoir's eyes gleamed with curiosity, but he stood still. "My friend," he said, "you said you'd sell your soul . . . you know . . . so would I. Yet we haven't. How—after all—how did this happen? That we're both men. No devils. No pacts in blood. Two men who've lived in this room . . . "

"I don't know," said Barry. "We'll think that out later. Can I stay with you, Jehan?"

"Consider this your home," Lenoir said with a gracious gesture around the room, the stacks of books, the alembics, the candle growing pale. Outside the window, gray on gray, rose up the two great towers of Notre Dame. It was the dawn of April 3rd.

After breakfast (bread crusts and cheese rinds) they went out and climbed the south tower. The cathedral looked the same as always, though cleaner than in 1961, but the view was rather a shock to Barry. He looked down upon a little town. Two small islands covered with houses; on the right bank more houses crowded inside a fortified wall; on the left bank a few streets twisting around the college; and that was all. Pigeons chortled on the sun-warmed stone between gargoyles. Lenoir, who had seen the view before, was carving the date (in Roman numerals) on a parapet. "Let's celebrate," he said. "Let's go out into the country. I haven't been out of the city for two years. Let's go clear over there—" he pointed to a misty green hill on which a few huts and a windmill were just visible—"to Montmartre, eh? There are some good bars there, I'm told."

Their life soon settled into an easy routine. At first Barry was a little nervous in the crowded streets, but, in a spare black gown of Lenoir's, he was not noticed as outlandish except for his height. He was probably the tallest man in fifteenth-century France. Living standards were low and lice were unavoidable, but Barry had never valued comfort much; the only thing he really missed was coffee at breakfast. When they had bought a bed and a razor—Barry had forgotten his—Lenoir introduced him to the landlord as M. Barrie, a cousin of Lenoir's from the Auvergne, their housekeeping arrangements were complete. Barry's watch brought a tremendous price, four gold pieces, enough to live on for a year. They sold it as a wondrous new timepiece from Illyria, and the buyer, a Court chamberlain looking for a nice present to give the king, looked at the inscription—Hamilton Bros., New Haven, 1881—and nodded sagely. Unfortunately he was shut up in one of King Louis's cages for naughty courtiers at Tours before he had presented his gift, and the watch may still be there behind some brick in the ruins of

Plessis; but this did not affect the two scholars. Mornings they wandered about sightseeing the Bastille and the churches, or visiting various minor poets in whom Barry was interested; after lunch they discussed electricity, atomic theory, physiology, and other matters in which Lenoir was interested, and performed minor chemical and anatomical experiments, usually unsuccessfully; after supper they merely talked. Endless, easy talks that ranged over the centuries but always ended here, in the shadowy room with its window open to the spring night, in their friendship. After two weeks they might have known each other all their lives. They were perfectly happy. They knew they would do nothing with what they had learned from each other. In 1961 how could Barry ever prove his knowledge of old Paris, in 1482 how could Lenoir ever prove the validity of the scientific method? It did not bother them. They had never really expected to be listened to. They had merely wanted to learn.

So they were happy for the first time in their lives; so happy, in fact, that certain desires always before subjugated to the desire for knowledge, began to awaken. "I don't suppose," Barry said one night across the table, "that you ever thought much about marrying?"

"Well, no," his friend answered, doubtfully. "That is, I'm in minor orders . . . and it seemed irrelevant . . . "

"And expensive. Besides, in my time, no self-respecting woman would want to share my kind of life. American women are so damned poised and efficient and glamorous, terrifying creatures. . . .

"And women here are little and dark, like beetles, with bad teeth," Lenoir said morosely.

They said no more about women that night. But the next night they did; and the next; and on the next, celebrating the successful dissection of the main nervous system of a pregnant frog, they drank two bottles ot Montrachet '74 and got soused. "Let's invoke a woman, Jehan," Barry said in a lascivious bass, grinning like a gargoyle.

"What if I raised a devil this time?"

"Is there really much difference?"

They laughed wildly, and drew a pentagram. "*Haere, haere,*" Lenoir began; when he got the hiccups, Barry took over. He read the last words. There was a rush of cold, marshy-smelling air, and in the pentagram stood a wild-eyed being with long black hair, stark naked, screaming.

"Woman, by God," said Barry.

"Is it?"

It was. "Here, take my cloak," Barry said, for the poor thing now stood gawping and shivering. He put the cloak over her shoulders. Mechanically she pulled it round her, muttering, "*Gratias ago, domine.*"

"Latin!" Lenoir shouted. "A woman speaking Latin?" It took him longer to get over that shock than it did Bota to get over hers. She was, it seemed, a slave in the household of the Sub-Prefect of North Gaul, who lived on the smaller island of the muddy island town called Lutetia. She spoke Latin with a thick Celtic brogue, and did not even know who was emperor in Rome in her day. A real barbarian, Lenoir said with scorn. So she was—an ignorant, taciturn, humble barbarian with tangled hair, white skin, and clear gray eyes. She had been waked from a sound sleep. When they convinced her that she was not dreaming, she evidently assumed that this was some prank of her foreign and all-powerful master the Sub-Prefect, and accepted the situation without further question. "Am I to serve you, my masters?" she inquired timidly but without sullenness, looking from one to the other.

"Not me," Lenoir growled, and added in French to Barry, "Go on; I'll sleep in the storeroom." He departed.

Bota looked up at Barry. No Gauls, and few Romans, were so magnificently tall; no Gauls and no Romans ever spoke so kindly. "Your lamp" (it was a candle, but she had never seen a candle) "is nearly burnt out," she said. "Shall I blow it out?"

~

For an additional two sous a year the landlord let them use the storeroom as a second bedroom, and Lenoir now slept alone again in the main room of the garret. He observed his friend's idyll with a brooding, unjealous interest. The professor and the slave girl loved each other with delight and tenderness. Their pleasure overlapped Lenoir in waves of protective joy. Bota had led a brutal life, treated always as a woman but never as a human. In one short week she bloomed, she came alive, evincing beneath her gentle passiveness a cheerful, clever nature. "You're turning out to be a regular Parisienne," he heard Barry accuse her one night (the attic walls were thin).

She replied, "If you knew what it is for me not to be always defending myself, always afraid, always alone . . . "

Lenoir sat up on his cot and brooded. About midnight, when all was quiet, he rose and noiselessly prepared the pinches of sulfur and silver, drew the pentagram, opened the book. Very softly he read the spell. His face was apprehensive.

In the pentagram appeared a small white dog. It cowered and hung its tail, then came shyly forward, sniffed Lenoir's hand, looked up at him with liquid eyes and gave a modest, pleading whine. A lost puppy.

Lenoir stroked it. It licked his hands and jumped all over him, wild with relief. On its white leather collar was a silver plaque engraved, "Jolie. Dupont, 36 rue de Seine, Paris VIe."

Jolie went to sleep, after gnawing a crust, curled up under Lenoir's chair. And the alchemist opened the book again and read, still softly, but this time without self-consciousness, without fear, knowing what would happen.

~

Emerging from his storeroom-bedroom honeymoon in the morning, Barry stopped short in the doorway. Lenoir was sitting up in bed, petting a white puppy, and deep in conversation with the person sitting on the foot of the bed, a tall red-haired woman dressed in silver. The puppy barked. Lenoir said, "Good morning!" The woman smiled wondrously.

"Jumping Jesus," Barry muttered (in English). Then he said, "Good morning. When are you from?" The effect was Rita Hayworth, sublimated—Hayworth plus the Mona Lisa, perhaps?

"From Altair, about seven thousand years from now," she said, smiling still more wondrously. Her French accent was worse than that of a football-scholarship freshman. "I'm an archaeologist. I was excavating the ruins of Paris III. I'm sorry I speak the language so badly; of course we know it only from inscriptions."

"From Altair? The star? But you're human—I think—"

"Our planet was colonized from Earth about four thousand years ago—that is, three thousand years from now." She laughed, most wondrously, and glanced at Lenoir. "Jehan explained it all to me, but I still get confused."

"It was a dangerous thing to try it again, Jehan!" Barry accused him. "We've been awfully lucky, you know."

"No," said the Frenchman. "Not lucky."

"But after all it's black magic you're playing with—Listen—I don't know your name, Madame."

"Kislk," she said.

"Listen, Kislk," Barry said without even a stumble, "your science must be fantastically advanced—is there any magic? Does it exist? Can the laws of Nature really be broken, as we seem to be doing?"

"I've never seen nor heard of an authenticated case of magic."

"Then what goes on?" Barry roared. "Why does that stupid old spell work for Jehan, for us, that one spell, and here, nowhere else, for nobody else, in five—no, eight—no, fifteen thousand years of recorded history? Why? Why? And where did that damn puppy come from?"

"The puppy was lost," Lenoir said, his dark face grave. "Somewhere near this house, on the Île Saint-Louis."

"And I was sorting potsherds," Kislk said, also gravely, "in a house site, Island 2, Pit 4, Section D. A lovely spring day, and I hated it. Loathed it. The day, the work, the people around me." Again she looked at the gaunt little alchemist, a long, quiet look. "I tried to explain it to Jehan last night. We have improved the race, you see. We're all very tall, healthy, and beautiful. No fillings in our teeth. All skulls from Early America have fillings in the teeth. Some of us are brown, some white, some gold-skinned. But all beautiful, and healthy, and well-adjusted, and aggressive, and successful. Our professions and degree of success are pre-planned for us in the State Pre-School Homes. But there's an occasional genetic flaw. Me, for instance. I was trained as an archaeologist because the Teachers saw that I really didn't like people, live people. People bored me. All like me on the outside, all alien to me on the inside. When everything's alike, which place is home? But now I've seen an unhygienic room with insufficient heating. Now I've seen a cathedral not in ruins. Now I've met a living man who's shorter than me, with bad teeth and a short temper. Now I'm home, I'm where I can be myself, I'm no longer alone!"

"Alone," Lenoir said gently to Barry. "Loneliness, eh? Loneliness is the spell, loneliness is stronger . . . . Really it doesn't seem unnatural."

Bota was peering round the doorway, her face flushed between the black tangles of her hair. She smiled shyly and said a polite Latin good-morning to the newcomer.

"Kislk doesn't know Latin," Lenoir said with immense satisfaction. "We must teach Bota some French. French is the language of love, anyway, eh? Come along, let's go out and buy some bread. I'm hungry."

Kislk hid her silver tunic under the useful and anonymous cloak, while Lenoir pulled on his moth-eaten black gown. Bota combed her hair, while Barry thoughtfully scratched a louse-bite on his neck. Then they set forth to get breakfast. The alchemist and the interstellar archaeologist went first, speaking French; the Gaulish slave and the professor from Indiana followed, speaking Latin and holding hands. The narrow streets were crowded, bright with sunshine. Above them Notre Dame reared its two square towers against the sky. Beside them the Seine rippled softly. It was April in Paris, and on the banks of the river the chestnuts were in bloom.

∽

This is a horror story. Just as the Brothers Grimm often did, Margo Lanagan terrifies us with how cruel the world can be. But she strips us of the illusion there is anything supernatural that can change it—for better or worse. As young Hansel tells us in this powerful and gruesome tale: "And I knew there was no magic in the world, just trickery on the innocent." In the original Grimm version of "Hansel and Gretel," the witch is a witch because we are told she is. The only evidence of her alleged witchcraft is that she has an edible house that attracts children. Otherwise she is a cannibalistic serial killer: evil, but no sorceress.

In the days of the Western European witch hunts—an era of religious and socio-economic upheaval—the accused were often those with the most tenuous connection to the social order, usually old women living alone. Controlling the weak, the different, and the alien can be seen an attempt to maintain "proper," orderly society. This witch, however, is no innocent old lady living peacefully in the woods.

The Goosle
Margo Lanagan

"There," said Grinnan as we cleared the trees. "Now, you keep your counsel, Hanny-boy."

Why, that is the mudwife's house, I thought. Dread thudded in me. Since two days ago among the older trees when I knew we were in my father's forest, I'd feared this.

The house looked just as it did in my memory: the crumbling, glittery yellow walls, the dreadful roof sealed with drippy white mud. My tongue rubbed the roof of my mouth just looking. It is crisp as wafer-biscuit on the outside, that mud. You bite through to a sweetish sand inside. You are frightened it will choke you, but you cannot stop eating.

The mudwife might be dead, I thought hopefully. So many are dead, after all, of the black.

But then came a convulsion in the house. A face passed the window-hole, and there she was at the door. Same squat body with a big face snarling above. Same clothing, even, after all these years, the dress trying for bluishness and the pinafore for brown through all the dirt. She looked just as strong. However much bigger *I'd* grown, it took all my strength to hold my bowels together.

"Don't come a step nearer." She held a red fire-banger in her hand, but it was so dusty—if I'd not known her I'd have laughed.

"Madam, I pray you," said Grinnan. "We are clean as clean—there's not a speck on us, not a blister. Humble travellers in need only of a pig-hut or a chicken-shed to shelter the night."

"Touch my stock and I'll have you," she says to all his smoothness. "I'll roast your head in a pot."

I tugged Grinnan's sleeve. It was all too sudden—one moment walking wondering, the next on the doorstep with the witch right there, talking heads in pots.

"We have pretties to trade," said Grinnan.

"You can put your pretties up your poink-hole where they belong."

"We have all the news of long travel. Are you not at all curious about the world and its woes?"

"Why would I live here, tuffet-head?" And she went inside and slammed her door and banged the shutter across her window.

"She is softening," said Grinnan. "She is curious. She can't help herself."

"I don't think so."

"You watch me. Get us a fire going, boy. There on that bit of bare ground."

"She will come and throw her bunger in it. She'll blind us, and then—"

"Just make and shut. I tell you, this one is as good as married to me. I have her heart in my hand like a rabbit-kitten."

I was sure he was mistaken, but I went to, because fire meant food and just the sight of the house had made me hungry. While I fed the fire its kindling I dug up a little stone from the flattened ground and sucked the dirt off it.

Grinnan had me make a smelly soup. Salt-fish, it had in it, and sea-celery and the yellow spice.

When the smell was strong, the door whumped open and there she was again. Ooh, she was so like in my dreams, with her suddenness and her ugly intentions that you can't guess. But it was me and Grinnan this time, not me and Kirtle. Grinnan was big and smart, and he had his own purposes. And I knew there was no magic in the world, just trickery on the innocent. Grinnan would never let anyone else trick me; he wanted that privilege all for himself.

"Take your smelly smells from my garden this instant!" the mudwife shouted.

Grinnan bowed as if she'd greeted him most civilly. "Madam, if you'd join us? There is plenty of this lovely bull-a-bess for you as well."

"I'd not touch my lips to such mess. What kind of foreign muck—"

Even I could hear the longing in her voice that she was trying to shout down.

There before her he ladled out a bowlful—yellow, splashy, full of delicious lumps. Very humbly—he does humbleness well when he needs to, for such a big man—he took it to her. When she recoiled he placed it on the little table by the door, the one that I ran against in my clumsiness when escaping, so hard I still sometimes feel the bruise in my rib. I remember, I knocked it skittering out the door, and I flung it back meaning to trip up the mudwife. But instead I tripped up Kirtle, and the wife came out and plucked her up and bellowed after me and kicked the table onto the path, and ran out herself with Kirtle like a tortoise swimming from her fist and kicked the table aside again—

Bang! went the cottage door.

Grinnan came laughing quietly back to me.

"She is ours. Once they've et your food, Hanny, you're free to eat theirs. Fish and onion pie tonight, I'd say."

"Eugh."

"Jealous, are we? Don't like old Grinnan supping at other pots, hnh?"

"It's *not* that!" I glared at his laughing face. "She's so ugly, that's all. So old. I don't know how you can even think of—"

"Well, I am no primrose myself, golden boy," he says. "And I'm grateful for any flower that lets me pluck her."

I was not old and desperate enough to laugh at that joke. I pushed his soup-bowl at him.

"Ah, bull-a-bess," he said into the steam. "Food of gods and seducers."

~

When the mudwife let us in, I looked straight to the corner, and the cage *was still there*! It had been repaired in places with fresh plaited withes, but it was still of the same pattern. Now there was an animal in it, but the cottage was so dim . . . a very thin cat, maybe, or a ferret. It rippled slowly around its borders, and flashed little eyes at us, and smelled as if its own piss were combed through its fur for pomade. I never smelled that bad when I lived in that cage. I ate well, I remember; I fattened. She took away my leavings in a little cup, on a little dish, but there was still plenty of me left.

So that when Kirtle freed me I *lumbered* away. As soon as I was out of sight of the mud-house I stopped in the forest and just stood there blowing from the effort of propelling myself, after all those weeks of sloth.

So that Grinnan when he first saw me said, *Here's a jubbly one. Here's a cheese cake. Wherever did you get the makings of those round cheeks?* And he fell on me like a starving man on a roasted mutton-leg. Before too long he had used me thin again, and thin I stayed thereafter.

He was busy at work on the mudwife now.

"Oh my, what an array of herbs! You must be a very knowledgeable woman. And hasn't she a lot of pots, Hansel! A pot for every occasion, I think."

Oh yes, I nearly said, *including head-boiling, remember?*

"Well, you are very comfortably set up here, indeed, Madam." He looked about him as if he'd found himself inside some kind of enchanted palace, instead of in a stinking hovel with a witch in the middle of it. "Now, I'm sure you told me your name—"

"I did not. My name's not for such as you to know." Her mouth was all pruny and she strutted around and banged things and shot him sharp looks, but I'd seen it. We were in here, weren't we? We'd made it this far.

"Ah, a guessing game!" says Grinnan delightedly. "Now, you'd have a good strong name, I'm sure. Bridda, maybe, or Gert. Or else something fiery and passionate, such as Rossavita, eh?"

He can afford to play her awhile. If the worst comes to the worst, he has the liquor, after all. The liquor has worked on me when nothing else would, when I've been ready to run, to some town's wilds where I could hide—to such as that farm-wife with the worried face who beat off Grinnan with a broom. The liquor softened me and made me sleepy, made me give in to the old bugger's blandishments; next day it stopped me thinking with its head-pain, further than to obey Grinnan's grunts and gestures.

~

How does yours like it? said Gadfly's red-haired boy viciously. *I've heard him call you "honey," like a girl-wife; does he do you like a girl, face to face and lots of kissing? Like your boy-bits, which they is so small, ain't even there, so squashed and ground in?*

He calls me Hanny, because Hanny is my name. Hansel.

Honey is your name, eh? said the black boy—a boy of black skin from naturalness, not illness. *After your honey hair?*

Which they commenced patting and pulling and then held me down and chopped all away with Gadfly's good knife. When Grinnan saw me he went pale, but I'm pretty sure he was trying to cut some kind of deal with Gadfly to swap me for the red-hair (with the *skin like milk, like freckled milk,* he said), so the only thing it changed, he did not come after me for several nights until the hair had settled and I did not give off such an air of humiliation.

Then he whispered, *You were quite handsome under that thatch, weren't you? All along.* And things were bad as ever, and the next day he tidied off the stragglier strands, as I sat on a stump with my poink-hole thumping and the other boys idled this way and that, watching, warping their faces at each other and snorting.

～

The first time Grinnan did me, I could imagine that it didn't happen. I thought, I had that big dump full of so much nervous earth and stones and some of them must have had sharp corners and cut me as I passed them, and the throbbing of the cuts gave me the dream, that the old man had done that to me. Because I was so fearful, you know, frightened of everything coming straight from the mudwife, and I put fear and pain together and made it up in my sleep. The first time I could trick myself, because it was so terrible and mortifying a thing, it could not be real. It could not.

I have watched Grinnan a long time now, in success and failure, in private and on show. At first I thought he was too smart for me, that I was trapped by his cleverness. And this is true. But I have seen others laugh at him, or walk away from his efforts easily, shaking their heads. Others are cleverer.

What he does to me, he waits till I am weak. Half-asleep, he waits till. I never have much fight in me, but dozing off I have even less.

Then what he does—it's so simple I'm ashamed. He bares the flesh of my back. He strokes my back as if that is all he is going to do. He goes straight to the very oldest memory I have—which, me never having told him, how does he know it?—of being sickly, of my first mother bringing me through the night, singing and stroking my back, the oldest and safest piece of my mind, and he puts me there, so that I am sodden with sweetness and longing and nearly-being-back-to-a-baby.

And then he proceeds. It often hurts—it *mostly* hurts. I often weep. But there is a kind of bargain goes on between us, you see. I pay for the first part with the second. The price of the journey to that safe, sweet-sodden place is being spiked in the arse and dragged kicking and biting my blanket back to the real and dangerous one.

～

Show me your boy-thing, the mudwife would say. *Put it through the bars.*

I won't.

Why not?

You will bite it off. You will cut it off with one of your knives. You will chop it with your axe.

Put it out. I will do no such thing. I only want to wash it.

Wash it when Kirtle is awake, if you so want me clean.

It will be nice, I promise you. I will give you a nice feeling, so warm, so wet. You'll feel good.

But when I put it out, she exclaimed, *What am I supposed to do with that?*

Wash it, like you said.

There's not enough of it even to wash! How would one get that little peepette dirty?

I put it away, little shred, little scrap I was ashamed of.

And she flung around the room awhile, and then she sat, her face all red crags in the last little light of the banked-up fire. *I am going to have to keep you forever!* she said. *For* years *before you are any use to me. And you are expensive! You eat like a pig! I should just cook you up now and enjoy you while you are tender.*

I was all wounded pride and stupid. I didn't know what she was talking about. *I can do anything my sister can do, if you just let me out of this cage. And I'm a better wood-chopper.*

Wood-chopper! she said disgustedly. *As if I needed a wood-chopper!* And she went to the door and took the axe off the wall there, and tested the edge with one of her horny fingertips, and looked at me in a very *thoughtful* way that I did not much like.

~

Sometimes he speaks as he strokes. *My Hanny,* he says, very gentle and loving like my mother, *my goosle, my gosling, sweet as apple, salt as sea.* And it feels as if we are united in yearning for my mother and her touch and voice.

She cannot have gone forever, can she, if I can remember this feeling so clearly? But, ah, to get back to her, so much would have to be undone! So much would have to un-happen: all of Grinnan's and my wanderings, all the witch-time, all the time of our second mother. That last night of our first mother, our real mother, and her awful writhing and the noises and our father begging, and Kirtle weeping and needing to be taken away—that would have to become a nightmare, from which my father would shake me awake with the news that the baby came out just as Kirtle and I did, just as easily. And our mother would rise from her bed with the baby; we would all rise into the baby's first morning, and begin.

~

It is very deep in the night. I have done my best to be invisible, to make no noise, but now the mudwife pants, *He's not asleep.*

Of course, he's asleep. Listen to his breathing.

I do the asleep-breathing.

Come, says Grinnan. *I've done with these, bounteous as they are. I want to go below.* He has his ardent voice on now. He makes you think he is barely in control of himself, and somehow that makes you, somehow that flatters you enough to let him do what he wants.

After some uffing and puffing, *No,* she says, very firm, and there's a slap. *I want that boy out of here.*

What, wake him so he can go and listen at the window?

Get him out, she says. *Send him beyond the pigs and tell him to stay.*

You're a nuisance, he says. *You're a sexy nuisance. Look at this! I'm all misshapen and you want me herding children.*

You do it, she says, rearranging her clothing, *or you'll stay that shape.*

So he comes to me and I affect to be woken up and to resist being hauled out the door, but really it's a relief of course. I don't want to hear or see or know. None of that stuff I understand, why people want to sweat and pant and poke bits of themselves into each other, why anyone would want to do more than hold each other for comfort and stroke each other's back.

Moonlight. Pigs like slabs of moon, like long, fat fruit fallen off a moon-vine. The trees tall and brainy all around and above—*they* never sweat and pork; the most they do is sway in a breeze, or crash to the ground to make useful wood. The damp smell of night forest. My friends in the firmament, telling me where I am: two and a half days north of the ford with the knotty rope; four and a half days north and a bit west of "Devilstown," which Grinnan called it because someone made off in the night with all the spoils *we'd* made off with the night before.

I'd thought we were the only ones not back in their beds! he'd stormed on the road.

They must have come very quiet, I said. *They must have been accomplished thieves.*

They must have been sprites or devils, he spat, *that I didn't hear them, with my ears.*

We were seven and a half days north and very, very west of Gadfly's camp, where we had, as Grinnan put it, *tried the cooperative life for a while.* But those boys, *they were a gang of no-goods,* Grinnan says now. Whatever deal he had tried to make for Freckled-Milk, they laughed him off, and Grinnan could not stand it there having been laughed at. He took me away before dawn one morning, and when we stopped by a stream in the first light he showed me the brass candlesticks that Gadfly had kept in a sack and been so proud of.

And what'll you use those for? I said foolishly, for we had managed up until then with moon and stars and our own wee fire.

I did not take them to use them, Hanny-pot, he said with glee. *I took them because he loved and polished them so.* And he flung them into the stream, and I gasped—and Grinnan laughed to hear me gasp—at the sight of them cutting through the foam and then gone into the dark cold irretrievable.

Anyway, it was new for me still, there beyond the mudwife's pigs, this knowing where we were—though I had lost count of the days since Ardblarthen when it had come to me how Grinnan looked *up* to find his way, not down among a million tree-roots that all looked the same, among twenty million grass-stalks, among twenty million million stones or sand-grains. It was even newer how the star-pattern and the moon movements had steadied out of their meaningless whirling and begun to tell me whereabouts I was in the wide world. All my life I had been stupid, trying to mark the things around me on the ground, leaving myself trails to get home by because every tree looked the same to me, every knoll and declivity, when all the time the directions were hammered hard into their system up there, pointing and changing-but-never-completely-changing.

So if we came at the cottage from this angle, whereas Kirtle and I came from the front, that means . . . but Kirtle and I wandered so many days, didn't we? I filled my stomach with earths, but Kirtle was piteous weeping all the way, so hungry. She would not touch the earth; she watched me eating it and wept. I remember, I told her, *No wonder you are thirsty! Look how much water you're wasting on those tears!* She had brown hair, I remember. I remember her pushing it out of her eyes so that she could see to sweep in the dark cottage—the cottage where the mudwife's voice is rising, like a saw through wood.

The house stands glittering and the sound comes out of it. My mouth waters; they wouldn't hear me over that noise, would they?

I creep in past the pigs to where the blobby roof-edge comes low. I break off a blob bigger than my hand; the wooden shingle it was holding slides off, and my other hand catches it soundlessly and leans it against the house.

The mudwife howls; something is knocked over in there; she howls again and Grinnan is grunting with the effort of something. I run away from all those noises, the white mud in my hand like a hunk of cake. I run back to the trees where Grinnan told me to stay, where the woman's howls are like mouse-squeaks and I can't hear Grinnan, and I sit between two high roots and I bite in.

Once I've eaten the mud I'm ready to sleep. I try dozing, but it's not comfortable among the roots there, and there is still noise from the cottage—now it is Grinnan working himself up, calling her all the things he calls me, all the insults. *You love it,* he says, with such deep disgust. *You filth, you filthy cunt.* And she *oh*'s below, not at all like me, but as if she really does love it. I lie quiet, thinking, Is it true, that she loves it? That I do? And if it's true, how is it that Grinnan knows, but I don't? She makes noise, she agrees with whatever he says. *Harder, harder,* she says. *Bang me till I burst. Harder!* On and on they go, until I give up waiting—they will never finish!

I get up and go around the pigsty and behind the chicken house. There is a poor field there, pumpkins gone wild in it, blackberry bushes foaming dark around the edges. At least the earth might be softer here. If I pile up enough of this floppy vine, if I gather enough pumpkins around me—

And then I am holding, not a pale baby pumpkin in my hand but a pale baby skull.

Grinnan and the mudwife bellow together in the house, and something else crashes broken.

The skull is the color of white-mud, but hard, inedible—although when I turn it in the moonlight I find tooth-marks where someone has tried.

The shouts go up high—the witch's loud, Grinnan's whimpering.

I grab up a handful of earth to eat, but a bone comes with it, long, white, dry. I let the earth fall away from it.

I crouch there looking at the skull and the bone, as those two finish themselves off in the cottage.

They will sleep now—but I'm not sleepy any more. The stars in their map are nailed to the inside of my skull; my head is filled with dark clarity. When I am sure they are asleep, I scoop up a mouthful of earth, and start digging.

～

Let me go and get the mudwife, our father murmured. *Just for this once.*

I've done it twice and I'll do it again. Don't you bring that woman here! Our mother's voice was all constricted, as if the baby were trying to come up her throat, not out her nethers.

But this is not like the others! he said, desperate after the following pain. *They say she knows all about children. Delivers them all the time.*

Delivers them? She eats *them!* said our mother. *It's not just this one. I've two others might catch her eye, while I feed and doze. I'd rather die than have her near my house, that filthy hag.*

So die she did, and our new brother or sister died as well, still inside her. We didn't know whichever it was. *Will it be another little Kirtle-child?* our father had asked us, bright-eyed by the fire at night. *Or another baby woodcutter, like our Hans?* It had seemed so important to know. Even when the baby was dead, I wanted to know.

But the whole reason! our father sobbed. *Is that it could not come out, for us to see!* Which had shamed me quiet.

And then later, going into blackened towns where the only way you could tell man from woman was by the style of a cap, or a hair-ribbon draggling into the dirt beneath them, or a rotted pinafore, or worst by the amount of shrunken scrag between an unclothed person's legs—why, then I could see how small a thing it was not to know the little one's sex. I could see that it was not important at all.

~

When I wake up, they are at it again with their sexing. My teeth are stuck to the inside of my cheeks and lips by two ridges of earth. I have to break the dirt away with my finger.

What was I thinking, last night? I sit up. The bones are in a pile beside me; the skulls are in a separate pile—for counting, I remember. What I thought was: Where did she *find* all these children? Kirtle and I walked for days, I'm sure. There was nothing in the world but trees and owls and foxes and that one deer. Kirtle was afraid of bats at night, but I never saw even one. And we never saw people—which was what we were looking for, which was why we were so unwise when we came upon the mudwife's house.

But what am I going to do? What was I planning, piling these up? I thought I was only looking for all Kirtle's bits. But then another skull turned up and I thought, Well, maybe this one is more Kirtle's size, and then skull after skull—I dug on, crunching earth and drooling and breathing through my nose, and the bones seemed to rise out of the earth at me, seeking out the moon—the way a tree reaches for the light, pushing up thinly among the other trees until it finds light enough to spread into—seeking out *me*, as if they were thinking, Here, finally, is someone who can do something for us.

I pick up the nearest skull. Which of these is my sister's? Even if there were just a way to tell girls' skulls from boys'! Is hers even here? Maybe she's still buried, under the blackberries where I couldn't go for thorns.

Now I have a skull in either hand, like someone at a market weighing one cabbage against another. And the thought comes to me: Something is different. Listen.

The pigs. The mudwife, her noises very like the pigs'. There is no rhythm to them; they are random grunting and gasping. And I—

Silently I replace the skulls on the pile.

I haven't heard Grinnan this morning. Not a word, not a groan. Just the woman. The woman and the pigs.

The sunshine shows the cottage as the hovel it is, its saggy sides propped, its sloppy roofing patched with mud-splats simply thrown from the ground. The back door stands wide, and I creep up and stand right next to it, my back to the wall.

Wet slaps and stirrings sound inside. The mudwife grunts—she sounds muffled, desperate. Has he tied her up? Is he strangling her? There's not a gasp or word from him. That *thing* in the cage gives off a noise, though, a kind of low baying. It never stops to breathe. There is a strong smell of shit. Dawn is warming everything up; flies zoom in and out the doorway.

I press myself to the wall. There is a dip in the doorstep. Were I brave enough to walk in, that's where I would put my foot. And right at that place appears a drop of blood, running from inside. It slides into the dip, pauses modestly at being seen, then shyly hurries across the step and dives into hiding in the weeds below.

How long do I stand there, looking out over the pigsty and the chicken house to the forest, wishing I were there among the trees instead of here clamped to the house wall like one of those gargoyles on the monks' house in Devilstown, with each sound opening a new pocket of fear in my bowels? A fly flies into my gaping mouth and out again. A pebble in the wall digs a little chink in the back of my head, I'm pressed so hard there.

Finally, I have to know. I have to take one look before I run, otherwise I'll dream all the possibilities for nights to come. She's not a witch; she can't spell me back; I'm thin now and nimble; I can easily get away from her.

So I loosen my head, and the rest of me, from the wall. I bend one knee and straighten the other, pushing my big head, my popping eyes, around the doorpost.

I only meant to glimpse and run. So ready am I for the running, I tip outward even when I see there's no need. I put out my foot to catch myself, and I stare.

She has her back to me, her bare, dirty white back, her baggy arse and thighs. If she weren't doing what she's doing, that would be horror enough, how everything is wet and withered and hung with hair, how everything shakes.

Grinnan is dead on the table. She has opened his legs wide and eaten a hole in him, in through his soft parts. She has pulled all his innards out onto the floor, and her bare bloody feet are trampling the shit out of them, her bare shaking legs are trying to brace themselves on the slippery carpet of them. I can smell the salt-fish in the shit; I can smell the yellow spice.

That devilish moan, up and down it wavers, somewhere between purr and battle-yowl. I thought it was me, but it's that shadow in the cage, curling over and over itself like a ruffle of black water, its eyes fixed on the mess, hungry, hungry.

The witch pulls her head out of Grinnan for air. Her head and shoulders are shiny red; her soaked hair drips; her purple-brown nipples point down into two hanging rubies. She snatches some air between her red teeth and plunges in again, her head inside Grinnan like the bulge of a dead baby, but higher, forcing higher, pummelling up inside him, *fighting* to be un-born.

In my travels I have seen many wrongnesses done, and heard many others told of with laughter or with awe around a fire. I have come upon horrors of all kinds, for these are horrible times. But never has a thing been laid out so obvious and ongoing in its evil before my eyes and under my nose and with the flies feasting even as it happens. And never has the means to end it hung as clearly in front of me as it hangs now, on the wall, in the smile of the mudwife's axe-edge, fine as the finest nail-paring, bright as the dawn sky, the only clean thing in this foul cottage.

~

I reach my father's house late in the afternoon. How I knew the way, when years ago you could put me twenty paces into the trees and I'd wander lost all day, I don't know; it just came to me. All the loops I took, all the mistakes I made, all laid themselves down in their places on the world, and I took the right way past them and came here straight, one sack on my back, the other in my arms.

When I dreamed of this house it was big and full of comforts; it hummed with safety; the spirit of my mother lit it from inside like a sacred candle. Kirtle was always here, running out to greet me all delight.

Now I can see the poor place for what it is, a plague-ruin like so many that Grinnan and I have found and plundered. And tiny—not even as big as the witch's cottage. It sits in its weedy quiet and the forest chirps around it. The only thing remarkable about it is that I am the first here; no one has touched the place. I note it on my star map—there *is* safety here, the safety of a distance greater than most robbers will venture.

A blackened boy-child sits on the step, his head against the doorpost as if only very tired. Inside, a second child lies in a cradle. My father and second-mother are in their bed, side by side just like that lord and lady on the stone tomb in Ardblarthen, only not so neatly carved or richly dressed. Everything else is exactly the same as Kirtle and I left it. So sparse and spare! There is nothing of value here. Grinnan would be angry. *Burn these bodies and beds, boy!* he'd say. *We'll take their rotten roof if that's all they have.*

"But Grinnan is not here, is he?' I say to the boy on the step, carrying the mattock out past him. "Grinnan is in the ground with his lady-love, under the pumpkins. And with a great big pumpkin inside him, too. And Mrs Pumpkin-Head in his arms, so that they can sex there underground forever."

I take a stick and mark out the graves: Father, Second-Mother, Brother, Sister—and a last big one for the two sacks of Kirtle-bones. There's plenty of time before sundown, and the moon is bright these nights, don't I know it. I can work all night if I have to; I am strong enough, and full enough still of disgust. I will dig and dig until this is done.

I tear off my shirt.

I spit in my hands and rub them together.

The mattock bites into the earth.

~

When the witch in Kelly Link's story gives Small, her favorite child, her hairbrush, it is no minor bequest. Hair was thought to contain an essential connection to the individual and was often used in spells.

Whether she is an old hag with wild tresses escaping from her conical hat or a beautiful young woman, the witch is most commonly portrayed with long hair. In eras where modesty or religion deigned a woman's hair be bound up or covered, this was another symbol of a witch's rebellion against the proper order of things.

Magic power was also thought to reside in a witch's hair. Some lore claims a witch shaking her hair while casting a spell strengthens the magic. The Malleus Maleficarum (The Witch's Hammer), *published in 1487 and, thereafter, used as manual to discover alleged witches, noted the Devil seemed "chiefly to molest women and girls with beautiful hair." In order for judges to protect themselves from a witch "the hair should be shaved from every part of her body" as this insures she is hiding no object that allows her to keep silent concerning her witchcraft. There are, not surprisingly, reports of those accused of witchcraft confessing after this procedure was carried out.*

Catskin
Kelly Link

Cats went in and out of the witch's house all day long. The windows stayed open, and the doors, and there were other doors, cat-sized and private, in the walls and up in the attic. The cats were large and sleek and silent. No one knew their names, or even if they had names, except for the witch.

Some of the cats were cream-colored and some were brindled. Some were black as beetles. They were about the witch's business. Some came into the witch's bedroom with live things in their mouths. When they came out again, their mouths were empty.

The cats trotted and slunk and leapt and crouched. They were busy. Their movements were catlike, or perhaps clockwork. Their tails twitched like hairy pendulums. They paid no attention to the witch's children.

~

The witch had three living children at this time, although at one time she had had dozens, maybe more. No one, certainly not the witch, had ever bothered to tally them up. But at one time the house had bulged with cats and babies.

Now, since witches cannot have children in the usual way—their wombs are full of straw or bricks or stones, and when they give birth, they give birth to rabbits, kittens, tadpoles, houses, silk dresses, and yet even witches must have heirs, even witches wish to be mothers—the witch had acquired her children by other means: she had stolen or bought them.

She'd had a passion for children with a certain color of red hair. Twins she had never been able to abide (they were the wrong kind of magic), although she'd sometimes attempted to match up sets of children, as though she had been putting together a chess set, and not a family. If you were to say *a witch's chess set*, instead of *a witch's family*, there would be some truth in that. Perhaps this is true of other families as well.

One girl she had grown like a cyst, upon her thigh. Other children she had made out of things in her garden, or bits of trash that the cats brought her: aluminum foil with strings of chicken fat still crusted to it, broken television sets, cardboard boxes that the neighbors had thrown out. She had always been a thrifty witch.

Some of these children had run away and others had died. Some of them she had simply misplaced, or accidentally left behind on buses. It is to be hoped that these children were later adopted into good homes, or reunited with their natural parents. If you are looking for a happy ending in this story, then perhaps you should stop reading here and picture these children, these parents, their reunions.

~

Are you still reading? The witch, up in her bedroom, was dying. She had been poisoned by an enemy, a witch, a man named Lack. The child Finn, who had been her food taster, was dead already and so were three cats who'd licked her dish clean. The witch knew who had killed her and she snatched pieces of time, here and there, from the business of dying, to make her revenge. Once the question of this revenge had been settled to her satisfaction, the shape of it like a black ball of twine in her head, she began to divide up her estate between her three remaining children.

Flecks of vomit stuck to the corners of her mouth, and there was a basin beside the foot of the bed, which was full of black liquid. The room smelled like cats' piss and wet matches. The witch panted as if she were giving birth to her own death.

"Flora shall have my automobile," she said, "and also my purse, which will never be empty, so long as you always leave a coin at the bottom, my darling, my spendthrift, my profligate, my drop of poison, my pretty, pretty Flora. And when I am dead, take the road outside the house and go west. There's one last piece of advice."

Flora, who was the oldest of the witch's living children, was redheaded and stylish. She had been waiting for the witch's death for a long time now, although she had been patient. She kissed the witch's cheek and said, "Thank you, Mother."

The witch looked up at her, panting. She could see Flora's life, already laid out, flat as a map. Perhaps all mothers can see as far.

"Jack, my love, my birdsnest, my bite, my scrap of porridge," the witch said, "you shall have my books. I won't have any need of books where I am going. And when you leave my house, strike out in an easterly direction and you won't be any sorrier than you are now."

Jack, who had once been a little bundle of feathers and twigs and eggshell all tied up with a tatty piece of string, was a sturdy lad, almost full grown. If he knew how to read, only the cats knew it. But he nodded and kissed his mother's gray lips.

"And what shall I leave to my boy Small?" the witch said, convulsing. She threw up again in the basin. Cats came running, leaning on the lip of the basin to inspect her vomitus. The witch's hand dug into Small's leg.

"Oh it is hard, hard, so very hard, for a mother to leave her children (though I have done harder things). Children need a mother, even such a mother as I have been." She wiped at her eyes, and yet it is a fact that witches cannot cry.

Small, who still slept in the witch's bed, was the youngest of the witch's children. (Perhaps not as young as you think.) He sat upon the bed, and although he didn't cry, it was only because witch's children have no one to teach them the use of crying. His heart was breaking.

Small could juggle and sing and every morning he brushed and plaited the witch's long, silky hair. Surely every mother must wish for a boy like Small, a curly-headed, sweet-breathed, tenderhearted boy like Small, who can cook a fine omelet, and who has a good strong singing voice as well as a gentle hand with a hairbrush.

"Mother," he said, "if you must die, then you must die. And if I can't come along with you, then I'll do my best to live and make you proud. Give me your hairbrush to remember you by, and I'll go make my own way in the world."

"You shall have my hairbrush, then," said the witch to Small, looking, and panting, panting. "And I love you best of all. You shall have my tinderbox and my matches, and also my revenge, and you will make me proud, or I don't know my own children."

"What shall we do with the house, Mother?" said Jack. He said it as if he didn't care.

"When I am dead," the witch said, "this house will be of no use to anyone. I gave birth to it—that was a very long time ago—and raised it from just a dollhouse. Oh, it was the most dear, most darling dollhouse ever. It had eight rooms and a tin roof, and a staircase that went nowhere at all. But I nursed it and rocked it to sleep in a cradle, and it grew up to be a real house, and see how it has taken care of me, its parent, how it knows a child's duty to its mother. And perhaps you can see how it is now, how it pines, how it grows sick to see me dying like this. Leave it to the cats. They'll know what to do with it."

All this time the cats have been running in and out of the room, bringing things and taking things away. It seems as if they will never slow down, never come to rest, never nap, never have the time to sleep, or to die, or even to mourn. They have a certain proprietary look about them, as if the house is already theirs.

The witch vomits up mud, fur, glass buttons, tin soldiers, trowels, hat pins, thumbtacks, love letters (mislabeled or sent without the appropriate amount of postage and never read), and a dozen regiments of red ants, each ant as long and wide as a kidney bean. The ants swim across the perilous stinking basin, clamber up the sides of the basin, and go marching across the floor in a shiny ribbon. They are carrying pieces of Time in their mandibles. Time is heavy, even in such small pieces, but the ants have strong jaws, strong legs. Across the floor they go, and up the wall, and out the window. The cats watch, but don't interfere. The witch gasps and coughs and then lies still. Her hands beat against the bed once and then are still. Still the children wait, to make sure that she is dead, and that she has nothing else to say.

In the witch's house, the dead are sometimes quite talkative.

~

But the witch has nothing else to say at this time.

~

The house groans and all the cats begin to mew piteously, trotting in and out of the room as if they have dropped something and must go and hunt for it—they will never find it—and the children, at last, find they know how to cry, but the witch is perfectly still and quiet. There is a tiny smile on her face, as if everything has happened exactly to her satisfaction. Or maybe she is looking forward to the next part of the story.

~

The children buried the witch in one of her half-grown dollhouses. They crammed her into the downstairs parlor, and knocked out the inner walls so that her head rested on the kitchen table in the breakfast nook, and her ankles threaded through a bedroom door. Small brushed out her hair, and, because he wasn't sure what she should wear now that she was dead, he put all her dresses on her, one over the other over the other, until he could hardly see her white limbs at all beneath the stack of petticoats and coats and dresses. It didn't matter: once they'd nailed the dollhouse shut again, all they could see was the red crown of her head in the kitchen window, and the worn-down heels of her dancing shoes knocking against the shutters of the bedroom window.

Jack, who was handy, rigged a set of wheels for the dollhouse, and a harness so that it could be pulled. They put the harness on Small, and Small pulled and Flora pushed, and Jack talked and coaxed the house along, over the hill, down to the cemetery, and the cats ran along beside them.

~

The cats are beginning to look a bit shabby, as if they are molting. Their mouths look very empty. The ants have marched away, through the woods, and down into town, and they have built a nest on your yard, out of the bits of Time. And if you hold a magnifying glass over their nest, to see the ants dance and burn, Time will catch fire and you will be sorry.

~

Outside the cemetery gates, the cats had been digging a grave for the witch. The children tipped the dollhouse into the grave, kitchen window first. But then they saw that the grave wasn't deep enough, and the house sat there on its end, looking uncomfortable. Small began to cry (now that he'd learned how, it seemed he would spend all his time practicing), thinking how horrible it would be to spend one's death, all of eternity, upside down and not even properly buried, not even able to feel the rain when it beat down on the exposed shingles of the house, and seeped down into the house and filled your mouth and drowned you, so that you had to die all over again, every time it rained.

The dollhouse chimney had broken off and fallen on the ground. One of the cats picked it up and carried it away, like a souvenir. That cat carried the chimney into the woods and ate it, a mouthful at a time, and passed out of this story and into another one. It's no concern of ours.

The other cats began to carry up mouthfuls of dirt, dropping it and mounding it around the house with their paws. The children helped, and when they'd finished, they'd managed to bury the witch properly, so that only the bedroom window was visible, a little pane of glass like an eye at the top of a small dirt hill.

On the way home, Flora began to flirt with Jack. Perhaps she liked the way he looked in his funeral black. They talked about what they planned to be, now that they were grown up. Flora wanted to find her parents. She was a pretty girl: someone would want to look after her. Jack said he would like to marry someone rich. They began to make plans.

Small walked a little behind, slippery cats twining around his ankles. He had the witch's hairbrush in his pocket, and his fingers slipped around the figured horn handle for comfort.

The house, when they reached it, had a dangerous, grief-stricken look to it, as if it was beginning to pull away from itself. Flora and Jack wouldn't go back inside. They squeezed Small lovingly, and asked if he wouldn't want to come along with them. He would have liked to, but who would have looked after the witch's cats, the witch's revenge? So he watched as they drove off together. They went north. What child has ever heeded a mother's advice?

~

Jack hasn't even bothered to bring along the witch's library: he says there isn't space in the trunk for everything. He'll rely on Flora and her magic purse.

Small sat in the garden, and ate stalks of grass when he was hungry, and pretended that the grass was bread and milk and chocolate cake. He drank out of the garden hose. When it began to grow dark, he was lonelier than he had ever been in his life. The witch's cats were not good company. He said nothing to them and they had nothing to tell him, about the house, or the future, or the witch's revenge, or about where he was supposed to sleep. He had never slept anywhere except in the witch's bed, so at last he went back over the hill and down to the cemetery.

Some of the cats were still going up and down the grave, covering the base of the mound with leaves and grass and feathers, their own loose fur. It was a soft sort of nest to lie down on. The cats were still busy when Small fell asleep—cats are always busy—cheek pressed against the cool glass of the bedroom window, hand curled in his pocket around the hairbrush, but in the middle of the night, when he woke up, he was swaddled, head to foot, in warm, grass-scented cat bodies.

~

A tail is curled around his chin like a rope, and all the bodies are soughing breath in and out, whiskers and paws twitching, silky bellies rising and falling. All the cats are sleeping a frantic, exhausted, busy sleep, except for one, a white cat who sits near his head, looking down at him. Small has never seen this cat before, and yet he knows her, the way that you know the people who visit you in dreams: she's white everywhere, except for reddish tufts and frills at her ears and tail and paws, as if someone has embroidered her with fire around the edges.

"What's your name?" Small says. He's never talked to the witch's cats before.

The cat lifts a leg and licks herself in a private place. Then she looks at him. "You may call me Mother," she says.

But Small shakes his head. He can't call the cat that. Down under the blanket of cats, under the windowpane, the witch's Spanish heel is drinking in moonlight.

"Very well, then, you may call me The Witch's Revenge," the cat says. Her mouth doesn't move, but he hears her speak inside his head. Her voice is furry and sharp, like a blanket made of needles. "And you may comb my fur."

Small sits up, displacing sleeping cats, and lifts the brush out of his pocket. The bristles have left rows of little holes indented in the pink palm of his hand, like some sort of code. If he could read the code, it would say: *Comb my fur.*

Small combs the fur of The Witch's Revenge. There's grave dirt in the cat's fur, and one or two red ants, who drop and scurry away. The Witch's Revenge bends her head down to the ground, snaps them up in her jaws. The heap of cats around them is yawning and stretching. There are things to do.

"You must burn her house down," The Witch's Revenge says. "That's the first thing."

Small's comb catches a knot, and The Witch's Revenge turns and nips him on the wrist. Then she licks him in the tender place between his thumb and his first finger. "That's enough," she says. "There's work to do."

So they all go back to the house, Small stumbling in the dark, moving farther and farther away from the witch's grave, the cats trotting along, their eyes lit like torches, twigs and branches in their mouths, as if they plan to build a nest, a canoe, a fence to keep the world out. The house, when they reach it, is full of lights, and more cats, and piles of tinder. The house is making a noise, like an instrument that someone is breathing into. Small realizes that all the cats are mewing, endlessly, as they run in and out the doors, looking for more kindling. The Witch's Revenge says, "First we must latch all the doors."

So Small shuts all the doors and windows on the first floor, leaving open only the kitchen door, and The Witch's Revenge shuts the catches on the secret doors, the cat doors, the doors in the attic, and up on the roof, and the cellar doors. Not a single secret door is left open. Now all the noise is on the inside, and Small and The Witch's Revenge are on the outside.

All the cats have slipped into the house through the kitchen door. There isn't a single cat in the garden. Small can see the witch's cats through the windows, arranging their piles of twigs. The Witch's Revenge sits beside him, watching. "Now light a match and throw it in," says The Witch's Revenge.

Small lights a match. He throws it in. What boy doesn't love to start a fire?

"Now shut the kitchen door," says The Witch's Revenge, but Small can't do that. All the cats are inside. The Witch's Revenge stands on her hindpaws and pushes the kitchen door shut. Inside, the lit match catches something on fire. Fire runs along the floor and up the kitchen walls. Cats catch fire, and run into the other rooms of the house. Small can see all this through the windows. He stands with his face against the glass, which is cold, and then warm, and then hot. Burning cats with burning twigs in their mouths press up against the kitchen door, and the other doors of the house, but all the doors are locked. Small and The Witch's Revenge stand in the garden and watch the witch's house and the witch's books and the witch's sofas and the witch's cooking pots and the witch's cats, her cats, too, all her cats burn.

~

You should never burn down a house. You should never set a cat on fire. You should never watch and do nothing while a house is burning. You should never listen to a cat who says to do any of these things. You should listen to your mother when she tells you to come away from watching, to go to bed, to go to sleep. You should listen to your mother's revenge.

~

You should never poison a witch.

~

In the morning, Small woke up in the garden. Soot covered him in a greasy blanket. The Witch's Revenge was curled up asleep on his chest. The witch's house was still standing, but the windows had melted and run down the walls.

The Witch's Revenge woke and stretched and licked Small clean with her small sharkskin tongue. She demanded to be combed. Then she went into the house and came out, carrying a little bundle. It dangled, boneless, from her mouth, like a kitten.

~

It is a catskin, Small sees, only there is no longer a cat inside it. The Witch's Revenge drops it in his lap.

~

He picked it up and something shiny fell out of the loose light skin. It was a piece of gold, sloppy, slippery with fat. The Witch's Revenge brought out dozens and dozens of catskins, and there was a gold piece in every skin. While Small counted his fortune, The Witch's Revenge bit off one of her own claws, and pulled one long witch hair out of the witch's comb. She sat up, like a tailor, cross-legged in the grass, and began to stitch up a bag, out of the many catskins.

Small shivered. There was nothing to eat for breakfast but grass, and the grass was black and cooked.

"Are you cold?" said The Witch's Revenge. She put the bag aside and picked up another catskin, a fine black one. She slit a sharp claw down the middle. "We'll make you a warm suit."

She used the coat of a black cat, and the coat of a calico cat, and she put a trim around the paws, of grey-and-white-striped fur.

While she did this, she said to Small, "Did you know that there was once a battle, fought on this very patch of ground?"

Small shook his head *no*.

"Wherever there's a garden," The Witch's Revenge said, scratching with one paw at the ground, "I promise you there are people buried somewhere beneath it. Look here." She plucked up a little brown clot, put it in her mouth, and cleaned it with her tongue.

When she spat the little circle out again, Small saw it was an ivory regimental button. The Witch's Revenge dug more buttons out of the ground—as if buttons of ivory grew in the ground—and sewed them onto the catskin. She fashioned a hood with two eyeholes and a set of fine whiskers, and sewed four fine cat tails to the back of the suit, as if the single tail that grew there wasn't good enough for Small. She threaded a bell on each one. "Put this on," she said to Small.

Small puts on the suit and the bells chime. The Witch's Revenge laughs. "You make a fine-looking cat," she says. "Any mother would be proud."

The inside of the cat suit is soft and a little sticky against Small's skin. When he puts the hood over his head, the world disappears. He can see only the vivid corners of it through the eyeholes—grass, gold, the cat who sits cross-legged, stitching up her sack of skins—and air seeps in, down at the loosely sewn seam, where the skin droops and sags over his chest and around the gaping buttons. Small holds his tails in his clumsy fingerless paw, like a handful of eels, and swings them back and forth to hear them ring. The sound of the bells and the sooty, cooked smell of the air, the warm stickiness of the suit, the feel of his new fur against the ground: he falls asleep and dreams that hundreds of ants come and lift him and gently carry him off to bed.

～

When Small tipped his hood back again, he saw that The Witch's Revenge had finished with her needle and thread. Small helped her fill the bag with gold. The Witch's Revenge stood up on her hind legs, took the bag, and swung it over her shoulders. The gold coins went sliding against each other, mewling and hissing. The bag dragged along the grass, picking up ash, leaving a trail of green behind it. The Witch's Revenge strutted along as if she were carrying a sack of air.

Small put the hood on again, and he got down on his hands and knees. And then he trotted after The Witch's Revenge. They left the garden gate wide open and went into the forest, towards the house where the witch Lack lived.

～

The forest is smaller than it used to be. Small is growing, but the forest is shrinking. Trees have been cut down. Houses have been built. Lawns rolled, roads laid. The Witch's Revenge and Small walked alongside one of the roads. A school bus rolled by: The children inside looked out their windows and laughed when they saw The Witch's Revenge walking on her hind legs, and at her heels, Small, in his cat suit. Small lifted his head and peered out of his eyeholes after the school bus.

"Who lives in these houses?" he asked The Witch's Revenge.

"That's the wrong question, Small," said The Witch's Revenge, looking down at him and striding along.

Miaow, the catskin bag says. *Clink*.

"What's the right question, then?" Small said.

"Ask me who lives under the houses," The Witch's Revenge said.

Obediently, Small said, "Who lives under the houses?"

"What a good question!" said The Witch's Revenge. "You see, not everyone can give birth to their own house. Most people give birth to children instead. And when you have children, you need houses to put them in. So children and houses: most people give birth to the first and have to build the second. The houses, that is. A long time ago, when men and women were going to build a house, they would dig a hole first. And they'd make a little room—a little, wooden, one-room house—in the hole. And they'd steal or buy a child to put in the house in the hole, to live there. And then they built their house over that first little house."

"Did they make a door in the lid of the little house?" Small said.

"They did not make a door," said The Witch's Revenge.

"But then how did the girl or the boy climb out?" Small said.

"The boy or the girl stayed in that little house," said The Witch's Revenge. "They lived there all their life, and they are living in those houses still, under the other houses where the people live, and the people who live in the houses above may come and go as they please, and they don't ever think about how there are little houses with little children, sitting in little rooms, under their feet."

"But what about the mothers and fathers?" Small asked. "Didn't they ever go looking for their boys and girls?"

"Ah," said The Witch's Revenge. "Sometimes they did and sometimes they didn't. And after all, who was living under *their* houses? But that was a long time ago. Now people mostly bury a cat when they build their house, instead of a child. That's why we call cats house-cats. Which is why we must walk along smartly. As you can see, there are houses under construction here."

~

And so there are. They walk by clearings where men are digging little holes. First Small puts his hood back and walks on two legs, and then he puts on his hood again, and goes on all fours: He makes himself as small and slinky as possible, just like a cat. But the bells on his tails jounce and the coins in the bag that The Witch's Revenge carries go *clink, miaow,* and the men stop their work and watch them go by.

~

How many witches are there in the world? Have you ever seen one? Would you know a witch if you saw one? And what would you do if you saw one? For that matter, do you know a cat when you see one? Are you sure?

~

Small followed The Witch's Revenge. Small grew calluses on his knees and the pads of his fingers. He would have liked to carry the bag sometimes, but it was too heavy. How heavy? You would not have been able to carry it, either.

They drank out of streams. At night they opened the catskin bag and climbed inside to sleep, and when they were hungry they licked the coins, which seemed to sweat golden fat, and always more fat. As they went, The Witch's Revenge sang a song:

> I had no mother
> and my mother had no mother
> and her mother had no mother
> and her mother had no mother
> and her mother had no mother
> and you have no mother
> to sing you
> this song

The coins in the bag sang too, *miaow, miaow,* and the bells on Small's tails kept the rhythm.

~

Every night Small combs The Witch's Revenge's fur. And every morning The Witch's Revenge licks him all over, not neglecting the places behind his ears, and at the backs of his knees. And then he puts the catsuit back on, and she grooms him all over again.

~

Sometimes they were in the forest, and sometimes the forest became a town, and then The Witch's Revenge would tell Small stories about the people who lived in the houses, and the children who lived in the houses under the houses. Once, in the forest, The Witch's Revenge showed Small where there had once been a house. Now there were only the stones of the foundation, upholstered in moss, and the chimneystack, propped up with fat ropes and coils of ivy.

The Witch's Revenge rapped on the grassy ground, moving clockwise around the foundation, until both she and Small could hear a hollow sound; The Witch's Revenge dropped to all fours and clawed at the ground, tearing it up with her paws and biting at it, until they could see a little wooden roof. The Witch's Revenge knocked on the roof, and Small lashed his tails.

"Well, Small," said The Witch's Revenge, "shall we take off the roof and let the poor child go?"

Small crept up close to the hole she had made. He put his ear to it and listened, but he heard nothing at all. "There's no one in there," he said.

"Maybe they're shy," said The Witch's Revenge. "Shall we let them out, or shall we leave them be?"

"Let them out!" said Small, but what he meant to say was, "Leave them alone!" Or maybe he said *Leave them be!* although he meant the opposite. The Witch's Revenge looked at him, and Small thought he heard something then—beneath him where he crouched, frozen—very faint: a scrabbling at the dirty, sunken roof.

Small sprang away. The Witch's Revenge picked up a stone and brought it down hard, caving the roof in. When they peered inside, there was nothing except blackness and a faint smell. They waited, sitting on the ground, to see what might come out, but nothing came out. After a while, The Witch's Revenge picked up her catskin bag, and they set off again.

For several nights after that, Small dreamed that someone, something, was following them. It was small and thin and bleached and cold and dirty and afraid. One night it crept away again, and Small never knew where it went. But if you come to that part of the forest, where they sat and waited by the stone foundation, perhaps you will meet the thing that they set free.

~

No one knew the reason for the quarrel between the witch Small's mother and the witch Lack, although the witch Small's mother had died for it. The witch Lack was a handsome man and he loved his children dearly. He had stolen them out of the cribs and beds of palaces and manors and harems. He dressed his children in silks, as befitted their station, and they wore gold crowns and ate off gold plates. They drank from cups of gold. Lack's children, it was said, lacked nothing.

Perhaps the witch Lack had made some remark about the way the witch Small's mother was raising her children, or perhaps the witch Small's mother had boasted of her children's red hair. But it might have been something else. Witches are proud and they like to quarrel.

When Small and The Witch's Revenge came at last to the house of the witch Lack, The Witch's Revenge said to Small, "Look at this monstrosity! I've produced finer turds and buried them under leaves. And the smell, like an open sewer! How can his neighbors stand the stink?"

Male witches have no wombs, and must come by their houses in other ways, or else buy them from female witches. But Small thought it was a very fine house. There was a prince or a princess at each window staring down at him, as he sat on his haunches in the driveway, beside The Witch's Revenge. He said nothing, but he missed his brothers and sisters.

"Come along," said The Witch's Revenge. "We'll go a little ways off and wait for the witch Lack to come home."

Small followed The Witch's Revenge back into the forest, and in a while, two of the witch Lack's children came out of the house, carrying baskets made of gold. They went into the forest as well and began to pick blackberries.

The Witch's Revenge and Small sat in the briar and watched.

⁓

There was a wind in the briar. Small was thinking of his brothers and sisters. He thought of the taste of blackberries, the feel of them in his mouth, which was not at all like the taste of fat.

The Witch's Revenge nestled against the small of Small's back. She was licking down a lump of knotted fur at the base of his spine. The princesses were singing.

Small decided that he would live in the briar with The Witch's Revenge. They would live on berries and spy on the children who came to pick them, and The Witch's Revenge would change her name. The word *Mother* was in his mouth, along with the sweet taste of the blackberries.

"Now you must go out," said The Witch's Revenge, "and be kittenish. Be playful. Chase your tail. Be shy, but don't be too shy. Don't talk too much. Let them pet you. Don't bite."

She pushed at Small's rump, and Small tumbled out of the briar and sprawled at the feet of the witch Lack's children.

The Princess Georgia said, "Look! It's a dear little cat!"

Her sister Margaret said doubtfully, "But it has five tails. I've never seen a cat that needed so many tails. And its skin is done up with buttons and it's almost as large as you are."

Small, however, began to caper and prance. He swung his tails back and forth so that the bells rang out and then he pretended to be alarmed by this. First he ran away from his tails and then he chased his tails. The two princesses put down their baskets, half-full of blackberries, and spoke to him, calling him a silly puss.

At first he wouldn't go near them. But, slowly, he pretended to be won over. He allowed himself to be petted and fed blackberries. He chased a hair ribbon and he stretched out to let them admire the buttons up and down his belly. Princess Margaret's fingers tugged at his skin; then she slid one hand in between the loose catskin and Small's boy skin. He batted her hand away with a paw, and Margaret's sister Georgia said knowingly that cats didn't like to be petted on their bellies.

They were all good friends by the time The Witch's Revenge came out of the briar, standing on her hind legs and singing:

> I have no children
> and my children have no children
> and their children
> have no children
> and their children
> have no whiskers
> and no tails

At this sight, the Princesses Margaret and Georgia began to laugh and point. They had never heard a cat sing, or seen a cat walk on its hind legs. Small lashed his five tails furiously, and all the fur of the catskin stood up on his arched back, and they laughed at that too.

When they came back from the forest, with their baskets piled with berries, Small was stalking close at their heels, and The Witch's Revenge came walking just behind. But she left the bag of gold hidden in the briar.

∼

That night, when the witch Lack came home, his hands were full of gifts for his children. One of his sons ran to meet him at the door and said, "Come and see what followed Margaret and Georgia home from the forest! Can we keep them?"

And the table had not been set for dinner, and the children of the witch Lack had not sat down to do their homework, and in the witch Lack's throne room, there was a cat with five tails, spinning in circles, while a second cat sat impudently upon his throne, and sang:

Yes!
your father's house
is the shiniest
brownest largest
the most expensive
the sweetest-smelling
house
that has ever
come out of
anyone's
ass!

The witch Lack's children began to laugh at this, until they saw the witch, their father, standing there. Then they fell silent. Small stopped spinning.

"You!" said the witch Lack.

"Me!" said The Witch's Revenge, and sprang from the throne. Before anyone knew what she was about, her jaws were fastened about the witch Lack's neck, and then she ripped out his throat. Lack opened his mouth to speak and his blood fell out, making The Witch's Revenge's fur more red now than white. The witch Lack fell down dead, and red ants went marching out of the hole in his neck and the hole of his mouth, and they held pieces of Time in their jaws as tightly as The Witch's Revenge had held Lack's throat in hers. But she let Lack go and left him lying in his blood on the floor, and she snatched up the ants and ate them, quickly, as if she had been hungry for a very long time.

While this was happening, the witch Lack's children stood and watched and did nothing. Small sat on the floor, his tails curled about his paws. Children, all of them, they did nothing. They were too surprised. The Witch's Revenge, her belly full of ants, her mouth stained with blood, stood up and surveyed them.

"Go and fetch me my catskin bag," she said to Small.

Small found that he could move. Around him, the princes and princesses stayed absolutely still. The Witch's Revenge was holding them in her gaze.

"I'll need help," Small said. "The bag is too heavy for me to carry."

The Witch's Revenge yawned. She licked a paw and began to pat at her mouth. Small stood still.

"Very well," she said. "Take those big strong girls the Princesses Margaret and Georgia with you. They know the way."

The Princesses Margaret and Georgia, finding that they could move again, began to tremble. They gathered their courage and they went with Small, the two girls holding each other's hands, out of the throne room, not looking down at the body of their father, the witch Lack, and back into the forest.

Georgia began to weep, but the Princess Margaret said to Small: "Let us go!"

"Where will you go?" said Small. "The world is a dangerous place. There are people in it who mean you no good." He threw back his hood, and the Princess Georgia began to weep harder.

"Let us go," said the Princess Margaret. "My parents are the King and Queen of a country not three days' walk from here. They will be glad to see us again."

Small said nothing. They came to the briar and he sent the Princess Georgia in to hunt for the catskin bag. She came out scratched and bleeding, the bag in her hand. It had caught on the briars and torn open. Gold coins rolled out, like glossy drops of fat, falling on the ground.

"Your father killed my mother," said Small.

"And that cat, your mother's devil, will kill us, or worse," said Princess Margaret. "Let us go!"

Small lifted the catskin bag. There were no coins in it now. The Princess Georgia was on her hands and knees, scooping up coins and putting them into her pockets.

"Was he a good father?" Small asked.

"He thought he was," Princess Margaret said. "But I'm not sorry he's dead. When I grow up, I will be queen. I'll make a law to put all the witches in the kingdom to death, and all their cats as well."

Small became afraid. He took up the catskin bag and ran back to the house of the witch Lack, leaving the two princesses in the forest. And whether they made their way home to the Princess Margaret's parents, or whether they fell into the hands of thieves, or whether they lived in the briar, or whether the Princess Margaret grew up and kept her promise and rid her kingdom of witches and cats, Small never knew, and neither do I, and neither shall you.

~

When he came back into the witch Lack's house, The Witch's Revenge saw at once what had happened. "Never mind," she said.

There were no children, no princes and princesses, in the throne room. The witch Lack's body still lay on the floor, but The Witch's Revenge had skinned it like a coney, and sewn up the skin into a bag. The bag wriggled and jerked, the sides heaving as if the witch Lack were still alive somewhere inside. The Witch's Revenge held the witchskin bag in one hand, and with the other, she was stuffing a cat into the neck of the skin. The cat wailed as it went into the bag. The bag was full of wailing. But the discarded flesh of the witch Lack lolled, slack.

There was a little pile of gold crowns on the floor beside the flayed corpse, and transparent, papery things that blew about the room, on a current of air, surprised looks on the thin, shed faces.

Cats were hiding in the corners of the room, and under the throne. "Go catch them," said The Witch's Revenge. "But leave the three prettiest alone."

"Where are the witch Lack's children?" Small said.

The Witch's Revenge nodded around the room. "As you see," she said. "I've slipped off their skins, and they were all cats underneath. They're cats now, but if we were to wait a year or two, they would shed these skins as well and become something new. Children are always growing."

Small chased the cats around the room. They were fast, but he was faster. They were nimble, but he was nimbler. He had worn his cat suit longer. He drove the cats down the length of the room, and The Witch's Revenge caught them and dropped them into her bag. At the end there were only three cats left in the throne room and they were as pretty a trio of cats as anyone could ask for. All the other cats were inside the bag.

"Well done and quickly done, too," said The Witch's Revenge, and she took her needle and stitched shut the neck of the bag. The skin of the witch Lack smiled up at Small, and a cat put its head through Lack's stained mouth, wailing. But The Witch's Revenge sewed Lack's mouth shut too, and the hole on the other end, where a house had come out. She left only his earholes and his eyeholes and his nostrils, which were full of fur, rolled open so that the cats could breathe.

The Witch's Revenge slung the skin full of cats over her shoulder and stood up.

"Where are you going?" Small said.

"These cats have mothers and fathers," The Witch's Revenge said. "They have mothers and fathers who miss them very much."

She gazed at Small. He decided not to ask again. So he waited in the house with the two princesses and the prince in their new cat suits, while The Witch's Revenge went down to the river. Or perhaps she took them down to the market and sold them. Or maybe she took each cat home, to its own mother and father, back to the kingdom where it had been born. Maybe she wasn't so careful to make sure that each child was returned to the right mother and father. After all, she was in a hurry, and cats look very much alike at night.

No one saw where she went—but the market is closer than the palaces of the kings and queens whose children had been stolen by the witch Lack, and the river is closer still.

When The Witch's Revenge came back to Lack's house, she looked around her. The house was beginning to stink very badly. Even Small could smell it now.

"I suppose the Princess Margaret let you fuck her," said The Witch's Revenge, as if she had been thinking about this while she ran her errands. "And that is why you let them go. I don't mind. She was a pretty puss. I might have let her go myself."

She looked at Small's face and saw that he was confused. "Never mind," she said.

She had a length of string in her paw, and a cork, which she greased with a piece of fat she had cut from the witch Lack. She threaded the cork on the string, calling it a good, quick, little mouse, and greased the string as well, and she fed the wriggling cork to the tabby who had been curled up in Small's lap. And when she had the cork back again, she greased it again and fed it to the little black cat, and then she fed it to the cat with two white forepaws, so that she had all three cats upon her string.

She sewed up the rip in the catskin bag, and Small put the gold crowns in the bag, and it was nearly as heavy as it had been before. The Witch's Revenge carried the bag, and Small took the greased string, holding it in his teeth, so the three cats were forced to run along behind him as they left the house of the witch Lack.

~

Small strikes a match, and he lights the house of the dead witch, Lack, on fire, as they leave. But shit burns slowly, if at all, and that house might be burning still, if someone hasn't gone and put it out. And maybe, someday, someone will go fishing in the river near that house, and hook their line on a bag full of princes and princesses, wet and sorry and wriggling in their catsuit skins—that's one way to catch a husband or a wife.

~

Small and The Witch's Revenge walked without stopping and the three cats came behind them. They walked until they reached a little village very near where the witch Small's mother had lived and there they settled down in a room The Witch's Revenge rented from a butcher. They cut the greased string, and bought a cage and hung it from a hook in the kitchen. They kept the three cats in it, but Small bought collars and leashes, and sometimes he put one of the cats on a leash and took it for a walk around the town.

Sometimes he wore his own catsuit and went out prowling, but The Witch's Revenge used to scold him if she caught him dressed like that. There are country manners and there are town manners and Small was a boy about town now.

The Witch's Revenge kept house. She cleaned and she cooked and she made Small's bed in the morning. Like all of the witch's cats, she was always busy. She melted down the gold crowns in a stewpot, and minted them into coins.

The Witch's Revenge wore a silk dress and gloves and a heavy veil, and ran her errands in a fine carriage, Small at her side. She opened an account in a bank, and she enrolled Small in a private academy. She bought a piece of land to build a house on, and she sent Small off to school every morning, no matter how he cried. But at night she took off her clothes and slept on his pillow and he combed her red and white fur.

Sometimes at night she twitched and moaned, and when he asked her what she was dreaming, she said, "There are ants! Can't you comb them out? Be quick and catch them, if you love me."

But there were never any ants.

One day when Small came home, the little cat with the white front paws was gone. When he asked The Witch's Revenge, she said that the little cat had fallen out of the cage and through the open window and into the garden and before The Witch's Revenge could think what to do, a crow had swooped down and carried the little cat off.

They moved into their new house a few months later, and Small was always very careful when he went in and out the doorway, imagining the little cat, down there in the dark, under the doorstep, under his foot.

~

Small got bigger. He didn't make any friends in the village, or at his school, but when you're big enough, you don't need friends.

One day while he and The Witch's Revenge were eating their dinner, there was a knock at the door. When Small opened the door, there stood Flora and Jack. Flora was wearing a drab, thrift-store coat, and Jack looked more than ever like a bundle of sticks.

"Small!" said Flora. "How tall you've become!" She burst into tears, and wrung her beautiful hands. Jack said, looking at The Witch's Revenge, "And who are you?"

The Witch's Revenge said to Jack, "Who am I? I'm your mother's cat, and you're a handful of dry sticks in a suit two sizes too large. But I won't tell anyone if you won't tell, either."

Jack snorted at this, and Flora stopped crying. She began to look around the house, which was sunny and large and well appointed.

"There's room enough for both of you," said The Witch's Revenge, "if Small doesn't mind."

Small thought his heart would burst with happiness to have his family back again. He showed Flora to one bedroom and Jack to another. Then they went downstairs and had a second dinner, and Small and The Witch's Revenge listened, and the cats in their hanging cage listened, while Flora and Jack recounted their adventures.

A pickpocket had taken Flora's purse, and they'd sold the witch's automobile, and lost the money in a game of cards. Flora found her parents, but they were a pair of old scoundrels who had no use for her. (She was too old to sell again. She would have realized what they were up to.) She'd gone to work in a department store, and Jack had sold tickets in a movie theater. They'd quarreled and made up, and then fallen in love with other people, and had many disappointments. At last they had decided to go home to the witch's house and see if it would do for a squat, or if there was anything left, to carry away and sell.

But the house, of course, had burned down. As they argued about what to do next, Jack had smelled Small, his brother, down in the village. So here they were.

"You'll live here, with us," Small said.

Jack and Flora said they could not do that. They had ambitions, they said. They had plans. They would stay for a week, or two weeks, and then they would be off again. The Witch's Revenge nodded and said that this was sensible.

Every day Small came home from school and went out again, with Flora, on a bicycle built for two. Or he stayed home and Jack taught him how to hold a coin between two fingers, and how to follow the egg, as it moved from cup to cup. The Witch's Revenge taught them to play bridge, although Flora and Jack couldn't be partners. They quarreled with each other as if they were husband and wife.

"What do you want?" Small asked Flora one day. He was leaning against her, wishing he were still a cat, and could sit in her lap. She smelled of secrets. "Why do you have to go away again?"

Flora patted Small on the head. She said, "What do I want? That's easy enough! To never have to worry about money. I want to marry a man and know that he'll never cheat on me, or leave me." She looked at Jack as she said this.

Jack said, "I want a rich wife who won't talk back, who doesn't lie in bed all day, with the covers pulled up over her head, weeping and calling me a bundle of twigs." And he looked at Flora when he said this.

The Witch's Revenge put down the sweater that she was knitting for Small. She looked at Flora and she looked at Jack and then she looked at Small.

Small went into the kitchen and opened the door of the hanging cage. He lifted out the two cats and brought them to Flora and Jack. "Here," he said. "A husband for you, Flora, and a wife for Jack. A prince and a princess, and both of them beautiful, and well brought up, and wealthy, no doubt."

Flora picked up the little tomcat and said, "Don't tease at me, Small! Who ever heard of marrying a cat!"

The Witch's Revenge said, "The trick is to keep their catskins in a safe hiding place. And if they sulk, or treat you badly, sew them back into their catskin and put them into a bag and throw them in the river."

Then she took her claw and slit the skin of the tabby-colored cat suit, and Flora was holding a naked man. Flora shrieked and dropped him on the ground. He was a handsome man, well made, and he had a princely manner. He was not a man that anyone would ever mistake for a cat. He stood up and made a bow, very elegant, for all that he was naked. Flora blushed, but she looked pleased.

"Go fetch some clothes for the prince and the princess," The Witch's Revenge said to Small. When he got back, there was a naked princess hiding behind the sofa, and Jack was leering at her.

A few weeks after that, there were two weddings, and then Flora left with her new husband, and Jack went off with his new princess. Perhaps they lived happily ever after.

The Witch's Revenge said to Small, "We have no wife for you."

Small shrugged. "I'm still too young," he said.

～

But try as hard as he can, Small is getting older now. The catskin barely fits across his shoulders. The buttons strain when he fastens them. His grown-up fur—his people fur—is coming in. At night he dreams.

The witch his mother's Spanish heel beats against the pane of glass. The princess hangs in the briar. She's holding up her dress, so he can see the catfur down there. Now she's under the house. She wants to marry him, but the house will fall down if he kisses her. He and Flora are children again, in the witch's house. Flora lifts up her skirt and says, see my pussy? There's a cat down there, peeking out at him, but it doesn't look like any cat he's ever seen. He says to Flora, I have a pussy too. But his isn't the same.

At last he knows what happened to the little, starving, naked thing in the forest, where it went. It crawled into his catskin, while he was asleep, and then it climbed right inside him, his Small skin, and now it is huddled in his chest, still cold and sad and hungry. It is eating him from the inside, and getting bigger, and one day there will be no Small left at all, only that nameless, hungry child, wearing a Small skin.

Small moans in his sleep.

There are ants in The Witch's Revenge's skin, leaking out of her seams, and they march down into the sheets and pinch at him, down under his arms, and between his legs where his fur is growing in, and it hurts, it aches and aches. He dreams that The Witch's Revenge wakes now, and comes and licks him all over, until the pain melts. The pane of glass melts. The ants march away again on their long, greased thread.

"What do you want?" says The Witch's Revenge.

Small is no longer dreaming. He says, "I want my mother!"

Light from the moon comes down through the window over their bed. The Witch's Revenge is very beautiful—she looks like a Queen, like a knife, like a burning house, a cat—in the moonlight. Her fur shines. Her whiskers stand out like pulled stitches, wax and thread. The Witch's Revenge says, "Your mother is dead."

"Take off your skin," Small says. He's crying and The Witch's Revenge licks his tears away. Small's skin pricks all over, and down under the house, something small wails and wails. "Give me back my mother," he says.

"Oh, my darling," says his mother, the witch, The Witch's Revenge, "I can't do that. I'm full of ants. Take off my skin, and all the ants will spill out, and there will be nothing left of me."

Small says, "Why have you left me all alone?"

His mother the witch says, "I've never left you alone, not even for a minute. I sewed up my death in a catskin so I could stay with you."

"Take it off! Let me see you!" Small says. He pulls at the sheet on the bed, as if it were his mother's catskin.

The Witch's Revenge shakes her head. She trembles and beats her tail back and forth. She says, "How can you ask me for such a thing, and how can I say no to you? Do you know what you're asking me for? Tomorrow night. Ask me again, tomorrow night."

And Small has to be satisfied with that. All night long, Small combs his mother's fur. His fingers are looking for the seams in her catskin. When The Witch's Revenge yawns, he peers inside her mouth, hoping to catch a glimpse of his mother's face. He can feel himself becoming smaller and smaller. In the morning he will be so small that when he tries to put his catskin on, he can barely do up the buttons. He'll be so small, so sharp, you might mistake him for an ant, and when The Witch's Revenge yawns, he'll creep inside her mouth, he'll go down into her belly, he'll go find his mother. If he can, he'll help his mother cut her catskin open so that she can get out again and come and live in the world with him, and if she won't come out, then he won't, either. He'll live there, the way that sailors learn to live, inside the belly of fish who have eaten them, and keep house for his mother inside the house of her skin.

⁓

This is the end of the story. The Princess Margaret grows up to kill witches and cats. If she doesn't, then someone else will have to do it. There is no such thing as witches, and there is no such thing as cats, either, only people dressed up in catskin suits. They have their reasons, and who is to say that they might not live that way, happily ever after, until the ants have carried away all of the time that there is, to build something new and better out of it?

⁓

About the Authors

ELIZABETH BEAR was born on the same day as Frodo and Bilbo Baggins, but in a different year. She is the Hugo and Sturgeon Award-winning author of over a dozen novels and nearly a hundred short stories. Her hobbies include rock climbing and playing passably bad guitar. She lives in Southern New England with a giant ridiculous dog and a cat who is an internet celebrity. Her most recent novel is *Range of Ghosts*, from Tor.

LEAH BOBET drinks tea, plants gardens in alleyways, and wears feathers in her hair. Her short fiction has appeared in venues including *On Spec*, *Realms of Fantasy*, and several year's best anthologies, and her first novel, *Above*, will be published by Arthur A. Levine Books in April 2012. Find her at www.leahbobet.com.

NEIL GAIMAN is the *New York Times* bestselling author of novels *Neverwhere*, *Stardust*, *American Gods*, *Coraline*, *Anansi Boys*, *The Graveyard Book*, and (with Terry Pratchett) *Good Omens*; the Sandman series of graphic novels; and the story collections *Smoke and Mirrors*, *Fragile Things*, and *M Is for Magic*. He has won numerous literary accolades including the Hugo, the Nebula, the World Fantasy, and the Stoker Awards, as well as the Newbery medal.

THEODORA GOSS was born in Hungary and spent her childhood in various European countries before her family moved to the United States. Her publications include the short story collection *In the Forest of Forgetting*; *Interfictions*, a short story anthology co-edited with Delia Sherman; *Voices from Fairyland*, a poetry anthology with critical essays and a selection of her own poems; and, most recently, *The Thorn and the Blossom: A Two-Sided Love Story*. She has been a finalist for the Nebula, Locus, Crawford, and Mythopoeic Awards, as well as on the Tiptree Award Honor List, and has won the World Fantasy and Rhysling Awards.

Four-time Bram Stoker Award-winner NANCY HOLDER has published seventy-five books and more than two hundred short stories and essays. She has written or co-written dozens of Buffy the Vampire Slayer, Smallville, Saving Grace, and Angel projects. Novels from her series,

Wicked, appeared on the *New York Times* bestseller list. Her two new dark young adult dark fantasy series (with Debbie Viguié) are Crusade and Wolf Springs Chronicles. She teaches in the Stonecoast MFA in Creative Writing Program, offered through the University of Southern Maine. She lives in San Diego with her daughter, Belle, and their growing assortment of pets. Visit her at nancyholder.com.

ELLEN KLAGES is the author of two acclaimed YA novels: *The Green Glass Sea*, which won the Scott O'Dell Award, the New Mexico Book Award, and the Lopez Award; and *White Sands, Red Menace*, which won the California and New Mexico Book Awards. Her short stories have been have been translated into Czech, French, German, Hungarian, Japanese, and Swedish and have been nominated for the Nebula Award, the Hugo, World Fantasy, and Campbell awards. Her story, "Basement Magic," won a Nebula in 2005. She lives in San Francisco, in a small house full of strange and wondrous things. Her website is www.ellenklages.com.

MERCEDES LACKEY has written over one hundred books in a career that has spanned two decades—and she hasn't slowed down yet. In her "spare" time, the bestselling author is also a professional lyricist and a licensed wild bird rehabilitator. Lackey lives in Oklahoma with her husband and frequent collaborator, artist Larry Dixon, and their flock of parrots. Her website is www.mercedeslackey.com.

URSULA K. LE GUIN has received five Hugo Awards, six Nebula Awards, nineteen Locus Awards (more than any other author), the Gandalf Grand Master Award, the Science Fiction and Fantasy Writers of America Grand Master Award, and the World Fantasy Lifetime Achievement Award. Her novel *The Farthest Shore* won the National Book Award for Children's Books. Le Guin was named a Library of Congress Living Legend in the "Writers and Artists" category for her significant contributions to America's cultural heritage and the PEN/Malamud Award for "excellence in a body of short fiction." She is also the recipient of the Association for Library Service for Children's May Hill Arbuthnot Honor Lecture Award and the Margaret Edwards Award. She was honored by The Washington Center for the Book for her distinguished body of work with the Maxine Cushing Gray Fellowship for Writers in 2006.

MARGO LANAGAN's latest novel is *The Brides of Rollrock Island*. She is a four-time World Fantasy Award winner, and her work has also been nominated for Hugo, Nebula, International Horror Guild, Bram Stoker, and Theodore Sturgeon awards, and twice been placed on the James Tiptree Jr. Award honor list. She attended the Clarion West Writers' Workshop in 1999, and has taught at Clarion South three times and also at Clarion West. Margo lives in Sydney, Australia.

TANITH LEE was born in 1947, in London, England. She worked at various jobs until in 1974-75 DAW Books began to publish her sf and fantasy, beginning with *The Birthgrave*. Since then she has published over ninety books and over three hundred short stories, written for TV and BBC Radio. Her latest novels are available from the Immanion Press and reprints—such as Flat Earth sequence and The Birthgrave Trilogy via Norilana Books. Much of her work will soon be available in ebook form via Orion, and other houses. She lives on the Sussex Weald with her husband writer/artist/photographer/model maker John Kaiine.

MADELEINE L'ENGLE (1918-2007) is best known for her Newbery Medal-winning novel *A Wrinkle in Time*, and its sequels *A Wind in the Door*, *A Swiftly Tilting Planet*, *Many Waters*, and *An Acceptable Time*. In addition to the numerous awards, medals, and prizes won by individual books, L'Engle's honors include being named an Associate Dame of Justice in the Venerable Order of Saint John, the USM Medallion from The University of Southern Mississippi, the Smith College Award "for service to community or college which exemplifies the purposes of liberal arts education," the Sophia Award for distinction in her field, the Regina Medal, the ALAN Award—presented by the National Council of Teachers of English—for outstanding contribution to adolescent literature, and the Kerlan Award. She also received over a dozen honorary degrees naming her not only as a Doctor of Humane Letters, but a Doctor of Literature and a Doctor of Sacred Theology. She was recognized with a World Fantasy Award for Lifetime Achievement and received the National Humanities Medal.

KELLY LINK is the author of three collections of short stories, *Stranger Things Happen*, *Magic for Beginners*, and *Pretty Monsters*. Her short stories have won three Nebulas, a Hugo, and a World Fantasy Award. She was born in Miami, Florida, and once won a free trip around the world by answering the question "Why do you want to go around the world?" ("Because you can't go through it.") Link and her family live in Northampton, Massachusetts, where she and her husband, Gavin J. Grant, run Small Beer Press, and play ping-pong. In 1996 they started the occasional zine *Lady Churchill's Rosebud Wristlet*.

SILVIA MORENO-GARCIA grew up in Mexico and now makes Canada her home. Her work has appeared in *Evolve 2*, *The Book of Cthulhu*, and many other places. She's even won and been nominated for a couple of literary awards. She owns and operates the horror micro-press Innsmouth Free Press. She is currently working on a novel about magic, music, and Mexico City. You can find her at silviamoreno-garcia.com or on Twitter @silviamg.

ANDRE ALICE NORTON, née Alice Mary Norton (1912-2005) is often called the Grande Dame of Science Fiction and Fantasy. The first woman to receive the Gandalf Grand Master Award from the World Science Fiction Society, she was also named as a Grand Master by the Science Fiction Writers Association. SFWA created the Andre Norton Award, to be given each year for an outstanding work of fantasy or science fiction for young adults beginning in 2006. She wrote novels for over seventy years and her three hundred or so published titles have had a profound influence on at least four generations of science fiction and fantasy readers and writers.

RICHARD PARKS has been writing and publishing sf/f longer than he cares to remember . . . or probably can remember. His work has appeared in (among many others) *Asimov's*, *Realms of Fantasy*, *Lady Churchill's Rosebud Wristlet*, and several year's bests. His second novel, *To Break the Demon Gate*, is due out in late 2012 or early 2013 from PS Publishing. He blogs at "Den of Ego and Iniquity Annex #3"—also known as www.richard-parks.com.

T.A. PRATT has written seven novels (and a few stories) about ass-kicking sorcerer Marla Mason, beginning with *Blood Engines*. The most recent book, *Grim Tides*, is being serialized for free at MarlaMason.net in the first half of 2012. He lives in Berkeley, CA. "Ill Met in Ulthar" owes a debt of inspiration to the works of Fritz Leiber, H.P. Lovecraft, and Peter Phillips.

LINDA ROBERTSON is the author of five books about Persephone Alcmedi; *Vicious Circle* was the first, *Wicked Circle* is the most recent; a sixth will be published in late 2012. She is also the mother of four awesome boys, owns four guitars, and has one goofy dog. Once upon a time, she was lead guitarist in a heavy metal cover band. She has worked various other jobs over the years, but writing has always been her passion. Her website is www.authorlindarobertson.com and she blogs at www.word-whores.blogspot.com.

DELIA SHERMAN writes short stories and novels for both adults and younger readers. Her short stories have appeared in numerous anthologies and magazines, most recently in the YA anthology *Steampunk!* and Ellen Datlow's *Naked City*. Her adult novels are *Through a Brazen Mirror*, *The Porcelain Dove*, and *The Fall of the Kings* (with Ellen Kushner). Her middle-grade novels, *Changeling* and *The Magic Mirror of the Mermaid Queen* are set in the magical world of New York Between. Her newest novel, *The Freedom Maze*, is a time-travel historical about antebellum Louisiana. When she's not writing, she's teaching, editing, knitting, and cooking. She lives in New York City with partner Ellen Kushner and a whole lot of books

CORY SKERRY lives in the Northwest U.S. and works at an upscale adult boutique. In his free time, he writes stories, draws comics, copy edits for *Shimmer Magazine*, and goes hiking with his two sweet, goofy pit bulls. He's been published in *Fantasy, Ideomancer*, and *Strange Horizons*. For more see: plunderpuss.net.

CYNTHIA WARD (www.cynthiaward.com) has published fiction in *Asimov's* and *Pirates & Swashbucklers*, among other anthologies and magazines, and nonfiction in *Locus Online* and *Weird Tales*, among other magazines and webzines. With Nisi Shawl, she coauthored *Writing the Other: A Practical Approach* (Aqueduct Press), which is based on their diversity writing workshop, Writing the Other: Bridging Cultural Differences for Successful Fiction (www.writingtheother.com). Cynthia lives in Los Angeles, where she is not working on a screenplay.

DON WEBB has published twenty books ranging from the nonfiction occult classic *Uncle Setnakt's Nightbook* to a mystery series from St. Martins Press. A Texan born and bred, he dwells in Austin, the Live Music Capital of the world, with his lovely wife and two cats. In addition to having written four hundred short, stories, he wrote a curse against witch hunting and persecution of occultists called the Mass of Terrible Justice, performed at the Temple of Set Conclave in Salem in 1992, the 300th anniversary of the Salem witch trials.

LESLIE WHAT is a Nebula Award-winning writer and the author of the novel *Olympic Games*. Her story collection, *Crazy Love*, was a finalist for the Oregon Book Award. She is the fiction editor of *Phantom Drift: New Fabulism* and the nonfiction co-editor of the forthcoming anthology, *Winter Tales: Women Write About Aging*. Her writing has appeared in numerous journals and anthologies, including *Fugue, The Los Angeles Review, Best New Horror, Parabola, Mammoth Book of Tales from the Road, Bending the Landscape, Asimov's, Flurb, Calyx, Utne Reader*, and other places.

JANE YOLEN has been called the Hans Christian Andersen of America and the Aesop of the twentieth century. She has written over three hundred books, been awarded six honorary doctorates in literature, the Caldecott Medal, two Nebula Awards, two Christopher Medals, the World Fantasy Award, three Mythopoeic Fantasy Awards, the Golden Kite Award, the Jewish Book Award, the World Fantasy Association's Lifetime Achievement Award, and the Association of Jewish Libraries Award among many others. She once got to spend a day in a studio with Kevin Kline while he did voice-over for one of her animated stories.

∼

Acknowledgements

"The Cold Blacksmith" © 2006 by Elizabeth Bear. First publication: *Jim Baen's Universe*, June 2006. Reprinted by permission of the author.

"The Ground Whereon She Stands" © 2011 by Leah Bobet. First publication: *Realms of Fantasy*, June 2011. Reprinted by permission of the author.

"The Witch's Headstone" © 2007 by Neil Gaiman. First publication: *Wizards: Magical Tales From the Masters of Modern Fantasy,* ed. Jack Dann & Gardner Dozois (Berkley). Reprinted by permission of the author.

"Lessons with Miss Gray" © 2006 by Theodora Goss. First publication: *Fantasy Magazine 2*, April 2006. Reprinted by permission of the author.

"The Only Way to Fly" © 1995 by Nancy Holder. First publication: *100 Wicked Witch Stories* edited by Stefan Dziemianowicz, Robert A. Weinberg & Martin H. Greenberg (Barnes & Noble, 1995). Reprinted by permission of the author.

"Basement Magic" © 2003 by Ellen Klages. First publication: *The Magazine of Fantasy & Science Fiction*, May 2003. Reprinted by permission of the author.

"Nightside" © 1990 by Mercedes Lackey. First publication: *Marion Zimmer Bradley's Fantasy Magazine*, Spring 1990. Reprinted by permission of the author.

"April In Paris" © 1962, 1990 by Ursula K, Le Guin. First publication: *Fantastic*, September 1962. Reprinted by permission of the author.

"The Goosle" © 2008 by Margo Lanagan. First Publication: *Del Rey Book of Science Fiction and Fantasy* edited by Ellen Datlow (Del Rey, 2008). Reprinted by permission of the author.

"Mirage and Magia" © 1982 by Tanith Lee. First Publication: *Hecate's Cauldron* edited by Susan M. Schwartz. (Daw, 1982). Reprinted by permission of the author.

"Poor Little Saturday" © 1956 by Madeleine L'Engle. First publication: *Fantastic Universe*, October 1956. Reprinted by permission of Crosswicks, Ltd.